FACING THE FAERIES 1906

DEBRA KORNFIELD

BOOK THREE OF THE CALLY AND CHARLIE SERIES

EABooks Publishing
Your Partner In Publishing

Author: Debra Kornfield
Facing the Faeries 1906, Book Three of the Cally and Charlie Series
1. Fiction/Historical/General
2. Fiction/World Literature/Ireland/19th Century

Published by EA Books Publishing, a division of
Living Parables of Central Florida, Inc. a 501c3
EABooksPublishing.com

Cover image by Marissa Bowles
Cover design and interior formatting by Robin Black

ISBN: 978-1-963611-00-7

For Chris and Elise Massa
You helped me believe I could write fiction.

CONTENTS

Are not angels ministering spirits,
sent to serve those who will inherit salvation?
Hebrews 1:14

The Malcomson Family in this book

Historical/***Fictional***

Peter Malcomson *(deceased)* m. ***Cathleen O'Connell***

Their children: ***Daniel, Margaret, Thomas, Charles***

Cathleen's *"adopted" grandchildren and their parents* ***Dugan*** *and* ***Aisling (Cally's*** *uncle and aunt)*

Peter's uncle: William Malcomson I

William I's son: William Malcomson II; his youngest children Llewellyn, Susan

William I's *son with* ***Melody Avery: Billy Malcomson***

Melody's *mother* ***Minnie*** *and brother* ***Cecil*** *m.* ***Mary****; their daughter* ***Ebony***

Thomas *and* ***Cora Malcomson's*** children: ***Shane, Shauna, Josie***

Thomas and ***Cora's*** adopted sister and niece: ***Callandra (Cally)*** and ***Felicity***

Cally's *brother* ***Teddy*** m. ***Starlight***; *their daughter* ***Aiyana***

Charles (Charlie) Malcomson m. ***Laoise Murphy***

Laoise's *parents* ***Colin*** *and* ***Muriel Murphy***

Laoise's *brother* ***Desmond*** m. ***Deirdre***

PROLOGUE

Quaker Meeting House, Waterford, Ireland, May 1877

WILLIAM MALCOMSON II CLIMBED FROM the carriage, stretched, walked up and down the street, glared at the closed door of the Meeting House, sighed, and climbed back into the brougham beside his father.

"When thee invited me to come with thee, I didn't imagine it would take this long," young William complained. "Tell me again what is making this so complicated?"

The elder William shifted in his seat and looked out the window at the still-closed door. "As I've said, son, several of our extended family believe the Malcomson Brothers bankruptcy is all my fault. The Society of Friends takes seriously the accusations they have made against me, because the sterling Quaker business reputation depends on absolute honesty and integrity. The elders hope to determine whether the failure of our businesses was due to moral irresponsibility on my part, by not caring enough about the rights and needs of our creditors."

"But thee have told me about the many factors against thee, Father. The American Civil War interrupting production of the cotton our mills depend on. Our relatives pulling their money out of our companies to build their fancy houses. Surely the elders will see it was not thy fault."

"I thank thee for thy confidence, son. We'll soon find out what the elders think."

"If the Society of Friends disowns thee, will they exclude me as well?"

"No. In thy twenty-two years thee played no role in the bankruptcy. Thee will remain a member in good standing."

"Well, I'll be embarrassed if they make thee leave. I might not want to stay."

The younger William climbed out of the carriage and again walked up and down the street. The Meeting House door still did not open. He stepped into the carriage once more.

"Father, I have another question. Please don't be angry."

The elder William's eyebrows shot up. "Why might I be angry?"

"Well, thee have said we need to live differently, not be so careless and extravagant with our money. What does that mean, exactly?"

"The details aren't clear to me yet, son. The bankruptcy court will be months yet determining the settlements with our creditors. We may or may not come out of this personally solvent. Meanwhile we must only spend what is essential and take on no new debt. I'm glad we're talking about this, because thee must make some decisions about thy life, William."

"What decisions?"

"I believe I have raised thee too leniently, William, assuming we would always be prosperous and able to do anything we pleased. I have not prepared thee well to make thy own way, without a family fortune to carry thee along. Now that thee have graduated from Trinity College, it is time for thee to choose a career. What would thee most like to do to earn thy living?"

"I never thought about earning my living, Father. I assumed I would work for Malcomson Brothers as much or little as I wished, more as a hobby, I suppose. I can be good at business, I think. Perhaps in imports and exports." The younger William's voice rose. "This can't have happened suddenly, Father. Why didn't thee tell me Malcomson Brothers was in trouble? I might have made different choices about what to study at Trinity!"

"Thee mean to say, thee might have chosen to study, instead of wasting thy years at Trinity in diversions and pranks," his father retorted.

"How was I to know I would have to earn money?" yelled the son.

His father pointed out the window. "Calm thyself, please. An elder is coming for us." He exited the carriage, donned his hat and straightened his clothing. Young William took a deep breath and followed him.

The elder greeted the two Malcomson men and gestured toward the Meeting House. "Thee may enter now. We have reached a decision."

"We thank thee," said William I. The three walked in silence into the gathering, inclined their heads in greeting to the elders, and took the seats indicated.

An older gentleman rose. "We have sought the guidance of the Lord, and have considered all we understand about thy situation, William. While we regret the grievous decline of Malcomson Brothers, we have concluded that a variety of factors have converged to cause its downfall, including a failure of support from thy extended family. We see that they acted extravagantly in promotion of their own interests, thus draining away capital necessary to the survival of the company."

William bowed his head almost to his lap, fighting for control. *Finally, someone understands what I've been up against. It's been hard, so hard. The weight of it unbearable . . .*

"We believe thee to be fully cognizant of thy responsibilities to thy creditors," the elder continued. "And we have every confidence thee will make the adjustments in thy own family's arrangements to compensate inasmuch as thee are able for the losses those who believed in Malcomson Brothers have suffered. It may be that thy brother Joseph could have rescued the company. But we cannot construe it as thy fault God did not give thee the business acumen Joseph enjoyed. Nor art thee to blame for his untimely demise and his failure to adequately prepare thee to assume his role and responsibilities."

Another elder stood. "In short, Brother William, we have decided thy membership in the Waterford Society of Friends will remain in good standing. And we are prepared to assist thee in the working out of the bankruptcy. Thee must not make thy decisions independently. Instead, rely on us for advice and counsel. We all stand to lose should thee not take wise actions in the settlement of these affairs. We expect thee to communicate with us often until this is resolved. Do thee accept our conclusions, William?"

William the first stood, so his son stood with him. "I do, with humble gratitude."

"Then thee may be excused while we consider other concerns."

The elder who had brought them from the carriage escorted the two Williams to the door, bowed, and closed the door behind them. Father and son took their seats. As the carriage pulled away, the older William bowed his head again, his body shaking with tears as his son stared at him in amazement.

"Father, I have never seen you weep. Not even when Mummy died."

William senior patted his son's leg, then pulled a handkerchief from his pocket and turned away, seeking control.

His son stared out his window as the houses of Waterford dissolved into rich countryside, bathed in the warm glow of sunset. *The world is falling apart. Nothing will ever be the same. I'm on my own now. Clearly, Father is in no condition to help me. And those old men only cared about Father and about their precious Quaker reputation. They offered no assistance to me, none at all.*

CHAPTER 1

CALLY

Kansas City, Saturday, November 12, 1904

CALLY SAT AT HER DESK reviewing her pharmacology notes, her brow furrowed. *Why do medications have to be so complicated? Side effects on the liver or kidneys, or irritation of the intestines . . . I wonder whether Falling Water's natural treatments have fewer negative impacts on our bodies. I want to learn whatever she taught Flora. Before Falling Water was killed.*

Someone knocked on her bedroom door. "Come in," said Cally. *Is my study time up already?*

Cora poked her head around the door. "Cally, Thomas had to go into work to deal with a train derailment east of here. Max is free now to take me shopping for art supplies. It's still raining, but the children are all happily occupied. It's Nora's day off, so you're the only adult in the house."

"No problem, Cora. Happy shopping!"

Cally turned back to her notes. *Where was I—oh yes, side effects. I wonder how much of this will be on the exam Monday.*

She was deep into review of the pros and cons of bloodletting when someone else knocked. Cally's ten-year-old niece poked her head around the door. "Aunt Cally, may we talk to you?"

"Of course, Shauna."

Her twin, Shane, followed Shauna into the room. "Mama has gone to the art store, so this seemed a good moment to ask for your help," he said, sitting on Felicity's bed. "We have an idea."

"Our birthday is coming in a couple of weeks, and we've been thinking," said Shauna.

"Do you want me to help with your party?" asked Cally.

"Not exactly," said Shane. "We want to do something special for Mama, because actually, she's the one who worked hard to birth us. So, we think she should be honored on our birthday."

"We didn't do anything to deserve gifts and treats," said Shauna. "Mama did."

"What do you have in mind?" asked Cally.

"We want to get up early on our birthday and make Mama breakfast in bed," said Shauna.

"We're thinking about French crepes, but we don't know how to make them. Can you help us, Aunt Cally?" asked Shane.

"Let me check my schedule. . . . Your birthday is on a Thursday. I'll have to leave early that day for the hospital. I already asked for Saturday, December 3 off for your birthday party. If we can surprise her that morning, I can help you. But I've never made French crepes. Have you talked to Nora about this? Maybe she knows how to make them."

"We asked her. She doesn't know either," said Shauna, frowning. "How can we learn, Aunt Cally? Mama loves them."

"Hmm . . . Have you checked your mother's cookbooks?"

"No. Let's go do that now, Shauna, while Mama is gone. We'll let you know if we find a recipe, Aunt Cally."

"If you don't, we can try the library."

"Yes! We're going there next Saturday, after Mama's art show. I'm sure we can secretly look at recipes while she's helping Josie and Felicity choose their books to borrow."

Cally smiled as the twins ran out of her room. *What a thoughtful idea! Cora will be delighted even if the crepes don't turn out perfectly. Now, where was I . . . Oh yes. The history of bloodletting . . . George Washington probably died from too much of it . . . The diagnoses that still require it now are hemochromatosis, too much iron in the blood, and polycythemia vera . . .*

Her door opened without a knock. Six-year-old Felicity ran in, trailed by her seven-year-old cousin Josie.

"Mummy, we finished coloring our paper dolls and their clothes. Can you help us cut them out? We already cut off one of the doll's arms."

"We're not good at the curves," explained Josie.

Cally sighed and stood. *I'll have to study more after the children are in bed. I want a good grade on this exam.* "Sure, I'll be glad to help you. Shall we give your doll's arm a bandage?" She pulled a roll of gauze from her nurse's bag and snipped off a small bit.

"Thank you, Mummy! I'm glad you're learning to be a nurse!"

"Was it a bad train wreck?" Cally asked her brother by adoption that evening at dinner. "You look tired, Thomas."

"Very bad, yes. A train taking people from Kansas and Missouri to the World's Fair in St. Louis collided with a westbound Missouri Pacific freighter. Thirty people were killed and dozens more injured. The investigation into what caused the accident has only begun."

"How awful, Thomas!" exclaimed Cora. "Anyone we know?"

"The names of the dead and injured have not yet been released by the Missouri Pacific. Families will be notified first. It's a nightmare. I must return to the office after dinner. I may not be home tonight or tomorrow, Cora."

"I understand, darling. I'll pack you some food and coffee."

Cally stood too. "I'll help you, Cora. So very sorry, Thomas. Children, I'll read you the next chapter of George MacDonald's *Fairy Tales* once you're all ready for bed."

"When you finish eating, you may be excused, children," said Thomas. "I may not see you until Monday night."

"We're sorry about the train wreck," said Shane.

"We'll pray for you and for the people who were hurt," said Shauna.

"Dr. Tann and his wife Eliza were on the train," Thomas told Cora and Cally Sunday evening. Both women gasped. "They weren't hurt and were a big help at the scene. I'm so grateful for them. This was the worst accident I've ever had to deal with."

"What happened?"

"An extra train was scheduled to take passengers to Missouri Day at the World's Fair. The westbound freighter was sidelined at Knob Noster to allow four trains to pass on the main line. For some reason, the conductor only counted to three and then resumed his journey."

"How awful!"

"Yes. The Sedalia office realized the collision would happen, because there was no way to communicate with either train. They immediately dispatched emergency personnel to the site where they estimated the wreck would occur, so help was available soon after. But they couldn't prevent it."

"Did the conductor die?"

"No. But he was near the end of his usual seventeen-hour shift. I'm guessing he erred from being too tired. Ever since I started working in the Kansas City office, I've been saying seventeen hours is too long for anyone to maintain alertness. Perhaps this tragedy will lead to more reasonable working conditions for the crews."

"You must be exhausted, Thomas."

"Yes. I'll eat, bathe, and sleep, and return to the office in the morning."

"Doctors and nurses often work the same long hours," said Cally. "Mistakes are bound to happen. I've heard of people taking drugs to stay awake."

"You've had shifts like that yourself. It's not sensible," said Thomas. "This must change, for every type of worker. Good night."

CHAPTER 2

BILLY

Coolroe, Portlaw, County Waterford, Ireland,
Tuesday, November 15, 1904

"EXCUSE ME, SIR. IS THIS the house of William Malcomson?" Billy asked. He interrupted a gardener bent over a bed of multicolored dahlias surrounding a signpost saying "Coolroe."

The man glanced up, looked Billy up and down, said "So it is," and returned to his weeding. Billy thanked him and turned to gaze at a house larger than any he had ever seen. The gardener stood and stretched. "What's yer business with Master Malcomson, then, lad? Ye're not from these parts."

"I'll explain it to him," said Billy, starting toward the front door.

"Ye best try the back," advised the gardener. "Himself only welcomes his own class at the front."

"I am his class," said Billy over his shoulder as he climbed the porch steps.

Shaking his head, the gardener bent to another flowerbed as Billy rang the doorbell.

"Yes?" asked the butler.

"I'm looking for my father, William Malcomson," said Billy.

"Yer father, is he? I doubt it," replied the butler. "Easy there, Master Llewellyn, Miss Susan." Two warmly dressed children, a bit younger than Billy, pushed past the butler and ran laughing around the house.

"He's probably not their father," said Billy. "My father might be their grandfather."

"Their Grandfather William is dead," said the butler.

"No!" Billy crumpled onto the porch, sobbing. "I've traveled so far to find him. Looked so long." He buried his face in his arms, his whole body shaking.

"I'll speak to Mr. William." The butler closed the door. A few minutes later, the door opened. A middle-aged man frowned at Billy, the butler hovering behind him.

"As you say, Doyle, it's not possible. I'd heard a rumor, years ago when my father visited America . . . But no. Not possible. Send him to the kitchen for his supper and a jacket and cap. Else he'll not survive in this weather."

The man disappeared, and the butler took his place. Billy leaped to his feet. "No, wait, Mr. Malcomson! Let me explain! Your father is my father too! It wasn't a rumor. I'm here! I exist! My name is William Joseph Malcomson!"

"Stop this nonsense," said the butler, grasping Billy's arm and walking him down the steps. "You heard the master. Follow this path around back and tell Cook, Doyle asks her to give you some supper. I'll look for a jacket. Mr. William is generous, so he is, but he doesn't suffer fools. Go on, now. I can see you're hungry." Doyle gave Billy a push,

Billy looked around desperately. *What shall I do? I can't let my search end like this!* The gardener stood watching, shaking his head.

"Go on," repeated the butler. He pushed Billy again, then reentered the house and closed the door.

Billy took a reluctant step, then another. *My father is dead. And he never told his family about me. Mr. Malcomson—William—my brother—doesn't believe me any more than that lady Cathleen on the ship. All of it—this whole long search—has been a waste. What will I do now?*

Billy stopped and wiped his nose on his sleeve. The gardener said, "Go on now, lad."

Reaching the back entry, Billy raised his hand to knock, but the door opened to reveal the butler and a woman wearing a white apron. Doyle pulled Billy inside and held up a well-worn jacket and cap. "This'll do ye, I reckon. Eat yer supper now. And never come back here again."

Doyle nodded at the cook and turned. As he walked away, Billy heard him mutter, "Sure, don't that beat all. A dark-skinned boy claiming old Mr. William as his da. Well, I never . . ."

Billy just had time to think, "How interesting the way his speech changed from the front door to the back door" before the cook pulled him to a seat and set a heaping plate on the table in front of him. Billy's eyes widened, then overflowed. He brushed the tears away and set to.

Behind him, a pile of pans clattered into the sink. Billy paused, put down his fork, and turned to look at the kitchen maid blushing as she fought to restore order. "Brigid!" exclaimed the cook as the maid quailed.

Billy leaped to his feet. "Ma'am, do you have work I could do, in exchange for a warm place to sleep? Just for tonight? I'm so tired . . ."

The cook looked him up and down. "I suppose ye could finish those pots, and then milk the cows, and sleep in the barn. Just for tonight."

"Thank you, ma'am. I never milked a cow before, but I'm a fast learner."

The maid threw Billy a look of gratitude, then addressed the cook. "If he'll help me with the pots and pans, I can teach him the milking. It is dreadful cold out there."

"As ye wish," said the cook. "Find him a blanket. Ye can feed him breakfast too if he manages to milk a cow. But then he must be on his way, never to return to this house."

❧

Killeagh, County Cork, Ireland, Friday, November 18, 1904

Billy gripped the handle of Old Thatch Inn's heavy wooden door just as someone shoved it open from inside. A man crashed into Billy, almost knocking him over.

"Steady on, mate," the man said, fishing Billy's cap out of a puddle and giving it a shake. "Are ye all right then?"

Billy nodded, settling his wet cap back on his head. For a moment, kind green eyes gazed into his as the man straightened his own cap over red curls. Then he was gone.

Billy stood for a moment, savoring his brief brush with benevolence. *It's kindness I'd hoped for from my half-brother William. But he wouldn't let me explain. Just shuffled me off like any poor beggar.* The memory scrunched Billy's face into a frown. His shoulders sagged as he pulled again at the door of the Old Thatch. *At least it will be warmer inside. The wind's chilly now the sun is setting.*

The tavern was dim, crowded with animated talkers and drinkers. *The right back corner, near the fireplace. That's what Mr. Doherty told me.* Billy squeezed past a hurrying barmaid and stood listening to the conversation at what might be the right table. *I have to concentrate to understand their accent. And I'm soooo tired.*

"What did Dugan say?" asked a middle-aged man with a balding head.

"He's gone to fetch the midwife for his wife Aisling. It's too soon for her to be birthing. He'll be staying home in case things go badly."

That one with the pipe is Mr. Doherty.

"Himself will be missed, but it can't be helped. A half 'un for ye then, Eamon?" The balding man turned to look for the waiter and saw Billy.

Mr. Doherty stood. "This is the lad I told ye about, Connor, who I met at the Gathering this morning. Billy, is it?"

Connor, his pate glistening, pointed to a chair. "Beastly out there. This'll warm ye up." He pushed a half 'un of ale toward Billy and turned again to look for the waiter. "Another for each of us, please, Tiernan."

Billy took a deep breath and nodded to each of the men. Tears threatened but he forced them back.

"So," said Mr. Doherty, sitting again. "I was just explaining to my mates that ye recently came to Ireland from America. Did I remember that right?"

"Mr. Doherty, I think?" said Billy.

"I apologize, lad. Ye can call me Eamon. The man serving us is my son, Tiernan Doherty. This is Connor. Next to ye is Toby."

They're all old. Except the waiter.

"Tell us about yerself, Billy," invited Connor, removing his damp jacket to reveal muscular arms. "Give me yer jacket." He turned toward the fireplace and added his jacket and cap and Billy's to several others hanging on hooks nearby.

"I was born in Idaho, in America. But my father is—was—Irish," said Billy as Connor sat again.

"Yer father is no longer living, then?" asked Eamon.

"No. I just found that out, three days ago, from my half-brother," said Billy, tearing up despite himself. "I've been walking west since then, to get far away from Portlaw. I don't even know where I am."

"I'm sorry for yer loss, mate," said Connor, bowing his head.

"Ye aren't close to yer half-brother?" asked Eamon.

"No. Until I went to my father's house, I didn't know he existed. He didn't even speak to me. Just told his butler to send me to the kitchen for a plate of food. The butler told me never to come back." Billy put his hands over his face and wept. Toby placed a large hand on Billy's shoulder.

"We're all brothers here, lad," said Eamon. "We look out for each other."

Billy wiped his eyes.

"How long since ye've eaten?" asked Connor.

"T—two days," said Billy. *This man beside me, Toby, hasn't said a word.*

Connor waved to catch the young waiter's attention. "Soup for all of us. And soda bread, Tiernan."

Toby made a grunting sound and did something with his hands.

"Toby wants to know why ye came to Ireland from America," said Eamon. "And how old ye are. And he says I should tell ye ye're in the town of Killeagh."

Oh. Maybe Toby can't talk. Billy turned toward Toby. "We—my mother and I—hadn't heard from my father for a long time, so I came to find him. We didn't know he was dead." Billy's eyes teared up again and he pressed his hands against his eyes.

"We understand. We've all lost someone," said Eamon. "And how old are ye?"

"Sixteen," Billy lied. *I've said that enough times I'm starting to believe it myself.* "Wh—what do you do?" Billy directed his question to Connor. *He seems to be the leader of whatever this group is.*

"I'm a metalworker by trade," said Connor.

"And I'm a farmer," said Eamon. "Sheep."

Toby moved his hands.

"Toby's a blacksmith," explained Eamon.

"I meant—what do you do together?" Billy gestured around the circle as Tiernan arrived with two bowls of soup. Connor pointed to Billy and Toby.

"I'll be right back with the others," said Tiernan.

"Go on, lad," said Connor. "We know ye're hungry. While ye eat, I'll explain. We are Irishmen who believe we should be our own masters, not ruled by the English. Do ye know anything about our history?"

Billy swallowed, savoring the salty warmth of the soup. "I know there was a terrible famine, and many Irish people went to America to escape it. I had a friend in school who was Irish. His grandparents lost their farm and took their family to New York. Their son, my friend's father, went to Idaho to work on the railroad."

"Did ye know we've been under the English fer centuries, and they have treated us cruelly?" asked Eamon.

"I heard you talk about that at the Gathering," said Billy. "I saw the crowd and went to see what it was about. Then you spoke to me and told me it was a Gathering. But I didn't know what that meant."

Toby did his hand thing again.

"Toby says I can tell ye the English cut out his tongue after he was caught spying," said Eamon. "But he's not sorry he tried."

"Ye see, Billy, we want independence from England," said Connor. "Over the centuries people have tried to achieve this all kinda ways, and paid a high price, but nothing has worked. So far. A group of us from Killeagh—many of those here now"—he gestured toward the others in the pub—"decided to travel to Cork City tomorrow to hear a man named Arthur Griffith speak about his ideas of what to try next. Can ye read, Billy?"

"Of course," retorted Billy.

"Then read this." Connor pulled a newspaper from under his chair. "It's an article by Mr. Griffith. Himself started the *United Irishman*. If it interests ye at all, ye could join us on our trip to hear him speak."

Billy squinted at the article in the darkness of the pub. "I don't have anything else to do. I'll go, sure." *I wonder what my father would have thought about this. He wasn't poor like these men. He lived in a mansion.*

"Many people across Ireland and in America and Canada believe as we do, that Ireland should belong to the Irish. Mr. Griffith wants to organize us in some way," said Eamon. "There's strength in numbers, ye see. Killeagh is a small town. We can't do much by ourselves, so we must join with others. Why don't ye come home with me tonight to sleep. We'll leave early tomorrow for Cork City."

"Where is Cork City?" asked Billy.

"It's twenty miles west, the biggest city in our county," said Connor. "We'll walk all morning, 'cept them as have horses and wagons, aiming to get there by noon. All right then, mates. We'll see ye back here at 4:00 in the morning."

"Yer jacket nice and warm now?" asked Eamon as they walked toward the door.

"At least until it gets wet again," said Billy.

"Here's my wagon. Climb in the back and pull the tarpaulin over ye. My farm is a coupla miles away."

Billy rested his head on a sack, lifted the tarpaulin over himself, and wrapped his arms around his chest. *I am tired to my bones. In that barn last night, I was too hungry to sleep ...*

Billy woke to someone pulling the tarpaulin away. Eamon spoke through the darkness. "Come eat, lad, before we go. Ye were sound asleep last night so I left ye in the wagon. My lad Aidan'll go with us, but Tiernan must mind the tavern. We'll load provisions and hitch up the horses while ye eat breakfast. Take yer jacket off and hang it by the fire again."

Billy blew on his cold fingers and climbed stiffly from the wagon. *I don't know what I'm getting into. But so long as these people want to feed me, I'll go along and learn what this Gathering thing is about. If I don't like it, I'll leave.*

"No, thanks. I'll walk. Aidan can have my turn," Billy told Eamon. *Walking is better than bumping and shaking in that wagon. The roads are terrible. Must be all the rain. This is the third time we've pulled the wagon out of a mudhole.* He sidestepped a puddle only to be splashed by a wagon wheel going through the same muddy water.

These people must feel strongly about this Gathering, to put up with this messy journey. Oh, there's Toby. I wish I could understand what he says with his hands. He sure is kind, though.

Billy watched Toby striding ahead of him, "talking" to Connor. *Good thing Toby can hear. Connor doesn't have to know how to speak with his hands. I think I'm beginning to get the hang of some of Toby's expressions, based on what Connor is saying back.*

Connor glanced behind him and gestured to Billy. "Come walk with us, lad."

Billy smiled and ran to catch up to the men. Over the next hour, responding to their gentle questions, he told Connor and Toby about the old man who had been his father. "I only have a few memories of him. Mother told me it was her fault, not mine, that he left us."

Billy described growing up in a brothel, where the other women cared for him—spoiled him, actually—though his own mother paid him little attention. "There was one other child in the house, a small, sweet five-year-old girl. She died of some kind of infection. That's why I want to become a doctor, to keep little ones from dying."

"If you want to become a doctor, you must go to school," signed Toby. Relaying this, Connor added, "And we don't have a school yet in Killeagh."

"What about that kind woman who adopted Dugan's *leanaí* as her grandchildren?" signed Toby. "She lives in Waterford, I think. Maybe Billy could go to school there."

"Good man, Toby. When we get home, we can ask Dugan how to contact her."

"So, you left your mother hoping to find your father, is that it?" asked Toby.

Billy's eyes brimmed. "Yes. Mother always told me how much my father loved me. And now he's—" Sorrow flooded him. He ran to the side of the road, squatted, and hid his face in his arms as he wept.

A man on horseback rode slowly by, shouting, "We're but half a mile from Cork City. All stop. Rest. Eat. We've made good time. All stop . . . " The man's voice faded as he rode on beside the long caravan of wagons and walkers. Others had joined them as they walked through Castlemartyr, Midleton, Carrigtwohill, Glounthaune Village.

Across from him, a lake shimmered. Turning, Billy saw buildings in the distance, the road packed with walkers. A group on bicycles sped past him, yelling for people to move. The sun flashed through racing clouds, a widening band of blue stretching down toward the city. *Maybe it won't rain on the Gathering as everyone feared.*

"Billy, come eat with us." Billy startled at a gentle touch on his shoulder. Eamon helped him to his feet and guided him toward the wagon, its tailgate flat and spread with the food Mrs. Doherty had provided for them. Aidan entertained them with farm stories. Billy found himself laughing. *What kind people. I never knew I would feel so grateful for a full stomach.*

Munching his soda bread and goat cheese sandwich, Billy noticed Toby looking at him. His smile seemed to say, "We're glad you're with us. Everything will be all right. You'll see." Billy took a deep breath and smiled back.

CHAPTER 3

CHARLIE

Note: Laoise is pronounced lee-sha. Aisling is ash-ling. Caoimhe is kee-va. Killeagh is Kill-la.

Waterford City, Ireland, Friday, December 2, 1904

"THAT WAS A DELIGHTFUL REHEARSAL, don't you think, Laoise?" said Charlie as they settled into his sister Margaret's carriage. "Now I can greet you properly. Come here."

Laoise scooted across the seat to his kiss and embrace. "Mmm, it's good to see you."

Charlie sighed. "It's been only three weeks this time, but to me it felt like an eternity. Thank you for making the extra, inconvenient trip from Galway to attend this rehearsal. What time is your train to Derry?"

"Not until ten p.m. I chose the overnight train to have the whole day with you."

"Then let's have lunch downtown. How about the Reginald Bar?"

Laoise laughed. "Charlie the traditionalist. Sure. Then we can decide whether we think the ground is too sodden for a walk along the river."

Charlie stuck his head out to signal the driver. After the carriage changed course, he said, "Speaking of tradition, I've been playing for the Christmas concert with the Waterford Ensemble for fifteen years, since I was ten. Hard to believe!"

"They love you, darling," said Laoise. "And they were responsive to our preferences of interpretation. I appreciate that."

"Yes, especially your change of tempo in the middle of the 'Gloria,'" said Charlie with a slight frown.

"I could tell you weren't happy about that," said Laoise.

"I'll get there. You know changes are hard for me, dear heart." Charlie shifted to look out the window as they passed the huge Waterford glass factory. "What would you think of living here, Laoise? We've talked about New York, Paris, Vienna, Kansas City, Dublin. . . . We need to figure this out."

"It would be nice to be near Margaret and her family. It's a port, and within Ireland we can travel anywhere by train. Perhaps later, after . . . "

"You're thinking about your mum."

"I am, Charlie. Wherever we live, part of my heart will always be straining towards her." Tears sprang to Laoise's sapphire eyes.

"Then let's decide now. We'll live in Dublin for as long as your mother is with us." Charlie hugged Laoise as she wept. "While we're there for Christmas, let's start looking around for a place. All right?"

"Th—thank you, Charlie. I s—so hope she'll still be alive when we marry."

"I think anticipating and planning your wedding will energize her," said Charlie. "As will knowing you'll be close by whenever you're not touring. She may have years yet, rather than the months we've been fearing."

"May—maybe. I hope so." Laoise straightened, blew her nose, took some deep breaths, and tidied her dark hair. "We still haven't settled on a wedding date, Charlie."

"It's complicated, given your itinerary and mine," Charlie said, pulling a small notepad from his pocket. "June 17th, I think, is the earliest possible Saturday, but it would give you only a week at home after Frankfurt. Will that be enough time, or would later in June or July be better? Since we're both taking three months off from touring after the wedding, we could set a later date and perhaps feel less pressured going into it. I want you to decide, my love. I'll support whatever date you choose."

"Charlie, I've been thinking of a slightly different approach—"

Charlie grinned. "Eloping?"

Laoise laughed. "Not exactly. This will stretch you, but please hear me out."

"I'm listening."

"Charlie, what if we get married civilly while we're with my family in Dublin for Christmas? We can keep it a secret, to not scandalize people."

Charlie sat up straight. "You mean, a month from now? Laoise, how can we? I mean . . . "

"All we have to do is sign some paperwork, wear any old nice-ish clothes, and show up at the registry office."

"You've been researching this."

"Yes. Along with my parents, we could invite your mum and maybe your Dublin cousins, if they'll keep our secret. I know the idea is unconventional—"

"But Laoise, your mum has her heart set on a gorgeous wedding gown and—"

"We can still have the church ceremony and reception in June, with all the frills Mum wants for her only daughter. She's already hired someone to help her plan and carry out the most memorable wedding ever. But should God take her sooner than June, I'll know she was present for what matters most, my legal commitment to be your wife."

Charlie sat back, staring at Laoise. "Would we then—I mean—when we see each other between concerts after—"

"Would we consummate our marriage? I don't see why not. We'll be man and wife." Laoise snuggled into Charlie's arms, lifted his hand, and kissed the tips of his fingers.

"Oh my," said Charlie.

The carriage passed the huge, ancient Reginald's Tower and drew up in front of the old Reginald Bar. The driver opened Laoise's door and extended his hand.

"Thank you, sir," smiled Laoise.

"Please return for us in three hours," instructed Charlie.

After selecting a table near a window and ordering food, Charlie turned to Laoise with a smile. "It's going to be amazing being married to you, darling. I'll never know what to expect."

"Perhaps we'll loosen you up a bit," grinned Laoise. "I noticed you ordered shepherd's pie, soda bread, and salad. That's my Charlie, the traditionalist. But I'm glad. I'm hungry, and they'll have your choices ready to serve."

"If you loosen me up just a bit at a time, I think I can handle it. I love your innovative spirit, Laoise. Ah, here's our food already. Thank you, miss."

"You have the rest of the day to decide about my idea, darling." Laoise took a big bite of shepherd's pie. "Yum!"

"I must decide today?"

"Um hmm." Laoise swallowed. "I have the paperwork in my valise, all filled out except your signature. Their only open date is January 3. Applying on such short notice, I had to beg for an exception. I'll have to mail it tonight from the train station."

"You've gone to a lot of trouble already," said Charlie. "What if I say no?"

"I'll be disappointed, certainly. I've been thinking about this since we were together in Prague a month ago. But I don't see any down sides. Do you?"

"You caught me off guard, that's all. I've been thinking so much about June or July."

Laoise sipped her ale. "I understand, dear. Remind me of your plans for the rest of December."

"I only have one commitment, a series of Christmas benefit concerts for the children's hospital in Belfast. I'll return to Margaret's house after that for some personal time of review and planning and practice."

Charlie buttered his soda bread and added, "Mum wants me to make a trip with her to Killeagh tomorrow."

"Killeagh? Where is that?"

"It's a village in County Cork."

"How long will it take you to get there?"

"About fourteen hours, I think."

"Did I tell you I rode in an automobile when I was in London? It went so fast—fifteen miles an hour, I think! We were all terrified!"

"Fifteen miles an hour! That's almost four times as fast as a horse!" exclaimed Charlie.

"Yes. Imagine the trip to Killeagh in an automobile. You could be there in four hours instead of fourteen."

"If the automobile didn't get stuck in the mud. The roads weren't made for automobiles."

"I know. And Da told me there are only fourteen automobiles in all of Ireland so far. They're all imported and dreadfully expensive. But why are you going to Killeagh?" Laoise ate the last bite of her salad.

Charlie swallowed and replied, "Our friends Dugan and Aisling lost a child last month, born prematurely. It's been terribly hard for them and their three other children. And, Dugan thinks he may have seen Billy. In Killeagh!"

"Billy? . . . Oh, the laddie you all decided was the treasure in your Idaho treasure hunt. He ran away, right?"

"Good memory, Laoise. Yes. Mum feels personally responsible for his disappearance."

"You told me. On the ship, she failed to recognize Billy as part of your family, right?"

"Yes. She's excited that he may have turned up here in southern Ireland."

"What do you know about it?" asked Laoise, looking around for the waiter. "I'd like tea."

Charlie signaled, ordered tea for them both, then answered Laoise's question. "All I know is that Dugan literally ran into a dark-skinned lad as he left Killeagh's Old Thatch Inn a couple of weeks ago. Friends told him later the lad called himself Billy. There aren't many people with dark skin in southern Ireland, so he was noticed."

"Dugan and Aisling are Cally's aunt and uncle, right? And for some reason no one understands, Cally refused to return to them after her father died."

"That's right," said Charlie. "Her da's name was Frank. I'm impressed you remember all this. I met Dugan and Aisling when I went with Mum and Father to tell them about Frank's death. Despite their grief, they've been our friends ever since. Mum fills in as honorary grandmother to Dugan and Aisling's children, since all four of their parents are dead."

"So much loss. And such kindness on the part of your mother."

"Yes. Mum says it's life-giving for her, since she misses my father. And apart from Margaret's three, her other grandchildren live far away. She truly loves Dugan and Aisling and their family."

Charlie sat back and placed his utensils on his plate. "That was delicious."

"I'm glad you can go with your mum, Charlie."

"Me too. You've polished off that whole plate. Would you like dessert?"

"No thanks."

"Then let's take a long walk by the river," said Charlie. "We have all afternoon to enjoy before we go to Margaret's house for dinner."

Laoise looked through the thick glass window as Charlie helped her don her wrap. "Sunshine in winter is a treat."

They turned onto a path beside the quay, Laoise snuggling Charlie's arm.

"This is where your family once built ships, isn't it."

"Yes, the largest fleet of steamers in the world, back then. Neptune Shipyards and Neptune Ironworks still functioned for a few years after the bankruptcy, but they closed in 1882, three years after I was born. I have a vague memory of my father bringing me to see the shipyard before it was sold. I think I remember it because he was so sad. He loved everything to do with shipbuilding and sailing."

"And passed that on to your brother Daniel, right?"

"The building part, not the sailing. Too bad Daniel moved to Belfast. I miss him."

"But your father was able to keep his ship?"

"Yes, the *Lion III.* And he was smart enough to leave the ship to his first officer, Paudeen, who still allows our family to sail to and from America free of charge. Paudeen is a wonderful man. One day we'll sail on the *Lion III* together, and you can meet him."

"I want to hear about your time in Switzerland with your mentor, Herr Paderewski. I know he means the world to you."

Charlie guided Laoise around a large puddle. "He does, yes. I hope you can meet him someday too. . . ."

Laoise clapped and then hugged Sally and Cait. "I love hearing you sing. Perhaps you and your cousins could sing for our wedding. What do you think?"

The girls, beaming, turned to their mother. "May we, Mummy?" asked Sally.

"What would they sing?" asked Margaret.

"We'll figure it out and let you know," said Laoise. "Girls, did you know your cousin Molly directs a children's choir in Belfast? My brother Desmond attended a concert with his girlfriend and when they saw the name Molly Malcomson, they went to talk with her. That's what gave me the idea for our wedding."

Charlie stood up from the sofa and stretched. "This has been lovely, Margaret. It's almost time for Laoise's train, and Mum and I must rise early for our long trip to Killeagh."

Cathleen stood as well. "I'd best go to bed. Thank you for the delicious dinner and delightful evening, dear. Give me a hug, children." Sally, Cait, and wee Peter ran to say good night.

"The carriage will be ready at 5:00, so you shouldn't have to drive too long after dark," said Margaret. "Cook will have breakfast for you at 4:30, and food for you to take on your journey. Give my love and condolences to Dugan and Aisling. I'll see you on your return. Good night. Mum."

"We won't be back until at least Monday night. Maybe Tuesday or Wednesday, depending on what we learn when we get to Killeagh. Don't worry if we're delayed," said Cathleen.

"You're hoping for more news about Billy, right? I understand, Mum. I hope you find him." Margaret hugged her mother, then turned to her children. "All right, first one in bed gets to choose a story. Da will read to you tonight. He'll help you, son, while the girls and I choose their clothes for tomorrow."

"Let's go, Da!" yelled four-year-old Peter, running after Sally and Cait.

When they were alone, Laoise turned to Charlie. "Dearest, it's time to decide. My carriage leaves for the train station in fifteen minutes."

Charlie took a deep breath. "Let's do it. I'll sign the application."

Laoise gave him a radiant smile and opened her valise. "I'm glad, Charlie."

Her look of love took Charlie's breath away. "I'm glad too, my precious, darling lassie."

"You can invite your mum to the ceremony while you're on your trip to Killeagh. You're sure she'll keep our secret?"

"She's good at that, Laoise. I know she'll want to be there to share our joy."

"Whew, I'm tired," said Cathleen, as their carriage slowed in front of Killeagh's Old Thatch Inn a few minutes after sunset.

"It's been a long journey," agreed Charlie. "Dugan is meeting us here?"

"Yes. He'll have supper with us, and tomorrow we'll go out to the farm to see Aisling."

As they gathered their things, the inn door opened. Red hair curled from beneath a man's duncher. "It's good of ye to come Cathleen, Charlie," he said, green eyes crinkling as he hugged them both. "Let me take yer luggage to yer room, and we can talk over supper. I took the liberty of ordering for ye."

"Thank you, Dugan. Allow me just a few minutes to freshen up," said Cathleen.

"Of course. Take all the time ye need."

"I'll be with you shortly, gentlemen."

"Can I tell Dugan your secret, Charlie?" Cathleen asked when they were settled at a corner table in the bar.

"Umm . . ." said Charlie, looking up from his salmon pie.

"Charlie's getting married, Dugan!" exclaimed Cathleen. "In Dublin, in June. You'll come, won't you? With Aisling and the children?"

Charlie breathed a sigh of relief. *Why did I doubt Mum would keep the true secret.*

"Of course. We would love to. Who is the fortunate bride, Charlie?"

"Her name is Laoise. I met her at the Dublin Music Academy when we were both students there, and we reconnected when the New York

Philharmonic invited us to do a series of concerts with them, Irish classics. Laoise plays the violin."

"I've met her," said Cathleen. "She's as gracious as she is lovely."

"I'm delighted for ye, Charlie," said Dugan, standing and pulling Charlie up into a hug. "Does this mean—I mean to say, is there any possibility—"

"That Cally and Felicity will come to the wedding? I expect they will, Dugan. I'm her brother now, you know."

"This is the best news in the world," said Dugan. "If this doesn't cheer Aisling, nothing will. She'll be counting the days."

"196," said Charlie. "A very long time yet."

Everyone laughed, then Cathleen said, "Please tell me more about Aisling, Dugan. I'm so very sorry for your loss of the baby."

For a moment, Dugan looked at his plate. "As ye know, the baby came early. He was already dead. It was the hardest thing Aisling and I have experienced. Even harder than losing Cally and Teddy since we still have hope of seeing them again. I'm worried about Aisling. I've never seen her so sad. She hardly gets out of bed."

Cathleen's eyes filled with tears. She put her hand on Dugan's forearm. "I can imagine, Dugan. I am so very sorry."

"It's been two weeks. The children and I need her, but she seems—what can I say . . . She's different than I've ever seen her," said Dugan.

"That's a very short time, given the immensity of her loss," said Cathleen. "How is she with Caoimhe, Cathal, and Christopher?"

"That's just it. She's not talking to any of us. She turns her face away when we go into her bedroom. Caoimhe is managing meals and the house, with some help from her brothers and me."

"A heavy load for a just-turned-thirteen-year-old," said Cathleen.

"Ya, it is. The babby was a surprise, but we were all looking forward to its birth, and of course Caoimhe hoped for a girl. Aisling refused to attend his burial. Truly, I don't understand—it's almost as if she is punishing the rest of us for the babby's death."

"Please don't think of it that way, Dugan. A mother can bond with the child in her womb, even before meeting him or her. I reacted much the same way when we lost our child."

Charlie gasped. "We lost a child, Mum? You never told me this!"

Cathleen extended her other hand to Charlie. "Yes, son. We lost a baby; you were not yet two and can't possibly remember. Your father and I saw no reason to burden you with it."

"But—but it's my brother. Or sister. How could you think I wouldn't care?"

"A wee girl, Charlie. I believe God gave us Cally to take her place in my heart."

"Oh, Mum. I'm disappointed you never thought to share this with me. Surely Daniel, Margaret, and Thomas knew about it and remember. Yet no one ever mentioned it to me."

"Our baby wasn't premature. When the time came close, we sent you four children to Priscilla and Silas in Dublin. When the baby died, Priscilla simply extended the time she cared for you. It may have been hard on you, Charlie, since you were so young, but for the other three it was simply a wonderful holiday. We never talked about it after the four of you came home. That's the way things were done back then."

"Well, I want to talk more about this, Mum. Perhaps on our ride back to Waterford?"

"Yes, let's plan on that, Charlie. Right now, we must focus on Aisling. I'm glad I'll have time with her tomorrow."

"And we want to know about Billy," said Charlie.

"Oh yes. Billy," said Dugan. "Sure, I interacted with him for only a few seconds. I didn't know his name until I talked later with my friend Eamon. But it all fits. He told Eamon he grew up in Idaho, America, and came to Ireland to find his father. He had just walked from Portlaw to Killeagh. He learned from his half-brother, as he believed him to be, that his father had died years ago. He and his mother never knew."

"Where is Billy now?" asked Charlie.

Dugan frowned. "I wish we knew. He went with Eamon and his lad Aidan to a Gathering in Cork City to hear Mr. Griffith. I had planned to go, but that was the night Aisling—" Dugan's eyes teared.

Charlie pulled a handkerchief from his pocket and handed it to Dugan, who sat for a moment staring at the table. Finally, giving himself a little shake, Dugan took a sip of his ale and continued. "Eamon told me they lost sight of Billy in the crowd. They searched for him a long time after the speeches were over, but never saw the lad again."

"I've heard that name, Griffith," said Charlie. "He started a newspaper or something?"

"Yes, *The United Irishman.* It's all about gaining independence from England."

"Sounds dangerous," said Charlie.

"Could be," said Dugan, his brow furrowed. "But Mr. Griffith believes in achieving his goals peacefully. We in Killeagh are only starting to learn what he has in mind. We're all reading his paper."

"So that's the last you or your friend Eamon heard or saw of Billy?" asked Cathleen.

"Sadly, yes."

"Oh my," said Cathleen. "Then the next thing we must do is find Mr. Griffith. Perhaps Billy is with him."

"It's worth a try, I suppose. I've heard Mr. Griffith is traveling all over Ireland advocating for his ideas and his newspaper. Eamon thinks he's brilliant, that there might truly be a new chance to work for independence."

Cathleen brightened. "My grandfather, Daniel O'Connell, also believed independence could be achieved through peaceful means."

"Begging your pardon, and meaning no offense, Cathleen, some people say nonviolence has never worked. They say, 'Look at us today, still subject to our English masters.' That's what people are discussing. Some say Mr. Griffith is misguided and the only way will be through a revolution. Like the Americans."

"But Mr. Gladstone achieved a great deal through peaceful means," said Charlie.

"That's as may be, but what kind of world are we leaving for our children? That's what Eamon and Connor and the others keep asking. Shouldn't we be willing to fight, even to lay down our lives, for our children's freedom?"

"I wonder whether Billy could be getting mixed up with all this," Cathleen said softly. "If only I had—"

"Mum, how could you possibly have known?" Charlie pulled his chair close and put his arm around her shoulders. "You'll pray, I know you will, and when we return to Dublin, we'll track down Mr. Griffith's itinerary. God willing, by locating him, we'll find our lad."

CHAPTER 4

CALLY

Note: Laoise is pronounced *lee-sha*. Aisling is pronounced *ash-ling.*

Kansas City, Saturday, December 24, 1904

AS USUAL, CALLY WOKE IN time to turn off her alarm clock before it would wake her daughter Felicity. But a headache pulled her head back to her pillow. *I'm so tired. I don't want to get out of bed.*

In what she had learned to consider sacred, the space between sleep and full wakefulness, Cally heard a familiar voice: "Don't be afraid."

Two weeks later, recording this message in her journal, Cally wrote, *I almost missed it, for my next thoughts were, "My head hurts, and I feel hot. But I've no time to be sick."*

Cally pushed herself out of bed. *Today I have home rounds with Nurse Everson and tomorrow, Christmas, I'm scheduled at the hospital. I'm needed. The hospital is overflowing with influenza patients.*

ଓଃ

Cally smiled her thanks as Nora set a stack of pancakes before her, along with a letter. *Oh, it's from Aisling. A treat for later.* The first bite of breakfast roiled her stomach. She pushed away her plate and tried to pay attention to the conversation at the table.

"We've received several Christmas letters," Thomas told the family. "We could read a couple of them each meal until we get through them. Who wants to read a letter from Charlie? He wrote to us from Margaret's house in Waterford."

Shauna's hand shot up a split second before her twin Shane's. "I do!"

"All right, Shauna. You can read the next one, Shane," said their father, handing Shauna an envelope.

"It's already open," protested Shauna.

"I opened it," said her mother, Cora. "I hoped there would be news about Charlie and Laoise's wedding, and I wasn't disappointed!"

"Read it, Shauna!" said Shane.

"Can I be in the wedding?" asked Josie.

"It's long," said Shauna. "Keep quiet, Josie.

Waterford

December 7, 1904

My very dear family, I love and miss you and wish Laoise and I could be with you this Christmastime. But first, Happy Birthday, Shane and Shauna!! I'm sorry I missed celebrating you two turning 11."

Shauna grinned at her brother across the table.

"Laoise and I will divide the Christmas holidays between Margaret and Percy's home in Waterford, with Mum, and the Murphy home in Dublin, with Laoise's parents. Both homes will have family visiting from Belfast! Daniel, Meghan and his children plan to spend Christmas at Margaret's, and Laoise's brother Desmond will introduce us to his just-announced fiancée Deirdre."

Shauna paused to ask, "Do the Murphys have other children besides Laoise and Desmond, Mummy?"

Cora looked to Thomas for help.

"No, just the two of them," said Thomas.

"Keep reading, Shauna," said Cora.

"I haven't heard whether Desmond and Deirdre have chosen a wedding date. But we have! June 17th at 10:00 a.m. at St. Catherine's, Laoise's family's church in Dublin. You must all come! We'll have a reception in Mrs. Murphy's beautiful garden. We'll send more details soon, but for

now, please block out time in June for traveling and for several days with us in Dublin."

Cally blanched. She gripped the edge of the table, blinking her eyes, trying to focus as Shauna continued.

"As you know, one of our conundrums has been where we should live: Dublin? Waterford? New York? Kansas City? Both of us tour in Europe, and I in America, and we're not fond of the Atlantic crossing. We've finally settled on Dublin, because Laoise's mum's health is fragile. Please pray Mrs. Murphy will be well enough to participate in our wedding. It will be heartbreaking for Laoise if she can't."

"We're going to Dublin!" shouted Shane. Josie and Felicity, seven and six, took up the chant, "We're going to Dublin! We're going to Dublin! We're—"

"All right, children," said Thomas. "Let Shauna finish reading the letter."

"We came to Waterford to practice for the Christmas concert with the Waterford Ensemble. Laoise will play with me! Both of us have concerts the next three weeks, but only here in Ireland, thank God. She sends her love and Christmas greetings along with mine. Give each other hugs from us. Love, Charlie"

"Why are you frowning, Mummy?" Felicity asked Cally. "Isn't this good news? We get to go to Ireland for Uncle Charlie's wedding!"

Max knocked on the dining room door. At Thomas's nod, he entered. "I'm sorry to interrupt, sir. Miss Cally, we must leave for the hospital now. The snowfall will disrupt traffic."

Cally stood. A wave of dizziness swept over her. She touched the table for balance and turned back to Felicity. "Charlie and Laoise's wedding is good news, Felicity. But I don't know whether the hospital will give me that much time off. You can go, though, even if I can't."

"Of course, you can, Felicity," said Cora, after a hard look at Cally.

Cally touched Felicity's shoulder. "Have a wonderful Christmas, all of you. I'll see you in two days, Felicity."

As Cally walked out, Thomas said, "We'll save the next letter for luncheon. We don't often have this much snow. Who wants to build a snowman?"

"I would!" yelled each child as all four jumped up from the table. Their excitement trailed Cally to the front door as she pulled on her coat and boots.

"I'll ask Nora for a carrot for the nose!" yelled Shane.

"And I'll get coal for the buttons," said Shauna.

"Mummy has a red scarf. That will keep him warm," said Felicity.

Cally pulled off her red scarf and substituted a green one. *Though I'm so hot I hardly think I need a scarf.*

"Can we use your hat, Daddy?" Josie asked Thomas.

"Don't forget our plan to take food to the Turners," Cora said to Thomas as he walked to the coatrack, its contents now largely a heap on the floor.

"I haven't forgotten. This will be a good experience for our children."

I wish I could go. The Turners suffered so much from the Jim Crow laws. I'm glad Thomas is helping people escape the south. Cally handed her valise to Max. Turning for a last look at the gay Christmas decorations, she realized Cora stood there, watching her.

Cora shook her forefinger at Cally. "After Christmas, Cally, we need to talk."

❧

As Max maneuvered the carriage through traffic and snow to the hospital, Cally pulled Aisling's letter from her pocket. Aisling described the tragic loss of her child. At the end, she practically shouted her joy that Cally would come to Ireland for Charlie's wedding. "Please bring Teddy with you. I long to see you both."

Cally gazed unseeing out the window of the carriage. *She must have heard about the wedding from Cathleen even before Charlie wrote to us. What can I tell her? I can't go back to Ireland. I can't.*

The carriage rocked as Max pushed through a crowd of pedestrians, intent on their final Christmas shopping. *Lord, help! I think I might throw up!*

Cally pressed her handkerchief to her mouth. *Cora saw through my excuse that I might not be able to get away from the hospital for the wedding.*

She knows my time there will end the last day of May, and I'm not expected in Idaho until the end of June. I need Flora to invent a reason I must go directly to Idaho at the beginning of June. But what will I say to Cora in the meantime?

The carriage slowed and stopped. "I'm sorry you must work on Christmas Eve, Miss Cally," said Max, grasping her gloved hand to help her step over a pile of snow. He put her valise in her hand and tipped his hat.

"I work Christmas Day also," said Cally. "I'll sleep at the hospital tonight. Thank you, Max. Merry Christmas. Enjoy your day off."

"Merry Christmas, Miss Cally." Max climbed to the bench and drove away.

Cally stepped into the busy hospital lobby, leaned against a wall, and looked around for Nurse Everson.

Later, she didn't remember crashing to the floor. She did remember a dream playing over and over in various permutations through the next days and nights of fever. Faeries made a ruckus at Charlie and Laoise's wedding. Each time, Mrs. Murphy fainted dead away. In her dreams, Cally knew it was her fault.

CHAPTER 5

BILLY

Cork City, Ireland, November 19, 1904

HUNDREDS OF PEOPLE JOSTLED EACH other crossing St. Patrick's bridge spanning the River Lee, as a stiff wind scuttled clouds across the sun. Billy and his caravan pressed forward with the crowd onto the grounds surrounding Saints Peter and Paul Church. Billy managed to turn in a full circle, taking in the spires of an elegant church across the channel to the south and a huge stone construction on a bluff high above the city.

"That's Elizabeth Fort," Eamon said, following Billy's gaze up the embankment. "It's built in the shape of a star. And those spires are Saint Fin Barre Cathedral, built forty years ago by the Church of Ireland. Isn't it grand? A Catholic monastery once stood there, but the Anglicans took over the land during the Protestant Reformation. That's when the Catholics built Saints Peter and Paul's."

"I don't know what Protestant and Catholic mean," said Billy, but Eamon apparently didn't hear him. Billy turned to follow him as their group pushed closer to a wooden platform erected in front of the church. A wave of new arrivals forced him to the side, away from the stage, and knocked him into a bush. As he struggled to his feet, several men emerged from the church through a side door. They turned away from Billy, following the church wall to mount the stage from the back.

Rain began to fall. Billy looked around for shelter. He followed the men to the back of the stage, crept under the wooden platform and sat leaning against a post. *I know they're talking up there, but I can't hear the words. Whew, I'm tired. That was a long walk.* Sheltered from the rain and chill wind, he fell asleep.

A scraping sound woke Billy. Suddenly two wood planks above him were pulled away, and then two more. It was dark. The rain had stopped, but a cold wind still blew into his quickly disappearing shelter. Billy jumped to his feet. *I don't want them to see me. I might get in trouble.*

"Who is this, then," a strong voice asked. "Grab him, lads. He may have had evil intentions toward our speakers. Tie him up."

Billy ran straight into the arms of two workmen, who made short work of tying his hands and feet. "He's but a lad," one of them said.

"Lads can be used to carry out the plans of their elders," the original voice said. "Carry him to Father Barrett."

"More likely he was just trying to get out of the rain," said the other workman. But they obeyed, and Billy found himself plunked on the floor of a small room before an old man in a long robe.

"We found him hiding under the stage, Father Barrett," reported the first workman. "Mr. MacDonagh thinks he had evil intentions."

Father Barrett peered at Billy through thick glasses. "Why ye're but a lad," he said. "And a sort of lad we don't often see in these parts. What's yer name, son?"

"B-B-Billy," he said, scooting backward toward the door. "I-I didn't mean any harm. It was warm and dry, and I fell asleep."

"Don't be afraid. I believe ye." Father Barrett rang a bell on a small table beside his chair. "Tea for two, please," he said to the curate who answered his call. "But first, untie this child."

I'm not a child! I'm sixteen—well, fourteen . . .

"I'm Father Barrett," the priest said. "I came from Enniskeane Parish to attend and speak at the Gathering. It's too late to ride thirty miles home, so I'm enjoying the hospitality of Peter and Paul overnight. You?"

"I came with friends from—from a small town, I forget its name." Billy rubbed his wrists. *I wonder why he calls himself "Father."*

"Ye're not from Ireland."

"N-no, sir. I'm from America. I came to find my father."

"Yer father is Irish, then?"

"He-he was. He's dead."

"I'm sorry for yer loss, lad. Where is yer mother?"

"She's in Idaho. At least she was. When I left."

"I see. Ye left her to find yer father. And after traveling a very long way to get here, ye found out yer father was gone."

"Ye-yes, sir."

"What are yer plans now, then? Will ye return to yer mother?"

"I-I don't know. She doesn't care much about me. I want to go to school and become a doctor. I don't care whether I do that in Ireland or in America."

"Ah, our tea. Thank ye, Robert. Would ye like a cup of tea in yer hand, Billy? I see Robert brought us some cakes as well. Pull up that chair and I'll say the blessing. Ye must be hungry. And then we'll find ye a corner to sleep in tonight."

"Ye-yes, sir. Thank ye, sir." *What does he mean, say the blessing? I guess I'll find out. The Irish always want to feed me. I'm glad for that!*

Men were talking. Billy kept his eyes closed and strained to hear.

"Did Mr. Griffith get off all right?"

That's the old man wearing the funny robe speaking.

"Yes, he caught the stage to Limerick in good time. I think he was pleased with the Gathering. Tell me about the lad."

That's the man who tied me up.

"His name is Billy. He wants to go to school and become a doctor. Why not take him back with you to St. Colman's, Thomas? Surely there is space in your school for a charity case. He has nothing but the clothes he's wearing, which clearly have not seen water and soap for a long while. But he's intelligent. I want to help him."

"I can take him to Fermoy and have him examined, Father. But whether the school accepts him as a student is not up to me. I'm just a teacher."

The old man's voice dropped. "Ye know, Thomas. Such a lad could be useful to us. He could earn his keep as a messenger."

"But if he were discovered, they would have no mercy." The man called Thomas also lowered his voice.

"Well, it's a thought. He would need an alias and being a student at St. Colman's would be a good one, especially if he's an apt scholar."

"We'd have to find him a bicycle. He's too big to carry on mine all the way to Fermoy."

Don't I have a choice about going to Fermoy, wherever that is? But this is a chance for me to go to school! Now that I know Father is dead, I want that more than anything. I wonder how hard it is to ride a bicycle.

The voices faded. Billy pushed back a blanket and stood up from the bench where he had slept. A dim multi-hued light shone through a window above him. *I better find Father Barrett.* He walked through an open door into a large room full of benches. At his end there were steps leading up to a platform and a cross. Father Barrett knelt before the cross. The other man walked rapidly toward the other end of the long room and out a set of double doors.

"And bless the lad, Billy. Guide him into yer plan for his life," the priest said out loud. He turned his head and smiled, then pushed himself up and walked across the platform toward Billy.

"Good morning, son. I have happy news—I've found ye a school! But first things first. Ah, there ye are, Robert. Please bring breakfast for the lad."

Ha—I know school is a bribe for me to become their messenger boy, and that might be dangerous. I'm going to let him know I overheard that part.

"I don't know how to ride a bicycle," Billy said.

"Bless me, did I mention a bicycle? Oh, but ye're a likely lad. Ye'll learn quickly. Mr. MacDonagh will teach ye. He's gone to find one for ye. Once ye get yer balance, ye'll love riding. Ye must both travel to Fermoy this afternoon because Mr. MacDonagh has classes to teach tomorrow morning."

"How far is Fermoy?"

"Only about twenty miles from Cork City, I believe. Ah, here we go. Thank ye, Robert. Eat yer breakfast, Billy, and then we'll see if we can clean ye up a mite before mass. Robert, do ye have any clothes in the charity box for a lad the size of Billy? Eat and drink, Billy, and then Robert will see to a bath for ye."

Twenty miles! I'm still tired from that long walk yesterday. This old man is used to getting his way, I can tell. But do I have a choice? I bet I could take the bicycle once I learn to ride it and escape back to Killeagh. I remember the name now, Killeagh is Eamon's town. But they don't have a school. I do want to go to school. I better tell them I'm fourteen. Otherwise, they'll put me in a class with work I'm not ready for. I wonder if Eamon and the others missed me and looked for me . . .

"Mr. MacDonagh is an excellent teacher," Father Barrett was saying. "His students love him. I expect soon ye will too. And St. Colman's has an excellent reputation. I believe ye'll make a fine physician one day, Billy lad. Finish yer porridge and we'll prepare ye for mass."

But that Mr. MacDonagh thought I had evil intentions! He tied me up! Should I tell Father Barrett I have no idea what a mass is, or just wait to find out?

St. Colman's School, Fermoy, County Cork, Ireland, Monday, November 21, 1904

Mr. MacDonagh's voice reached Billy on the couch just before he felt a large hand shaking his shoulder. Billy pulled the blanket over his head. *Oh, my muscles are sore. I'm sooo tired. Don't make me get up yet.*

"Billy, listen to me, and then you can go back to sleep. I must go now to my morning classes. At lunchtime I will come back to fetch you to a meeting with the director of the school. I've left breakfast for you on the table. Do you hear me, Billy? You're on your own for the morning, but don't leave my room. You'll get lost. St. Colman's is a big place."

Billy grunted.

Three men sat together looking over the tests Billy had taken. Mr. MacDonagh sat silent beside him on an identical wooden chair while the men talked.

"He's notably behind in history and literature."

"Not surprising, I suppose, since he's from some remote part of America. Do either of you know where Idaho is?"

Both shook their heads.

"His writing is good. He expresses himself well. He's clearly a careful reader."

"And he's at age level in maths and science."

"We could place him in first form, if MacDonagh would agree to tutor him in history and literature."

It sounds like they want to keep me. I wonder what first form is.

"I wonder how he'll fit in with the other lads."

"Socially, you mean?"

"Yes. He's—different. Is he Catholic?"

"I assume he must be, since Father Barrett recommended him."

Billy turned toward Mr. MacDonagh with a frown. The teacher put his finger to his lips.

They talk as if I'm not right here listening to them.

"He may need some coaching in that area as well. I wonder is he any good at sports? He's tall and well developed for fourteen."

All three men raised their heads and looked at Billy, who looked steadily back at them.

As if I'm not even here. I don't even know what kind of sports they play.

Finally, the man who seemed to be the leader addressed Mr. MacDonagh. "We'll give him a trial period, Thomas, if you will help him catch up in his weak areas. There will be an adjustment period, no doubt, but a lad like William will be good for our students educationally. They're too insulated from the wider world. Perhaps William can teach them something about America."

I've never been called William before. I like it—makes me feel I'm truly my father's son.

"Where shall we place him for boarding?" asked another of the men.

"We have a vacant bed in Harry's room, since Anthony went home injured," volunteered Mr. MacDonagh.

"Harry can teach him rugby."

"And hurling."

All three men stared again at Billy. He squirmed. Mr. MacDonagh put a hand on Billy's leg.

They stare at me as if they're hungry. I wonder what they see.

The men stood. The leader said, "All right, MacDonagh. He'll begin classes tomorrow. Take him to Coach O'Brien for his athletic evaluation, to Mistress Everson for measurements for his uniforms, and when afternoon classes are over, introduce him to his roommates. In one month, we'll evaluate his progress."

On his way out the door, the leader stopped. "I expect you to make us proud, William."

Billy blushed scarlet but managed to mumble, "I'll do my best, sir."

The leader nodded and moved on. When the door closed, Mr. MacDonagh turned to Billy. "Welcome to St. Colman's, William. That went extremely well. I'm pleased. Tomorrow after classes we'll have your first tutoring session. Are you ready to work hard?" He pulled out his pocket watch without waiting for a response from Billy.

"Let's take a quick tour before you see Coach O'Brien. Boarding rooms are on the third floor, classrooms on the second, and administration, the dining hall, and activity rooms on the first. We host the Gaelic League. In fact, there's a musical event tonight. Some of your classmates will be performing, along with people from the town. You'll enjoy it. I'll ask Harry to be sure you find the right hall."

I've no idea what the Gaelic League is, or rugby, or hurling. I wonder what kind of boy Harry is. I wonder when Mr. MacDonagh will talk to me about the other part of this deal—the messenger boy part.

By the time Mr. MacDonagh finished showing Billy the school, and then took him for uniform measurements and to meet Coach O'Brien, it was suppertime. Mr. MacDonagh scanned the dining hall and walked Billy toward a red-haired boy a full head taller than most of the students around him. He stood when the teacher addressed him.

Harry turned bright blue eyes toward Billy as Mr. MacDonagh said, "I'm entrusting William to you because you're a leader, Harry. I expect you'll make him welcome and teach him everything about St. Colman's. Including rugby and hurling. The other students will take their cues from you, so don't let me down. I'm confident William will make us all proud one day."

"Yes, sir. Hey you lads. Make room for our new classmate, William."

Mr. MacDonagh smiled and made his way to the head table, where Billy recognized the three who had evaluated him earlier. "I'll do my best," he said again under his breath, then turned his attention to the boys around him and his supper.

☙❧

To his surprise, the music was all sung in a language Billy did not understand, not one word. "It's Gaelic. We're all learning it," whispered Harry. "You will too. It's what the Irish spoke before England banned our native tongue."

Billy tried to listen but fell asleep halfway through. Harry elbowed him in good humor.

When they arrived at his new room on the third floor after the concert, a paper-wrapped package lay on the floor by the door, labeled "William" in large letters. It was a school uniform, with crisply ironed white pants and a green jacket. A note promised two more by the end of the next day.

What a relief! Now I won't look different from the other boys my first day of classes. Well, not much different.

The other boys went straight to their homework. Billy fell onto the bed Harry pointed out as his and remembered nothing more.

CHAPTER 6

CHARLIE AND LAOISE

Dublin Train Station, Monday, January 2, 1905

"THERE YOU ARE, MUM! WHO'S the baby?" Charlie reached out to steady his mother, carrying a wee child as she descended the steps from the train.

Cathleen's laugh trilled. "His mother is corralling his older brother and sister. There they come. Let's help them to their carriage and then we can find my bag."

"Let me help, ma'am. I'm Cathleen's son." Charlie took a valise from a young mother's arm, gaining a look of gratitude as she grasped a child's arm before the wee lassie darted away.

"I don't know how I would have made it without your mum's help." The woman hefted her young son into one arm. "She was a godsend."

"She often is," nodded Charlie. "Shall I call a carriage for you?"

"My brother Sean is meeting us. There he is." She let go of her daughter's arm to wave at a tall man walking onto the platform.

"Oh no, you don't," laughed Charlie, grabbing the child before she disappeared into the crowd. "You get to stay here with us until your uncle can help your mummy."

When Sean reached them, Charlie and Cathleen said goodbye, located her bag, and settled into their own carriage.

"The Royal Hibernian Hotel, please," instructed Charlie.

"Now, son, let me look at you. How are you feeling about this wild scheme Laoise came up with?"

Charlie blushed. "I've quite adapted to the idea, Mum."

"I feel privileged to be included in your elopement. Or are you calling it something else?"

"We've been calling it our 'first vows,' and the June wedding our 'second vows.'"

"Not every marriage gets off to such a solid start, repeating their vows a few months into the adventure. Tell me, how is Mrs. Murphy?"

"I think she'll want you to call her Muriel. She believes we're doing this for ourselves, so please don't dissuade her, Mum. She doesn't need to know Laoise fears she won't still be with us come June."

"Of course not. She's weaker, then?"

"She is. I noticed the change when I arrived. I'm quite concerned about how Laoise will take it when the time comes."

Cathleen put her hand on Charlie's arm. "I'm sorry, Charlie. This is hard."

"Yes, especially as attached as Laoise is to her mum. But the doctor says this could be but a bump in the road. She may rally and have a long time yet. She says she intends to be here to welcome our first child."

"Which, I understand, may be quite far in the future, as both of you continue to invest in your careers."

"That's what we think now, yes, Mum." *I won't tell her right now that Laoise doesn't want to have children.*

"Tell me the order of things tomorrow. Who from Laoise's family will be there?"

"Her parents, of course, Colin and Muriel. And her brother Desmond with his fiancée Deirdre. They're planning to get married in August."

"A busy season for the Murphy family."

"Yes. Our time at the registry office is 8:40. Couples are scheduled every twenty minutes, so we can't be late. We'll need to leave the hotel at eight o'clock. The Murphys have planned a late breakfast at their home afterward."

"Will we check out of the hotel before we go to the registry office?"

"Yes, but we can leave our things in the care of the hotel and pick them up on our way to the train station after breakfast. Laoise and I will see you off to Waterford and then catch a train to Bray. Laoise wants to spend a couple of days at the beach. I'm praying for sunshine."

"Can you only spend two days there?"

"Sadly, yes. Our concert schedule wasn't planned with a honeymoon in mind. We'll take a proper honeymoon in June, though, after our wedding."

"Will you be playing together from now on?"

"No. We'd no idea of getting married in January when we planned our schedule. But we have arranged encounters whenever each of our itineraries allows it. They will keep us going until June."

Cathleen shook her head. "I've never heard of anything like this."

Charlie laughed. "Nor have I, Mum. Nor have I. Here we are at the hotel."

"You may kiss the bride," proclaimed the registry official.

Everyone cheered as Charlie gave Laoise a hearty kiss. Muriel's smile was especially brilliant.

Charlie and Laoise splashed in the shallow, chilly waves lapping the Bray beach, relishing rare warm winter sunshine. Charlie pointed to a man dressed in their hotel's livery scanning the beach.

"I wonder if he's looking for us," Laoise said.

"I'll go find out," said Charlie.

A couple minutes later he was back. "We need to return to the hotel, Laoise. Your father called."

The color drained from Laoise's face. "Oh no."

"We don't know anything yet, Laoise." said Charlie. He held a sweater for her and then anchored her sandals while she stepped into them. Quickly gathering their things, he put his arm around her shoulder as they walked across the sand to the hotel. Laoise looked straight ahead, her mouth clamped shut.

"Here you are, sir. The call has gone through." The hotel operator handed the telephone to Charlie. He offered it to Laoise, but she shook her head. "You. Please, Charlie."

"Mr. Murphy? This is Charlie."

Laoise's eyes didn't leave his face. She startled when he began to smile.

"That's wonderful news. Thank you for calling to let us know. Yes, we'll be home tomorrow. We can celebrate together then, but please congratulate him for us. Would you like to speak to Laoise? All right then. Until tomorrow."

Charlie handed the telephone back to the operator and pulled Laoise into his arms. "It was good news, my precious. Your mum is fine. I'll tell you all about it when we reach our room, all right? We must get you warm."

Tears streamed down Laoise's face as they climbed the stairs. As soon as they were in their room, Charlie took her in his arms and held her as she sobbed. After a time, he said gently, "Laoise, take a bath, dress warmly, and then we can talk about what happened. It's about Desmond. He got the job he applied for. He's moving to Dublin. Your father was so pleased he wanted to share the news with us right away. Take your bath now, please, before you catch your death of cold."

"The shivering wasn't from cold. It was from—from—"

"I know. But your skin is cold. I'll order hot tea."

"Thank you, Charlie. I'll be quick."

"Take your time, dear. We're in no hurry."

Alone, Charlie sagged onto the settee, his head in his hands. *I was as afraid as Laoise that her mother had died. One of these days it's going to happen. I need to prepare myself. This has been a wee taste of what it might be like for Laoise when the real thing happens. I feel totally inadequate to help her. Lord, have mercy. She may not have the courage to travel to the continent for her concert series.*

He pushed himself upright, walked across the room and rang the bell. When the knock came on the door, he told the bellboy, "Tea please."

Charlie stretched and crossed to the double windows. Wind stirred the bay into waves, the sky clouding over. *What if Mrs. Murphy goes into crisis—or, God forbid, dies—while I'm not in the same city with Laoise? What then? I think she needs a traveling companion. But who would be free to go with her?*

His mind flitted over the people they both knew, rejecting each in turn. Suddenly, a memory popped into his head, of buying pastries in Munich for those who served him and his mother on a train headed to Vienna. *Mum! Would she be free to travel with Laoise?*

In the distance, rain suddenly poured down. As he watched, a rainbow appeared, grew, and strengthened. It seemed to him a sign. *I'll ask Laoise. If she says yes, I'll ask Mum.*

A knock sounded on the door. Charlie went to open it for the tea service just as Laoise emerged from the bathroom, a towel around her head.

"I'm fine now, Charlie. I've forgiven my father for scaring me so. Oh, how lovely. A cup of tea in my hand is perfect. Thank you, my darling."

Charlie tipped and thanked the bellboy. Laoise poured the tea.

"Come sit by me, sweet Laoise. I have an idea . . ."

While she listened to Charlie on the telephone, Cathleen smiled at her four-year-old grandson Peter trying to turn somersaults on the living room carpet.

"I understand, Charlie. Yes, I think it makes sense that Laoise can handle the January concerts in Ireland, especially since you'll be with her twice during that time. Can you hold on for a moment while I fetch my diary? I think I remember my plans, but it will be good to note the commitments I will need to change."

As she stood, Peter succeeded in turning a perfect somersault. He came up grinning, and Cathleen gave him a big hug and congratulations on her way to her bedroom. Within moments she was back.

"So, Charlie, I think this is workable. I'm writing down what you told me. You both travel to the Continent February 7, correct? You to Paris and she to Frankfurt. You plan to meet in Vienna February 28th, and in Livorno March 13. You have two weeks together in Switzerland the end of April, where you'll play two concerts together in Geneva thanks to Mr. Paderewski. Then a long stretch apart in May until you both travel to London for two concerts together, then return to Dublin June 5 to prepare for the wedding June 17. Do I have all that right?"

"Those are our plans right now, Mum. I'll prepare a written copy of our concert schedules for you."

"So, I have almost a month to prepare for traveling with Laoise for most of four months. I'll make plans of my own for the dates you two will have together. This sounds fun, Charlie."

Cathleen heard Charlie's breath come out in a whoosh. "I'm so relieved, Mum. I can't tell you how grateful I am already. If you had seen how Laoise reacted when her father telephoned—"

"I can imagine, Charlie. This is terribly challenging for you both. How about this: I will travel to Dublin Friday, February third, so I have time over the weekend to discuss with you, Laoise, and her parents how we will handle things should her mother take a turn for the worse along the way. I'll arrive bag and baggage, prepared for four months, yet aware her itinerary could be cut short."

"Thank you for your flexibility, Mum. Yes, that sounds good. I'll check with Laoise and her parents to confirm February third. But I think a few days with them before we travel will be wise. Better to make plans we don't use than not be prepared should the worst happen."

"All right, then. Please tell Laoise I am delighted with this opportunity to travel together. I love Europe, as you know. I'm sure we'll have a great deal to share with each other."

"Thank you, Mum. I'll look forward to seeing you about a month from now."

"Give Laoise and her parents my love."

CHAPTER 7

CALLY

St. Joseph Hospital, Kansas City, January 3, 1905

"GOOD MORNING, CALLY. ARE YOU feeling better this morning? I've brought you breakfast!" Nurse Saunders spoke through a mask. "Doctor Stephens wants you to drink this, dear."

Cally turned toward the wall and didn't open her eyes. She felt the nurse's hand on her shoulder.

"Cally, how will you get well without nourishment? You have no fever today. Let me help you sit up."

"I'm not hungry. My tummy hurts," said Cally, her eyes still closed.

"Come now. You're a nurse. You know how important nutrition is for healing."

"Just a student nurse," said Cally. "Maybe not even that—." A fit of coughing interrupted her speech.

"You mean because you got sick? You have typhoid fever, Cally. No one blames you for that. When you're well, they'll give you a chance to make up what you've missed in your training. I'm sure of it."

Cally turned her head and opened her eyes. "You really think so?"

"Of course. You've been in isolation, Cally. You've been very ill. Sister Irmena has come by twice to see you, but she could only look at you from the doorway."

Cally let Nurse Saunders help her sit up. "Sister Irmena came? How embarrassing. I don't remember."

The nurse handed Cally a glass of milk. "Cally, if one of your patients was very sick, would you think they should be embarrassed by their illness?"

"Of course not. But I was supposed to meet Nurse Everson and—"

"Nurse Everson saw you fall and responded quickly to get you out of the crowded lobby. You were burning up with fever."

Cally's brow wrinkled. She swallowed a mouthful of milk, then asked, "How can I have typhoid fever again? I had it when I was fourteen. And anyway, I hadn't heard of people having typhoid here."

The nurse folded a blanket and readied supplies for a bed bath. "I'm told you cared for an ill visitor from New York City. Is that right?"

"Yes, about three weeks ago, in the home of his daughter."

"There's an epidemic of typhoid fever in New York. Your patient brought it to Kansas City. We've had four more cases since you got sick, including his daughter. And yes, it is possible to get typhoid fever more than once."

"Do you know whether my family is all right?" Cally set the still half-full glass on her bedside table.

"Yes. Your entire household was put under quarantine. But your sister—Cora, is it?—has been begging to see you. Since you're better and no one from your family has symptoms, the doctor will allow her to visit today, wearing a mask and standing in the doorway. Finish your milk and then I'll help you bathe and tidy up a bit. She'll be here at 10:00."

"I'm glad no one else in the family got this."

"Yes, well, they're still under quarantine. The doctor is allowing your sister's visit only because she has news she insists she must tell you in person."

"Bad news?"

"I don't know. Ready for your bath?"

"Oh, Cally, we've been so worried!" said Cora from the doorway. She burst into tears. "We were afraid—"

"Afraid I would die? Why? What made you so frightened?"

"Cally, there's no easy way to say this. Our Malcomson cousins, Nathanael and Sarah, they both—" Cora dabbed at a fresh wave of tears with her already sodden handkerchief.

"What happened to Nathanael and Sarah? Just tell me, Cora."

"Th—they both died, the same week. From ty—typhoid fever. Their children are orphans. We—we thought you might die too."

Cally slumped against her pillow. "Oh, poor Matilda. And Toby. And Florry and Ben. And wee Jimmy. And all the grandchildren. Does Felicity know?"

"Yes. She's quite sure we should bring Lizzy and her family here to take care of them."

"How is Felicity? Can I see her?"

Cora waited while Cally coughed.

"Not yet. The doctor says we must be extra protective of the children. But I can take her a note if you want to write one." Cora opened a small valise. "I brought you paper, a pen, and ink. And other things I think you might want—including a letter from Ryan that arrived the day after Christmas. I'll ask Nurse Saunders to give them to you."

Cally closed her eyes. *Nathanael and Sarah were always so kind to me.* She frowned, tears seeping from beneath her eyelids. *Is this how you reward goodness, God? Snatching lovely, generous people away from their family, their work? You don't need them in heaven. We need them here! I feel angry, God! How could you do this?*

Cora's voice came again from the doorway. "Nurse Saunders says you must rest now. I'll tell Felicity you're getting better. And I'll come again soon for your letter to her." Cora paused and swallowed. "Get well, please, dear Cally. This has been so hard."

Hearing tears once more in Cora's voice, Cally opened her eyes. Cora pulled her mask aside to wipe her face with a clean handkerchief.

"Cora, thank you for all you are doing to care for your own family and for Felicity. Please tell everyone I love them. I'll write to Felicity and to Matilda too. Don't worry. I'll be well before you know it."

"I hope so. Goodbye, sweet sister. I miss you."

"Goodbye, Cora. Please rest when you can."

Cally leaned back against her pillow. *I was afraid Cora would question me about Charlie's wedding. But she's dealing with so much else! I'll write to Felicity and Matilda right now and save Ryan's letter for bedtime.*

But halfway through her note to her daughter, the pen dropped from Cally's hand, spilling ink across her letter as she fell fast asleep once more.

"Well, I'd say your sister's visit was exactly what you needed," said Nurse Saunders the next day, walking in to find Cally sitting in a chair. "Now, though, I must ask you to take it a little easier. These next days are critical, the doctor says."

"My daughter needs me," said Cally. "We've had a tragedy in our family. I want to be there for her. My sister is exhausted. How soon can I go home?"

"I'll speak to the doctor, but I expect you'll be with us for a while yet. I want you to drink your breakfast and then rest for a while."

"All right." Cally put aside the book Cora had brought her and stood. The nurse leaped to catch her before she fell.

"You see? You're not strong yet, Cally. Let me help you back into bed. Convalescence from typhoid fever takes several weeks."

"But perhaps I can recover at home?"

"You'll have to speak with the doctor about that."

"I need to find out from Sister Irmena how I can make up the time I've lost in my training."

"Write her a note—*after* your nap—and we'll be sure she receives it. Now, I'm hanging the Do Not Disturb sign on your door."

Before the door clicked, Cally's eyes closed.

Nurse Saunders touched Cally's shoulder. "Cally, are you awake? Sister Irmena is here to see you."

Cally's eyes popped open, and she struggled to sit up. Sister Irmena stood in the doorway.

"Thank you for coming! I know you are very busy, Sister."

Sister Irmena approached the bed, her white mask matching her coif. She nodded at Nurse Saunders, who held a chair for her, made a small curtsey and left.

"How are you, Cally? Dr. Stephens says you have been very ill."

"So I'm told. I don't remember. I do know I'm getting stronger. I hope I can return to my duties soon."

"That's what I came to discuss with you. I hear you're anxious about losing your place in our nursing school."

"Yes. I did wonder . . . "

"Cally, I have no intention of removing you from our program. At the same time, we must evaluate where this illness leaves us in regard to the special training we've designed for you."

"Then it might take longer than we thought for me to return to Idaho?" asked Cally.

"That's what we need to determine. After we talk today, I plan to write to your mentor, Dr. Flora. Does she know you've been sick?"

"I don't think so. I haven't yet written to her. I doubt my sister Cora has had time to do so."

"I've been wondering whether you should consider convalescing in Idaho instead of here. Dr. Stephens does not feel it would be safe for the children in your family for you to go home to them. If Dr. Flora is willing to care for you, he might release you from the hospital sooner."

"But I would have to travel . . . "

"True. I'm not thinking this can happen for another week or two, and of course it depends on your progress. But if someone could travel with you, and if you confine yourself to a private car, I think it could be doable, once Dr. Stephens is confident you are stable."

"But then I would be a burden to Dr. Flora." Cally frowned.

"Hence our need to communicate with her about this idea. My thought is that you could take books with you, and though you would not be able to attend our lectures, I believe you could, with Dr. Flora's guidance, proceed with the theoretical assignments of our classes. I could send Dr. Flora exams for her to administer."

"How long do you imagine I might take to convalesce?"

"I asked Dr. Stephens this question and he suggests two months might be reasonable once you are able to leave the hospital. It will depend, of course, on your compliance with the protocols he will give you. If you don't follow them, your recovery will be longer."

"What about my daughter? Would she go with me?"

"I think not, Cally. It would take her out of school and her normal routine, and it would put her at risk. This would be another question to discuss with the doctor before you talk about it with your sister. Cora would, of course, need to understand why I want you to go to Idaho and agree to continue caring for Felicity."

She remembers Cora's name! And my daughter's!

"Nurse Saunders told me the next two weeks are critical to my recovery," said Cally.

"Yes, most typhoid patients who die make an initial recovery, then relapse and don't recover. That's the main reason your doctor wants to keep you here for the next several weeks."

"I see." Cally tipped her head. "I doubt I will relapse. I would like to speak with him about this plan before I write to Dr. Flora. Or will it be you who will write to her, Sister?"

"I would like both of us to write her, and perhaps Dr. Stephens as well. That way she can consider the proposal from the perspective of each of us."

Sister Irmena stood and opened her bag. "I've brought you a textbook, Cally. When you feel up to reading it, pay most attention to the chapters I've listed for you. But rest comes first. You must pay attention to and honor what your body tells you. When you're tired, rest. Do not feel obligated yet to achieve any reading goals." Sister Irmena placed the textbook on Cally's bedside table. "Please repeat back to me what I've just told you, Cally."

"I'm to read when I have energy, but I should rest anytime I am tired. As yet I have no deadlines."

"Correct. Cally, I will be tracking your progress through Dr. Stephens, and will come to see you again in a week. Meanwhile, you could write Dr. Flora your letter, and I will write mine. If you continue improving, I'll ask Dr. Stephens a week from now to write her as well."

"And then I can talk about it with Cora and with Felicity," said Cally.

"Yes. God willing, everyone will agree." Sister Irmena took a step toward the door, then turned back. "I do think this is in your best interest, Cally, even though it will separate you from your daughter for another extended period."

"Thank you for your visit, Sister Irmena. Thank you for your concern about my training."

"God be with you, my dear. I am praying for you daily and will see you again in a week."

"Thank you, Sister. Goodbye."

Cally lay back and closed her eyes, tears seeping from beneath her eyelids. Footsteps approached her bed.

"My dear, what is the matter?" asked Nurse Saunders. "Are you feeling worse?"

Cally wiped her eyes. "Oh no, I'm fine. But I've become a burden to the people I love, most especially my sister Cora. And now Sister Irmena suggests adding to Cora's burden, by asking her to care for my daughter for two more months. How can that be the right thing to do?"

"You've time to think and pray about it, Cally."

Cally sighed and brushed away a tear. "She says I'll be here at least two more weeks."

"I see she left you an anatomy book to study. That should distract you. Anatomy was my favorite subject when I was in training, though I must say I had trouble understanding kidney function. Are you good at memorization?"

"Quite good, I suppose. When I'm functioning normally."

"Well, if at any point you want me to quiz you, I can do that. Let me know."

"Thank you, Nurse Saunders! I will."

"How about a rest now?"

"Yes, ma'am." Cally pulled the covers over her.

I have too much to think about to go to sleep. If I go to Idaho, I'll be able to see Ryan again! But he's made it clear his heart still belongs to Bethany. His letter was a Christmas card for me and Felicity signed by many of our Idaho friends. Brian must be so big. Let me think. He was born on St. Patrick's Day, so he's now . . .

Under the bedclothes, Cally counted on her fingers. *Ten months! He'll be walking soon.*

Cally turned over, pulling the blankets more tightly around her. *Felicity will be upset that I get to see Brian and she doesn't. She'll probably mind that more than she'll mind being away from me. I miss her so much already. I can't imagine planning to be away from her for two months more!*

St. Joseph Hospital, Saturday, January 14, 1905

"Cally, you have a visitor."

Cally closed her anatomy book. "Cora? Did she bring Felicity?"

"Not Cora. A man."

Cally's brow furrowed. *Thomas? I hope it's not more bad news.* She straightened her gown and ran her fingers through her hair. Her eyes narrowed as a tall, masked man with a paunch and a cane appeared in her doorway. *You look vaguely familiar. It's so hard to tell with a mask . . .*

"Cally, I'm not sure you remember me. My name is Toby Finelli."

Cally gasped. "Felicity's owner! Is she all right?"

"Felicity? Yes, she's fine. I imagine you know she won second place in the Derby last year."

"Yes, she did well! Of course, I wanted Felicity to win. But I was proud that Lasca Durnell made history as the first female owner of a Kentucky Derby winner."

Mr. Finelli chuckled. "Elwood deserved to win. But maybe it will be Felicity's turn this year."

"Mr. Finelli—" Cally stopped. *Would it be rude for me to ask?*

"Why am I here, is that what you're wondering? May I sit down? My leg . . . "

"Oh, yes. Please. Forgive my poor manners."

Mr. Finelli pulled a chair just inside Cally's room.

"Cally, I'm here because of what you said to me during the trial. You asked me to forgive you for taking Felicity. Even had the judge given me the opportunity, I was too shocked to respond."

Cally's hand went to her lips. "Oh my."

"But later, I couldn't get it out of my mind. I've never been a forgiving kind of man. That cost me my marriage and my relationship with my son. I kept remembering your face as you looked at me with such sorrow over my injured leg. Yet I tried to kill you! And would have done so, had Felicity not been spooked by the gunshots."

Mr. Finelli stopped and wiped his eyes. "Cally, I'm the one who needs to ask you to forgive me. For my rage. For my greed. For my total lack of concern for your life. For not believing your note saying you would return Felicity. For my desire to hurt you—just a child—even after Felicity came back to me unharmed."

"But—"

"Please let me finish, Cally. This is not something I have much practice saying. I was wrong. Your request for my forgiveness in the middle of a trial when I was determined you should be punished to the fullest extent of the law—it woke me up, Cally. I began to see what a despicable, self-centered person I have been. When I read in the papers about your illness—"

Cally sat up straight. "My illness has been in the papers?" She reached for her blankets. *I feel cold.*

"Yes. I believe the whole of Kansas City is praying for your recovery."

Tears filled Cally's eyes. "But why—"

"You're a famous person in this town, Cally. Don't you realize that? People care about you."

"That's very kind, but I don't see why—I'm sorry. I interrupted you, Mr. Finelli."

"Cally, your kindness and decency shine through all you do and say. Your life gives people hope."

"I don't see why—" Cally frowned. "Sir, please continue with what you were trying to say before I interrupted. Again." She leaned back into her pillows and pulled the covers over her. *Why did the room suddenly get so cold?*

"All right. Let's take this in parts. First, yes, I fully forgive you, Cally, for taking Felicity without permission and for your indirect role in the injury of my leg."

Cally blew out a breath. "Thank you, sir. I am grateful to be released from my wrongdoing."

"Part two, can you forgive me for all of the wrong I did against you?"

"Oh, yes, sir. With all my heart."

A tear trickled down Mr. Finelli's cheek. When he spoke, his voice was gruff. "Thank you. You can't know what that means to me."

I'm shivering even with these blankets. "I'm so glad, sir."

"Part three: I would like, if you are willing, to introduce you to my wife and son."

Cally sat up straight. "Your wife and son, sir? Then you—"

"Yes. Thanks to you, I found the courage to repent of all the harm I did them, and they have graciously forgiven me. We are a family once more."

"I-I would love to m-meet them, sir."

Mr. Finelli stood and gave Cally a brilliant smile before walking to the door.

My teeth are chattering. He didn't seem to notice. That's good. But suddenly I feel hot. Cally pushed off her blankets.

"Cally, it gives me great pleasure to introduce to you my beloved wife, Sandra, and my dear son, Philip."

Cally managed, "I-I'm delighted, ma'am. Philip." Forgetting they couldn't come close to her, she stretched out her hand. And toppled off the bed.

"Nurse! Nurse!"

Cally heard Mr. Finelli shout. She heard running footsteps.

Don't be afraid.

Everything went black.

Kansas City, Monday, January 16, 1905

Telegram from Thomas Malcomson to Theodore Donnelly, Grove, Oklahoma: "Cally very ill. Come at once."

Telegram from Theodore Donnelly to Thomas Malcomson: "On my way. Teddy."

Telegram from Theodore Donnelly to Dr. George Tann, Independence, Kansas: "Cally very ill. On my way to Kansas City."

Telephone call from Dr. George Tann to Richard Williams, Olathe, Kansas: "Cally very ill. Can you go?"

Telegram from Richard Williams to Thomas Malcomson: "Athena and I will arrive this afternoon by carriage. Let us help. Will stay at The Eldridge."

Telegram from Thomas Malcomson to Cathleen Malcomson, Waterford, Ireland: "Cally very ill. Please pray."

Telegram from Cathleen Malcomson to Thomas Malcomson: "Oh no! Praying constantly. Informing family. Please update daily. Margaret sends love."

Telegram from Cathleen Malcomson to Dugan McCarthy, Killeagh, Ireland: "Cally very ill. Please pray."

Telegram from Cathleen Malcomson to Charles Malcomson, Dublin, Ireland: "Cally very ill. Please pray."

Telephone call from Charles Malcomson to Grattan home, Waterford, Ireland: "May I speak with Mum, please, Margaret? . . . What should we do, Mum? Laoise is in Derry and travels tomorrow to Belfast. I'm to leave tomorrow for a concert in London. I'm guessing these next few days are critical. By the time we could get there, she'll be improving, or she'll be . . . " Charlie choked back a sob.

Telephone call from Charles Malcomson to Laoise, Northern Counties Club, Derry: "Cally is very ill. Please pray for her—and for me to know what to do about my concert schedule."

Telephone call from Charles Malcomson to cousins Silas and Priscilla Malcomson, Dublin: "Cally is very ill. Please pray for her—and for me to know what to do about my concert schedule."

Telegram from Silas and Priscilla Malcomson to Thomas Malcomson: "Praying for Cally and all of you with much love."

Telegram from Cathleen Malcomson to Daniel Malcomson, Belfast, Ireland: "Cally very ill. Please pray."

Telegram from Daniel Malcomson to Thomas Malcomson: "Praying for you and for Cally with much love."

Telegram from Charles Malcomson to Matilda Jackson, New York City: "Cally very ill. Please pray."

Telegram from Matilda Jackson to Thomas Malcomson: "Lizzy and I arriving by train Friday. Can stay at hotel. Will help with children."

Telegram from Charles Malcomson to Mary Anthony, Rochester, New York: "Cally very ill. Please pray."

Telegram from Mary Anthony to Thomas Malcomson: "Praying for my girl with much love and concern. Please keep me informed. Mary."

Telegram from Thomas Malcomson to Dr. Flora Spencer, Hansen, Idaho: "Cally very ill. Please pray."

Dr. Flora at a hastily gathered community meeting, Hansen, Idaho: "Someone should go. I think that person should be you, Ryan. Does everyone agree? Will you care for Brian, Priscilla?"

Telegram from Ryan Byrne, Twin Falls, Idaho to Thomas Malcomson: "Arriving Thursday by train. Will stay at The Eldridge. Whole community sends love and prayers."

Telegram from Thomas Malcomson to Cecil Avery, Fish Haven, Idaho: "Cally very ill. Please pray."

Telegram from Cecil Avery to Thomas Malcomson: "Mother and Melody praying. Ebony arriving KC Thursday. Can stay at hotel. Let her help with the children."

Richard and Athena conversing with Thomas upon their arrival in Kansas City: "We're here to help thee and Cora. Athena can help Nora run the house and meals. I'll manage communications and transportation. Tell me who is coming and when. I'll send the daily telegrams and make telephone calls for thee."

Thomas, tearing up: "Thank you, dear friends. We have other friends arriving in the next few days who want to help with the children—Matilda, Lizzy, and Ebony."

Athena: "We'll both help with the children until the others arrive."

Thomas: "Our main concern, of course, is for Felicity. We're grateful Cora was able to take her to visit her mother while she was doing well. That's the image she has in her mind. I'm glad the doctor has forbidden visits from the children since Cally's relapse. I wouldn't want Felicity to see her now, unresponsive."

Athena: "These coming to serve the children—does Felicity know them?"

Thomas: "Oh yes. She knows and loves them all. Lizzy is her age, her special friend. She'll be delighted too that Ryan is coming."

Richard: "Ryan is Cally's friend from Idaho?"

Thomas: "That's right. We suspect there is more to that relationship than Cally has admitted."

Thomas rising as he hears sounds in the hallway. "I believe that is Cora arriving from the hospital now. My dear, you look exhausted. Richard and Athena have come to help us."

Cora, weeping as she hugged them: "Oh, friends, I don't know whether Cally will survive this relapse. It's so good of you to come."

"Have thee brought laundry from the hospital, Cora? If so, please let me wash it." Athena reached for a bag Cora had set on the floor.

"It's not laundry. It's cards and gifts. Cally became something of a celebrity in this town because of her trial. And now the *Star* means to publish an update daily until she's better. I brought all this home to keep for her until she's able to read the cards for herself. You should see her room—it's like a floral shop!"

Richard: "Her fame has spread to Olathe as well. People truly care about her, but it's also a diversion."

Athena: "We read the paper on the train. Today's story was an interview with Mr. Finelli, Felicity the horse's owner. He was visiting with Cally when she fainted with fever."

Cora: "Mr. Finelli visited Cally in the hospital?"

Richard: "Yes, with his wife and son. Here's the paper—thee can read it for thyself."

Athena: "Why don't thee both sit down and relax, Cora and Thomas. I'll bring thee hot drinks. Thee can read the story together. I've met thy sweet Nora. We'll get along famously."

Richard: "Thomas, after thee read the article, please make a list for me of who is arriving, by what means, and when, so I can organize their transportation here and to the hotel using our carriage and thine. I've already been talking to Max. And make another list of those who will expect daily updates by telegram. When are thee two heading back to the hospital?"

Cora: "Not until after supper. I need to sleep for a while. I'm too tired to think straight."

Athena and Richard, sharing a look, said at the same moment: "That's why we're here."

"We'll take it a day at a time," said Athena.

"I know you have experience doing so," said Cora. "Thank you for the strength you bring to us. We will likely have many fraught days ahead of us."

"God's mercies are renewed every morning," said Athena.

☙❧

Telegrams from Richard to all those praying for Cally:

Wednesday, January 18: "Day 5. Fever still high. Rash. Unresponsive."

Friday, January 20: "Day 7: No change."

Monday, January 23: "Day 10: Still no change. Doctors concerned."

Wednesday, January 25: "Day 12: Fever finally broke. Rash receding. Hope."

☙❧

St. Joseph Hospital, Thursday, January 26, 1905

The first thing Cally noticed was the fragrance of flowers. She breathed in the scent, registering at the same time a man's voice singing a lovely

Irish ballad. *Am I in heaven? But my head hurts. I thought in heaven I would have no more pain.*

Cally tried to raise a hand to her head, and discovered it was tethered somehow. So was her other hand. Making a great effort, she blinked open her eyes. *Ryan! He's singing with his eyes closed. Why is he in heaven with me? Who will care for wee Brian?*

Cally stretched her toes and then her ankles and legs. She tried again to raise her hands. *Why am I tied down?* She cleared her throat, and Ryan's eyes popped open, his singing stopping mid-phrase. Tears sprang to his eyes and ran down his cheeks.

"Are you sad, Ryan? Why are you sad?" asked Cally. At least that's what she tried to say. Her voice came out so hoarse the sounds were not fully intelligible.

Ryan set aside his guitar and leaned toward her, slowly stretching his hand out to touch her cheek. "Cally, are you truly awake?" he said softly through his mask. "I can hardly believe it."

"I think I'm in heaven," Cally said, though only she understood her words. "Why are you here with me, Ryan?"

"Sweetheart, may I tell your nurse you woke up?" asked Ryan.

"Why do I have a nurse if I'm in heaven?" Cally asked. But Ryan seemed to take her response as assent, and ran into the hallway shouting, "Nurse! Nurse! Come at once! Cally's awake!"

CHAPTER 8

BILLY

St. Colman's, Fermoy, December 20, 1904

BILLY CLOSED HIS TEXTBOOK AND gathered the notes spread across Mr. MacDonagh's table, scribbled during his tutoring session.

"You are doing well with your studies, William. I hadn't thought to ask you this. Do you have a place to go for the Christmas holidays? I'm sure you've heard the lads talk about going home on Friday." Mr. MacDonagh gazed at Billy through his thick glasses.

"No, sir. I have no family in Ireland." Billy coughed to cover the emotion that still gripped him when he thought about his dead father and the rejection of his half-brother.

"Well then, you'll join me and some of the other teachers and a half dozen other students who stay here for hols. That gives me an idea. How would you like an adventure?"

"An adventure, sir?"

"Yes. A bike ride and the delivery of a message."

Aha. He hasn't forgotten the deal he made with that priest.

"Where would I go?"

"I'll let you know later. You will come to me the day after Christmas."

"Yes, sir."

"Now, before tomorrow, I want you to finish reading *The Battle of Aughrim* and come ready to discuss Patrick Sarsfield's controversial choices within his political context."

"Yes, sir."

"And William?"

"Yes, sir?"

"Good first effort with the hurling. Coach O'Brien thinks you have potential."

"Thank you, sir. But—sir—"

"Yes?"

"Why do you and St Colman's think sports are so important?"

"Well, we believe they teach us many things, such as teamwork, giving your all for a cause larger than yourself, good sportsmanship, and the value of keeping our bodies healthy. And the value of simply having fun with your mates. Do you not enjoy being part of a team?"

"Yes, sir—that is, I'm beginning to, now that I understand better what it's all about. I never had exposure to sports in Idaho. Good day, sir."

"William, one more thing. This Christmas holiday has made me think about your mother. Have you told her where you are?"

"No, sir."

"Don't you think it would be an appropriate Christmas gesture to write her a letter? I know you think she doesn't care, but in my experience, every mother wishes to know where her son is and whether he is well. Especially when he is only fourteen. I urge you to do this."

"I'll think about it, sir."

"You are dismissed."

"Thank you, sir."

December 26, 1904

Billy knocked, then stood nervously before Mr. MacDonagh's door. *He hasn't said anything about this being dangerous, but I haven't forgotten what Father Barrett said. What a lot I've learned since then, when I didn't know his funny clothes meant he was a priest and didn't know what a mass was!*

The door opened. *Here we go . . .*

"William, the task I have for you today is simple, if you're not still too stuffed from our Christmas feast."

"No, sir."

"You will cross the River Blackwater to the British barracks and ask to speak to the rugby coach. His name is Mr. Allen. He will give you tickets for me for the big game against Cork City. Don't open the envelope. Inside will be a smaller envelope, which you will take to the Catholic priest of Lismore in the village of Tallow. You will head east fourteen miles out of Fermoy and turn south when you reach Tallowbridge. He will meet you at the Mill Road Bar and will buy you lunch. Hand him the envelope. He will take his message and return the rugby tickets to you. You needn't know his name, nor he yours. You'll recognize him by his vestments."

"Vestments, sir?"

"The priestly clothes he wears. He'll know you by—"

"By the color of my skin."

"Yes. You should be back here in time for supper. Your reward will be attending the rugby match with me on Saturday. I look forward to teaching you the fine points of the game."

Billy brightened, then sobered. "It's raining today. And cold."

"Yes. Here, you can wear my rain cape. The cycling will keep you warm. Watch out for puddles. Any questions?"

"No, sir."

"Then repeat back to me the instructions I've given you."

So, it begins. I'm getting an idea of what Mr. MacDonagh is involved with because of our history discussions. I'm happy about the rugby game. I'll have something to talk about with Harry.

Early morning Tuesday, January 31, 1905

Mr. MacDonagh responded immediately to Billy's knock, as if he were waiting by the door. "Come sit down, William. You've had your breakfast?"

"Yes, sir."

"I hear you took first in your biology exams. Well done!"

"Thank you, sir. I'm especially interested in every subject which contributes to my hope of going to medical school."

I don't think he called me here to talk about biology.

"Tell me, William. Did you write to your mother?"

"I decided to write to my uncle instead. He will know what to say to my mother."

"And have you heard back from your uncle or your mother?"

"Not yet, sir."

"I believe writing to your family was a wise decision, William."

"Yes, sir."

I don't think I'm here to discuss my family, either. He doesn't need to know I never sent the letter.

"William, I am releasing you from classes for the rest of the week."

Billy sat straighter. "Sir?"

"I need you to go on an errand for me. This will be a long trip and a delicate one."

"Delicate, sir?"

"I'm sending you first to Clonmel, and then to Kilkenny, where the police are particularly antagonistic toward our endeavors. You will need to be more careful than usual."

"Yes, sir. May I know more about what you are calling 'our' endeavors?"

"Not yet, William. The less you know, the better. You'll have less to reveal should you be questioned."

"Questioned, sir?"

"Yes. Should anyone inquire as to your purpose in either Clonmel or Kilkenny, simply say you are visiting friends, the Malcomson family in Clonmel, and the O'Keefe family in Kilkenny. You will stay overnight with the Malcomsons in Clonmel tonight and Thursday night, and in Kilkenny with the O'Keefes Wednesday night. I'm taking advantage of the St. Brigid school holiday, so you won't miss as many class days as it sounds."

"The Malcomsons, sir? That's my name."

"Yes, an interesting coincidence. Malcomsons have lived in Clonmel for generations. I doubt there's any connection. I remind you, William, that on these errands you are simply Billy. I don't want you to reveal your last name or any personal information to anyone, including the Malcomsons of Clonmel. I don't want you to be traceable back to St. Colman's."

Billy swallowed hard to avoid saying, "But they might be my relatives!" Instead, he asked, "How far is Clonmel, sir?"

"Thirty-four miles. Clonmel is halfway to Kilkenny. I'll give you money to stop and eat lunch in Clogheen, halfway to Clonmel, and in Ardfinnan, on the way from Clonmel to Kilkenny. A young lady named Lucy Malcomson will be waiting for you at the cotton mill as you approach the town of Clonmel. I believe her family lives just outside of town near the mill. You will give Lucy's father this first envelope, with an M in the corner."

"Yes, sir."

"Repeat that part back to me."

"I'll eat lunch in Clogheen. Lucy Malcomson will meet me at the cotton mill outside of Clonmel. I'll give her father the first envelope, stay overnight with her family and go tomorrow to Kilkenny. I'm to say only that my name is Billy."

"Yes. In Kilkenny, you will meet a man in the Rothe family side chapel of St. Mary's Church. You will know him by his green duncher. He'll know you by—"

"The color of my skin."

"Yes. You will give him the second envelope, marked O'K, then follow his directions to his house, which you will enter by the back door after leaving separately from St. Mary's. At no time will you be seen in the streets with the man in the green duncher."

"Yes, sir."

"You will sleep there, then cycle back to Clonmel, sleep one more night at the Malcomsons', and return here by supper time Friday. You will take with you nothing but a change of clothes in this small pack."

"I only have one set of clothes, sir. Otherwise just my uniforms."

Mr. MacDonagh frowned and rang his bell. "I'll see about another set for you."

"Yes, sir."

"You will not speak to anyone at St. Colman's about this trip. If anyone asks where you've been, say there was a death in your family."

"But that would be a lie."

"True, but it's for a worthy cause."

"I wish I could know the cause, sir."

"Someday I'm sure you will know and will be very proud of the important part you are playing, William. I am not telling you now for your own protection."

"And for your protection too, I think, sir."

"True. You are never to mention my name in connection with any of these errands." A knock sounded on his door. Mr. MacDonagh spoke to an old woman at the door. "Do we have any clothes William's size in the charity bin? Please check and bring me what you find."

Mr. MacDonagh closed the door and turned back to William. "I've had your bicycle oiled and the tires changed and inflated. I believe it will serve you well."

"Yes, sir. But what if I have a flat tire? I've never taken care of a bicycle."

"If you have any problems with the bicycle, you must walk it to the nearest town and ask for help. After you return from this trip, I'll give you some basic instruction in bicycle care, but we don't have time for that today. I want you to be on your way."

A knock sounded again on the door. "That was fast," said Mr. MacDonagh, opening it. "Yes, that will do nicely. Thank you." He extended a small packet to Billy. "Until Friday supper, then. I will be watching for your return. Your reward this time will be your choice of books from the Fermoy bookshop."

"Thank you, sir."

Mr. MacDonagh extended his hand. Billy shook it and started toward the door. Then he turned and said, "Should I be afraid, sir?"

"No. Just careful. Avoid policemen and soldiers."

"Yes, sir."

How will I choose just one book?

ଓଃ

Even with Mr. MacDonagh's rain cape, Billy shivered so violently by the time he located the mill outside of Clonmel he could hardly manage his bicycle. He slid off it gratefully to greet the girl waiting for him. His shoulder ached from a fall. The girl Lucy looked him over and without even asking, took the handlebars to guide the bicycle to her home. Fortunately, it was but a half-mile walk, and Lucy did not press Billy to talk.

"Mother!"

"Oh my," said the woman who responded to Lucy's call. "Take him right over by the fire, Lucy, and take off his cape and shoes. I'll prepare a hot toddy." The woman bustled away.

Billy sank into the chair and closed his eyes, savoring the warmth. A gentle hand touched his sore shoulder.

"Drink this, lad. It will warm thee up inside. Thee may rest here until suppertime, about half an hour. Come help me clean the mud off Billy's cape, Lucy. He must have fallen into a puddle. Maybe more than one."

An indefinite time later, Billy felt another hand touch his shoulder. "I'm Lucy's father. Welcome to our home, lad," rumbled a deep voice.

Billy opened his eyes. The man was slender. His body didn't seem to match his voice.

"Thank you, sir."

"Feeling better now?"

Billy sat up straighter. "Much better, sir."

The man glanced around, then said, "I believe thee brought something for me."

"Yes, sir, Mr. Malcomson." Billy found the envelope with the M in his jacket pocket, mashed but not wet. "Here you are, sir."

The man had just tucked the envelope in his pants pocket when Lucy appeared. "Dinner is ready, Papa."

"I imagine thee would like to wash up, eh, lad? Come with me. Have thee clean clothes?"

It wasn't difficult at dinner for Billy to avoid saying what Mr. MacDonagh had told him to keep to himself. He could hardly focus on his food, much less the conversation, and didn't even try to learn the names of Lucy's brothers and sisters. Everyone was friendly, but they asked few questions. *As if they're used to messenger boys showing up at their house. I'm exhausted. All I want is a bed.*

Billy stopped eating, considering. *At the same time, I feel warm and happy, as if in some way I've come home. Maybe it's because I think these people might be my relatives, even though they dress and talk funny.*

"Billy, thee are falling asleep at the table," said Mrs. Malcomson. "Won't thee take him to the guest room, husband? And Billy, Lucy will walk thee back to the mill in the morning to continue thy journey. She suspects thee were too tired to notice the way. We will wake thee for breakfast at 7:00."

"Goodnight, Billy!" chorused everyone at the table.

Morning dawned cold but clear. His muddy clothes from the day before were folded, clean and dry, at the foot of his bed. Billy still needed Mr. MacDonagh's cape, now also clean and dry, for warmth. But the sunshine cheered him, as did his conversation with Lucy on the walk back to the mill. She chatted about their family's life as if she and Billy were old friends.

Suddenly Billy blurted, "Lucy, I want to tell you something that is supposed to be a huge secret. If I tell you, will you promise not to say anything about it to anyone ever? It's important."

"Then maybe thee shouldn't tell me," said Lucy. "Sometimes secrets can be burdens."

"This one is a burden for me," said Billy.

"If it's important, thee can find the strength to carry it a wee bit longer," said Lucy. "Thee should not break trust with whoever asked thee to carry it."

Billy looked at Lucy in amazement. *I've never heard anyone talk like this. I thought she would feel honored that I wanted to tell her.*

"If we see one another again, and if circumstances have changed, thee can tell me."

"If? Why do you say if? I'm coming back here tomorrow night."

"Then we shall see whether circumstances have changed. Here we are and it's time for my shift at the mill; I mustn't be late. I will pray for thee, Billy. Godspeed." She disappeared into the building.

Billy stood looking after her for a long time. Then he shook himself, stretched his muscles, and climbed on the bike for the long ride to Kilkenny. The heavy rains of the day before had left the road puddly, but he didn't have to deal with rain driving into his face. He found himself humming a tune they sang every day in chapel at St. Colman's.

Praise God from whom all blessings flow. Praise him all creatures here below.

Billy smiled as a rabbit hopped across the road in front of him, and birds called to each other in the bushes. *We are all God's creatures, aren't we. And God is smiling at us today. I'll make better time without wind and rain, so I don't have to be in a hurry.*

Yet when there were straight, relatively puddle-free and traffic-free stretches of road, Billy peddled as fast as he could, and even experimented with riding hands-free. Stretching his arms out beneath the cape, he yelled at the top of his lungs, "I'm flying!"

Billy dawdled so long over his lunch in Ardfinnan, stuffing himself on Mr. MacDonagh's money, it was late afternoon when he rounded a curve and saw the buildings of Kilkenny. Dusk was falling when he arrived at St. Mary's Church, following the written directions Mr. MacDonagh had provided. He parked his bicycle in the graveyard at the side of the church and entered through a side door, referring once more to his instructions.

The side chapel closest to the altar, on the left. Ha, I've learned some church-y words since starting at St Colman's. When I got there, I didn't even know what an altar was, or a chapel inside a church. Now I look forward to mass at school. Father Jancey always says something to encourage us. He says God loves us, each lad individually. I wonder if that's true. Here we are.

A man dressed as a businessman, a green duncher beside him, knelt in the Rothe chapel, otherwise empty. The man did not move, apparently absorbed in his prayers. Billy wandered around the small room, reading the inscriptions on the memorial stones in the wall. *I like this one. This priest must have been a wonderful pastor to his people. The other stones don't say all these nice things.*

The man praying looked up. "I believe your name to be Billy," he said.

"Yes, sir."

"Then you have something to give me."

"Yes, sir." Billy pulled the O'K envelope from his pocket, smoothed it as well as he could, and handed it to the man, who pocketed it, handed him a folded paper, donned his duncher, bowed, and walked away.

Bill opened the paper. Instructions for getting to his house. *Wait. What?? I'm not his servant. Why do I need to go to the back door? I wish I knew what this is all about. Why does everything have to be secret? Why did Mr. MacDonagh say it would be dangerous for me to talk with a policeman or a soldier? Hmm. I'll recognize the house by its three turrets on the front. I hope it won't be too dark to see them.*

Emerging from the chapel, Billy awkwardly bowed toward the altar as he had seen his classmates do at school, walked back out the side door, and collected his bicycle. *My shoulder is still sore, but nothing like yesterday. I wonder what tonight will be like. I know the family's name is O'Keefe. But if I get lost finding the house, I better not mention that. At least I have the address.*

In the gathering darkness, Billy took one wrong turn down a narrow lane and had to retrace his steps over a bridge with the sound of rushing water beneath it. He saw one policeman, who simply nodded at him. Finally, by the light of the moon, he saw a house with three turrets. The back door of the man's house opened at a single knock.

"Where have ye been? I've been standing here waiting for ye this half hour," scolded a middle-aged woman dressed as a maid. "What, ye think I've nothing better to do? Ye've delayed my service to Cook. I'll have ye scrubbing the pots and pans to pay for yer tardiness."

"Yes, ma'am," Billy said meekly. *It's true; I have been lazy today. I could have gotten here much earlier.*

"Come eat yer supper, then, so ye can get to work."

Billy followed the maid into the kitchen, where a stern, skinny woman in a once-white apron put food away from the family's supper. A footman entered with a large stack of soiled ceramic plates. The cook pointed Billy to a full plate of food at the end of the kitchen table. The maid poured him a cup of tea. Both the maid and the footman exited to continue clearing the table upstairs.

"I'm to give ye this," said the cook, handing Billy an envelope. "Open it only when ye are by yerself. Ye'll sleep in the storage room; I've made ye a pallet. I'll wake ye for breakfast and then ye'll be on yer way. Ye are to speak to no one. Now eat."

Frowning, Billy began to eat his meat pie. *It's some kind of fish, I think. Tastes all right, though. Beggars can't be choosers, Mother used to say. They're certainly treating me like a beggar.*

On her return, carrying a heavy tray of crystal glasses, the maid said, "Help me set this down, lad. Finished with yer supper? Then here's the scrub brush. Set to."

Billy looked at the huge collection of pots and pans in the large sink. *It'll take me all night to clean all these. And my shoulder is sore.* He looked around to protest, but the room was empty. He didn't yet know how to find the storage room where he was to sleep. He took up the scrub brush and tackled the first pot.

An hour later, a footman entered to show him his pallet. Billy looked with satisfaction at the gleaming pots and pans drying on the sideboard. *That'll show them I'm not a sissy.*

The footman handed Billy a candle and directed him to a room behind the kitchen, closing the door after him. Billy tried the handle and frowned as he discovered it was locked. *Clearly, they don't trust me. I suppose someone will let me out in the morning, but I don't like this at all.*

The candle revealed a room nearly full of apples, potatoes, carrots, turnips, some vegetable he couldn't name, and boxes and bags, with a pallet and blanket in one corner. Billy shivered. He helped himself to an apple, testing the only small, high window—firmly closed from the outside—as he chomped. He pulled off his shoes and sat down on the pallet, huddled into his cape for warmth. Inside the envelope the cook had given him, he found a smaller, sealed envelope, and a note instructing him to go the next day to Waterford.

No! What should I do? Mr. MacDonagh didn't tell me anything about this! I've no idea how far Waterford is. Will I be able to do this and still get back to Fermoy by Friday supper? Let me think. I left St. Colman's on Tuesday, spent the night last night in Clonmel, and rode here today, So, tomorrow is Thursday.

Scrunching his face, by the flickering light of the quickly shrinking candle, Billy read the note again:

"You will deliver this to the ticket clerk at the Waterford train station. He will give you further instructions. Speak about this to no one." The initials were barely decipherable but seemed to be "PJ O'K."

Does this man have the right to tell me what to do? What would Mr. MacDonagh say? Wait—isn't Waterford the county where my rude half-brother lives, in Portlaw? I swore I would never go back there. I don't know what to do. Whatever this messenger thing is about, it must be bigger than Mr. MacDonagh and Father Barrett. I wish someone would tell me what's going on.

When the candle sputtered out, Billy tossed and turned on the hard pallet, agonizing over whether to go to Waterford or simply return to Clonmel and then Fermoy. He slept at all only because of the extra warmth of the cape.

When a knock sounded on the storage room door, Billy leaped up in a fright. The door opened and the cook said softly, "Time for ye to be on yer way. I've yer breakfast ready, and a sandwich for yer journey. Come quietly, now."

Billy ate quickly, tucked the sandwich into his small pack with his clothes, and slipped out into the still, pre-dawn darkness. His bicycle, the cook whispered before closing the door, was behind a bush in the side yard. It took him several attempts, and a bang to his head on the low-hanging branch of a tree, to discover which bush. A slight graying of the sky in one direction told him which way must be east. *I'm to go south, said the cook. That is, if I'm going to Waterford. It's time to decide.*

Billy wheeled his bicycle to the street and decided to walk, since he could hardly see where he was going. East or west? *Toward the sunrise, I think.* He turned right and had just taken his first steps when a dark figure appeared from nowhere and grasped his bicycle.

"Where do ye think ye're going?" a gruff voice whispered. "Wherever it is, ye ain't going there. Ye're coming with me."

CHAPTER 9

CHARLIE AND LAOISE

Charlie and Laoise's apartment, Dublin, January 31, 1905

CHARLIE OPENED THE MAIL. "LAOISE, we've received an intriguing invitation. Do you remember meeting my friend Liam at the Waterford Christmas concert? He's been coming to Dublin whenever he can to attend an evening of conversation at the home of Mr. George Russell. He invites us to go with him Sunday evening."

"George Russell—the controversial poet who calls himself AE?" asked Laoise.

"You've heard of him?"

"I read *The Nuts of Knowledge.* Lovely poems. 'We must pass like smoke or live within the spirit's fire . . . ' I can loan it to you if you like."

"I would like that. Thank you. Liam says at the last Conversation James Joyce was there, and Yeats! Imagine! I want to go, though it will be our last Sunday in Dublin before we both travel."

"A nice way, though, to celebrate our successful Irish and English January tours," said Laoise. "Let's do it!"

"Mum will be in town to discuss your travel plans. Shall we ask her to go with us?"

"Or I could ask Da and Mum to invite some of their friends over to meet her. That will free us to go just the two of us. That would be nice."

"I agree. I must remember, though, to introduce you as my fiancée."

"I will smile and nod and secretly savor how thrilled I am that's not the case," said Laoise, grinning as she hugged Charlie.

"Welcome, welcome. We're delighted you've joined us," rumbled AE, bowing over Laoise's hand. "Liam's depth of understanding of economics has instructed us all. Are you two also economists?"

"Not at all," laughed Laoise. "We're musicians. I play violin and Charlie the piano."

"Why of course! I thought your names familiar. You just toured Ireland, did you not, Miss Murphy? To rave reviews, I understand. And you, Mr. Malcomson. Are you not associated with Maestro Paderewski?"

"You know Mr. Paderewski?" exclaimed Charlie.

"Only because I was privileged to attend a concert in America featuring him and a young pianist who played an encore with him. A number of years ago," said AE, stroking his beard.

Charlie's eyes had grown wider and wider. "Unbelievable!" he said, as images from the concert AE referenced flashed through his mind.

"I love your poetry, Mr. Russell. Or do you prefer AE?" asked Laoise.

"AE, if you please. Allow me to introduce you to our other guests, and then you can raid the refreshment table. Standish, come and meet our new guests, Miss Laoise Murphy and her—"

"Fiancé," said Laoise.

"Congratulations. Her fiancé Charles Malcomson."

"The pianist?" asked a dignified older middle-aged gentleman, bowing. "Standish O'Grady, at your service."

"You write Celtic fairy tales," said Charlie, delighted. "I've enjoyed them all my life."

"And this young man is Bulmer Hobson. I suspect you may be approximately the same age," said AE. "Bulmer has been traveling around Ireland organizing youth meetings for the Gaelic League, where young patriots can socialize and support one another. He's trying to reconcile his Quaker beliefs with his more recently acquired nationalist interests."

"I'm from a Quaker background as well!" said Charlie. "My father's family—"

"Is esteemed in Quaker circles and beyond," said Bulmer. "May I extend my sympathies for the decline and fall of Malcomson Brothers? Such a tragedy, the early death of your grandfather Joseph. Allow me to present painter Miss Alice Jacob, another Quaker wrestling with Ireland's enigmas. She teaches design and lacemaking at the Dublin Metropolitan School of Art."

"I'm pleased to meet you, madam. What an amazing experience, to walk into a gathering of strangers and discover they know all about me," said Charlie. "Please tell us about your youth meetings, Mr. Hobson."

"Bulmer, please."

"Then call me Charlie. And this is my fiancée, Laoise."

"I've seen your orchid drawings," Laoise was saying to Miss Jacob. "So precise, yet artistic at the same time. Have you studied botany? Oh, how nice to meet you, Bulmer."

"Yes, informally," said Miss Jacob. "Dr. Perceval Wright, professor of botany at Trinity College, has guided me."

"Liam, thank you for inviting us!" exclaimed Charlie, looking around for Laoise, who had walked away with Miss Jacob. "What a fascinating group of people!"

"Come meet the others," said Liam. "Father Barrett, I would like you to meet my friend Charlie. Father Barrett comes to Dublin occasionally from Enniskeane Parish. He is involved with the nationalist efforts in western Ireland. I look forward to learning more about what you do, Father Barrett."

Father Barrett bowed.

"And it's a particular honor to introduce Professor Alfred Marshall, who guided me through my thesis in economics at Cambridge," continued Liam. "He is visiting Ireland because he's deeply interested in what he considers the essential role of economics in providing the preconditions for the improvement of the working class. Professor Marshall, my friend, renowned pianist Charles Malcomson."

"Mr. Marshall, this fascinates me," said Charlie. "With apologies to my friend Liam, I confess I've always considered economics a theoretical endeavor, with little application to real life."

Professor Marshall nodded. "That is regrettable, though I suspect more common than we economists like to believe, Mr. Malcomson."

"Charlie. Please continue, Professor."

"In my view, the duty of economics is to improve the material conditions of the people. But this will only occur in connection with social and political forces genuinely concerned about improvement of the lot of ordinary citizens, including the education of women, the development of trade unions to protect workers from exploitation, and sensible investment to create opportunities for the poor to work and prosper." Mr. Marshall took a sip of wine. "Sadly, my viewpoints are not always embraced by my colleagues. I hope to discover more compatible viewpoints here in Ireland."

"We look forward to discussing all of this in-depth next week," said AE, who had joined the group. "Can you join us again, Mr. Malcomson?"

"Charlie, please. No, both Laoise and I depart Tuesday for separate tours on the Continent. We will return to Dublin only in June, for our wedding. But we would love to visit again following our honeymoon."

"You can see why I'm excited by Professor Marshall's visit," said Liam. "I have plans to introduce him to several people here who I believe can profit from what he has to say. I'll be spending this week with him here in Dublin."

"Please tell me more about what you hope to achieve, Professor Marshall," said AE.

"Shall we avail ourselves of the refreshments before the discussion begins?" Liam asked Charlie. He guided Charlie to a table at the side of the room, saying, "Last week the Conversation was about the launching of the *Lillebonne*, a triumph for Dublin shipbuilding but controversial due to the treatment of the employees who built it. And we discussed Synge's play "The Well of the Saints," soon opening at the Abbey Theatre. It's about two blind beggars who believe they are beautiful until they regain their sight."

"Sadly, we'll miss the opening," said Charlie. "I already look forward to coming again this summer. Laoise and I have been hungry for this kind of intellectual stimulation."

"Me too," said Liam. "You should hear them when they start getting off on nationalism and economics. It's refreshing to be in an environment where people can discuss disparate views without fear of recrimination. Amazing, truly. In my experience there are few such places in Ireland outside of college campuses. There's too much fear in the air to allow free sharing and mutual learning and growth in friendship between people with differing political perspectives."

"We'll be back!" said Charlie, helping himself to fruit, cheeses, and wine. "A lovely side benefit to coming tonight is reconnection with you, my friend. Do you still ride?"

"Every time I can make time. You?"

"Not for ages. Our family lost Mayfield when my father died. Midnight is elderly. She lives at my sister Margaret's in Waterford. I live in an apartment now, with no place to keep a horse."

"You could board a horse with me, should you choose to acquire one," said Liam. "I know how much you love your gallop."

"Why thank you! I'll give that some thought, after Laoise and I marry. You're coming to the wedding?"

"Wouldn't miss it," said Liam. "Let's sit down. They're about to start."

"We look forward to a special guest contributing to our Conversation next week," said AE once the group had settled. "Professor Alfred Marshall, whom I hope you have all met already, will discuss with us the practical applications of economics for the betterment of the poor. And in March—I'm not sure which week yet—Arthur Griffith will tell us about the new political party he wants to begin, Sinn Féin, 'Of the people.' I'm sure many of you have been reading *The United Irishman* and are aware of some of his ideas. Our thanks to Father Barrett for inviting him to join us."

Charlie and Laoise looked at each other, disappointment showing in both their expressions. AE noticed and inclined his head to them.

"This will not be your only opportunity to acquaint yourselves with their views, friends. I hope both Professor Marshall and Arthur Griffith will become frequent visitors to our evenings," said AE. "For tonight, I've invited our friend Miss Jacob to introduce the topic, 'the importance of beauty to our national conversation.' Miss Jacob?"

"In recognition of our growing friendships, I would be honored if you would all call me Alice. As you know, I have made a career out of creating beauty through painting and lacemaking, and I have the joy of teaching others to explore their gifts in these areas. Our new friend Laoise Murphy has just been telling me what it means to her to create beauty with her violin. I found it fascinating. Will you begin our Conversation by sharing with the group on this topic, Miss Murphy?"

Laoise smiled and nodded.

Alice continued, "And then perhaps Father Barrett could give us some theological insights from the Catholic perspective to balance my Quaker beliefs. To complete that discussion, is there anyone here who could give us a Church of Ireland point of view on the topic?"

Everyone looked around the circle. No one raised their hand until Laoise tentatively raised hers. "I have been raised in the Church of Ireland. So perhaps my comments will reflect that perspective."

"Please continue, Miss Murphy," said Alice.

"If you are Alice, I am Laoise." She looked around the circle. "I am intrigued with this topic, as you can imagine. For me, lovely music represents so much that is good in our humanity: Order. The ability to harmonize divergent voices. The nurture of our souls through a language that though nonverbal yet speaks to our emotions so powerfully that we can leave a musical presentation soothed, or empowered, or challenged, or even disturbed."

Charlie stared at Laoise. *She's speaking eloquently and confidently, without prior notice or opportunity to prepare. I've never seen her like this.* He glanced around the room, noting each person's gaze fixed on Laoise's face. *Suddenly I don't feel I know her at all. Or have only scratched the surface of who she is. Coming here this evening would have been worth it just for this. Yet there is such wealth awaiting us in relation to each person here.*

He looked across the room at Liam and caught his eye. "Thank you," he mouthed. Liam smiled and nodded. Charlie focused again on what Laoise was saying.

"So, isn't God as Creator the first thing Scripture teaches us about him? And he made man in his own image. Thus we are all meant to be creators, each in our own way, according to the gifts and interests we each have received. Charlie's mother, Cathleen, told me that Quakers say, 'There is that of God in each of us.' For that reason, she, a Catholic, is a pacifist. Rather than do violence against one another, we who wish to honor our Creator must encourage and draw out the yearnings and gifts of beauty in one another by developing our various creative callings. This resonates deeply in me. I hope to spend the rest of my life doing just that, soothing and healing some of the wounds of our tortured history. Thank you."

The group took a collective deep breath and shifted in their chairs, then turned their attention to Father Barrett.

"As Laoise expressed so well, the starting place for each of us—Roman Catholic, Church of Ireland, Quaker, or Presbyterian—must be the Creator's purposes in making mankind. Can we not find here common ground that could help heal our schisms and inform the crafting of a more harmonious and balanced future, with space for each of us on our beautiful island?"

As Father Barrett talked, Charlie's mind flitted back to the concert with Mr. Paderewski in the church in Albany, New York, which, he had just learned, AE had attended. *I was twelve. I played traditional Irish music as an encore. Amazingly, that brought the congregation—mostly Irish—to tears.*

Then he remembered Laoise playing her violin to help him stabilize after hearing of the destruction of the Danish ship, the *SS Norge.* Reaching further back, he recalled Mr. Paderewski encouraging him to throw into his playing all his feelings of distress and confusion over the death of his childhood mentor, Mr. Barrow.

These personal experiences illustrate what Laoise is talking about, the healing role of beautiful music. I've never thought about my work quite in this way before, as a sort of partnership with God. So often I think of my music as simply self-indulgent, doing what I love. How humbling. And motivating at the same time, to be the very best pianist I can be.

He took Laoise's hand, this hand capable of creating powerful, passionate, life-giving music, his heart flooded with gratitude.

CHAPTER 10

CALLY

Kansas City, St. Joseph Hospital, January 26, 1905

"OH NO. SHE'S ASLEEP AGAIN," Ryan told Nurse Saunders. His shoulders slumped as they reentered Cally's room.

Nurse Saunders felt Cally's forehead and checked her breathing and vital signs. Cally sighed and turned over. The nurse smiled. "See—this is normal sleep, Ryan, not coma. I won't do it just to show you, but it would be possible to wake her up. Don't be discouraged. This is all good!"

"Could I use a hospital telephone to tell her family?" asked Ryan. "As you know, we've been taking turns sitting with Cally. I'm to be here two more hours before Cora comes, but I don't want to wait that long to share this wonderful news."

"You can ask to use a telephone in the patient services office downstairs. Don't worry. I'll keep a close eye on Cally while you're gone."

"Can Cally have more than one visitor at a time? Everyone will want to see her awake."

Nurse Saunders laughed. "Who is 'everyone'? All the people who have taken turns sitting with Cally?"

"Well, yes. Cora and Thomas. Felicity. Her brother Teddy. Richard and Athena. Matilda—"

"I see. I'll check with the doctor when he comes by on evening rounds, but until then, let's limit to two at a time, all right? No reporters. No one not directly tied to Cally. And Ryan, you should let people know she still has a long recovery ahead. She'll need a great deal of rest, and I for one am not going to wake her up just to greet visitors."

"Not even her daughter?"

"Well, I might make an exception for Felicity. But only when the doctor decides Cally is no longer contagious. For today, I'll allow Cora to be here with you, and we'll re-evaluate tomorrow once the doctor sees her this evening and gives us his guidelines. You must all practice patience for some time yet as she begins to regain her strength."

"I understand. Thank you, Nurse. I'll go call Cora." Ryan surprised her with a big hug before bouncing out of the room. *I'm the one who was with her when she woke up! I'm so glad!*

௸

"You called me 'sweetheart.' What did you mean by that?" Cally's clear, coherent words startled Ryan from a nap. His eyes flew open to see her green ones fixed on his face.

Ryan sat up, rubbed his eyes, and smoothed his hair. "Hello, Cally. It's nice to see you awake."

"I asked you a question."

"I—I don't remember. I've been sitting by your bed for days, taking my turn watching you sleep. I was so thrilled to see you wake up that I even hugged Nurse Saunders."

"You did?"

"Yes. And then you fell asleep again and slept right through Cora's visit and Athena's. They were disappointed, but Nurse Saunders wouldn't let them wake you. So, Teddy and I are still the only ones who have seen you awake, after all those days when we weren't sure—we weren't sure—I mean we didn't know—" Ryan brushed away the tears that flooded his eyes.

"You thought I might die?"

"We feared that, yes. You were so sick, Cally."

"When I woke up, I thought I was in heaven. But I'm still in the hospital."

"It seems God still wants you here with us. That's what Cathleen said in her telegram yesterday."

"This is a lot for me to sort out, Ryan. Where is Cathleen? How many days have I been sick? What day is today? When can I see Felicity?"

"Cathleen is in Waterford with Margaret and her family. You were unconscious for ten days. Today is Saturday, January 28th, 1905. You may be able to see Felicity next week if you continue to improve."

"I need to study anatomy."

Ryan laughed. "I have no idea what will next come out of your mouth. All in good time, Cally. When you have more energy."

"I thought you were in heaven with me," Cally said again.

"Not yet." Ryan smiled.

"Why can't I see Felicity? And Cora?"

"Cora was here for hours Thursday and came again yesterday, but you didn't wake up. She's coming again this afternoon. Your doctor still feels he must protect Felicity from getting typhoid. It won't be long though, Cally. She's as anxious to see you as you are to see her."

Cally frowned again. "Did she already learn to read, without me?"

"Ah, Cally," Ryan chuckled. "No, not quite, though she's making progress. You'll still be able to help her."

"Who else has been here?"

"Your brother Teddy—don't you remember talking with him?"

Cally scrunched her face. "I thought that was part of a dream."

"He'll come again this afternoon. With Cora."

"Teddy has been here all these days? He's neglecting his wife. And his baby!"

"Cally, we didn't know from one hour to the next whether you would still be alive. Teddy didn't want to leave while you were so sick."

"I'll tell him to go home."

"Richard and Athena Williams have been helping Thomas and Cora manage everything. Ebony Avery came from Idaho to help with the children. Matilda and Lizzy also, from New York."

"So many wonderful people! And I've missed them all!"

"You'll still get to see them, I believe, one or two at a time. Nurse Saunders keeps reminding us not to wear you out."

"Is Priscilla taking care of Brian?"

"Yes. He's doing well."

"So big—ten or eleven months, I think? Is he walking yet?"

"Almost. He pulls himself up and sidesteps holding on to furniture. I hope he waits for his first steps until I'm back with him."

"Then you must go home soon!"

"I will. Probably next week."

"You called me sweetheart, Ryan," Cally said again. "What about our agreement?"

Ryan reached out and took her hand. "Cally, our agreement is still intact. I was happy that you came back to us. We all thought we were losing you."

"But—"

"Cally, I already went through the pain of losing the love of my life, Bethany. And during all those hours sitting here with you, I didn't know whether that would be the last time I saw you alive. That doesn't mean I'm breaking our agreement. Not at all."

Cally lifted Ryan's hand to her cheek. "Dear Ryan. I know your heart still belongs to your beautiful Bethany. I understand."

"I know you do. Thank you. I think I will always miss her." *This isn't the right time to say I had no idea how strong my feelings were for Cally until I feared I might lose her. Or that I realized I need to entrust Bethany to God and move forward with my life.*

"Ryan, I'm tired. Can I sleep now?" Cally's eyes closed before she completed her question.

"Of course. Sweet dreams." He watched her breathing deepen. "Sweetheart," he whispered.

Ryan had no idea whether she heard him. He kissed his fingers and gently touched her forehead, now miraculously cool. He stood, stretched, and walked to the door to receive a stack of mail for Cally. *She doesn't know the impact she's had, just by being herself. I don't deserve her, God. But if you give her to me, I will love her as long as we're both alive.*

He set the stack of cards on a table, picked up a book and took his seat again. *While I'm talking to you, God, could you please give Bethany a hug for me? And tell her about Cally?*

CHAPTER 11

BILLY

By the River Nore, Kilkenny, Thursday, February 2, 1905

BILLY SMACKED HIS ASSAILANT'S HANDS as hard as he could, jerked the bicycle from his grip, threw himself onto the seat, and pedaled as fast as he could down the street. The man gasped, cradled his hands for a moment, then ran after him, yelling, "Stop!"

Billy turned down the next street he came to, then left, then right, then right again, always keeping the brightening sky in his sights. Suddenly he realized the river was in front of him, with no bridge in view.

One direction or the other, there must be a bridge. Billy turned left onto a path by the river. The sound of pounding feet told him his pursuer had not given up. Suddenly Billy remembered Toby, his tongue cut out. Panic flooded him and he pedaled faster than ever. A bridge came into view, but a man was crossing it, coming in Billy's direction.

I'll hide under the bridge until it seems safe to cross.

Billy directed his bicycle down a grassy slope that proved steeper than it had seemed in the grey light. He lost his balance and slid down the embankment, his bicycle clattering behind him.

"I've got ye now!" came a growly voice from above.

Billy looked desperately around, thinking about Toby's tongue. *My bicycle is probably useless now, all banged up.* He grabbed the small pack, holding the envelope he was to deliver to the Waterford train station, buckled it around his middle, and threw himself into the river.

The water was so cold, and the current so fast, Billy lost his breath. He could not touch bottom. He dived in time to miss hitting his head on a boat moored ahead of him, but conked his head on another vessel when he came up for air. Gasping, spitting, coughing, trying desperately to keep his head above water, Billy tumbled downstream. His head hit a rock and he passed out.

The sun had peeked over the horizon when Billy came to on a small flat rocky area beside the river, which rushed noisily on its way beside him. Billy sat up, shivering. He touched his forehead and felt a gash. His finger came away bloody. *The cold water must have helped me not bleed too much, but now it will bleed more. I need help. I've lost my bicycle for sure. And the cape as well. But at least I got away from that man.*

He sat trembling, looking around. *Well, the river took me south. Should I take that as a sign? Father Barrett did say this messenger business could be dangerous. Who was that man, and why was he chasing me?*

Billy stood and surveyed the embankment, which continued steep as far in each direction as he could see. *I think I'm on the opposite side of the river from where I went in. The only way to get out of here is to climb.* Blood dripped now into his right eye. *I'm starting to feel more pain. I think I was too frozen in the water to feel much of anything. I better tie my extra shirt around my head. Maybe that will stop the bleeding.*

His shirt, and all the contents of the small pack, were soaked through. Billy grunted trying to tie a knot with the wet cloth. *It's not good, but that's the best I can do.* He went to the edge of the river to rinse the blood from his hands. Turning to look up, considering his best path up the embankment, he saw a face gazing down at him. An old woman's face. Billy caught his breath, his eyes widening. *Oh no! Is she friend or foe? Ha, I made a rhyme. But should I try to hide?*

The face disappeared. Billy called out, but there was no answer. He examined the bushes at the foot of the embankment seeking a hiding place, but they seemed such a tangle of thorny branches he could not find his way in. He backed away to consider the embankment again and almost ran into the old woman.

"Wha—what? Who? H—how?" Billy sputtered, looking wildly around for a way of escape other than the river.

It seemed she could not talk. She beckoned with one finger, and when he simply frowned, she took his arm and pulled him toward what seemed an impenetrable mat of bushes. Puzzled, Billy allowed her to pull him along. When they reached the bushes, the woman let go of him, went to her knees, then crawled. The bushes seemed to open before her. Billy followed. Behind the bushes he saw a cave, large enough for them to stand. And inside the cave, a set of stone steps ascended to a hole cut in its roof.

The old woman nimbly climbed the steps, beckoning him to follow her. At the top she looked around, then beckoned again, and disappeared.

Billy climbed, shivering. The woman stood at the door of a small cottage a short distance away. He ran across the grass, losing his makeshift bandage. His head bled freely now. The old woman pulled him into the cottage, closed the door, and pointed to a chair. She wet a rag and held it tight against his forehead, his head pulled into her chest.

Billy could hear her heart beating, fast. She hummed as she held his head. He recognized the tune: *Praise God from whom all blessings flow . . .*

Warmth enveloped Billy from a fire burning in the hearth. Gradually, his shivering eased. The woman checked the bleeding and returned the rag to his forehead.

How long they stayed like this, the old woman humming, her heart beating, the fire crackling, Billy could not later remember. He grew drowsy.

Finally, the woman was satisfied and threw her bloody cloth in a pail. She sorted through a pile of rags in the corner, choosing the longest, thinnest one, and bound it around his head. She gestured for Billy to rise and moved his chair closer to the fire. She filled a kettle and tucked it into the coals, then bent and wrestled with Billy's shoelaces with her gnarled fingers.

"I can do it," said Billy. She nodded. *There seems to be nothing wrong with her hearing.* Giving up on the shoelaces, Billy pulled his shoes off still tied, and placed them and his socks near the fire. Suddenly, he felt faint. *I wonder how much blood I—*

He toppled from the chair.

When Billy woke, he found a pillow under his head and a blanket over his body, almost naked. He lay in the place he had fallen, his clothes spread over a rack by the fire.

Billy lifted his head and tried to sit up. The woman appeared immediately, motioning for him to lie still. She returned moments later with a cup of tea.

"I should drink," Billy said, interpreting her gestures. "So my body can make more blood." *Hmm. This tea has something in it. It's sweet and salty at the same time.* He drank it all, and she refilled the cup. He drank that also, then lay down and fell back to sleep.

This process repeated several times. Sleep. Wake. Drink. Sleep again. Finally, he woke feeling refreshed. Shadows filled the room, the last colors of sunset visible through what must be a west-facing window. *I've spent the whole day in this woman's hut. I should go or I won't make it back to St. Colman's by suppertime tomorrow. Mr. MacDonagh will be worried.*

Billy started to get up, but the old woman pushed him back down. She brought him a bowl of soup. Billy ate it hungrily, sitting by the fire, then carefully stood up. The woman shook her head, pushed him down, and brought him another cup of the sweet/salty tea. Pointing to the window, dark now, she gestured to indicate he should sleep where he was.

It's true that I'll be stronger in the morning. And it will be easier to find my way. Billy handed the woman the teacup and lay back on the pillow. He noticed the wet clothes from his small pack spread out before the fire; the clothes he had worn in the river now folded into a neat pile. *She must have found the envelope. I wonder if the message is still readable. Perhaps she doesn't know how to read.*

The woman hummed again, this time a tune he didn't recognize but thought the most beautiful he had ever heard. *Interesting. Thinking about Toby losing his tongue is what motivated me to escape that man. And now I've met another person who can't talk. But both apparently have good lives.*

Billy gazed at the fire, listening and trying to memorize the old woman's music, until he fell asleep once more.

❧

Bright sunshine streamed through a small eastern window. Billy stirred, turned over, and then touched the bandage on his forehead. *No blood.* He opened his eyes. The old woman hummed softly as she poured something into a pot hanging over the fire. She turned and smiled as he sat up. She pointed to her own head, so he touched his.

"It doesn't hurt anymore." Billy pushed to his feet then grabbed the back of a chair. "I didn't expect to feel wobbly!"

The old woman smiled and pointed to the stack of clothes, which now included his spare set.

Billy let go of the chair and dressed, then took a few tentative steps toward the front door. "I'm walking! I feel so much better. I'll be right back." Outside he stretched in the cold air and walked slowly to a place where he could relieve himself. *I've never drunk so much tea in my life.*

Returning, Billy noticed an old, rusty bicycle propped against the back of the cottage. *I wonder whether it's functional. I need to get to Waterford and back to school. But wait—I can't just take her bicycle. Maybe this is how the old woman gets food! Perhaps it's her only form of transportation.*

The bicycle had once been green. Billy noticed a small insignia on the handlebars. He looked at it more closely, rubbing away a bit of dirt. *A dragonfly. I think.*

Grasping the handlebars, Billy walked the bicycle a few steps. Its wheels turned smoothly. *I don't hear any scraping or rubbing sounds. The tires are inflated. The chain turns like it's just been oiled. It's a good bike—just old and a bit rickety.* He mounted, rode a full circle around the cottage, and propped the bicycle back in its place.

"So, you like my bicycle," the old woman said as he reentered the cottage.

Billy gasped and backstepped out the door. "Ye--yes, ma'am. You can talk? Yesterday it seemed you couldn't talk." *And how did she know I rode her bicycle?? The windows are too high to see out of, and the door was closed! So much about this old woman doesn't make sense. Should I run away?*

"You're wondering how I knew you rode my bicycle," the woman stated, not responding to Billy's question about her ability to speak.

"Ye-yes, ma'am," said Billy, backing away another step.

"What *would* a lad do, who had lost his own and has responsibilities? Some things, Billy, are easy to deduce."

"Yes, ma'am, but—"

"But what?"

"How do you know I had a bicycle before—"

"Before ye jumped in the river to escape that threatening man?"

"Ye-yes, ma'am." Billy looked around wildly. *Which direction should I run?*

"Why else would ye have been in that swift, cold river? Surely not for a swim. That tells me ye were escaping for yer life. But enough of this silly conversation. Sit down and eat yer porridge and drink another cup of my tea. We must make plans." She turned to set a steaming bowl and cup on the table. Hesitantly, Billy entered, sat at the table, and picked up the spoon. He sniffed the porridge before putting it in his mouth.

"Now, ye must take my bicycle to Waterford. Walking would take too long. I'll give ye money for a coach from Waterford to Fermoy. That's the only way ye'll get back to school by dinnertime, as yer teacher told you. Don't worry about the bicycle. I'll get it back."

"Bu-but how do you know—"

"Bright lad like ye, of course ye would be in school."

Billy set down his spoon and stood. "Ma'am, you know too much about me to have conjectured it all. Who are you? I demand to know."

The old woman harrumphed. "The lad arrives here half dead and this is the thanks I get? We've no time for this, Billy. Ye must be off to Waterford."

"Bu-but ma'am, I was expected in Clonmel last night and—"

"Ah yes, the lass. Yer third cousin twice removed. Lucy. Have ye not the ability to write letters?"

Billy's whole body shook. The old woman ignored him.

"Now, I've packed food for ye. Yer body is not restored altogether, so ye'll be right tired by the time ye deliver yer message at the Waterford train station. Don't worry—the writing's dry. At the station, buy tea and mix one of these packets into it. If ye still feel weak, drink a second packet before ye board the coach."

"Ho-how will I find the Waterford train station?"

"Head straight west until ye reach the road, then straight south into Waterford. Ask anyone there to direct ye to the train station. Ye'll find the coach station next to the train station. Any more questions?"

"Who are you? How do you know so much about me?"

"I meant relevant questions. We must get ye on yer way lest yer teacher fret. Let me look at yer forehead."

The woman removed the bandage and clucked with satisfaction. "Just a small patch is all ye need now. Good thing I've sticking plaster on hand."

She applied a small bandage to his forehead. "Now, ye'll need more warmth, seein's ye've lost yer teacher's cape in the river. I mended this old jacket of mine for ye. Try it on."

Shaking his head as if to clear it, Billy said, "How did you—"

The old woman pressed the jacket into his hand. He pulled it on, fastened its buttons, and immediately felt strength pouring into his body. He started to exclaim but the old woman overrode him.

"That'll do, I believe. Now, tuck these packets into yer pocket, along with the message ye are to deliver, and yer money for the coach. Button the pocket, that's right. Here's yer lunch. Ye mustn't dawdle. Don't forget to drink yer tea before ye board the coach to Fermoy."

"Ma'am, thank you for—"

"No thanks needed. We're on the same team. Off ye go."

On the same team? What team? Not one bit of this makes sense.

Billy ran for the bike, mounted, and rounded the cottage heading west. He waved to the old woman standing in the doorway, shouting his thanks. The old woman waved back.

It was a glorious day. Billy turned his head to wave again at the old woman and skidded to a stop, shielding his eyes from the bright sun. The cottage had disappeared. It was simply not there. Panic washed through him. He lay his bike on the grass and ran back to where the cottage had been. He found no trace of it. *This is impossible. I have completely lost my mind.*

Looking carefully in every direction, Billy reached up to touch his forehead. *The bandage is gone! And so is my wound!* He took a deep breath, trying to still his racing heart. *Did I imagine this whole thing? Am I still in the middle of a dream?*

Billy slapped himself. He ran to the abutment over the river, searching for a hole and steps leading down into a cave. Nothing. The river still tore through the countryside, its current as rapid and deep—and doubtless just as cold—as he remembered.

Turning, Billy saw in the distance a small heap on the grass. *That's the bicycle. That at least is still here.* He walked in a circle, staring at the countryside in every direction, trying to calm his out-of-control feelings.

I can't think of anything to do except ride to Waterford. Assuming the old woman gave me accurate directions.

Billy ran to the bicycle, mounted, and pedaled west. *Who can I talk to about this? Who would believe me? Even I think I'm crazy! I have no idea what just happened to me. I only know I feel more physically fit than I ever have. I feel like I could ride to Waterford and then all the way to Fermoy without a problem. But I'm to leave the bicycle and take the coach from Waterford. The bicycle—the old woman said not to worry, she would get it back. WHAT OLD WOMAN?"*

With one hand, Billy managed to unbutton his pocket and feel the contents. *Yes, packets to add to my tea. Money.* He pulled out the envelope. *It looks as clean and new as when the cook gave it to me. What if it disappears just like the cottage? What if I disappear?*

Still pedaling, Billy tucked the envelope back in his pocket and refastened the button. He reached the road and turned left.

How am I to understand any of this? The only thing I know to do next is to follow the old woman's directions. Even if she's not—what, not real? But I'm wearing her jacket, one I've never seen before in my life!"

Billy emerged from the train station fortified by a cup of tea, bearing yet one more message sealed into an envelope, this one for Mr. MacDonagh. As he crossed the road to enter the coach station, the train, which had been boarding while he was drinking tea, began to move. He looked up as the train slowly gathered speed. A woman looked at him through a window of the train. She lifted her hand and was gone. Billy stared as the train cars flicked by him.

That woman—she looked familiar. I'm sure I've seen her before... A memory surfaced: a woman on a ship, telling him he couldn't possibly be himself. *That was Mrs. Malcomson! The first one who refused to believe I'm a Malcomson too!* Billy started pedaling his bicycle beside the track, as if he could catch up to her.

The train rumbled faster and faster. As the last car rushed past him, Billy stopped and drooped over the bicycle, panting, exhausted. *I used up all my energy.*

Slowly he turned, walking the bicycle back to the coach station. *I don't know whether Mrs. Malcomson boarded the train here in Waterford or was just passing through. I think that train is headed to Dublin. Does she live there? Or here? Or somewhere else?*

Billy checked his pocket. *One tea packet, and the money for the coach, along with the message for Mr. MacDonagh.* He propped the bicycle near the entrance to the coach station, purchased a ticket to Fermoy to leave in fifteen minutes, then bought a cup of tea and stirred in the old woman's powder. *Perhaps this last packet will revive me. A twelve-hour ride to Fermoy. I'll be late. But I'm glad now I'm not doing this by bicycle. How will the old woman get her bicycle back? Ha. What old woman?*

Once he boarded, squeezing into the small space by the window left by a rotund couple, Billy collapsed. *The packet didn't work. I have zero energy. But nothing to do the rest of this day, until I reach Fermoy. I wish I had brought a book to read.*

Billy promptly fell asleep and woke only briefly at stage stops all the way to Fermoy. He dreamed of a long walk and talk with Lucy, ending at an old woman's cottage. The old woman had Mrs. Malcomson's face.

CHAPTER 12

CHARLIE AND LAOISE

The Murphy home, Dublin, Friday, February 3, 1905

LAOISE MET CHARLIE AT THE door of her parents' home just as the bell announced dinner. "Your mother has arrived and it's time to eat, my love," she said with a hug.

"I need just a minute to change my jacket. I'll be right there."

Cathleen opened the door to the entranceway and smiled at them both.

"I'll be right with you, Mum," Charlie said, and ran up the stairs behind Laoise.

"She has news she can't wait to tell us," said Laoise.

"That's intriguing. We already know Cally is better. Today's telegram was full of optimism." Charlie washed his face and hands and slipped into the jacket Laoise held for him. "Thanks for bringing this over for me. How is your mother today?"

"She's fine. Cheerfully reviewing with Mrs. Davis, the marvelous woman she has hired to help her, a long list of her ideas for the most splendiferous wedding ever."

"Thanks for doing all that without me."

Laoise grinned. "I expect we were all grateful not to include you."

Charlie swatted her with a hand towel and adjusted his bow tie.

"Let's go hear Mum's news."

"Are you sure it was him, Mum? At the train station in Waterford?"

"Positive. He was on an old bicycle, waiting for the train to pass. He stared back at me as though he recognized me, then pedaled alongside the train until I lost sight of him. I've already sent a telegram to Margaret to keep an eye out for him. He must be living in Waterford!"

"Or nearby, perhaps?" Charlie speared a sprig of broccoli. "This is delicious, Mother Muriel."

"I love hearing you call me that, dear," said Muriel. "Isn't it a delightful secret we all share? Yet the wonderful wedding awaits us. They say one can't have his cake and eat it too. We're proving them wrong."

Laoise kissed Charlie on the cheek. "The best of all worlds! But back to Billy, Mother Cathleen, please tell me again why this lad means so much to you all."

Cathleen smiled at Laoise then looked at her son. "Would you like to tell her, Charlie?"

"Sure. You all know about the treasure hunt my sister Cally, my brother Thomas, and I undertook last year. We—"

"Along with the children," said Cathleen.

"Yes, along with Cally's daughter Felicity and Thomas's three children," agreed Charlie. "We learned along the way that old Uncle William fathered a child in Idaho. He left us a packet to deliver to this child, but when we located his mother, we learned Billy had run away. His mother, Melody, suspected he had gone to Ireland to search for his father."

"Billy probably doesn't know his father has died. Until we find him, we can't deliver his packet and fulfill the treasure hunt," said Cathleen. "Also—" she stopped and looked at her plate.

"Also, Mum met Billy on the ship coming from Ireland to visit us for Josie's birthday," said Charlie. "She didn't believe his story, that he was Uncle William's son. That's not surprising, because he has dark skin."

"God forgive me, I couldn't imagine any situation in which Billy's story could have been true. I turned him away. I feel it's my fault this young lad is wandering around Ireland alone." A tear ran down Cathleen's cheek. She wiped it away.

"Billy does seem to be moving around," said Laoise. "Didn't you tell me, Charlie, that someone saw him in Killeagh a few weeks ago?"

"That's right," said Charlie. "Other than notifying Margaret, which you've already done, Mum, I don't know what else we can do. If he's living in Waterford, sooner or later she'll hear about it, don't you think? There aren't many lads with dark skin in Waterford. Or anywhere in Ireland."

"I think we should let Cecil and Melody and Minnie know we've seen him. I doubt they've heard from Billy. Thomas at least hasn't told us so." said Cathleen.

"Cecil and Melody and Minnie?" asked Laoise.

"Billy's uncle, his mother, and his grandmother," said Charlie. "I agree, Mum. A telegram, do you think, or a letter?"

"A telegram followed by a letter," said Cathleen. "I'll do it tomorrow. Cecil's daughter Ebony is still in Kansas City helping with the children while Cally convalesces. Cora says she's been wonderful and may stay on longer term."

"We met Miz Minnie, Billy's grandmother, first. She was our first clue." said Charlie. "And we found Billy's mother, Melody, in Pocatello. It's an amazing story. We got to participate in reuniting Melody with her mother. With Mr. Martin's help. Really, the heart of the treasure hunt was Billy the whole time."

"Shane recognized that before the rest of us," said Cathleen. "I think the most important thing we can do for Billy now is pray for him."

"As you have been doing all along, I'm sure, Cathleen," said Colin. "I'm confident this will all come right in time. The Malcomson family is a formidable force."

Charlie laughed. "It's true we don't give up easily when we set our mind to something. Right now, my mind is set on discussing plans for Mum and Laoise's tour. We can do so with free spirits now that Cally is on the mend."

"Let's retire to the drawing room," suggested Muriel. "Cathleen, it's such a comfort to us that you are willing to accompany Laoise."

"For me, it's pure pleasure. I love music, I love Europe, and most especially, I love Laoise."

"And me," grinned Charlie.

"And you, dear." Cathleen hugged him as they walked to the drawing room. "So, what's our first destination?"

"First Frankfurt, then Munich, then Vienna," responded Laoise.

"I go first to Paris, then Zurich, then Salzburg. I'll meet you two in Vienna—I already can't wait," said Charlie, pulling papers from his valise as they all settled into sofa and chairs. "I've made four copies of our travel plans and accommodations, with telephone numbers, addresses, the trains we plan to take, and the concert halls where we will play. What else should I have thought of?"

cs ৯ɔ

"Well, it's good to have all that figured out," Muriel said. "Now we can all relax and enjoy the lives God has given us. I have no immediate plans to transfer to Heaven, but I understand everyone's concerns about a peaceable process whenever it happens."

"Have you made plans of your own in Europe, Cathleen?" asked Colin.

"I have, yes. While our two lovebirds are together in Vienna the end of this month, I shall visit my friend Olga Wisinger-Florian."

"The artist? She's your friend? I think her flowers live and breathe!" exclaimed Muriel. "Is there any possibility . . . "

"That I could bring back a painting for you? I shall inquire with joy," said Cathleen. "Then while Charlie and Laoise are together in Livorno mid-March, I plan to make a Catholic retreat in Florence, on the topic of meditation. And during their two weeks together in Switzerland the last half of April, Margaret and the children will join me for a Mediterranean Easter holiday. She's working out the details—probably Nice, since it's close to Monaco where I'll reconnect with Laoise. Perhaps you will be well enough to join us, Muriel. That would be delightful."

Muriel brightened. "I would love that. I haven't been to France for oh, years and years."

"Lovely!" said Cathleen. "I wish I could include my daughters-in-law Cora and Meghan as well. And Cally. We'll find another time, though, when Laoise can be with us. This April she'll have other priorities."

"I will, true," said Laoise, coloring. "But it's a lovely idea, Mother Cathleen. It's a joy to think Cally could join us. What a scare that was!"

Muriel, Cathleen, and Charlie heaved a collective sigh.

"Cally still faces a long convalescence. But God has a plan for her life, that is clear. Now Muriel, Colin, Charlie, Laoise, will you join me in entrusting to God our plans and the journeys we have ahead of us?" Cathleen bowed her head.

On the train from Frankfurt to Munich, February 13, 1905

"You seem troubled, my dear," Cathleen said to Laoise once they had settled into their train compartment. "Were you not pleased with the concert last night? I thought your playing was stunning."

"It's not that," said Laoise, her sapphire eyes brimming. "I dreamed my mother died and I completely fell apart and became a burden to everyone. The dream left me questioning myself. Am I such a weak and self-centered person that I make everything, and everyone, revolve around me? Here I am taking up so much of your time and energy. Weeks and weeks. I'm sure you would rather be in Kansas City with Cally."

"Oh, my dear, I do love Cally very much, and I'm looking forward to having time with her when she comes for your wedding. But I love you, too. And I fully believe this is where God wants me right now, here with you, sharing your concerns for your mother. Don't worry, dear. I'm here because I would rather be nowhere else. I'm proud of you for being capable of creating gorgeous music at the same time your heart is breaking. That is no easy feat."

Laoise closed her eyes and breathed deeply, then looked at Cathleen. "I can't tell you what your words—and your presence—mean to me. Could you pray that whenever the time comes, I can find the strength to behave myself in a way that honors my mum?"

"I will do that right now, dear. Shall we pray together?"

The Wisinger-Florian home, Vienna, Monday, February 27, 1905

"What a delight to see you again!" exclaimed Cathleen, hugging Olga. "Though I saw you from afar at Laoise's concert last night."

"A delight indeed. I fear, though, our coveted time together may be cut short." Olga extended a telegram to her friend.

The color drained from Cathleen's face. "Mrs. Murphy's doctor doesn't think she has much time," said Cathleen. "We are all to return at once."

"Do you want to telephone Charlie and Laoise's hotel?" asked Olga.

"No. I need to deliver this news in person," said Cathleen.

"You will take our carriage," said Olga. "Trains depart hourly. I'm sure you can arrange at the station the most efficient way to reach Dublin. Don't worry, my friend. We will find another time to spend together."

"Thank you, Olga. I will look forward to that."

"Refresh yourself while Emil brings the carriage. He will wait at the hotel to take all three of you to the train station."

"You are most kind. Thank you."

଄ଃ

Charlie told them, "While we wait for the train, I will telegraph Florence to cancel our joint concerts March 10-12. Perhaps if Mother Muriel recovers enough, we can still enjoy some time at Livorno."

"Thank you, Charlie." Laoise grasped Cathleen's hand and tried to smile.

଄ଃ

Dublin, Thursday, March 2, 1905

"Papa!" Laoise ran from the carriage into her parents' home, trailed by Charlie and Cathleen.

"Here I am, Laoise," Colin said calmly, walking into the front room from his study. "Your mother is asking for you. Come with me."

"Should I go too?" Charlie whispered to Cathleen.

"Let's wait. She'll call you when she needs you," said Cathleen. "Meanwhile, we'll pray."

Minutes passed. An hour. Then Charlie heard a shriek. He startled. Tears flooded his eyes.

"Go, son," said Cathleen.

଄ଃ

"The funeral will be Sunday afternoon at our church," said Colin. "It will be posted in the paper tomorrow. I see no reason to delay. Everything has been prepared already."

"Laoise won't be capable of discussing next steps until after the service," said Charlie. "I'll cancel our Livorno plans, and the next weekend as well, Bologna for Laoise, Rome for me."

"And I my Florence retreat plans," said Cathleen. "When will Desmond arrive?"

"He and Deirdre will catch the first train from Belfast tomorrow," said Colin.

"Would it be better for Charlie and me to stay at Charlie's apartment to make more space for your family?" asked Cathleen.

"You are our family," said Colin. "Please don't leave us."

CHAPTER 13

CALLY

St. Joseph Hospital, Kansas City, February 3, 1905

"THANK YOU FOR COMING, RYAN. Hug Brian for me. Tell Priscilla thank you from me for caring for him so you could be here. And give my letter to Flora. And tell everyone I'll be there as soon as I'm strong enough to travel. Probably by the end of the month, the doctor says. Though he keeps telling me that even then I'll need to rest a lot. I know Flora will understand."

"I'm sure she will. I'll see you in a few weeks then. Cally." *I almost said sweetheart again. I need to be more careful.*

Cally reached out for a hug. Ryan kissed her cheek, then left, closing her door gently behind him. Cally climbed out of bed and watched through her window until he emerged below and climbed into the carriage Richard held for him. He looked up and waved. *That was sweet, though I'm sure he can't see me.*

Cally stared after the carriage as Richard drove away. *Clearly, Ryan isn't ready yet to let go of Bethany. He's thoughtful, but he holds himself at a distance. Will that ever change, God? How long before I can tell him how I really feel about him?*

She breathed a huge sigh, then turned away from the window and climbed back into bed and closed her eyes. *Funny how easily I tire. Another week or so in this room—mostly to be sure I'm no longer contagious—before I can go home. Most everyone has already left: Teddy back to his family, Ebony to hers, Matilda and Lizzy too. Now Ryan is leaving. Richard and Athena are still here, helping Thomas and Cora until I'm home from the hospital. How good and kind they have all been! Thank you, God, for the friends and family you have given me. After a nap, I'll tackle another stack of cards. And maybe, finally, look again at my anatomy book . . .*

Hansen, Idaho, February 28, 1905

"Look at the crowd, Athena! What's today, a holiday?" Cally stared out her window as the train slowed and stopped and the conductor intoned, "Hansen."

"I suspect they are thy friends, Cally. Do thee not recognize anyone?"

"Of course, I do. I know them all—well, most of them. But—"

"I saw thy friend Ryan near the front. I suspect he will help us with thy luggage."

"I'm sure he will. Whew, I'm tired. I hope Flora doesn't have any plans for me today." Cally didn't move.

"I will ask Ryan to come help thee. And tell the conductor we need a few more minutes to get thee safely off the train."

"Thank you, Athena."

"As thee are aware, Cally, I will stay overnight and catch the train east tomorrow."

"Thank you for making this journey with me, Athena. I couldn't have done it alone."

"Thee are most welcome, dear."

Cally leaned back and closed her eyes, spent. A gentle touch and Ryan's voice roused her.

"Can you walk, Cally? Here, lean on me. Flora's wagon is close by. I can carry you once we're off the train."

"Thank you, Ryan." Tears sprang to Cally's eyes. *I didn't want my return to Idaho to be like this. How embarrassing. And disappointing. How can I be so tired just from sitting for two days?*

A cheer erupted when Ryan appeared with Cally at the top of the steps to the platform. Cally lifted her free hand and tried to smile. When they had managed the descent, Ryan lifted her, and she breathed a sigh of relief. As he walked toward the wagon, she heard Flora explaining to the crowd that Cally was recuperating well but needed to rest after her long journey. Cries of "Get well soon, Cally," "We love you, Cally!" and "Welcome back, Cally" followed her.

Flora had layered the back of the wagon with blankets and pillows, and Cally sank into them gratefully. *She does understand. Maybe because she was so sick herself, back when we first met her. Thank you, God, for Flora. And for Ryan.* She opened her eyes in surprise. *Dear Ryan, who is climbing in beside me . . . Where will they put the luggage? I miss Felicity . . .*

"Cally, do you remember Falling Water's daughter-in-law, Sunrise?" asked Dr. Flora.

"Of course! How lovely to see you again. How is your baby?"

"He is asleep right now." Sunrise laughed. "He is almost eight months old. Learning to crawl! Getting into everything!"

"Sunrise has offered to stay with us to care for you when I am out doctoring," said Flora.

Cally rubbed tears from her eyes. "Thank you. It will be almost like—like—"

Flora touched Cally's shoulder. "Like having Falling Water back with us. I know. Fortunately, Falling Water taught Sunrise a great deal about healing. I am greatly blessed by her assistance."

"Thank you," Cally said again. "I hope I will soon be well enough to give you some assistance too, Flora."

"That day will come, dear. For now, you must be patient with yourself. Now I must go, but I leave you in good hands. Do you remember Constance Tatum? She's in labor with her fourth child. That means the baby could come quickly."

"Go!" said Cally.

"And while my child sleeps, I will help you bathe," said Sunrise.

CHAPTER 14

BILLY

Fermoy, February 3, 1905

"FERMOY! LAST STOP!"

The coachman's voice rang in the midnight stillness. He opened the coach door and caught Billy before he tumbled out onto the ground. The passengers grumbled, stirred, untangled themselves, and emerged blinking in the light of the lantern held aloft by the stage assistant.

Billy moved aside, stretched, yawned, and looked around him. *Where am I? I don't know the station's location in Fermoy, nor how far it is from St. Colman's.*

He waited until the others had gone their way, then approached the coachman, filling out papers at a desk in the station. "Sir, I'm sorry to disturb you. I don't know where I am. Can you tell me how to get to St. Colman's? How far is it? I'm afraid it will be locked when I get there."

"Are ye a student at the school, then? How come ye to be arriving so late?"

"I was sick, and this was the first coach I could take in Waterford."

The coachman looked him up and down. "Ye don't look likely to be a St. Colman's student, yer jacket all patched and all. Where is yer luggage?"

"I don't have any with me. It's a long story."

"But ye can swear to me that if I take ye to St. Colman's, they will receive ye? Ye aren't spinning a tale for me now, are ye? Because I don't fancy getting into trouble on yer account if yer telling me falsehoods."

"I swear I'm telling you the truth." Billy crossed his heart as he had seen children do in Idaho.

"Well, ye do talk like them, ye have that. Tell Chester—never mind."

The coachman got up and flung open the door. "Chester, stop with the horses. I need the coach a mite longer. Ye can go home. I'll care for them when I get back. Just give them a drink of water while I finish this paperwork. I'll see ye tomorrow." He stomped back to the desk. "I swear to ye, lad, if ye are telling tales, I'll take ye before the magistrate, so I will."

"Yes, sir."

"Well, go and make yerself useful to Chester. I'll be out shortly."

"Thank you, sir." *I have no idea how to care for a horse. I suppose Chester will tell me."*

By the time Chester explained to Billy how and where to fetch water, the coachman appeared, ordered Billy into the coach, and drove off, urging the horses to a trot. Billy peered out the coach window to the empty streets going by. *I'm glad I don't have to walk all this. I'll have to figure out a way to thank the coachman for going so many extra miles.*

Billy had almost fallen asleep again when the coachman pulled up at the gatehouse of St. Colman's. He jumped from his bench and pulled the bell. Billy climbed stiffly from the coach. The gateman appeared yawning and frowning.

"It's me, sir, William Malcomson. I'm sorry to be arriving so late. I know it's long past hours. Can you let me in?"

"In some kind of mischief, are ye, William Malcomson? Come on then. I'll let my betters tend to ye. They won't be pleased, no, indeed, they won't. Climb back in the coach, lad."

Grumbling all the while, the gateman pulled a key from his pocket and unlocked the gate, then selected another key and climbed up beside the coachman. They trotted down the long lane to the front door of the school. The gateman unlocked the front door, let Billy in, then locked it again. *I suppose he'll ride the coach back to the gatehouse.*

Billy walked as quietly as he could to his third-floor room. A folded note with WILLIAM in large letters was tied to the door handle. Billy read it in the light of the hall lantern, "William, present yourself to me immediately upon arrival, no matter the hour. MacDonagh."

"Yes, sir!" Billy saluted in exaggerated fashion, then walked to the end of the hallway. He knocked softly on Mr. MacDonagh's door. It opened immediately.

"Where on earth have you been?" demanded Mr. MacDonagh, pulling him inside. "Did I not tell you to be back in time for dinner?"

"I'll tell you the whole story, but can it be tomorrow, sir? It's the middle of the night! Here, I have this for you." He extracted a wrinkled note from his pocket. "I'll explain everything, but I'll do a better job of it in daylight."

"Come to me right after breakfast, then. Before rugby practice. Goodnight."

"Goodnight, sir."

cs෴ഊ

"What is the meaning of this note you gave me, William? I gave you no order to Waterford! And what was that jacket you were wearing? Where is my rain cape? What have you been up to these days? Do you not realize how dangerous it can be for you to disobey orders and take things into your own hands? You do not have enough information to make independent decisions! You—"

Billy sighed. "Sir, as I said last night, I will be glad to tell you the whole story. But I'm too tired to fight with you. Please call me when you're ready to listen." He opened the door handle and walked out. Mr. MacDonagh pushed against the door he was trying to close behind him.

"No, wait. I'm ready. I apologize, William. I ordered tea. There is so much I don't understand—"

Billy sighed again and reentered Mr. MacDonagh's quarters. For the next half hour, his teacher allowed him to talk, interrupting only occasionally with a pertinent question. As Billy came to the end of his recital, he stood, took a deep breath, and gathered his courage.

"I've come to a decision, Mr. MacDonagh. I refuse to risk my life for the sake of these 'messages' when I am not trusted enough to know what they are about. I don't want to die. I want to become a doctor, a pediatrician. My life has value, at least to me."

Mr. MacDonagh stared at Billy. "You have no right—" he said softly.

"I understand, Mr. MacDonagh, that in your mind, playing the role of messenger is my payment for my attendance at St. Colman's. I don't know whether the directors of the school are aware of this arrangement of yours, or whether they believe they are teaching me out of charity. I am willing to go to them to find out my true status. If they do not want me apart from my delivery of these messages, I will leave. I will find another school. I don't know what you are up to, sir, but it has no meaning to me. What does matter to me is preparing myself for medical school. If St. Colman's is not prepared to help me do that, I will find a school that will. With no life-threatening conditions. You can think about that while I go to rugby practice."

Billy turned to walk out, passing an old servant woman who had come to collect the tea service. She winked. Billy gasped. "You—how—"

She put a finger to her lips, turned from him, and reached for Mr. MacDonagh's teacup.

Billy stared at the closed door to Mr. MacDonagh's rooms for a long time, then raised his head and strode down the hall. *I feel—good. Strong inside, like I've grown too big for my skin. Like a dragonfly molting its exoskeleton to free its wings. I read about that once at my old school in Idaho. They have to get rid of what imprisons them in order to fly. I need that too.*

But who is that old woman?

CHAPTER 15

CHARLIE AND LAOISE

[Reminder: Laoise is pronounced *lee-sha.*]

The Murphy home, Dublin, Wednesday, March 8, 1905

"LAOISE DEAR, CAN WE TALK?"

Colin Murphy opened the drapes, then pulled a chair next to Laoise's bed in her old room, where she had isolated herself since her mother's funeral. She blinked in the sudden light of a bright spring day and sat up.

"What is it, Papa?"

"My dear, you've hardly eaten since your mother died. You've refused to see me, or Charlie, or Desmond. Until now. I'm happy we're talking now."

"I'm sad, Papa. I don't know how to live without Mummy."

"I understand, Laoise. It's hard for me, too. But we knew this time would come. And we know she's no longer suffering."

"I know. Is it selfish of me not to find comfort in that fact?"

"Does my saying those things feel to you like I'm denying your pain, and my own? No, dear. She's left a hole in our hearts nothing and no one else can fill. We will miss her terribly the rest of our lives."

Tears streamed down Laoise's face. Colin handed her his handkerchief.

"I—I keep telling myself I must think about what's next. About Charlie and our life together. About my tour. But I have no energy for any of that." Laoise lay back on her pillows.

"It's only been five days since she died, dear one. You know that Charlie cancelled your vacation plans in Livorno, as well as your joint concerts in Florence the following weekend, to give you time to grieve. Now he needs to know what to say to the people in Bologna and Genoa. They've been trying to contact you, alarmed over the other cancellations in your itinerary."

"I don't care about any of them," said Laoise. She turned over and squeezed her eyes shut.

"All right. But before we cancel, I suggest we take another day for you to think about it, Laoise. It may be that returning to your music is the most healing thing you can do for yourself."

Colin stood, placed his hand on Laoise's shoulder, moved his lips in prayer for her, and quietly left the room.

"She's not ready to decide yet," Papa said to someone outside her door.

That must be Charlie or Cathleen. Laoise frowned and sat up, holding her aching head in her hands. A melody filled her mind, not one of her concertos, but a lullaby her mother had sung to her as a child. She lay down and listened to her mother's voice in her head.

Sleep, my child, and peace attend thee
All through the night
Guardian angels God will send thee,
All through the night . . .
Though our hearts be wrapt in sorrow,
From the hope of dawn we borrow
Promise of a glad tomorrow
All through the night . . .

For the first time since hearing the news in Vienna of her mother's decline, Laoise slept without dreams or distress.

Dublin, Tuesday, March 21, 1905

Colin Murphy went straight from his office at Nigel and Murphy, Solicitors, to a meeting of the St. Catherine's Church of Ireland Parish Trustees. Upon entering the Chapel of Ease on Donore Avenue, he greeted Vicar Fergus Greer and nodded to the other men already gathered. No one seemed to notice the tiny slip of paper the vicar pressed into Colin's hand.

"How are you and your family, Colin?" asked a man at the table.

"Well enough, Sean, thank you. My son Desmond returned last week to his work in Belfast. But he and his fiancé plan to move back to Dublin. I'm happy about that. And my daughter Laoise left today to resume her concert tour in Europe."

"We are deeply sorry for your loss," said another man at the table. "Muriel will be missed."

"Thank you. What about that tie with England, then?" said Colin, changing the subject.

"It's my opinion our lads would have won had they played at home instead of in Middlesbrough," replied Sean. "But we'll see how they fare in Glasgow Saturday, yes?"

"We'll see," the vicar affirmed. "Shall we begin, then, Curate Bradshaw?"

A young man stood, adjusted his collar, and read the Collect of the day. After a suitable silence, he said, "Our agenda concerns the large number of evictions occurring among our parishioners from the new tenements on Thomas Street." He looked around the assembly with a smile. "As you all know, we use the income from those tenements to care for our poor, who, ironically, we are evicting because they have failed to supply through rental the funds we use to care for such as them."

"Have you a proposal for how to deal with this circular situation?" asked Vicar Greer.

"I do, Father. The first step, surely, is to evaluate the situation of each family evicted, to determine the cause of their financial difficulties. We must identify the problem in each case. Only then can we determine appropriate action."

A gentleman across from Colin stood. Vicar Greer nodded and said, "Mr. Guinness."

"Edward will do, Vicar. I agree with Curate Bradshaw's first step, certainly. But does it not seem necessary to establish a separate fund for aid to the poor? The interest could be used to help with situations such as you describe. I propose that each gentleman of the vestry contribute to this fund, to be managed by yourself and Curate Bradshaw. I offer one thousand pounds as a self-perpetuating endowment."

"Thank you for your generosity, Mr. Guinness," said the vicar.

"Edward," said Mr. Guinness. "Secondly . . . "

Colin found himself distracted, desperately wanting to find out what message the Vicar had penned on the slip of paper now in his pocket. *Since Muriel died, nothing has interested me as much as this.* He looked up and saw the vicar's eyes on him, a passing glance, but full of meaning. *Until I can read his message, though, I've no idea what meaning he is trying to convey.*

He slid the paper from his pocket and glanced at it under the edge of the table. "Arthur Griffith wants to meet you. I will take him to your house tomorrow evening at 9:30."

A balcony of Le Petit Manoir, Morges, Switzerland, Friday, April 21, 1905

Charlie sighed with pleasure, pulling his attention from a glorious sunset over Lake Geneva long enough to grin at Laoise. "Getting married before our wedding was such a grand idea, Laoise! The thought of meeting you here kept me going through these last difficult weeks. I'm glad we were able to reschedule. We'll do Livorno another time. I promise."

Laoise toasted him, then took a sip of champagne. "Our joint concert in Florence last weekend was the truly grand idea, Charlie. Took me right back to our Irish concerts with the New York Philharmonic."

"Good practice for Geneva next weekend. I'm sad though that Mr. Paderewski is in Canada. I wanted you to meet him. I want him to hear you play."

"I would love to know him, Charlie. He's had such an impact on you."

"This is the beginning of our joint repertoire, sweet Laoise. We can build it gradually without any pressure, since we have these pieces perfected."

"Well, about that . . . "

"I know. Your sense of timing doesn't agree with mine when it comes to the Trio. Laoise, what if we try to see Hamilton Harty in London? Since we disagree on this, we can ask his opinion as the composer."

"Mr. Harty was friendly when we attended the 'Irish Symphony' debut in Dublin last year. Maybe he would like to see us, especially if we're asking for advice about playing his music," said Laoise. "Do you know what else I would like to do in London?"

"No, what?"

"I'd like to attend the new London Symphony. We could go to one of their very first concerts. And I want to see 'The Scarlet Pimpernel.' It's been playing at the New Theatre since January. I've seen rave reviews."

"Both of those sound delightful!" Charlie set down his champagne glass and pulled a small date book from his pocket. "Since London is our last concert before our wedding, shall we extend our time there by a few days? A kind of pre-wedding pre-honeymoon?"

Laoise laughed, then sobered. "Why not? Mrs. Davis will have everything ready for our wedding. All I must do is put on my gown." A tear trickled down her cheek. "I wish my mum . . . "

Charlie pulled her close. "I know, dear heart. It's so hard not having her with us—another reason I'm grateful we went ahead to get married. The wedding ceremony will be nice, I'm sure of that. But I'll always remember your mum's smile as we turned from saying our vows at the registry office. For me, that smile was the true blessing of our marriage."

Laoise took a deep breath. "It's getting dark and a bit chilly, Charlie. Shall we go in?"

ଔଓ

Charlie woke with a jerk to Laoise screaming and thrashing. Before he could react, she fell off the bed with a thump. He scrambled across the bed and to the floor beside her, gathering her into his arms.

"Laoise, I'm here. You've had a bad dream. You're safe. I'm with you, my darling."

Gradually her sobs eased, and she sat up, leaning against the bed beside him.

"I'm glad this floor is carpeted. Do you want to tell me about your dream, Laoise?"

"I was running on a path, like the loop we walk through the trees at St. Stephen's Green. I passed a bench I used to sit on with my mum, and-and—I felt flooded with grief. I-I couldn't breathe."

Charlie hugged Laoise closer and said again, "I'm with you, darling."

Laoise swallowed. "I—I had to keep running. I couldn't stop!" She sobbed.

Charlie held her and waited.

"As I ran away from the bench, my grief eased, and I could breathe again." Laoise blew her nose. "But running brought me back around to the bench, and grief devastated me again. And again. And again."

Laoise's voice rose into a wail. "I couldn't get off the track. I couldn't stop running!"

Charlie pulled a blanket from the bed and wrapped it around the two of them, rocking her in his arms as she wept. After a while, he began singing to her, a song that seemed to come into his mind of its own accord.

Jesus, Lover of my soul, Let me to Thy bosom fly,

While the nearer waters roll, While the tempest still is high:

Hide me, O my Savior, hide, Till the storm of life is past;

Safe into the haven guide; O receive my soul at last.

"What is that?" asked Laoise, her voice muffled by the blanket.

"It's a song my mum used to sing to me when I was frightened as a child," said Charlie. "I haven't thought about it in years. I'm surprised I still know the words."

"Like when there was a storm that reminded you of the ship? Is—is there more?"

"Yes. Do you want me to sing the second verse?"

"Yes, please."

Other refuge have I none; Hangs my helpless soul on Thee;

Leave, ah! Leave me not alone, Still support and comfort me.

All my trust in Thee is stayed, All my help from Thee I bring;

Cover my defenseless head with the shadow of Thy wing.

"Mummy used to tell me to imagine I was a wee chick safely sheltered under the wings of a mother hen. Though the storm raged around me, it couldn't touch me."

"And that helped?"

"It did, yes. Laoise . . . I know the terrible loss of your mother will take time to heal. My heart was with you every minute we were apart, following you to Bologna, Genoa, Milan . . . Mum probably told you, even when I can't be with you, Jesus is. He's our true refuge who never has to be somewhere else."

"You really believe that, don't you." Laoise's voice was so muffled by his chest, Charlie could hardly hear her.

"I do, yes. I don't know how much we can control our dreams. But when we're awake and feeling sorrow or fear or anguish, we can ask Jesus for help."

"I can imagine your mum saying that to you. It's like you're using her words. Will you teach me her song?"

"I'll be glad to, Laoise. But do you think we can go back to sleep now, and I could teach you the song tomorrow?"

"I'm afraid to go back to sleep," said Laoise, her voice rising. "I'm afraid I'll find myself back on the path, running toward that bench, unable to stop."

"Then how about if you say the second verse after me, like a prayer, asking Jesus to care for you even in your dreams?"

"All—all right. I—I'll try."

"Let's get back in bed. Then I'll say a line and you say it after me. Let me get the blanket back on top of us . . . Here we go: Other refuge have I none."

"Other refuge have I none," echoed Laoise.

"Hangs my helpless soul on Thee."

"Hangs my helpless soul on Thee.

"Leave, ah! Leave me not alone."

"Leave, ah! Leave . . . me . . . "

"Still support and comfort me."

Slow, deep breathing was her only response.

Morges, Tuesday morning, May 2, 1905

Charlie thanked the bellboy and opened a telegram. "Margaret and children left for Waterford. I leave Nice tomorrow. Meet Laoise Monaco. Mum." Charlie looked carefully into Laoise's sapphire eyes. "You'll have three days to practice at the Monte Carlo Opera House before your concerts there."

"I don't know if I can perform by myself. I wish you didn't have to go to Germany." Laoise stuck her tongue out at Charlie and laughed. "Let me act like a needy child just one more day. I'll rediscover my strength on the train to Monaco."

"These days with you have been magical," said Charlie, cuddling her hand as they walked down to lunch. "This month will be the last time we plan to travel separately. We can get through the next four weeks. I'm sure we can. Then we'll have London together, our wedding, and a whole long life to celebrate a day at a time. With no more secrets from the world."

"Let's not talk about it today. Let's just play," said Laoise.

CHAPTER 16

CALLY

Ryan's farm near Twin Falls, Idaho, April 22, 1905

"BRIAN'S SO DETERMINED TO MASTER walking. Look at him. He falls and gets right back up again. I'm inspired." Cally and Ryan sat on a picnic blanket in a meadow, newborn lambs nursing nearby and the blue, blue sky arching overhead.

"Me too," said Ryan. "I wonder what drives babies to work so hard."

"Did you know babies have a hundred more bones than adults?"

"How is that possible?" asked Ryan. He took a huge bite of his sandwich.

"I think it's God's design. It makes babies more flexible for the birthing process. Bones fuse as babies grow. I've been learning so many fun facts from my anatomy book!"

"Remember how little energy you had a few weeks ago, Cally? Now you're studying several hours a day. I'm sure Flora is pleased with your progress."

"Ryan, what have you been thinking about lately, while I've been consumed with anatomy and physiology?"

"I've been reading Irish history. Did you know there are more Irish people in America now than in Ireland itself? There's an American organization intent on achieving Irish freedom from England!"

"Where do you find this information?"

"I send away for books. One of them came with an advertisement for a newspaper called *The Gaelic American.* It opened my eyes to the plight of the Irish under British rule. They've been treated abominably. The paper argues against those who believe Ireland will be fine with what they call Home Rule, still under the British Empire but governing itself in many respects. An Irish politician named John Redmond is in favor of that solution. I receive the *Irish World* as well. It's a more moderate paper that doesn't support using violence to obtain independence. I find it all quite fascinating. I'm trying to figure out which approach might be most effective."

"You mean there are Irish who want to try to overthrow the British Empire? How could that be possible? It would be like—like the State of Idaho rebelling against the whole United States!"

Ryan laughed. "Absurd, right? Yet there are people writing regularly for *The Gaelic American* so passionate about this they are willing to lay down their lives for the cause. They regularly reference the American fight for independence from Britain."

"Ryan, you would never—"

"Of course not. I'm an American first and Irish second. But I am trying to understand them. *The Gaelic American* claims Irish independence will only come about through American support. Most Irish are very poor, whereas the immigrant Irish in this country have done better, some very well. I want to help. But first I must figure out which perspective I'm siding with."

"Can you do that just by reading about it?"

"I don't know. I'm thinking about traveling to Ireland, to understand the situation there firsthand."

"Do you know anything about your family, Ryan? If you go to Ireland, perhaps you could find relatives there!"

"I have no information about my family, Cally. I was little more than a baby when my parents and siblings died, and I imagine Byrne is a common name in Ireland."

"But you do know your family was Quaker. I've learned from the Malcomsons that the number of Irish Quakers is small. And they keep good records. I'll ask Cathleen who you could contact among the Quakers to ask about your family."

"That would be amazing, Cally. More than I ever hoped for. What if I have aunts, uncles, and cousins in Ireland—or even here in America!"

"Charlie and Laoise are getting married in Dublin in June," Cally said slowly. "Would you like an invitation to the wedding? You could travel with Thomas and Cora and their family. And after the wedding, you could investigate your family story. I don't know, but I would guess Quaker records might be kept in Dublin, since it's the largest city."

"Aren't you going to the wedding?"

"I don't know whether I'll be well enough. I don't want to get sick again and detract attention from Charlie and Laoise."

"You still fear a relapse?"

"I do. It happened to me once already. I thought I was getting well and then—"

"I think you should ask Flora how likely that is. This is your beloved Charlie's wedding, Cally! How can you even consider not being there? It could be an opportunity for you to reconnect with your own family, the aunt and uncle, niece and nephews you've told me about."

"I know, but as I said, I don't want to risk getting sick or requiring special attention. I want Charlie and Laoise's special day to be all about them."

"Please talk to Flora. Perhaps you're worrying unnecessarily. As for myself, I would be delighted to receive an invitation, if I can go with you. I would feel awkward inserting myself into your family without you. I'm just a distant friend."

"You're much more than that, Ryan! You've traveled twice to Kansas City on my behalf. You testified at my trial. You sat with me in the hospital. You shared so much with Cora and Thomas both there and here in Idaho. Felicity thinks you and Brian somehow belong to her."

"If you go, I'll be happy to go. And if you want to spend more time in Ireland, perhaps with your uncle and aunt, while I travel around learning about the nationalists, we could return together in time for your fall semester at St Joseph's."

Brian toddled over and fell into his father's lap. "Good job, Brian!" Cally clapped. "You're doing so well!"

Brian beamed.

"Does he look like Bethany, Ryan?"

"He does. A constant reminder to me of love and loss. Once in a while I see an expression that reminds me I'm his father. But his blond curls and blue eyes and dimples are all hers."

"Look—what he did just then, squinting his eyes. You do that."

"I do?"

"Yes, when you're thinking hard about something. So, what are you thinking about, baby Brian?"

Brian pounced and came up with an orange butterfly in his chubby fist.

"Oh no, Brian! You've squashed the poor butterfly! That American Lady will never fly again." Ryan pried open his child's fingers and looked sorrowfully at the butterfly's mashed body. "We must leave the butterflies to fly free, Brian. All right?"

Brian gazed intently at his father's face, as if trying to understand.

"Back to the idea of traveling to Ireland, Ryan, how could you leave your farm for that long?" Cally asked.

"I've been thinking about that. I could hire people to care for the sheep and the other animals and the garden. I'm quite sure Priscilla and Jerry would care for Brian. As you know, they consider him their grandchild."

"When were you thinking about going? Before you learned about the wedding."

"I'd thought of traveling with you when you return to Kansas City this fall—I thought you would be here all summer—then continuing east from there. But it would be even more fun to travel all the way to Ireland with you and the Malcomsons. Wouldn't it? Think about how enjoyable that would be, Cally. And if I'm with you, I could take care of you if you get sick, so you wouldn't have to worry about becoming a burden to others. Think about it, and if you'll go, yes, I would love to receive an invitation to the wedding."

Cally looked down. "I wonder what the family will think if we go to the wedding together."

"That's up to you, Cally. Tell them whatever you like. I would be proud to go with you."

Cally glanced at Ryan and blushed at the expression on his face. "Thank you, Ryan," she said softly.

Ryan stood and stretched. "This has been delightful. Sadly, I have chores to attend to. And this wee one needs a nap. Thanks for picnicking with me today, Cally. And engaging with my interest in Irish nationalism. I can loan you newspapers if you like—I've kept them all. I would love to have your perspective on the arguments of the two sides."

"We know the Quaker position," said Cally, folding the blanket. "They are totally against violence of every kind. Your parents would be horrified to know you're considering the perspective of *The Gaelic American*."

"Just considering. I haven't taken a position yet." Ryan picked up Brian for the walk back to his house. "It's interesting you say that, though. A Quaker man named Bulmer Hobson has been writing some articles. He's opposed to violence yet seems very committed to the cause of Irish independence. But not to Home Rule. He's trying to find a peaceful means of achieving full freedom without fighting with arms."

"A third position, then. Sure, I'll read some of your papers. It will be a nice break from anatomy and physiology, especially when Flora is called out in the evenings. Since I was judged well enough for Sunrise to go home to her family, but not well enough to go on calls with Flora, I find I often have time alone."

"Perhaps Brian and I could occupy some of that time, Cally. If you would enjoy that. I get lonely too. We can talk more about the Irish situation once you've formed your own thoughts."

"Lovely! Thanks for the picnic, Ryan. I'm glad Flora could drop me off here. She'll be by to pick me up any time."

"I'm glad you came. Let me get you some lemonade. You can wait for Flora on the porch swing while Brian sleeps and I do my chores."

"Will I see you two tomorrow at the Hansens' Easter dinner?"

"I wouldn't miss it. Until then, Cally" He walked toward the barn whistling.

I don't think I told Ryan a lie—I AM concerned about whether I can travel to Ireland without getting sick. I remember what it was like on the ship when Da—when Da died. Sailing on the very same ship doesn't sound at all appealing right now. But I can't tell Brian—or Cora—the real reason I can't go back to Ireland. They would think it silly that I'm afraid of the faeries. But I am. I saw what they can do when they're miffed.

Cally fingered the small round mirror in her pocket, a frown creasing her face. *Now Ryan is excited about going to the wedding with me. But sailing again on the* Lion III*? I feel overwhelmed with grief and fear just thinking about it. And I'm afraid my presence in Ireland would attract the faeries' attention. I don't want them to cause harm to the Malcomsons or to the Donnellys. Or to anyone close to them, like Laoise's mum.*

Cally swallowed the rest of her lemonade as Flora's wagon trundled toward Ryan's house. *If the faeries still want it, I could give them my mirror... Would that satisfy them? I wish I could ask Miss Hilda.*

Felicity's teary voice on the telephone wrenched Cally's heart. "Mummy, I wish you were here with me for Easter. My new dress is so pretty. It's the first one I ever had that you didn't make for me."

"I know, my precious lassie. I miss you so much, and I can't wait to see your dress. It won't be long now. I'll be home in just three weeks!"

"Is Mr. Ryan coming too? And Brian?"

"No. I'm strong enough now to travel on the train by myself." *I won't tell her yet that he plans to go to Ireland for the wedding. One step at a time.*

"Tell you what, Felicity. Ask Shauna to help you make a paper chain."

"What's a paper chain?" Felicity's voice perked up.

"You cut strips of paper the same size, then glue the ends together in a long chain. Each morning before you go to school you can tear off one link. When you tear the last link, that's the day I'll be home!"

"Can I color the links?"

"Of course! Color them before you glue them."

"How many do I need to make?"

"Well, let's see. Today is April 23. I'll be home on May 13. You can look at a calendar and count how many days that is."

"Can I go make the chain right now?"

Cally laughed. "Yes! I'll make one too. Every link we tear off is one day closer to being together again. All right, sweetheart? I love you."

"Love you too, Mummy. Bye."

Cally sighed. *Each link will also be one day closer to the wedding. What am I going to do?*

Wednesday, May 10, 1905

At the sound of a knock, Cally set aside her textbook and rose to open the door of Flora's house, trailed by the doctor's pet wolf Fauna. *Her tail is wagging, so it must be someone we know. But then who don't we know in this community.*

"Ryan! And Brian! I didn't expect to see you again until next month! Is everything all right?"

"I need you to look at Brian's teeth. Do you think he has the right number for his age?"

"You need me to—" Cally laughed as she noted Ryan's twinkling eyes.

"We just wanted to see you again. We'll miss you, Cally."

Cally took the baby, gave him a hug and a kiss, and set him down. He immediately toddled toward Fauna, falling over her in a giggly heap.

"Is something on your mind, Ryan?"

Ryan blushed and turned toward the couch. "Can we sit down for a minute? I know you're busy studying for your exam. It's this evening, right, before you catch the train to Kansas City tomorrow morning?"

"Yes, when Flora gets back from her weekly clinic in Rock Creek. But I can take a few minutes. I think I know about all my brain can hold about the nervous system."

Ryan fidgeted. "Well, Cally, I have something I want to say to you, but I'm afraid it may upset you."

Cally's eyes widened and she frowned. "What could you say that would upset me? Did I hurt your feelings in some way? I didn't mean to."

"No. Yes, in a way, I suppose."

"Just tell me, Ryan." Cally jumped up and closed her bedroom door before Brian reached it. "I haven't babyproofed in there."

Back on the couch, Cally looked expectantly at Ryan. "Just tell me," she repeated.

"Cally, can't you tell that I love you? I've tried so hard to honor our agreement, but I couldn't sleep last night, so full of wanting to tell you before you leave. I've made my peace with Bethany. She's given us her blessing and I just have to know—"

Cally sucked in a breath. "How do you know Bethany gives us her blessing? And what do you need to know?"

"Do you love me too, Cally? Sometimes I think I see signs that you do. But then I wonder if I just imagined it. Do you ever think of us being together, for always? Getting married and—" Ryan stopped as tears streamed down Cally's face.

"How long?" she whispered. "How long have you felt this way?"

"Since I sat by you all those hours when you were so sick, not knowing—not knowing whether I might—I might lose you, Cally! I couldn't bear losing you too. I had a lot of time to talk with God and with Bethany about—about us. You and me. But I knew you would want to stick with our agreement, so I couldn't say anything then."

"You called me sweetheart," said Cally slowly. "Then you said it didn't mean anything."

"I didn't think you were ready to know what it meant to me." Ryan reached for her hand. "Cally, if you're still not ready, it's all right. I had to tell you. But I'm not in a hurry. We can wait as long as you need. And if you don't—don't want to even consider a serious relationship with me, you can tell me that, too."

Brian had toddled over and leaned against Cally, staring into her face as if trying to understand her tears. Cally wiped her eyes, giggled, picked up the baby, and cuddled him. "Brian seems to want to know my answer as much as you do, Ryan."

She took a moment to bury her face in Brian's soft hair, then took a deep breath and looked at Ryan, her eyes shining. "I thought this day would never come. I thought your heart belonged to Bethany forever. I love you too, Ryan. I feel overwhelmed by knowing you truly care for me."

"Oh, Cally!" Ryan scooted over to put his arms around Cally and Brian and planted a soft kiss on Cally's lips as she leaned into him. Brian gurgled and patted both their faces.

"How will I be able to focus on studying now?"

"Here's an idea: I need to buy groceries. How about if you study while Brian and I go do that. We'll come back and cook lunch for you, as a little celebration."

"That sounds lovely!"

"And maybe I can quiz you, if that would help you prepare for your exam."

"All right."

"We'll be back then, in a little while."

"Ryan."

"Yes?"

"It's all right if you call me sweetheart now."

Ryan blushed. "Then, we'll be back in a little while, sweetheart."

Ryan gave her another kiss, then lifted Brian. At the door he looked back. "I'm happy, Cally. So happy."

"Me too, my love."

"You can keep studying while I cook," Ryan told Cally, after tucking a sleeping Brian into her bed for his nap.

"No, I'll help you. Let me peel these carrots. There's so much we need to talk about!"

"What's first on your mind?"

Cally stopped peeling. "Ryan, are you thinking of telling other people? This is all so new and precious, I want to cherish it for a while, just the two of us. Is that all right with you?"

Ryan stopped chopping an onion. “It will be hard for me. I feel like shouting it from the rooftops: Cally loves me!!!”

Cally laughed. “It is amazing, isn’t it. Neither of us thought we would ever find someone to love and to love us.”

“Truly amazing. While I think my love for you is strong enough for anything that might happen. But I know it’s fragile just because it’s so new. Like a newborn baby that needs to be protected and cared for and carefully fed.”

“I like that analogy, Ryan. Won’t it be fun to see our love grow stronger as we nurture it?”

“Yes.” Ryan leaned over and kissed her head, bent once more over the carrots, then dumped his onions into a pan and picked up a potato. “So, for now, we’ll keep our love protected from the world.”

“Thank you, Ryan.”

“Now I have a question for you. I like the idea of asking permission to court you. Bethany expected that, so I asked her father. Who in your family could I ask?”

“What an interesting custom, Ryan! Is that something people often do? There’s so much I don’t know about how the world works!”

“I think it’s customary, yes. The idea is that a father is responsible for his daughter while she lives in his home. You were only seven, though, when your father died. So, who functioned as a parent to you when you were growing up?”

Cally leaned against the wall and thought. “I don’t think I can count Paddy. Cap was our employer. I don’t believe he thought in terms of being a father to us. As his drinking grew worse, it was more often us taking care of him. The Anthony sisters, though, did care for Teddy and me, especially Aunt Mary. She still calls me ‘her girl.’ I think she does think of me as a daughter.”

“Interesting. What about the Malcomson family?”

“Thomas and Cora took me in off the streets, a pregnant pauper recuperating from severe illness. They had no idea I already knew some of their relatives. They have been as kind and generous as it’s possible to be, but they are more like older siblings than parents. Legally, Thomas adopted me as a sister and Felicity as a niece."

"What about Cathleen?"

"Hmm. Perhaps if she lived in this country and I saw her more often . . . Felicity does think of her as her grandmother. But I guess I still think of her as Thomas and Charlie's mother, not my own."

"Tell me about your relationship with Charlie. I know you've been very close."

"Charlie was the first Malcomson to take an interest in me, when we were both children. He was a junior sailor on his father's boat when Da, Teddy, and I came over from Ireland. My da died, in fact, because he offered to take Charlie's place as a sailor in the middle of a terrible storm. It took Charlie a long time to get over that. He felt responsible for Da's drowning. Oddly enough, Charlie's father, Peter, also felt responsible, once he realized he expected from Charlie more than he was capable of at his young age, the reason Da stepped in. It was a huge emotional tangle. Of course, I didn't realize all that at the time. I just 'knew' it was somehow my fault."

"Your fault? How could that be?"

"I believed every terrible thing that happened was my fault. I still tend to assume that. But I don't want to talk about that right now."

"I'd like to come back to that, though, all right?"

Cally looked at Ryan and slowly nodded.

"When you're ready, Cally. I won't push you."

"Thank you."

"Tell me more about Charlie."

"He was terribly upset when I ran away from his family, and excited when Thomas and Cora took me in. That's still such a wonderment."

"A wonderment?"

"Well, in the whole big country of America, Charlie's brother and sister-in-law 'happened' to find me by the side of the road and feel the desire to take me into their home. With no idea of my history with Charlie and Cathleen. Yes, a wonderment."

"And then?"

"By then, Charlie was already a pianist, traveling around giving concerts. So, I didn't see him very often. He always treated me with great kindness, like a brother."

"Did you ever think of him differently?"

"No. I always felt how distinct his world is from mine. His care for me was pure grace, but it felt uneven. Do you know what I mean?"

"You mean you felt he was higher, and you were lower than him in some way?"

"Yes, I guess that's what I mean. The Malcomson family is wealthy, and educated, and accomplished. They take for granted ways of living and dressing and moving in the world I never imagined until I lived with them. I went to live with them as a servant. Only later did they adopt me and Felicity. And though they elevated us to be officially part of their family, I continued doing the same tasks and occupied much the same space in their home as I had before. When I started nursing school, they hired Nora to replace me. Do you see what I mean?"

"I honestly don't think *they* would see what you mean. From what I could tell last summer, Cora genuinely treated you as her sister."

"I know. But she wasn't born a Malcomson. It's something inside me, I guess. Anyway, I'm glad Charlie found Laoise. She's exactly the kind of person he needs—someone who shares his passion for music, who grew up much the same as he did, with the same expectations for how they will live. And she's gorgeous, and gracious, and—and perfect, as far as I can tell."

"No one is perfect, Cally. Though you seem perfect to me."

"Haha. Just wait until you know me better."

"I can't wait. I want to know every bit of you, perfect and imperfect. I love you, Cally."

"I'm trying to be serious, Ryan. I have a lot of problems."

"Well, maybe I can help you solve some of them. And maybe some of them aren't real problems, but instead are just in your head."

"Maybe . . . anyway, back to the question of who you should ask permission to court me . . . "

"From what you've said, it seems you think of Mary Anthony in the role of parent more than anyone else."

"I guess that's true."

"Should I write her a letter then? About my desire to court you?"

"Hmm. I think she would say she can't say yes without meeting you. Would you be willing to travel to Rochester, New York, to talk with her personally?"

"Would you come with me?"

"I would love to see her. So would Felicity. Aunt Mary is getting old. I don't know how much time she has left. Her sister Miss Susan Anthony already died."

"So . . . New York. How far is Rochester from New York City? Would we do this before or after our trip to Ireland?"

"Let me get a calendar." Cally ran to her bedroom and tiptoed in. Brian didn't stir.

"We sail from New York City for Ireland June tenth, right? It was kind of Thomas to buy a ticket for me along with the rest of your family," said Ryan.

"Yes, the tenth is a Saturday. The family has train tickets leaving Kansas City Tuesday, June sixth."

"Could Thomas swap our train tickets for another day?"

"Thomas IS the railroad in Kansas and Missouri. He can do whatever he wants, I think."

"Then how about this: I'll meet you in Kansas City on Thursday, June first so you, Felicity, and I can leave for Rochester the next day. We can spend a couple of days with Aunt Mary before we join the others in New York City to sail for Ireland."

"Let me think for a minute . . . yes, I think that will work. It will be a longer time for you away from Brian, though. I'll write to Aunt Mary inviting ourselves! I think she'll be delighted."

"Cally, I don't know how long I will spend in Ireland. I might not come back with you. You understand, don't you?"

"I do. But Sister Irmena expects me at the hospital the end of June. I have so much to make up from when I was sick."

"Well, one step at a time. Maybe I'll find out enough about my relatives and about the various nationalist perspectives ahead of the trip that I don't have to stay long after the wedding. I wrote to the Quaker people you told me about. Haven't heard back yet though."

"Correspondence takes time. Perhaps you can meet some Dublin Quakers while you're there. A personal conversation might be more helpful than letters."

"We can meet them together, and you can ask about your family too!"

"Maybe so. Mmm, the stew smells so good it's making me hungry."

"Here, have a taste."

"Yum!"

Cally waved at Ryan, Brian, Flora, and Fauna, and a collection of other friends until the train curved so she could no longer see the station. She wiped tears from her eyes.

"Happy tears, or sad?" asked the middle-aged woman sitting next to her.

"Both, I guess," said Cally. "We'll see each other again in three weeks, but right now that feels like a long time."

"Ah, young love," said the woman. "Or is he your husband?"

"Not my husband. We haven't figured it all out yet."

"A handsome baby," observed the woman.

"Yes. I'm told he looks like his mother. She died birthing him." Cally extended her hand. "My name is Cally."

"I'm Stacey, from Rock Creek."

"Oh, then you just boarded too. How far are you going?"

"All the way to New York City. My cousin recently died, and her family needs help for a while until they adjust to their new reality. She left three young children and her husband is beside himself."

"It's kind of you to go."

"This typhoid epidemic has been a terrible thing."

"Oh, did your cousin die of typhoid?"

"She did, yes, along with so many others."

"I'm just recovering from typhoid myself."

Stacey pulled back a little.

"Don't worry—I'm no longer contagious," Cally added hastily. "I got sick at Christmastime."

"Are you from New York too? What are you doing in Idaho?"

"I live in Kansas City. I'm a student nurse, and contracted typhoid from a patient visiting there from New York, before we realized the cause of his illness. A kind friend invited me to convalesce here, once my doctor was sure I wouldn't pass it on."

"And you met that young man here?"

"Well, yes, but we met a year ago. It's a long story . . . "

"I love stories. We've a long ride ahead of us."

Cally pulled from her valise a dress she wanted to finish as a surprise for Felicity. "All right, I'll tell you, as long as you then tell me more about your life."

"With pleasure," said Stacey.

Thank you, God, for this distraction from the pain of leaving Ryan.

"I love it, Mummy!" Felicity twirled in her new dress, then plopped down beside Cally. "Mummy, Aunt Cora told me Mr. Ryan is going with us to Ireland! Is Brian coming too?"

"Yes, Ryan is coming! But no, Brian will stay with Priscilla. The trip would be very long for him, and Ryan doesn't know how long he'll stay in Ireland. He wants to try to find his relatives there."

"Aunt Cora says we're going to meet lots of relatives in Ireland. Did you know I have more cousins? One is named Caoimhe, and she has two brothers, Cathal and Christopher. You never told me about them."

"I've never met them, Felicity. They were born after I left Ireland to come to America. You have other cousins there too."

"I know. Martin and Molly and Sally and Cait and Peter. And we get to see Grandma Cathleen! It's been ever so long since she was here."

"You're excited about this trip, aren't you."

"Yes! I've never been on a ship before. Uncle Thomas showed us on a map where we're going, from Kansas City to New York on a train and then we'll sail across a whole big ocean! And Aunt Cora says Uncle Charlie's wedding will be fancy, and Laoise is so beautiful. Josie and I think she will be the mostest beautifulest bride in the whole world!"

"You're probably right about that. It's a grand adventure! And I have a surprise for you. How would you like to go visit Aunt Mary Anthony before we go to Ireland? She lives in a city called Rochester, in the state of New York."

"New York is where we get on the ship to cross the ocean."

"That's right. To visit her, we'll leave a few days before the rest of the family. Ryan will go with us."

"But not baby Brian?"

"Not baby Brian," Cally agreed.

Felicity heaved a sigh. "I could help take care of him."

"I know, honey, but he'll be happy staying with his grandma Priscilla in Idaho."

"Mummy, do you know what I think?"

"No, dear."

"I think you should marry Mr. Ryan, and then baby Brian could be my brother and Mr. Ryan could be my daddy. That's what I think. Why don't you do it?"

Cally smiled. "That's an interesting idea, Felicity. Now, darling, it's time for bed."

"But Mummy, why won't you tell me you'll do it? Marry Mr. Ryan?"

"I promise I'll think about it, Felicity. Would you want to live in Idaho?"

"On Mr. Ryan's farm? With baby Brian and the sweet baby lambs? Yes!"

"Life would be very different there, Felicity. You would be far away from your cousins, and you would go to a small school."

Felicity heaved another sigh. "Oh Mummy. I know about Idaho. Don't you remember I was *there,* for weeks and weeks? I loved being there."

"But you wouldn't often see Josie and Shauna and Shane."

"They could come visit us."

Cally laughed. "Now I think you're just trying to delay bedtime. Off you go."

"You'll still be here in the morning?"

"I will. I promise. I don't have any plans to leave you again."

Felicity snuggled close. "That's good, cuz I missed you so, so much, Mummy. I'm glad you're not sick anymore."

"I'm glad too. I missed you terribly. Do you want help getting ready for bed?"

"No, but will you sing the songs you used to always sing to me?"

"I will. I'm going to bed soon too because I'm tired from the long train ride, but first I'm going to tell Auntie Cora our plans to visit Aunt Mary."

"Sing me the song about Ireland."

"All right."

Sure a little bit of Heaven fell from out the sky one day
and it nestled in the ocean in a place so far away
and when the angels found it sure it looked so sweet and fair
they said suppose we leave it for it looks so peaceful there.

So they sprinkled it with stardust just to make the shamrocks grow
it's the only place ye'll find them no matter where ye go
then they darted it with silver just to make the lakes look grand
and when they had it finished sure they called it Ireland.

CHAPTER 17

BILLY

St Colman's, Monday, February 6, 1905

AT THE END OF BILLY'S Irish Literature tutoring session, Mr. MacDonagh pushed his chair away from the table and said, "Well done, William. I'm proud of your hard work. I believe we can begin adding Gaelic lessons to your studies."

"Gaelic, sir? Will that help me become a pediatrician?"

"Not directly, no. But you're living in Ireland, and Gaelic, we hope, will soon become the national language."

"Replacing English, sir?"

"Probably not replacing English, but all citizens will learn it. I believe you will profit from getting a head start."

Billy shook his head. "I'm not an Irish citizen, sir. I don't know how long I will stay in this country. And I have another question, sir."

"Yes?"

"You haven't given me an answer to whether I should stay at St Colman's or look for another school."

"True. I haven't answered you because it's not just up to me. I must consult with other people."

"Father Barrett."

"Among others."

"Do the directors of the school know you invited me to St Colman's just so I could be your messenger boy?"

"No, they do not. And if the time comes to discuss your situation with them, I will do it myself. It's not your concern."

Billy jumped to his feet. "Not my concern? How can it not be my concern whether I continue studying here or not? You don't respect me very much, do you!"

"Calm yourself, lad. I only meant you needn't be concerned about arguing your own case. I fully believe the directors are well pleased with your work and will be happy for you to continue as a student here whether or not you continue delivering messages for the movement."

"Movement? What movement?"

"I am not at liberty to say more."

"Then I am also not at liberty to risk my life delivering more messages."

"Fine, William. I will not ask you to do so until I hear from my superiors what I may and may not tell you. Meanwhile, proceed with your studies as if you will stay at St Colman's. I will advise you if anything changes. Next time we will begin Gaelic. Your classmates are already far ahead of you, so you must work hard to catch up. You are dismissed."

"I still don't understand—"

"You are dismissed."

Stubborn man. Why can't he just tell me what this is all about and let me decide whether I want to serve his precious "movement"?

In the hallway, Billy glared at Mr. MacDonagh's closed door and raised his fist to knock. Then he sighed, lowered his hand, and ran down the hall to his room to dress for rugby practice.

St Colman's, Sunday, February 19, 1905

Billy sat on a bench at the edge of the practice field, doodling in the snow with a stick. *Sundays are the worst days. We're not allowed to study or play sports. That's my whole life denied me. Most of the lads write letters to their families. Who would I write to? Lucy, like the old woman suggested? Ha. I was just one in a series of strangers staying at their house. She won't remember who I am. Uncle Cecil? He'll pressure me to return to Idaho. I like St. Colman's. Except for Sundays.*

He stopped doodling and looked at the design he had made with his stick. *That's not half bad. I think I'll go try it with paper and pencil.*

He stood and threw his stick as far as he could. It landed upright in the snow. *I couldn't have done that if I had tried.*

He turned and jogged toward the school, brushing snow off his pants and shoes before entering. *No tracking in snow. I don't want to clean the whole entryway again.*

Billy nodded to an upperclassman who looked up from reading a book. Taking the stairs to the third floor two at a time, he opened the door to his hallway and almost crashed into Harry.

"Is buachaill aisteach thú," said Harry, shaking his head as he started down the stairs.

"Wait! What does that mean?" demanded Billy.

"Figure it out!" said Harry as he disappeared around the curve in the stairway.

"It means, 'You're a strange lad,'" said a boy walking toward him from their shared room. Fred, recently back at school after recovering from an injury, stopped beside Billy. "Learn your Gaelic and we won't be able to keep secrets from you."

"You keep secrets from me?"

"Not secrets, really. We just enjoy talking about you in Gaelic because we know you don't understand."

"What do you say?"

"That would be telling. Learn your Gaelic like Harry told you."

"Whatever you're going to do right now, could I do it with you? I hate Sundays."

"Sure. I'm going to the game room. Do you like to play games?"

"I don't know. I've never done it."

"Then come with me. We're going to play Vint, but we're not allowed to gamble. Do you know it?"

Billy shook his head.

"It's like bridge, with a few quirks like whist. I'll teach you."

"Thank you, Fred!"

"Pay attention so you don't embarrass me." Fred pulled a deck of cards from his pocket. "In this game the ace is high."

"What's an ace?"

Fred sighed. "This will be a long afternoon."

St Colman's, Thursday, March 16, 1905

"Billy, get some clothes together. I'm taking you home with me for the St Patrick's Day holiday. My mum will be here to pick us up in one hour."

Billy stared at Fred, who rapidly filled a small suitcase open on his bed.

"Sure, your English is as bad as your Gaelic now? What didn't you understand about what I said? Don't you want to go?"

"Of—of course I do," Billy stammered. "I'm surprised, that's all. No one ever invited me to their home before."

"Pull yourself together, lad, and think what you'll want with you for three days."

"I—I don't know what to put it in."

"You don't have any luggage?" Fred stuck his head under his bed and emerged with a small case. "Here, you can borrow this. Bring some decent clothes for Sunday church. And something green for the St. Patrick parade."

"This is all I have that isn't school uniforms," Billy said, holding out what he thought of as his "church clothes" since Father Barrett gave them to him in a church, and the set Mr. MacDonagh had procured for him from the school's charity bin.

"Those'll work for play. You can borrow something from me for Sunday. I probably have an extra green shirt too. Pack whatever else you want to take with you and meet me on the front steps at 4:30. I'm to meet with my maths teacher for tutoring until then."

Billy's face brightened. "Maybe I could help you. Maths is easy for me."

Fred bumped his fist and hurried out, carrying his suitcase.

Does he want to be my friend? Or is this what Mr. MacDonagh calls charity? Oh well, I won't worry about that. It will be grand getting out of this place for a few days. Ha! I just said "grand" instead of great. No one in Idaho says grand.

Billy sorted through his few possessions and saw the letter he had written Uncle Cecil at Christmas time. He threw it in the trash, then stopped, retrieved it and put it back in his cupboard. He whistled as he threw his Gaelic textbook, a drawing pad, and pencils into the case, along with his two sets of clothes. Then he retrieved the drawing pad and a pencil.

I have at least half an hour . . .

Billy sat at his desk and drew, giving up and crumpling one drawing after another. Finally, he sat back, satisfied. *This dragonfly actually looks like one. If I had colored pencils, I would make it bright green.*

Suddenly noticing the time, Billy closed Fred's case and ran downstairs. Another lad, a new student named Ben, tossed a ball with Fred at the front of the school. *Fred didn't tell me he invited Ben too.* Billy stood for a minute watching them. *I don't think I'll go after all. What if I make a fool of myself? I don't know how to behave around a family. And I haven't had a friend since leaving my school in Pocatello. I don't know how to be friends with Irish boys. What if his parents don't like me . . .*

"There you are, William!" said Fred, tucking the ball into a cloth bag bulging with other odd-shaped objects. "Ready to go? That's my mum now. Come on."

Fred's mother greeted Billy warmly. *She doesn't seem surprised or unhappy. Maybe this will be all right.* He gave her a timid smile and climbed into the carriage beside Ben.

St Colman's, Wednesday, March 22, 1905

"Today will be your last tutoring session with me," announced Mr. MacDonagh. "You have hard work ahead to keep up, but I think you're ready to fly on your own with history and literature."

"Thank you, sir. Could I still have tutoring in Gaelic?"

"I'm surprised. I thought you weren't interested in learning the Irish language."

"The other lads—they talk about me in Gaelic because they know I can't understand. I want to learn the language secretly, so I can know what they're saying."

"Ah, I see. No nationalist sentiments, then."

"This isn't my country, sir. At least not yet."

"I see," Mr. MacDonagh repeated. "I have discussed your situation with the directors of the school. You may stay here on the condition you continue to do well in your studies."

"Thank you, sir. That's easier than starting over somewhere else. They didn't mention sports?"

"They did, in fact. They are impressed with how much you are contributing in both rugby and hurling. What motivates you?"

"I think about that man who tried to kill me in Kilkenny. I want my body strong."

"I see," said Mr. MacDonagh a third time. "William, have you thought more about whether you would be willing to deliver messages for us?"

"Who is 'us?"

"It's not in your best interest for me to tell you that."

"It's also not in my best interest to risk my life for someone else's movement."

"You are dismissed."

April 12, 1905

Billy closed his Gaelic textbook and stood, stretching his muscles.

"Sit down, please, William. It's been almost a month since I asked you about delivering messages for us. We have a particularly urgent situation this weekend. Will you do it?"

"What's in it for me?" *I'm almost willing to consider it just to get out of here for a few days.*

"Your Gaelic tutoring."

Billy jumped to his feet. "You'll stop tutoring me if I say no?"

"Yes. I'm tutoring you as a favor, not because I must. If you're not willing to do a favor for me, why should I continue doing so for you?"

"B-but you're not risking your life! All it costs you to help me is a wee bit of time!"

"I'm not sending you back to Kilkenny, if that's what you're worried about."

"Where, then?"

"To Father Barrett in Enniskeane."

"Where's that?"

"It's about fifty miles southwest. You'll locate Father Barrett at St. Mary's Church. When he reads the message, he'll want to depart immediately for Cork City. You can ask him for a place to spend the night before returning to Fermoy."

"You think I can do fifty miles in one day?"

"Let me see. Today is Wednesday. If you leave early tomorrow, and take a break for lunch, I'm quite sure you can bicycle to Enniskeane and be back here Friday evening, in time for the hurling match Saturday morning."

"I'll be tired."

"You'll have the whole night to sleep and recover."

"What about my classes?"

"Go to breakfast tomorrow as usual and eat quickly. I'll come to you in the middle of the meal and tell you to come with me because there's been an emergency. Which is true. I'll tell your teachers the same thing. I doubt they'll ask questions."

I bet Fred will ask questions. "I didn't say I'll do it."

"But you want to, don't you. I can see it in your eyes."

"I don't have a bicycle."

"Oddly enough, an old bicycle showed up at the school that no one has claimed. It seems sturdy enough."

The old woman's bicycle?

"All right. I'll do it. But if someone attacks me again, that's it. I'm out."

"I understand, William. Now, here is the message, and your money for lunch. I do not wish to loan you my new cape."

"I can wear my old jacket." *The old woman's jacket . . . Will it give me energy again? It hasn't done so since I came back to school.*

"Any other questions?"

"Yes, sir. How will I know where to go?"

"Take the road south to Cork City. You can eat lunch there—it's about halfway. Then ask someone for directions to Enniskeane. You'll go west out of Cork City to Carrigrohane and southwest from there. St. Mary's Church will be easy to find."

Am I being stupid? But my hands and feet are tingling, thinking about riding fast down an open road . . .

As Billy left Mr. MacDonagh's rooms, he bumped into an old woman carrying a mop and bucket. She grinned at him before shutting the door behind her.

☙❧

Thursday, April 27, 1905

"Just a moment, please, William," said Mr. MacDonagh as Billy gathered his things after Gaelic tutoring.

Billy sighed and waited.

"Your trip to Cork City and Enniskeane went well. This time I need you to go northeast, to Cashel, in County Tipperary. You'll be gone over the weekend. With the May Day holiday, you won't miss any classes."

"But sir—the lads have been telling me about the Bealtaine bonfire! They say it's the most exciting day at St. Colman's! I don't want to miss it. Can't you send someone else?"

Mr. MacDonagh frowned and said loudly, "Not everything is about you and what you happen to want!"

Billy backed up and sat down on Mr. MacDonagh's sofa, trying to catch his breath. *I feel like he just punched me. Why did he do that? Is what he wants more important than what I want?*

Mr. MacDonagh glared at Billy, turned on his heel, walked from the sitting room into his bedroom, and slammed the door.

Tears sprang to Billy's eyes, and he scrubbed them away, breathing hard. *What right does he have to order me around with no explanation?*

Staring at Mr. MacDonagh's door, Billy remembered waking up in darkness under the platform outside Saints Peter and Paul Church, to Mr. MacDonagh's voice saying, "Grab him, lads. He may have had evil intentions. Tie him up."

Billy's body filled with heat. He leaped to his feet, snatched a marble bookend from the small table beside the sofa and heaved it at the closed door. He yelled, "You're not my boss!" then ran out of Mr. MacDonagh's sitting room into the hallway, slamming the door just as his teacher had done.

Boys in the hallway stared at Billy. He pushed his way past them, ran down the stairs, and out the door, running across the field until his legs collapsed under him. *I have to leave. I can't stay here after this. Mr. MacDonagh will never forgive me. He'll find some way to punish me. I can't go back, even for supper.*

For a long time, Billy lay in a heap, alternately sobbing and yelling. He shouted his anger at his mother who had never wanted him and his father who had abandoned him. He sobbed over his half-brother saying he could not be who he was. And Mrs. Malcomson's belief of the same. *And everyone on that ship treated her like she was the queen of England.* He yelled his outrage at Mr. MacDonagh's lack of trust in him, refusing to tell him what his "movement" was all about.

He cried over the color of his skin, the fact that he didn't belong anywhere, and the difficulty of learning Gaelic. He wept for the pretty child who had died in Idaho, because her mother was afraid to seek medical help and thus reveal she was a harlot. *I heard that word thrown at my mother in the streets. I'm the son of a harlot! That makes me a nobody!* Billy pounded the ground and wept until he had no more tears.

Finally, Billy grew still. He wasn't asleep, just spent. *I don't think I can move a single muscle in my body.*

How long Billy lay there he didn't know. After a time, he realized it was dark. He heard voices of his teachers and classmates calling, "William! William!" and saw torches bobbing across the field.

Billy pulled into himself, making his body as small as he could. *I don't want them to find me. Why are they looking for me anyway? What did Mr. MacDonagh tell them? I know they don't care about me. No one does. No one in the whole world.*

As he thought this, a vision formed in his mind of the face of an old woman, her lips pursed in concentration as she measured ingredients for her restorative tea. He remembered the kind eyes of a red-headed man fishing his hat out of a puddle in Killeagh, saying "Steady on, mate." He saw Toby's face, animated as he signed to Billy that if he wanted to become a doctor he must go to school. For a moment he felt Eamon's gentle touch as he said, "Come eat with us, lad." He remembered Lucy, prattling to him as if they were old friends.

One by one, he let warm memories soothe him, until he fell asleep.

It was Fred's voice that wakened Billy the next morning. Billy opened his eyes and saw Fred sitting cross-legged beside him, looking at him with a curious expression on his face.

"Go away," said Billy.

"I can't," said Fred. "I'm under orders."

"Orders? Whose orders?"

"Mr. MacDonagh's."

Billy turned over, away from Fred, and covered his face with his arm.

Fred put his hand on Billy's shoulder. "Mr. MacDonagh told me to tell you he's sorry. He was wrong."

"Oh yeah?" Billy muttered into the grass. "Why didn't he come tell me himself, then?"

"Something about needing to travel to Cashel."

Billy turned over and sat up. "He went to Cashel?"

"Yes. On that old bike that showed up here. He told me to tell you to enjoy the bonfire."

"He did? What else did he say?"

"Nothing else. That's all." Fred stood. "Now, I don't know about you, but I'm hungry. If you're willing to come, we should go to breakfast while it's still being served."

Billy looked at himself, his uniform stained and dirty. "Do you think you could sneak some breakfast out for me? I can't go to the dining room like this."

"No, you can't," agreed Fred, helping Billy to his feet and brushing him off. "I'll try, but you know how sharp-eyed those teachers are. If I can't, it's only a few hours until dinner. And then tea. And then supper. One good thing about this school, they know how to feed us. And we'll have all kinds of special foods for Bealtaine."

"It sounds wonderful," said Billy, walking with Fred toward the school.

"I'll race you back," said Fred. "Everyone is at breakfast so you can run up to our room without anyone seeing you." He took off with his gazelle-like lope and Billy pounded after him.

Curious glances met Billy as he slid into his seat in his first class. The teacher plunged them into algebra equations and Fred looked at him, his hands palm up in supplication. Billy nodded and smiled. *Yes, I'll explain this to you later.* He turned back to his teacher and scribbled as fast as he could.

CHAPTER 18

CHARLIE AND LAOISE

London, Floating on the Thames, Tuesday, June 13, 1905

"THIS HAS BEEN SUCH A great reprieve, after the intensity of our tours. Oh look—there's the royal barge, flying blue and gold streamers!" Charlie leaned over the railing to point out a vessel quickly overtaking theirs.

"Maybe it's an outing of the royal family from Sweden, in town for Princess Margaret's wedding! I've been pretending all the London pomp and circumstance is celebrating our wedding," Laoise said with a grin.

"Tomorrow we'll face our own version of pomp and circumstance. The family from America is due to arrive in Waterford today and will travel to Dublin tomorrow. I don't know whether they or we will get there first," said Charlie.

"I'm holding on to every minute here with you, my love. At the same time, I'm excited to see everyone, especially the reunion between Cally and her aunt and uncle." Laoise edged around the railing to keep the royal barge in sight.

Charlie followed her. "Yes! I'm glad Margaret offered to organize the supper Friday, so everyone can be together, including our Dublin cousins, Priscilla and Silas and their daughters. It's so kind of your father to host the supper in his home."

"It's risky. If it rains, we won't be able to use the garden. And it's too many people to fit comfortably in our dining room." Laoise smiled at a group in another boat as enthralled with the royal barge as she.

"But since it will be informal, people will be able to spread out into other rooms, right? I'm more worried about rain for the reception on Saturday," said Charlie.

"Oh, didn't you know? Mrs. Davis has rented a huge tent, which will cover most of the garden. It will be nicer, of course, if it doesn't rain, but we'll be fine either way."

"Mrs. Davis seems to have thought of everything."

"Yes," said Laoise. "And she has an army of people to make it all happen."

"As if we were royalty, eh?"

Laoise laughed. "Without all the fuss about protocol. The best of all worlds."

"Do you know what I'm most looking forward to?"

"No. What?"

"Being able to introduce you as my wife. No more secrets."

"Ye-es. But hasn't the secret been fun?"

"It has. Marvelous fun. Life with you will never be boring." *What is Laoise looking at?*

Charlie turned from Laoise to see the object of her nod and smile. "Mr. Paderewski! And Madame Paderewski! What—how did you—I can't believe it!"

Charlie and Laoise ran to hug the Paderewskis. *This is the best wedding gift Laoise could have given me! How did she manage it?!*

"I thought you were still in America on tour!" said Charlie as they settled at a table.

"I should be, yes. But I've had to take a leave from playing," said Mr. Paderewski. "I damaged some nerves in my arms and neck. I lost all feeling. I thought my life was over."

"But our Polish American doctor friend Francis Fronczak healed Ignacy," said Madame Paderewski. "And see—from the malady, we gained a holiday! And the chance to meet your charming Laoise."

"How did you—and she—"

"We've been planning this since April," said Laoise, laughing. "I can't believe I truly surprised you."

"Laoise discovered from the newspaper we would be in London these days, and contacted me," said Mr. Paderewski. "The rest was just logistics."

"It's better than if they came to our wedding, right, Charlie, with so many other people to pay attention to. We have the rest of the day and evening just with them!"

"I had JUST said to Laoise life with her will never be boring, when you appeared," laughed Charlie. "What do you think, Laoise? Shall we tell them our secret?"

"Why not?" said Laoise, beaming.

"We have hours and hours," said Madame Paderewski. "Tell us everything."

CHAPTER 19

CALLY

St. Joseph Hospital, Kansas City, Monday, May 15, 1905

CALLY OPENED THE DOOR TO Sister Irmena's office.

"You look well, Cally! What a delight to see your smile once again. Please, sit down. How was your journey from Idaho?"

"It was fine, thank you. It's lovely to see you again, Sister Irmena."

"I've been looking over the exams Dr. Spencer sent me, and I imagine you've brought another one or two with you."

"Yes, here they are."

"Hmm, a bit of confusion over the cranial nerves . . . Please review those, Cally. But overall, I'm pleased. I believe our plan for your convalescence in Idaho worked out well. Dr. Spencer wrote that you helped her understand more clearly our approach to training nurses. She wants to start a program in Idaho, tailored to the realities there."

"Yes, ma'am. She's quite passionate about it. She wants to include herbal treatments used by native Americans."

"Oh? That's unusual."

"Dr. Flora works closely with them and has learned many wonderful natural remedies. She has great respect for their beliefs."

"How interesting. So, Cally, I believe that if you work hard during the summer, you will be able to complete your classes here and be ready to return to Idaho in the fall for your second year, your internship with Dr. Spencer."

"Ma'am, you gave me permission to attend my brother's wedding in Ireland."

"So I did. I had forgotten. How long do you expect to be gone?"

"I will leave Kansas City June third and expect to be back by the twenty-fourth, ready for work on June twenty-sixth, as we discussed." *She doesn't need to know we're squeezing in a trip to Rochester.*

Sister Irmena frowned. "You must be gone so long?"

"Yes, ma'am, but I promise to study every chance I get. We'll have many days of travel by train and by ship."

"If it were anyone but you, Cally, I would never approve such a long absence, especially after you had so many weeks out sick. But you've shown me you can progress independently. I'll hold you to your promise to study while you're away."

"Thank you, ma'am."

"Meanwhile, you'll have three full weeks to study and work at the hospital. Do you feel strong enough for that?"

"I do, yes, Sister."

"Then begin the next unit, the circulatory system, and report for hospital duty at 7:00 tomorrow morning. You will take your next exam Friday afternoon. I know you'll work hard."

"I will, ma'am."

St. Joseph Hospital, Friday, June 2, 1905

Cally sat at a table waiting for Sister Irmena to give her an exam on the genitourinary system. *Whew, I'm tired. Between studying, working, giving extra time to Felicity, and helping Cora, I've had almost no time to rest. But this exam is my last responsibility. When I get home, Ryan will be there!* Cally's cheeks grew warm.

"Here you are, Cally. You have one hour. Open the window if it's too hot in here. These small rooms do tend to get stuffy." Sister Irmena placed the exam on the table and exited. Cally put her hands over her cheeks and smiled, then picked up her pencil and read the first question.

"Ryan, welcome back to Kansas City!" Cally's eyes flashed Ryan a warning as he jumped to his feet in Thomas and Cora's sitting room. He glanced at Felicity on the sofa and gave Cally a friendly sideways hug.

"I showed Mr. Ryan how much I can read!" said Felicity. "And I told him he should marry you so baby Brian can be my brother. But you came before he could answer me."

"That's an interesting idea, Felicity," Ryan told her, returning to sit beside her. "I'll think about it." He grinned at Cally over Felicity's head. She blushed.

Cora walked in and heard this interchange. She looked from Ryan to Cally, her eyebrows raised. "I suspect more happened in Idaho than you've told me," she whispered to Cally.

Cally's blush deepened. "How can I help with supper?" she asked out loud.

"Nora has supper well in hand. I'll call you in a few minutes," said Cora. "My children are doing their homework so they can spend some time with Ryan after supper. They're disappointed not to be traveling to New York with you, but I've assured them they'll have several days aboard ship to plague Mr. Ryan."

"I get you all to myself on the train," said Felicity, taking his arm possessively.

"Well, not entirely, young lady. Come sit with us, Cally," Ryan invited. "Felicity is going to read me one more book."

"I'll wash my hands first. Go ahead, though, Felicity. I'll be right back." *I'm starting to think that after Ryan receives Aunt Mary's blessing, we might as well tell everyone. It's so complicated trying to keep this to ourselves. Especially with Felicity trying to "convince" Ryan to marry me!*

Ryan entertained everyone at supper with stories about Brian's antics, mimicking the lambs on his farm. With all eyes on him, Cally could watch him without being conspicuous. *He's so alive, so engaged and entertaining. So different from the man I first met shortly after Bethany died, when he sat silent and sad at our Sunday suppers. This must be the real Ryan. It seems a huge weight has been lifted from him. I'm so glad.*

Cally missed a comment from Thomas. Cora, sitting beside her, poked her. "What dreamland are you in, sis? Thomas is talking to you."

"Oh, I'm sorry, Thomas. I'm—I'm quite tired."

"I understand, Cally. I was just saying that I've asked Max to have the carriage ready for you at six tomorrow morning."

"Thank you, Thomas. We'll have to get up early, Felicity."

"That's all right. I can sleep on the train. Remember I used to do that with Uncle Charlie when we traveled to Idaho?"

"I do remember. You're an old hand at train travel."

"Who wants dessert?" asked Cora.

"I do!" chimed all the children and Ryan.

Cora disappeared into the kitchen. Thomas addressed Cally quietly. "I've been thinking about Billy, and my mum's belief that she saw him from the train in Waterford. Do you think we should take his treasure hunt packet with us to Ireland? We could leave it with Mum or with Margaret, in case either of them sees him again."

"Would you be willing to take it, then, Thomas? It seems a big responsibility for me to carry all the way there, especially with this side trip to Rochester."

He nodded just as Nora arrived with a large tray laden with strawberry shortcake and whipped cream.

"My favorite!" exclaimed Cally. "Thank you, Nora!"

"We made it to celebrate your return to health, dear sister," said Cora, beaming and then tearing up. "I'm so very glad you're well again."

Cally jumped up and gave Cora a warm hug. "Thank you, thank you, thank you, for your care for Felicity, your hospital visits, your prayers—for everything you did for weeks and weeks. I owe you a debt I can never repay."

"Just stay well, Cally. That's all the payment I want."

Cally sat down to savor her delicious dessert. "I'll get you the packet right after supper," she told Thomas between bites.

Ryan stood and tapped his glass. "I have an announcement to make." *Oh no! Please don't, Ryan! We agreed not to say anything until after Rochester!*

Everyone looked at Ryan expectantly. Cora glanced back and forth from Ryan to Cally.

"In memory of the great treasure hunt when I met you all, I've created a treasure hunt of my own. If you would be willing to stay in the dining room for ten minutes, I'll set it up. It shouldn't take more than twenty minutes to complete. Is that all right, Cora and Cally?"

Why did I doubt him? "It's fine with me," Cally smiled.

"Sounds fun!" said Cora. "For the ten minutes Ryan needs, how about each of us tell the best moment of this week."

Ryan bowed and left the room.

"My best moment was Mr. Ryan coming here. And he said he would think about marrying my mummy so baby Brian can be my brother and I can have my very own daddy. That's my best moment," said Felicity. "But the bestest moment will be if he says yes."

Cally blushed scarlet. *I wish I didn't have such pale skin! This is embarrassing.*

"Well, that's a hard act to follow," said Thomas. "But my best moment this week was receiving a letter from my brother Charlie telling us more about why he's thrilled to be marrying Laoise. I was going to read it at the end of supper, but now I think I'll save it until tomorrow."

"But we won't be here tomorrow," said Felicity. "Can't you read it now?"

"Perhaps it will be a best moment for all of us," affirmed Cora. "After all, we're traveling a very long way to witness this wedding. I would love to know Laoise better."

"All right. I have it right here in my pocket."

Thomas pulled the envelope from one pocket and his spectacles from another.

Dear Thomas, Cora, Cally, and beloved children,

I want you to know I deeply appreciate your willingness to travel all the way to Ireland to participate in my wedding to Laoise. It's a costly trip in time, money, and energy. It means so much to me that you are supporting us in this life-changing sacred event.

Laoise and I want all the children—you four, Margaret's three, Daniel's two, and Dugan and Aisling's three (whom Mum considers her grandchildren as well) to participate in the wedding in a special way. Shane, Shauna, Josie, and Felicity, would you be willing to learn a song to sing during the ceremony, along with your cousins? You will be our own children's choir!

We had the idea because Molly, your oldest girl cousin, directs a children's choir, and we got to hear them perform. We've asked her to practice with you and be your director when you sing at the wedding. All right?

The song Laoise and I want you to learn is called "All Creatures of our God and King." You haven't heard it before, because it was only translated into English last year by a pastor named William Draper in England. When Laoise and I went to church in January in Dublin, we heard a choir sing it for the first time in Ireland, and we thought it was beautiful. We wrote Mr. Draper to ask permission to use it in our wedding, and finally received from him the words and the music and the story of the song.

Pastor Draper took the words from a longer poem written by St. Francis in 1225 called The Canticle of the Sun. He used a German hymn tune for the music. He expects it to be published in the English Hymnal next year, and then everyone will be able to sing it. I'll send the words and the music to you on a separate sheet.

"But I won't have time to learn it before we leave tomorrow!" said Felicity, jumping up.

"That's true, but we'll have many days on the ship together. You can learn it then," said Cora. "I'll try to learn it first, so I can teach you."

Felicity settled back in her seat.

"Shall I go on?" asked Thomas.

"Yes, please. I want to hear about Laoise," said Shauna.

Now, let me tell you more about Laoise. She is beautiful, as you all know. But I've been learning how lovely she is on the inside too. She is kind and gentle, of course. But did you know she is mischievous? She's always surprising me with her thoughts and ideas for fun. And that's good for me, because I can be too serious and intense and focused on my music. Laoise thinks our music should be a delight, not just a duty. She's a consummate professional—

"What does consummate mean?" asked Josie.

"It means she's extremely skilled and accomplished," said Cora. "She's very, very good at playing her violin. I would love to be described as a consummate artist. It's one of the highest compliments anyone can receive."

"Uncle Charlie's a consummate musician too," said Shane.

"Maybe that's why they go together so well," said Shauna.

"Shall I continue?" asked Thomas. "Just two more paragraphs."

"Please," said Cora.

She's a consummate professional, but what makes her music so special is her heart. She believes music should both heal and animate us to be the best people we can be. It's her way of honoring God, the Creator. Each of us has been given a special way to honor God, and music is the gift He has given to Laoise and me.

So, I'll leave this question with you, "What is your special way to honor God? What are the gifts He has given each of you?" You can think about that question and tell me your thoughts when we are together in Dublin for the wedding.

I love each of you so much. And Laoise sends her love as well.

(Uncle) Charlie

Ryan, who had come back in during the reading of this letter, clapped his hands. "That was precious! I feel even more privileged to be able to participate in Charlie and Laoise's wedding."

"Is the treasure hunt ready?" asked Cora.

"Yes! I'm going to give Shane the first clue, and then whoever finds the second can read it, and so on."

"How many clues are there?" asked Thomas.

"Six," said Ryan. "Here you go, Shane."

Cally found herself laughing as the treasure hunt progressed. *How long has it been since I laughed out loud? Ryan is good for me, just like Laoise is good for Charlie. Thank you, God.*

The last clue revealed a set of whistles, one for each of them, carved by Ryan himself. "I have lots of time on my hands once Brian is in bed for the night," he said, half-apologetically. "Each whistle is a different tone. Perhaps you can learn to play your song for the wedding as well as sing it!"

He pulled another whistle from his pocket. "I carved a complete octave. I don't know whether that's enough to play Charlie and Laoise's song, but we can try it and see! If you look at the back of your whistles, you'll see a letter. That's each one's note."

"Ryan, I didn't know you were a woodcarver!" exclaimed Cora. "This is wonderful! Tell you what, children. Let's keep all the whistles in a bowl on the mantelpiece, so we don't lose or break them. Look at the letter carved on yours, and then you'll know which one belongs to you."

Cally gazed at Ryan across the room as he showed the children how to play their whistles and lined them up to play an octave. *I wonder how many other skills Ryan has up his sleeve. My only skill is sewing. And I'm learning to take care of patients. But nothing as fun as carving instruments!*

"Come on, Aunt Cally! We need you to play a note!" called Shane.

Cally took her place between Josie and Thomas, her heart overflowing. *I must remember to give Thomas Billy's packet. I'll get it as soon as the children are sent off to bed.*

଒଼

"I noticed the way you looked at me when I stood to announce the treasure hunt," Ryan said to Cally before he left for his hotel. "You thought I was going to tell about us."

"I'm sorry. Yes, that was my first thought. You don't seem upset about it."

"I'm confident you'll learn to trust me. When I give my word, I stick to it. That's something Priscilla and Jerry drilled into me while I was growing up. I understand your difficulty with trust though, Cally. You've suffered many betrayals. Of course, that makes you wary. I hope over time trust will become easier for you. At least with me."

"Thank you. The way you've handled this helps me trust you more. If you had been angry, I would have punished myself. Instead, I feel like you're my ally, you understand. And watching you teach the children to play the whistles—that was so special for me, Ryan. You're a natural teacher. And the treasure hunt made me laugh. It was so much fun. I needed that. Thank you."

"I'm glad, dear heart." He kissed her cheek. "I'll see you in the morning. Max will pick me up at the hotel on your way to the train station. And then our adventure will begin!"

"Felicity is so excited to be traveling with us to see Aunt Mary. Imagine how she'll feel when she hears that you do want to marry me!"

"She'll be the first to know. After that, I suspect she'll handle telling the rest of the world."

Cally laughed. "I think you're right. Good night. I hope you sleep well."

"I'm sure I will. I'm tired. Sleep well yourself, sweetheart."

Cally stood looking after him as Max pulled away. *Thank you, God. I never imagined such a wonderful man would want me, after—well, you know; I don't need to tell you. I'm grateful. And happy. And excited about our future. That's an amazing feeling. Truly amazing.*

Port of New York, June 9, 1905

"Whew, that was close!" exclaimed Ryan, holding Felicity's hand tightly as they pushed through the crowded station to the wharf. "I was afraid they wouldn't accept our luggage."

"I think we were the last ones. I saw them take down the *Lion III* sign as we walked away," said Cally. "Now we need to find Thomas and family."

"Are you all right?" asked Ryan. "You don't look well."

"I had a bad dream last night. I can't get it out of my mind. Nothing to worry about. I'll feel better when we get out of this crowd."

Don't be afraid.

Cally gave her head a small shake. *How can I not be afraid? My dream was so vivid, so real. I think it was a warning.*

Ryan shielded his eyes from the sun. "I see them!" he said, pointing to the Malcomson family gathered near a post with the placard, "Lion III, Waterford, Ireland."

Felicity jerked her hand from Thomas's and darted away.

"Felicity!" shouted Cally and Ryan at the same time.

Ryan grabbed Cally's hand and took off after Felicity. They were slowed by a large cart full of luggage trundling across their way. Once they could see the family again, it was clear Felicity had spilled their news. Cora ran to give Cally a hug and congratulations. The others cheered.

"Have you made specific plans?" asked Thomas, shaking Ryan's hand.

"We'll wait until Cally finishes her nurse's training," said Ryan. "So, possibly next summer. The nice thing for me is that Cally will begin her internship with Flora this fall. I know she'll be busy, but we'll have more time together than if she stayed in Kansas City."

"It will be a big adjustment for us," said Cora. "We'll miss you and Felicity terribly."

"We'll be only a train ride away," said Cally.

Don't be afraid.

Cally replied in her mind, *You're not helping. I AM afraid. I'm terrified.*

"A long train ride," said Shane. "Mummy, am I old enough to take the train by myself to visit Aunt Cally and Felicity and—should I call you Uncle Ryan now, Mr. Ryan?"

"I would be honored," said Ryan.

"Hmm, let me think about that, Shane." Thomas ruffled his son's hair. "I'm not sure I'm quite ready for you to travel so far by yourself. But we can talk more about it. Anyway, Cally and Felicity will still be with us the rest of the summer after we get home from the wedding. We'll cherish that time, Cally."

"Thank you."

Don't be afraid. I am with you.

"Cally, what's wrong?" asked Ryan.

"I feel a wee bit sick. It must be nerves, or the crowd, or—" *I think I'm going to throw up.*

A whistle blasted from the *Lion III.*

"Oh, it's time to board!" said Cora. "Come, children. Do you have all your things?"

"I wonder when we'll get to see Paudeen," said Thomas as the long line of passengers boarding the *Lion III* moved slowly forward. "I should say, Captain Paudeen. Charlie and Mum see him every time they cross the Atlantic, but this is our first trip back to Ireland since we came to America."

"The last time we sailed on the *Lion III* I was pregnant with you two," said Cora, smiling at the twins. "I expect this to be a much more pleasant voyage than that one was for me."

The last time I traveled on the Lion III*—Oh, God! Don't you see I can't do this? What shall I do? What shall I do? Don't just tell me "Don't be afraid" again! I AM afraid!*

It was Cally's turn to enter the narrow gangway. Ryan climbed ahead of her holding Felicity's hand, following Thomas and Cora and their children. A few other passengers pressed her from behind, the last ones to board the ship. Reaching the top, Cally stepped down onto the deck and out of their way. Ryan looked back and smiled at her, still holding Felicity's hand.

I can't do this. I can't go to Ireland. I'll fall apart on the voyage. And I'll ruin the wedding. I'll hurt people. I know it!

Cally looked desperately around, seeking she knew not what. The engines revved. Gripping her small valise, Cally flung herself back onto the now-empty gangway and reached the bottom just as the ship started to move away from the pier. She took a flying leap and crumpled onto the dock. Gasping, she jumped to her feet and raced away from the ship.

The engines growled. Cally ran as fast as she could, dodging passengers milling around other piers. At the door of the station, she glanced back at the ship, its distance from the dock growing quickly. She couldn't hear him, but she could see Ryan's small figure shouting and waving his arms as the huge ship pulled away. Thomas and Cora joined him, shouting and pointing too.

They don't know I'm doing this for them.

Clutching her valise, Cally ran through the station and out the other side onto the street. She ran and ran, dodging walkers and the vehicles in cross streets, until she doubled over, gasping. Foot traffic flowed around her. She burst into tears.

What am I going to do now? Where should I go? Can they ever possibly understand I did this to protect them, because I love them and don't want to hurt them?

Cally stumbled to a low wall in front of a house and sat with her head in her hands. Images of each beloved person on the ship paraded through her mind, each one bringing more tears. Felicity. Ryan. Cora. Thomas. The twins. Josie. And then her loved ones in Ireland, Charlie, and Laoise, and Cathleen. Aisling and Dugan.

She wept until she had no more tears. For a long time, she simply sat there, exhausted, oblivious to people's glances as they walked past her.

Don't be afraid, Cally. I am with you.

CHAPTER 20

BILLY

Knocklong, County Limerick, Saturday, May 20, 1905

WITH SECONDS TO GO IN the hurling match against St. Michael's, Billy caught a pass from Fred on his hurley. He heaved the sliotar into the air and struck it forward as hard as he could just as an opponent's shoulder crashed into his and knocked him to the ground. Several other players tripped over him, and a stray elbow hit him in the mouth. Despite his face mask, Billy tasted blood before he passed out.

When he came to, Billy heard cheering before he tasted more blood. Opening his eyes, he saw legs, and cleats, then a figure bending over him. Shouts of "William! William! William!" mixed with "Benjamin! Benjamin! Benjamin!"

Billy put his hands over his ears and curled his body as small as he could. His head hurt. "Stop shouting! Please!" he managed, before someone turned him over on the ground. The sun pierced his eyeballs. He covered them with his arms and repeated, "Please."

"Might be a concussion," said the figure bent over him to someone beside him.

"For sure he needs stitches," said the other person after pulling off Billy's helmet. "Shall we do it right here, or move him to the bench?"

"Best do it here, I say."

Billy groaned and tried to turn away from them, his eyes squeezed shut.

"Hey, you, lads, give us some help here," shouted person number one. "Hold him still while we stitch him up."

Hands nailed his legs and pulled his arms, bloodied from the wound in his lip, to the grass. Gentler hands held both sides of his face. "We did it!" a familiar voice said softly. Fred. "We won the tournament. Thanks to your magnificent pass right into Ben's hands. Well done, William!"

"Point or goal?" managed Billy before he felt the stab of a needle in his lip.

"Goal! It was magnificent! The goalkeeper didn't have a chance," said Fred, still talking softly. "We're a fabulous team, me at back, you midfield, Ben forward. Everyone is saying so."

Pure luck. It's Ben who saw where the ball was going and caught it. It took everything he had for Billy not to squirm under the needle stabbing his lip.

"That's right, lad," said person number two. Coach O'Brien. "Ye three are heroes, sure enough. Now, Willam, ye must rest today and tomorrow. We're taking ye back to school in a carriage, and ye'll be in the infirmary overnight. There isn't time to carry ye to the station before the train comes."

"They're calling us," said Fred. "I'll see you back at school, William."

Billy squinted against the sun. The hands holding him released and the bodies around him disappeared. "I walk," he said around the swelling of his lip, trying to get up.

"No, no, lad," said voice number one. *He must be the medic.* "Lie still until the carriage arrives with ice for yer lip. Ye must rest. We think ye might have a concussion. The less ye move, the better all around. I'll ride with ye in the carriage back to Fermoy."

"Throw uh," said Billy, and did so.

"It's a concussion right enough," said another voice, number three. "Should we take him to the hospital?"

"There's no hospital closer than Fermoy," said voice number one. "We can decide on the way. Did ye see the hit? Could have been called foul but the referee's attention was already down the field where the lad struck the ball."

"I don't know. I judged it a fair tackle," said Coach O'Brien. "The defender was already in motion when the lad struck the ball. He couldn't have stopped himself."

"Well, it doesn't matter. The important thing is getting this lad back in shape for next Saturday's game against Cork." Voice number three. *I guess he's from Fermoy.*

"I doubt he'll be recovered enough for that one," said Coach O'Brien. "There's the carriage. Let's get some help carrying the lad and apply the ice once he's settled for the drive."

"What do we have for him to throw up in?" said number one. "They usually throw up in threes."

In fact, the motion of lifting him caused Billy to heave again.

"That's two," said number one. "Wait for the third before we put him in."

Billy obliged. And then passed out from the pain in his head.

❧

"Old woman. Tea," Billy tried to say when he woke in the infirmary Sunday morning. *My lips feel bigger than my whole face.*

"He's trying to say something." Fred's growly voice.

"Maybe he can write it." Ben's higher tones. A rustling.

"William, can you write what you're trying to tell us?" Fred.

Billy tried to open his eyes. "Ligh," he mangled, squinting.

"Turn off the light," said Ben. "There, see? His face relaxed and he opened his eyes."

"Billy, can you write what you wanted to tell us?" asked Fred again.

"Ty," said Billy, accepting a pencil. Ben held a notebook over him. "Head hurts. Old woman tea," Billy scrawled.

"What old woman? What tea?" asked Fred.

"I'll find the nurse and ask whether he can have more opium," said Ben, disappearing.

"Cleanth," managed Billy.

"An old woman who cleans the school?"

"Yeth."

"Today is Sunday. She might not be here today. But I'll try to find out." Fred also disappeared.

Billy closed his eyes. *If I lie perfectly still, the pain isn't as bad. But how will I drink the tea with my lips so swollen? How will I eat or drink anything?*

As he lay there, another thought came before he drifted off. *I won't be bicycling to Tallow today. Mr. MacDonagh will be upset. He needs another messenger lad for when I can't go. Maybe Ben?*

Sometime later, Billy heard the nurse say, "No more visits today, lads. We must let him rest."

All day, no old woman or tea appeared. Early the next morning, Billy woke to the sound of humming. *Praise God from whom all blessings flow,* his mind sang along.

He blinked at the first rays of the sun through the east window and turned over. A cup of tea rested on a small table beside his bed, next to a straw. *Ah. That's how I do it. For the first time I feel hungry and like I could eat and drink without throwing up.*

He tried to sit up. Gentle hands supported him and tucked another pillow behind his back. But Billy could see no one. "Are ou ere?" he asked. *Huh. I think the swelling is going down.*

"Shhh, don't try to talk. Drink yer tea before someone else comes in."

Billy heard a smile in her voice as she added, "Ye never saw me, right, lad?"

The tea rose from the table, the straw guided to his lips by invisible hands. "Slowly, now, Billy."

Billy tried, but he couldn't get his lips to close over the straw.

"All right. We'll do it this way."

Billy followed the movement of the straw with his eyes. *She's doing the sucking for me.*

The straw returned to his mouth, and he felt the trickle of warm tea on his tongue. He swallowed, twice, and the straw moved back to the cup, then returned to his lips. By the time the invisible woman set down the empty cup, the tea was cold.

"Hank you," Billy said.

"More later," said the woman's voice. Gentle fingers touched his forehead and his lips. Billy felt immediate relief from the pain. "Sleep now."

He did.

ଓଃ

Father Jancey's was the next voice Billy recognized. "How is he?"

"Remarkably better, Father." The nurse.

"I won't wake him. I'll just anoint and pray for him."

A cross traced on his forehead, his chin, his chest. "Loving Father, touch William now with Your healing hands, for I believe that Your will is for him to be well in mind, body, soul and spirit. Cover him with the Most Precious Blood of Your Son, our Lord Jesus Christ, from the top of his head to the soles of his feet."

A hand touched the top of Billy's head and the blanket over his feet.

"Let the fire of Your healing love pass through his entire body. Touch also his mind and his emotions, even the deepest recesses of his heart. Saturate his entire being with Your presence, love, joy, and peace and draw William ever closer to You every moment of his life. I ask this in the name of the Lord Jesus Christ. Amen."

"Thank you, Father," said the nurse.

"I'll check on him again tomorrow. Has his family been notified?"

"No family is named in his school records, Father."

"I see. Then we are his family. Good day, nurse."

"Good day, Father."

ଓଃ

"Remarkable." A voice Billy didn't recognize woke him Monday morning. "When I saw him Saturday, I'd have said he would need at least a week to recover. But the swelling is almost gone. Can you wake up, lad? I'm Dr. Foster. I would like to examine you."

I don't want to open my eyes. The light— But the light did not stab him as it had since his injury. Billy moved to sit up and felt no nausea as the doctor began his inspection.

"How is the pain in your head, lad?" asked Dr. Foster.

"Better, sir," Billy said clearly. "I'm hungry." *My lips only hurt a little when I said that.*

Dr. Foster laughed. “The best sign of healing. Give him milk, nurse, and if he can handle that, try some porridge, and later other soft foods. We’ll take it slowly, but if he can handle normal eating by the end of the day, perhaps we can release him from the infirmary tomorrow. Remarkable.”

It’s not anything you did. It’s the old woman’s tea. And Father Jancey’s prayer.

ଔଓ

As it grew dark, Mr. MacDonagh entered the infirmary.

“He’s sitting in a chair, nurse? Reading? I thought—”

The nurse’s laugh trilled. “We all thought it would be a long recovery. But Father Jancey prayed such a powerful prayer this morning—”

“The Padre Pio prayer, was it? I’ve heard him pray that before. But I haven’t seen this kind of immediate results.” Mr. MacDonagh moved toward Billy.

“Good evening, William. I’m happy to see you’re recovering so quickly. Everyone says you’re a hurling hero.”

“Just lucky, sir. Ben is the one who caught the sliotar and hit it over the crossbar.”

“It’s a team sport, William. Success is never a one-person endeavor. That’s why hurling has survived for two thousand years. At least.”

“Hurling is that old, Mr. MacDonagh?”

“Indeed. It was brought to Ireland by the Celts, but there’s evidence it was played before Christ walked the earth.”

“I’m sorry I couldn’t go to Tallow. I knew you would be upset about that.”

“How can I be upset at one of St. Colman’s heroes? I went myself. Just got back.”

“Sir, I think you need another messenger, not just me. In case something like this should happen again. I think Ben would be a good choice.”

“The new lad? Why do you think so?”

“He loves bicycling. He’s strong. He doesn’t talk much.”

Mr. MacDonagh smiled. “I’ll watch him and think about that. Do you know whether he has nationalist leanings?”

"Sir?"

"Never mind. I'll leave you, William. I came here directly when I got back, as you can see. I need a bath. Perhaps I'll see you in class tomorrow."

"The doctor said he'll decide in the morning."

"All right. I'm happy to see you're reading your Carrigan."

"Sir, are the stories he tells—the ones he says old people told him—are they true?"

"The folktales, you mean? I believe there is truth in them, William, even if they've been embellished over the years."

"Embellished, sir?"

"Extrapolated. Added to with imagination. Enhanced."

"So, you think there really are—or were—beings like faeries, and leprechauns, and púcas?"

"These 'beings,' as you call them, have been described by hundreds of people through the centuries, both in oral and written folklore. It's hard for me to believe so many people, in different ages and unrelated locations in Ireland, could have made up such similar stories."

"I don't think these beings live in Idaho," said Billy.

Mr. MacDonagh laughed. "They do seem quite attached to Ireland. I'm not aware that the Irish in other far-flung places—America, Australia, Argentina—have reported seeing faeries."

"Interesting."

"Well, I'm off to my bath and my supper. Glad to see you doing so well, William."

"Thank you, sir. Think about what I said. About another messenger."

"I will. Good night."

଼

St. Colman's, May 25, 1905

"May I say congratulations, Harry?" asked Billy, extending his hand to the lad named Best Scholar at the Sixth-Year graduation ceremony.

"Thank you, William. I say, you've been a surprise to me this year."

"A surprise?"

"We didn't know what to expect when you showed up. We never had a student from America. Not while I've been at St. Colman's, at least. You're smart, you're persistent, you became a hurling hero. You've even learned some Gaelic."

"The hurling was pure luck."

"That's not how I saw it. I saw skill and grand teamwork."

"Where do you head next, Harry?"

"Dublin. The Catholic University. I want to become a physician."

"I didn't know that. Me too."

"Indeed? What specialty?"

"Pediatrics."

Harry nodded. "I can see that. You have innate patience and kindness. Even toward those who mistrust and mistreat you. Not for me, though, the wee *storin*. They would drive me crazy."

"What are you interested in?"

"Not sure yet. Cardiology or neurology. I want to help those fields grow through research as well as practice."

"Best wishes to you, Harry."

"And to you, William. You're a credit to St. Colman's."

"Thank you!" *That's the nicest thing anyone has said to me since I got here.*

Billy watched Harry join the circle of his family and friends. *I wonder whether anyone will be here for me when I graduate. Fred's family will be kind. But it's not the same. Should I write to Uncle Cecil?*

Billy turned to leave the hall and bumped into his best friend. "I bet you'll be First Scholar when it's our turn," said Fred.

Billy laughed. "That's one thing I like about you, Fred. You have a grand sense of humor."

"I'm not jesting. You're smart in every area: history, maths, sciences, languages—even Gaelic. You've picked it up so fast."

Billy lightly punched Fred's arm. "I had to know what the lads were saying about me. And you have to admit I'm still terrible at cards."

"That's true," grinned Fred. "But you're learning . . . say, how about a game now? Some of the lads are gathering in the game room instead of hanging around here. Come with me."

"If you don't mind losing again."

"Hey, I didn't say you would be my partner. We'll draw straws. Loser gets you."

Billy laughed. "One of these days I'll surprise you. Might even be tonight!"

Friday, June 2, 1905

As he stood up from the breakfast table, Billy saw Mr. MacDonagh approach.

"We have a few minutes before classes, William. May I talk with you in my rooms?"

"Am I in trouble, sir?"

Mr. MacDonagh smiled. "No, not at all. Meet me there after you brush your teeth."

"Yes, sir."

Mr. MacDonagh opened immediately to Billy's knock.

"Do you have plans for this long weekend, William?"

"No sir. I planned to study for exams. What is the June Holiday anyway? It doesn't seem to stand for anything."

"It's meant to be a rest for working people during the long period between May Day and All Saints Day. There's another long weekend in August."

"What do you have in mind, sir?"

"This will be a different sort of trip for you. I want to send you by train to Dublin, to a man who calls himself AE. He's agreed to pass a message on for us to a participant in his Sunday Conversations. Before you ask—every Sunday evening people gather at his home to converse about a variety of topics. Interesting people from all walks of life."

"When would I leave, sir?"

"I've booked you on the evening train tomorrow."

"What will I do when I arrive in Dublin?"

"A man will meet you at the station and take you to AE's home. You'll recognize the man by his black top hat and red rose boutonniere."

"Boutonniere, sir?"

"A boutonniere is a flower worn in the lapel of a man's suit."

"Why don't I just pass the message on to this man, rather than going to AE's home?"

"Because I have received permission to allow you to learn more about our movement, and this man has volunteered to explain it to you. AE's home is well known for people coming and going, especially on Sundays, so it's considered a safe place for this conversation to take place."

"May I know the man's name, sir?"

"Yes. It's Mr. Colin Murphy. He's a solicitor."

"A solicitor, sir?"

"In America, you would call him an attorney, a lawyer."

William took a step back. "Sir, I—I don't have any papers for being in Ireland. I guess you could say I snuck into this country. Will he—could I—"

"Could Mr. Murphy get you in trouble with the law? I don't expect he will question your credentials, William. He has offered to help you, not to hurt you. However, that raises an interesting idea. At some point we should pursue getting papers for you. If you intend to stay in Ireland."

"I have no other plans, sir."

"Walk with me while we go down for classes. Did you ever write to your uncle, William?"

Billy blushed and looked away.

"No, sir."

"I suspected as much. Well, I'm going to make that a condition for you speaking with Mr. Murphy. By tomorrow afternoon, bring me a letter written and addressed to your uncle. I will personally mail it for you."

Mr. MacDonagh nodded and said good morning to students who passed them in the hallway. Beside Billy's first classroom, he stopped walking. "I'm not forcing you, William. You choose. Don't write the letter and stay here for the weekend, as you had planned. Or write the letter and travel to Dublin.

I want your response either way by the end of classes today, because if you're not going to Dublin, I must find someone else to go."

Mr. MacDonagh turned in the direction of his own classroom, then stopped and spoke over his shoulder. "Don't even consider putting a false address on the envelope, William. I am going to add a note asking your uncle to telegraph me when he receives your letter. If I don't receive a telegram from him within a reasonable time, I will know you tried to deceive me. I'll await your answer this afternoon."

CHAPTER 21

CHARLIE AND LAOISE

Aboard the Lion III, June 9, 1905

"MUMMY! DON'T GO! STAY WITH me!" Felicity dissolved into heart wrenching sobs. The family gathered around her, shock on all their faces.

"Cally! Cally! Stop!"

His voice hoarse from yelling, Ryan stared in dismay at the place he had seen Cally disappear, and at the rapidly growing distance from shore. He turned to Thomas. "I must go after her! Can you ask your captain friend to take the ship back to shore?"

"We can ask," said Thomas. "Are you all right to stay with Felicity, Cora? Let's go up to the bridge, then, Ryan."

"I must tell you, though," Thomas said as they walked, "Captain Paudeen has the entire ship to be concerned about. He's not likely to turn it around for a passenger who chose not to sail."

When they had explained their situation to Paudeen, and he had given the response Thomas expected, Ryan cried, "Can you at least give me a boat to row myself back?"

"I'm sorry, but no, I can't," said Paudeen gently. "We need every one of our boats in case something goes wrong on the voyage."

"Something HAS gone wrong!" shouted Ryan.

"Sir, I understand you are very upset and worried about your friend. I can offer you return passage after we arrive in Waterford. And we can send messages to anyone you know on shore who might be able to find and care for your friend."

Thomas put his hand on Ryan's arm. "Yes! At least that's something, Ryan. Where do we need to go to send messages, Paudeen?"

"We'll send them from here. Why don't you spend a few minutes thinking through your messages and who you want to send them to. Here is paper and a pencil. Write each message with the appropriate telephone number and bring your notes back here."

"Thank you, Captain." Thomas turned to leave the bridge, giving Ryan a nudge.

"But—but—" sputtered Ryan. "I don't know anyone in New York City."

"I do," said Thomas. "Come. Let's think it through together."

"All right," said Ryan, reluctantly following Thomas to the deck. "But just sending messages doesn't seem like enough. Cally could have gone anywhere. I won't attend the wedding. I'll be on the return voyage from Ireland."

"I understand," said Thomas. "In your place, I would do the same thing. It's terribly distressing. But let's think about the most likely actions Cally might take."

The two men sat together near the bridge. "Should we alert the police?" asked Ryan.

"New York is a big city," said Thomas. "If Cally doesn't want to be found, there are a thousand places she could hide. And police might frighten her more. Let's try instead to think where she might go."

"Doesn't your cousin Matilda live in New York City?" said Ryan. "She cared enough about Cally to travel to Kansas City to support us when Cally was so sick."

"Yes. Matilda." Thomas pulled a small notebook from his pocket and found his cousin's address and telephone number. "How about this: 'Cally is in New York City. She meant to travel with us to Ireland for Charlie's wedding, but she missed the ship. If she goes to you, please ask her to send us a telegram on the *Lion III*.' We'll ask when we return to the bridge how she can do that. Now, who else? I wish Nathanael and Sarah were still alive. It would be natural for Cally to go to them."

"True," said Ryan. "I don't think she would return to Rochester. She wouldn't want to upset Aunt Mary."

"I'll send a telegram to Max, telling him it will take Cally at least four days if she goes there."

"And one to Flora in case she goes to Idaho," said Ryan. "I can write down her address and telephone number for you."

"Good idea. And I'll send a message to the New York City train station, asking them to give her a message if she buys a ticket west." Thomas scribbled rapidly.

"Oh yes. You can do that, can't you."

"I can," smiled Thomas. "Anyone else?"

"Not that comes to mind," said Ryan. "Thank you for helping me with this."

"She's my sister," said Thomas. "I wish I could think of more we can do for her. My mother would say, pray. Cora and I will be doing so."

"Me too. Every moment."

Cora and the children were not where Thomas and Ryan had left them. "I imagine Cora is settling the children into our cabins. Let's look for them there."

Cora, sorting their luggage into three piles, nodded when Thomas relayed Paudeen's response. "That's what I expected. Thomas, the only way I can figure this out is for me to take Cally's place in the cabin with Felicity and bring Shauna over with me. That leaves Josie with you. Shane can stay with Ryan as we planned."

Thomas nodded slowly, "I see your reasoning, Cora. All right. While you organize the cabins, shall I take the children to run around the main deck? Please find Ryan and me there as soon as you can. We need to talk about what could possibly have been in Cally's mind to do such a thing. That might offer us a clue to where she'll go next. We've sent messages to several people, but perhaps you'll have another idea."

Cora nodded. "I'll be up as soon as I can. Children! Go up to the deck with your father!"

Felicity, sobbing again, clung to Cora, who sat down and gathered her into her arms. "It's all right, sweetheart. You can stay with me."

"She—she told me she wouldn't leave me again!" hiccupped Felicity.

"I fully believe she meant that when she said it," said Cora. "She loves you with all her heart. We're going to try to imagine why she might not have wanted to go to Ireland. Do you have any ideas?"

Felicity shook her head no and stuck her thumb in her mouth, a habit she had abandoned years before.

"Let's go find Uncle Thomas and Uncle Ryan," said Cora. "Maybe they have some ideas."

Thomas and Ryan had pulled four deck chairs together. Felicity sat, though, in Cora's lap, still sucking her thumb.

"I blame myself. Cally reacted strangely when the idea of going to Ireland first came up, when we read Charlie's letter the day before Christmas," said Cora. "I meant to ask her about it, but then she got sick, and Nathanael and Sarah died, and the house was full of company. And then Cally went to Idaho. And when she got back, it seemed she fully planned to go to the wedding. I thought I must have imagined her first reaction to Charlie's letter."

"Assigning blame won't help us," said Thomas. "What is there about Ireland that has always frightened Cally? Remember, she refused to go back when she was seven, when Father wanted to take her and Teddy back to Dugan and Aisling."

"And she hasn't returned since, not once," said Cora slowly. "But in the rush of life, it never occurred to me to think that was strange."

Ryan broke the silence he had fallen into after sending their messages. "Teddy!" said Ryan. "Perhaps she'll go to her brother!"

"It's worth sending him a telegram," said Thomas. "I'll do that."

"Cally told me how supportive Dugan and Aisling were to her after her mother died. It doesn't make sense. Why would a young child not want to go back to loving relatives, to a familiar situation? Instead, she chose to fend for herself and her little brother on the streets of Albany and on the canal! I don't understand." Cora stroked Felicity's back as she spoke.

"Something significant must have happened in Ireland before she left that terrified her," said Thomas. "Pity she never told us what that was. Clearly, it was powerful enough to still frighten her all these years later, as an adult, not just a wee child."

"So, none of us knows the reason she left us. Did you see her face just before she ran down the gangway? It was pure terror. I hate thinking of her dealing with that all by herself." Ryan stood and paced back and forth in front of the group.

"The question then is, what will she do now?" said Thomas. "If she abandoned the voyage out of overwhelming terror, rather than because she planned to do so, she herself probably doesn't know where to go. Can we try to think like her? Who might she go to?"

"I would have said Nathanael and Sarah, but they're gone," said Cora.

"That's exactly what I said," nodded Thomas.

"I don't think she would go to Mary." Ryan repeated what he had told Thomas. "Mary's not well. She's still grieving the loss of her sister Susan. Cally would not want to upset her more."

"Would she go back to Kansas City, without us there?" asked Thomas.

"That has to be one possibility," said Cora.

"Max will let us know if she shows up there. Would she go back to Idaho? What do you think, Ryan?" asked Thomas.

Ryan frowned. "We did send a message to Flora, but I think Cally would be embarrassed to go to Idaho. Everyone there knew I was joining her on this wonderful trip. There would be no end of explanations, and what could she say if she didn't want to tell them the truth?"

"Any other ideas?" asked Thomas.

"Teddy," said Ryan again. "I think she'll go to her brother. He might understand what happened in Ireland before they emigrated. He was only five. But he was there."

Thomas stood. "I'll send Teddy a message right now."

Waterford, Thursday, June 15, 1905

Cathleen, Margaret, and all three children—Sally, Cait, and Peter, jumping up and down—waved from the pier as the *Lion III* approached. The Kansas City Malcomsons scrambled to be the first down the gangway.

"Welcome!"

"It's soooo wonderful to see you!"

"We have a carriage and our new Brotherhood Tourer waiting to take us all to the train station. Percy will meet us there," Margaret told Thomas. "Wait! Where's Cally?"

"She didn't come," said Thomas. "I'll tell you about it on the train."

Margaret frowned, but extended her hand to the member of the party she didn't know. "You must be Ryan. I'm Thomas's sister, Margaret."

"I'm happy to meet you, ma'am."

"Oh, please. No ma'ams and sirs among us. I understand you're joining our family!"

"That's my intent, ma'am—er, Margaret."

"Can I ride in your automobile, Auntie Margaret?" asked Shane. The girls chimed in too.

"We can take four of you, if my children ride in the carriage," replied Margaret. She turned back to Cora. "I'm very sorry Cally didn't come. Mum doesn't seem to have missed her yet." Margaret looked over at Cathleen, surrounded by her grandchildren. Only Felicity hadn't joined that circle, clinging to Cora instead.

"It seems Felicity hasn't adjusted to her mum not being with her," observed Margaret. "Well, we must gather your luggage and be off. The Dublin train leaves in an hour."

"What are the plans when we get there?" asked Thomas.

"We'll go first to the hotel, get settled, and eat lunch. There will be time to rest for whoever needs that—I certainly would, after such a long voyage. Charlie and Laoise will join us for dinner at 6:00, at a nearby restaurant."

"Your grand dinner with everyone from both families is tomorrow night, right?"

"Yes, at the Murphys' home. They decided to put up the reception tent in their garden a day early, so we can eat there in comfort even if it rains. I've planned for thirty people—well, twenty-nine, now that Cally isn't with us. Fifteen adults and fourteen children. If we count Martin, Molly, Martha, and Abigail as children."

"They're not children anymore, but they are the next generation. So, the twenty-nine includes Dugan's family, the Murphys, Daniel and his family, cousin Silas and his family, and all of us," said Thomas.

"Yes. Dugan and Aisling will be devastated over Cally. Mum says the anticipation of seeing Cally has pulled Aisling out of her depression. They'll arrive tomorrow afternoon."

"What about the Belfast folks?"

"Tomorrow in time for lunch. We've planned an outing for the children tomorrow morning, and a rehearsal with Molly of their song for the wedding after lunch at the hotel," said Margaret.

"Thank you for all your planning," said Thomas, hugging his sister.

"It's what I do best, you know that," smiled Margaret.

"If it's all right, I'd like to spend time with Cousin Silas tomorrow morning."

"Oh?"

"I've been involved with him in the southeast United States, trying to help people adopt a just and charitable attitude toward former slaves. Things have gotten worse in the south. There have even been lynchings. I'm not sure Cousin Silas knows this."

"Oh. Always something going on with you, Thomas. I think we'll do fine without you at the zoo tomorrow. Now, though, can you deal with the luggage?"

"Of course! Where are the vehicles?"

"I'll gather everyone and start walking that direction. You can follow us."

"Ryan! Come help me." Ryan shook himself and followed Thomas and the two baggage lads he enlisted.

On the train, Thomas sat with his mother and sister so he could describe Cally's abrupt departure from the *Lion III.* "Ryan wanted to take the first ship back, but he didn't find space. The *Lion III* needs repairs and won't sail again for a week. So, he's coming to the wedding after all. But his heart, of course, is with Cally."

Margaret looked down the aisle to where Ryan sat with Felicity, Cora, and Josie. "What a sad story about Cally. I'm sure you're all worried about her. And Charlie will be so disappointed. We all know how much he loves her."

"Yes, but we've done all we can think of to do," said Thomas. "Cora and I mean to make Charlie and Laoise's wedding as happy as we can, even for Felicity and Ryan. There may be responses to our telegrams when we reach the hotel."

"I have an idea why she might have done this," Cathleen said slowly.

"You do, Mum?" said Thomas and Margaret at the same time.

"Yes. After the disastrous voyage when Cally's father Frank drowned, Peter, Charlie, and I went to Killeagh to tell Dugan and Aisling the news personally. We told them Cally didn't want to return to Ireland. We described what a woman who helped care for wee Cally on the ship said to us, that Cally sometimes cried out in her sleep, in fear of the Dubh Sidhe. We asked Dugan and Aisling whether they thought Cally might be afraid to return to Ireland because of a bad experience with the faeries."

Cathleen paused and took a deep breath.

"And?" said Margaret.

"They told us Miss Hilda, a local wise woman, would know. Miss Hilda confirmed that yes, Cally's fear of the faeries was probably behind her decision to stay in America."

"But Cally is no longer a child afraid of fairy tales. I don't understand," said Margaret.

"There's a lot we don't know about Cally," said Thomas. "She doesn't talk to us about the hard things that happened to her and Teddy in Ireland before coming to America. I think you've hit on something important, Mum. I wish Cora and I had taken time to sit with Cally and ask her to tell us more of her story."

"I share that wish, Thomas," said Cathleen. "She seemed to be doing well when I was with her in Idaho. And there was so much going on, and so many people . . . But like you, I wish now I had taken more time with Cally. We were so focused on Flora's recovery, and Josie's birthday, and the treasure hunt."

"And the art show, and the tragic murder of Falling Water, and then the trial," said Thomas.

"No use crying over spilt milk, Mum and Thomas," said Margaret. "The question is how we can salvage the wedding for Charlie and Laoise. They will only marry once."

"I wonder, Mum . . . Would it help Charlie if you remind him of what you just told us about Cally's possible fear of faeries? He would at least know Cally's actions are not a rejection of him and Laoise," said Thomas.

"I doubt he would think that, Thomas. Cally and Charlie have a very close relationship. He told me that even before he reconnected with Laoise, Cally suggested he marry a musician," said Cathleen. "I am confident there is no rejection or jealousy on Cally's part."

"I do believe she's happy for them, and completely in love with Ryan," agreed Thomas. "Well, we'll see how Charlie reacts to the news and respond as seems best at the time."

"My heart goes out to Felicity," said Margaret. "How can she make sense of her mother's actions, when not even the adults understand what Cally did? She hasn't let go of Cora for an instant, as if she fears losing her too. Cally's fear must have been overwhelming, to do this to her beloved daughter."

"With our last minutes on the train, let's pray for Cally, and Felicity, and Ryan, and Charlie, and for joy to yet reign over the events of the next days. And for Aisling, that this disappointment will not throw her back into depression," said Cathleen, and bowed her head.

❧

"We have responses from everyone we sent messages to," Thomas told the adults at dinner. "So far, no one has seen Cally. I asked each one to notify us if they have any news."

Ryan excused himself and went out for a walk by himself.

❧

The Murphy home, Friday afternoon

"Stunning!" exclaimed Margaret. "I'm not sure when I've seen a more beautiful garden. Even with this huge tent blocking out the sky. I'm glad I didn't invest a lot in floral arrangements for the tables—we're surrounded by flowers!"

"Where are my canvas and paints when I need them?" said Cora.

"No wonder Muriel was such a fan of Olga's," said Cathleen.

"Olga? Oh, your friend in Vienna," said Margaret.

"I remember her paintings from the World's Fair in Chicago. The flowers seemed so alive, I wanted to reach out and pick them!" said Cora.

"Having the dinner here is the perfect way to honor Muriel's memory," said Cathleen. "So, Margaret, how can we help you? The table settings are exquisite."

"I made place cards for each person. As you see, I requested three large round tables in addition to the food and beverage tables. They will serve double duty for food at tomorrow's reception, but Muriel wanted small, more intimate tables for that event. I need your help to decide who should sit where this evening."

"Muriel wanted smaller tables?" asked Cora.

"Yes. Muriel planned the entire wedding and reception, and Laoise says she did it with great delight. Laoise was so busy with her concert tours she was happy to let her do so. She told me yesterday she's quite sure her mum will be watching from heaven to be sure her plans are carried out just so," said Margaret.

"What have you thought so far about the table seating?" asked Cathleen.

"I've sorted the place cards into three possible groupings for the three tables. Tell me what you think of this: one table for the grandchildren, including Caoimhe, Cathal, and Christopher—that's twelve. The head table with Charlie and Laoise and the four young couples, that's ten. And the rest of us at the third table."

"Hmm. I don't know whether Felicity will sit with the other children. The only way I managed to detach myself from her was to put her down for a nap before I left."

"All right. We'll shift her to your table," said Margaret. "It's possible my Peter will want to be with me. But let's leave him with the other children for now. We can easily make the change if he prefers. What do you think of these other two?"

"The only one who doesn't really fit is Ryan," said Cora. It would be nice if he could be with the other young people. But that would make Cally's absence even more noticeable."

"Let's keep him with us—fewer new people to expect explanations from him," said Cathleen.

"How about if each of us arranges the seating at one table?" said Margaret. "Then we can each look at the other two tables and suggest changes."

"I'll take the children's table," said Cora.

"Then you do your table, Mum, and I'll do mine."

"Molly with Sally and Caoimhe," murmured Cora, placing the cards. "Martin with Shane and Cathal. Cait with Shauna. Josie with Christopher and Peter. That puts the youngest next to the oldest girl. I think that will work. And if by some miracle Felicity wants to join the children, we can squeeze her in between Shauna and Josie."

"I kept the couples together, alternating men and women," said Margaret. "Charlie and Laoise with Desmond and Deirdre on her side and Meghan and Daniel on his. Anthony and Cousin Abigail next to Deirdre, then Percy and me, which places me next to Daniel."

"Perfect!" said Cathleen. "I'm not as sure about mine, so feel free to suggest adjustments."

"Wait. Cousin Martha isn't coming?" asked Cora.

"Martha's on her own honeymoon! She and Stephen opted for a small wedding with their Quaker Meeting. We only learned about it when I talked with Priscilla about Charlie's wedding. All right, Mum. Tell us what you've done." Margaret followed Cora to Cathleen's table.

"I started with Felicity next to Cora, with me on her other side. Then Silas and Priscilla, Dugan and Aisling, Ryan, Colin, and Thomas."

"Do you think Colin will mind not being with his daughter?" asked Cora.

"I think when he sees their table is all young couples, he'll be happy to sit with us few older ones," said Cathleen. "I know he'll be missing Muriel terribly, as Ryan will be missing Cally. Perhaps they can comfort each other. And Thomas is so good at interesting conversation. I think he'll be able to distract them into having a good time."

"I see," said Margaret. "I would have expected you to put Dugan and Aisling beside you."

"The reason I didn't is so that Felicity can watch them and feel more comfortable around them before we ask her to interact with them. And I don't want her sadness to intensify Aisling's. Priscilla and Silas are so very good at engaging with people. I think this will go well."

"There we are, then. We did it!" said Margaret.

"What's next?" asked Cora.

"Could you help me decorate the basket for cards, while Mum decorates the stand for the guest book? The family can sign it tonight."

"Before we leave, I would love to walk the perimeter of the garden and just soak in the colors and fragrances," said Cathleen.

"Lovely idea, Mum. We'll join you."

☙❧

"I know you're sad that Cally didn't come. But, Charlie, can you please not let that spoil our wedding?" Laoise handed Charlie a handkerchief and waited patiently as he wiped his eyes and then sat for a time on the settee in her bedroom at the Murphy home, his head down.

"You've already written to her. The family is doing all they can," observed Laoise.

Charlie took several deep breaths, looked up, smiled at Laoise, and said, "I hear you, my darling. What can be done for Cally is being done. She'll be disappointed if we let this ruin our joy. I hope Mum will be able to console Dugan and Aisling. Especially Aisling."

"Are you ready, then, to enjoy the family dinner?"

Charlie took another deep breath. "I'm ready."

Laoise straightened his bowtie, took a fresh handkerchief from her drawer, adjusted her hair, and took Charlie's arm. "Here we go!"

"The most alluring, charming, wise, and beautiful bride in the world," said Charlie.

☙❧

"May I sit by you, Felicity?" Cathleen asked.

Felicity looked up at her and nodded.

Cathleen whispered to Priscilla and Silas, on her left as she sat, "I need to talk with Felicity for a moment."

Priscilla smiled and nodded.

"Thank you, Felicity. I've been wanting to tell you a story about your mummy," said Cathleen. "It's about her wee round mirror."

"The one she always takes with her?"

"Yes. Did you know Uncle Charlie and I first met your mummy when she was a tiny child, maybe three or four years old?"

"I didn't know that," said Felicity, her eyes fixed on Cathleen's face.

"Charlie and I were on a trip, and our carriage wheel broke as we rode into a village named Killeagh. We stopped at an inn for repairs. As we stepped out of our carriage, I pulled my wee mirror from my pocket to straighten my hair after our long journey. When I looked up, a girl holding a basket of eggs was looking at me."

"My mummy?"

"Yes. She was with her uncle Dugan, the man sitting across the table from us."

Felicity looked across the table into warm green eyes. The man smiled at her.

"That's my mummy's uncle?"

"He is. That makes him your great uncle. Kind of like a grandfather. He and Aisling want to be your friends."

Felicity pulled back a little, but said, "He looks like my mummy." She watched Dugan and Aisling as she nibbled a roll and listened to Cathleen.

"So, when I got out of the carriage in Killeagh I saw a child with red curls and big green eyes and freckles. Like you."

"My mummy!"

"Yes. She looked curiously at my mirror. I asked the man whether she could look at herself. He said yes. I believe it was the first time she had ever seen herself in a mirror. She was fascinated, so I told her she could keep the mirror."

"That how Mummy got her mirror? From you?"

"Yes. Long before we knew her name or that she and you would become part of our family. Isn't that lovely?"

"Does that man know he saw you by the inn?" asked Felicity.

"Yes. I've talked to him about it, and he remembers," said Cathleen. "He and Aisling took care of your mummy after her own mother died. They love her very much."

"Then why didn't Mummy want to come here and see them?" asked Felicity, her eyes brimming. "Why did she run away? Why didn't she want to come to Uncle Charlie's wedding?"

Cathleen glanced at Dugan and Aisling. Tears shone in their eyes as well.

"We're not sure, sweetheart. But we think when your mummy was a wee girl here in Ireland, something sad happened that we don't know about. We think she didn't want to come back and remember it all over again."

"I don't like to remember when Falling Water died."

"Yes. Like that. Your mummy never told us exactly what it is that she doesn't want to remember. But, Felicity, I am absolutely, totally, completely sure your mummy would be with you if she could be. She planned to come. But at the last minute she was too afraid. We think she's gone to spend some time with your Uncle Teddy."

"Mummy told me she would never leave me again. I think I did something wrong."

"It wasn't your fault, Felicity. It's a problem of her own she had to solve. If she possibly could, she would be with you. She loves you with all her heart."

Felicity breathed deep, her head down. Then she sat up straight and pointed across the tent at Laoise. "Isn't she beautiful, like a princess? Is she really my aunt now?"

"She is! And Dugan and Aisling want to be your uncle and aunt too. Or grandparents if you want to think of them like that."

Felicity looked at Dugan and Aisling. They smiled. "I didn't know I had any grandma besides you. And they're not old like you."

Cathleen laughed. "No, they're not. But grandparents can be young. Would you like to spend some time with them after supper?"

"Will you stay with me?"

"If you like."

"Then yes."

Dugan's and Aisling's eyes brimmed with tears again.

"All right, then. Would you like anything more to eat, Felicity? I'm going to get some more beef wellington and champ. I didn't know I was so hungry!"

"I'm hungry, too." For the first time since the *Lion III* sailed, Felicity attacked her plate.

Cathleen smiled across the table to Dugan and Aisling and held her thumb up.

"Thank you," mouthed Aisling.

Cathleen replenished her plate, then turned her attention to Silas and Priscilla.

☙❧

On the other side of Cora, Thomas introduced Ryan to Laoise's father, Colin Murphy.

"I met an American from Idaho a couple of weeks ago," Colin said between bites of beef and champ, after learning Ryan lived in Idaho.

Thomas straightened, He stared at Colin. "You did? That must be an unusual occurrence."

"Yes, a first for me. A remarkable lad, with dark skin. I wondered whether he might be one of your American natives. He wanted to discuss Irish nationalism."

For a moment, Thomas couldn't breathe. "Did you tell Charlie about him?"

"No. Charlie and Laoise got back only yesterday. Why? You seem interested in this lad."

"He may be—I think he might be—a lad we've been trying to find for months. A year. Do you know where he might be now?"

"I'm sorry. I don't really know anything about him. I was asked to meet with him to explain Irish nationalism. I wasn't told more, and the lad didn't volunteer information."

"Did you meet him here in Dublin?"

"Yes. I met him at the train station. A train coming from Cork City, but it makes stops all along the way. I don't know where he got on. I took him to the home of someone else for our conversation, as I was instructed. I left him there."

"May I know whose home that was?"

"Hmm, I'm not sure I'm at liberty to say. But I returned that evening, and the lad was no longer there. I presume he returned to wherever he came from."

"Did the lad tell you his name?"

"He only said his name was Billy."

"Oh my."

"You seem quite overcome."

"Billy is part of our family. He's been missing for more than a year. Almost two years—he'll turn fifteen on July fourth. He left home the day he turned thirteen."

"How extraordinary. He looked well. Tall and strong and well-fed. He asked intelligent questions. He told me he plans to become a doctor. A pediatrician. And that he's not sure how long he will stay in Ireland. That's all I can tell you."

Tears came to Thomas's eyes. "That's more than we've known for all these months. I believe it was God who prompted you to mention him to us."

"I was just making conversation, a connection with your America I found unusual."

Ryan looked across Colin to smile at Thomas. "Amazing. All because I live in Idaho."

Thomas said, "You can't know what this means to us, Colin. I wish I could have overheard your conversation with Billy. Irish nationalism is a topic I'm interested in myself. So is Ryan."

"Yes, I am very interested," said Ryan. "I've been reading Irish American papers representing several different points of view."

Desmond, returning to his table, stopped beside his father. "I overheard some of that. I also would like to participate in a conversation about nationalism, Father."

"You would? I didn't know you were interested."

"We must all figure out what we think about this."

"Then how about if we men gather for breakfast Monday morning at my club? Anyone is welcome: Daniel, Percy, Silas, Dugan. That other young man, married to your cousin—"

"Anthony," said Thomas. "I'm not sure how long everyone will be staying in Dublin, but sure, if you're willing, let's invite them all. I'll clear it with Cora and Margaret, of course, but I appreciate your offer, Colin. Charlie, of course, will be gone on his honeymoon."

"That's just as well. I don't want to upset Laoise with anything else. Going through this wedding without her mother is enough for her to deal with right now."

Thomas raised his eyebrows. *I wonder what he's involved with that might upset his daughter. Right now, I want to share the news about Billy!*

He turned to get Cora's attention and saw Felicity smile.

That's the first Felicity smile I've seen since Cally abandoned ship. No wonder Cora is riveted. I won't interrupt her now.

Thomas picked up his fork. *Imagine—Billy was right here in Dublin just a few days ago! He's well and strong! He wants to become a doctor! That means he must be in school . . .*

At the head table, Daniel stood and tapped his glass. When the room quieted, he said, "What a wonderful occasion this is, celebrating as a family the joining of Charlie and Laoise ahead of the official event tomorrow. If my father were here, he would be thrilled with this marriage. I'm confident I speak for him and for all our family when I say welcome, Laoise. Welcome to the Malcomson clan. We are so delighted Charlie found you."

Daniel stopped while all the Malcomsons cheered and clapped. Laoise blushed, inclined her head, and took Charlie's arm.

"My sister Margaret and I thought it would be nice to have time now for anyone to speak who would like to do so, to honor Charlie and Laoise. But before we do that, my daughter Molly has an announcement she has already discussed with the children."

A lovely, slim young woman stood and smiled at the children. "We had an enjoyable practice time today, didn't we, *weans*? But I think we will feel more confident if we go over our song a few more times. Parents, can we do that this evening, after supper? Mr. Murphy says we may gather by the piano in his living room after dessert. All right, mums and das? I won't keep them more than half an hour."

Everyone nodded and murmured assent. Molly said, "Thank you," and sat.

Colin stood. "My only sadness tonight is that my dear Muriel is not with me to welcome you to our home, Malcomson family. I wonder, can we all take a moment to be silent in her memory? Then we can proceed with what Daniel has suggested."

Around the tables, people nodded and bowed their heads. A tear trickled from Laoise's eye. Charlie wiped it with his thumb, then held her close. After a minute, Cathleen stood.

"Dear Laoise, for some time now I've thought of you as already part of our family." Cathleen winked at Charlie and Laoise.

Thomas's eyes widened as Cathleen continued. *Did Mum just wink? What was that about?* He looked at Charlie and Laoise, both blushing. *I'm going to get to the bottom of this.*

"You hold a special place in my heart, my dear newest daughter. As most of you know, I had the privilege of traveling with Laoise on her recent tour through Europe. I found her to be as lovely and gracious inside as she is outside. I've no doubt you will be a tremendous blessing to our Charlie. Welcome, precious Laoise. I love you."

Laoise nodded and smiled, tears coming to her eyes once more.

Thomas looked across to Margaret's table to catch her eye, wanting to ask, *Do you know the secret between Charlie and Mum?* Margaret pointed at herself and then him. He nodded. *Yes. After supper. I can't wait to tell her about Billy. And tell everyone else too!*

Retrieving his room key at the hotel, the attendant handed Thomas a telegram from Max:

"Cally came for clothes. Left note. Gone to Teddy. Says don't worry, enjoy wedding, love to Felicity, Ryan, Charlie, Laoise, Dugan, Aisling, everyone. All fine here. Max"

So, Ryan guessed right about what Cally would do. What a relief! I'll go find him right now.

Thomas sighed as he climbed the grand curving staircase. *What an evening! Margaret wanting me to help Percy decorate Charlie's getaway carriage. Mum's surprise—still meant to be a secret—that Charlie and Laoise have been legally married since January! Colin's connection with Billy! The laughter at the head table—apparently Deirdre is quite the comic. So much interest in Irish nationalism. And—oh yes. Mustn't forget the obvious happiness of the bride and groom, despite our missing parents, Father and Mrs. Murphy. And our missing Cally.*

Thomas found Ryan's room and knocked on the door. After a moment, Ryan opened, his hair tousled as if he had already gone to bed.

"I have good news for you, Ryan! You were right about Cally." Thomas handed Ryan the telegram and watched his face relax as he read it.

"Does this change your mind about your return to America?" asked Thomas.

"I'll think about it. Is there a way I can talk to Cally, do you think?"

"Hmm. I doubt Teddy and Starlight have a telephone. But you could send Teddy a telegram and ask him to arrange a call. Surely someone in Grove, Oklahoma has a telephone."

"I'll do it tomorrow morning. Thank you, Thomas. This has been an evening of good news."

"Yes?"

"Felicity went with Molly to practice their song without insisting Cora go with her. Then she had a happy conversation with Dugan and Aisling. And she wanted me to bring her back to the hotel to put her to bed, while Cora cared for her own—your—children. It's a huge breakthrough. I'm so grateful to Cathleen."

"Mum can work wonders. I'm glad for Felicity and for Cora as well, not having Felicity attached to her like a Siamese twin."

"Cora has been amazingly patient with Felicity."

"I agree she's quite wonderful," smiled Thomas.

"And the other great thing that happened for me tonight is the prospect of talking about nationalism with Colin Monday morning. I can't wait to hear what he has to say."

"I'm excited about that too. Say, Ryan. If you wake up early, you could help me and Percy decorate Charlie and Laoise's getaway carriage. We have some amusing ideas."

"I'd love to!"

"Then meet us in the lobby at 7:00. We want to do it before breakfast. I'm off to bed. Tomorrow's another big day."

"Good night, Thomas. Thank you."

Cathleen sat in the second pew at St. Catherine's Church watching her youngest child formally pledge his life to the woman he loved. *How I miss you today, Peter! Are you watching from Heaven? Do you know what happens to your family here on earth?*

She glanced across the aisle, to Colin mouthing the words Laoise spoke. *It must be even harder for Colin, his loss so recent. I'm glad Charlie and Laoise decided to settle in Dublin. And he'll soon have Desmond and Deirdre nearby too.*

As the vicar removed Charlie and Laoise's rings from the pillow her grandson Peter held, Cathleen glanced down at her own ring, a flood of memories filling her mind. She looked at her son's radiant face as he repeated, "With this ring I thee wed . . . " *Ha. Charlie thought he didn't need this ceremony, after marrying Laoise at the Registry Office. But it's such a different experience, being supported by the Church and the community, not just family.*

She looked around at the stained-glass windows, the gorgeous flowers, the pews filled mostly with the Murphys' friends. She watched her grandchildren line up to sing their song, each carrying a Ryan-crafted whistle. Even Felicity smiled, her new Cally-made dress on elegant display. *What a clever and charming couple they are, Cally and Ryan. I believe you have good plans for them, Lord God.*

Her heart sang along with the children:

"Ye who long pain and sorrow bear,
Praise God and on Him cast your care,
O praise Him, O praise Him ..."

Complete your healing in Cally's life, Lord. Free her to live with joy and peace.

"Let all things their Creator bless,
And worship him in humbleness,
O praise him, Alleluia . . . "

Cathleen's heart flooded with thankfulness.

"Praise, praise the Father, praise the Son,
And praise the Spirit, Three in One,
O praise Him, O praise Him!
Alleluia, alleluia, alleluia!

CHAPTER 22

CALLY

Grove, Oklahoma, Friday, June 16, 1905

CALLY STOOD BEFORE A CLAPBOARD bungalow and looked around. A profusion of flowers perfumed the still, hot air around the front porch, while a neat vegetable garden featuring foot-high corn, spreading squash, and flourishing beans took up most of the back yard. Bees and a swiftly darting hummingbird navigated a stately row of hollyhocks.

Perhaps no one is home. Cally took a deep breath, climbed the steps and knocked tentatively on the front door. When no one answered, she knocked more boldly. The door opened enough for a dark eye to peer around it.

"Cally? Is it you?" Starlight flung open the door and extended her arms. Cally took a step into her sister-in-law's embrace, fragrant with wood smoke, and burst into tears. Starlight patted her back and murmured soothingly until the outburst eased.

"Come in. I just put Aiyana down for her nap. Teddy is not here. He has gone to see River Runner, but he will be home for supper. He would have stayed home had he known you were coming today. Until we received Thomas Malcomson's telegram, we thought you had gone to Ireland for Charlie's wedding!"

Starlight's welcome evoked a fresh flood of tears. Cally sat on a pine chair and buried her face in her arms, her head bent over her lap as if she had no more strength to keep it upright.

"I will make tea," said Starlight. "And then you will tell me all about it."

To both young women's surprise, the front door opened, and Teddy walked in.

"Cally? Now I understand why Maiana urged me to come home now."

"River Runner's wife?" hiccupped Cally.

"Yes. Maiana is a seer," said Starlight. "I was just going to make tea. Will you join us, Teddy, while Cally tells us why she is here?"

"Yes, please. But first a hug," said Teddy, pulling Cally into his arms.

"I might start crying again." Cally clung to her brother for a long time, absorbing his strength and kindness.

"Sit with me on the sofa. Now then," said Teddy after Starlight served them all sweet tea and sat down opposite them. "You were on your way to Dublin for Charlie's wedding . . . "

"Yes. I fully intended to go. I did go to the port. But I—I couldn't—I—I—"

"Take a deep breath, Cally. Tell us what happened," said Starlight. "You're not alone anymore."

Cally swallowed and stared at her lap for a moment. She began speaking softly and slowly. Her voice grew louder and her speech faster as she talked. "I—I got on the ship with Felicity and Ryan and Cora's family. And then I panicked when the gate started to close. I ran down the gangway and jumped onto the pier. And then ran and ran and ran away from the ship."

"What happened then?" asked Teddy.

Cally took a deep breath, trembling. "When I could run no more, I cried out to God. He told me to come here."

Cally slumped into the sofa as if she had used all her strength.

"I'm glad you decided to come, and of course you can stay as long as you like," said Teddy. "But what made you so afraid?"

Cally looked down. "I don't think I can tell you," she said so softly both Teddy and Starlight leaned in to hear her. Both sat back frowning.

"I don't understand," said Starlight. "You can't tell us because you don't know? Or because you're afraid to say it?"

"Both," whispered Cally. "It doesn't make sense even to me."

Teddy was silent for a long moment. Then he said slowly, "Cally, does this have anything to do with why you refused to take me back to Ireland after Da died?"

Cally's body jerked. She looked at Teddy, eyes wide, and inclined her head in assent.

"Then . . . why were you so afraid to return to Ireland, then and now?"

"Nightmares," said Cally. "Over and over. I was afraid to go to sleep."

"Can you tell us about your nightmares?" asked Starlight. "Maybe between us we can make some sense of their message."

"I don't want to remember them," said Cally. "They were too terrible."

"Perhaps it's too soon," said Starlight. "Perhaps after you get some rest, and grow more comfortable here, you'll find the courage to face them. Come see the sleeping place I have prepared for you. I'm sorry we don't have beds—we're used to sleeping on the floor. You look weary, sister of my husband."

"I will care for our wee blossom," said Teddy. "She's waking up."

"Thank you, my husband," said Starlight.

"Wee blossom?" asked Cally.

"Aiyana means blossom," said Starlight. "Come. I will ask God to let you nap without nightmares."

As she stretched out on her pallet and closed her eyes after Starlight's prayer, Cally heard Teddy say, "Shall I ask Maiana to come?"

"Let's wait a day or two. Perhaps Cally is just too tired to think clearly."

For the first time in weeks, Cally slept without dreams.

☙❧

At supper, Teddy talked lightheartedly about his construction work, and Starlight asked him to help her judge whether it was too soon to harvest the beans in her garden. Baby Aiyana entertained them by dropping one pea at a time over the side of her highchair and saying "Boom." By the end of the meal peas circled her chair.

Cally played peek-a-boo with her niece while Starlight and Teddy washed the dishes, then they all went for a walk by the river. The air was still sticky hot, but a light breeze blew by the time they returned home, Aiyana's sleepy head resting on her father's shoulder.

"I'm ready to sleep again myself, if you don't mind," Cally said.

"Of course. Sleep for as long as you like. I'll be off to work at sunrise. We like to take advantage of the morning coolness," said Teddy.

"And I will spend the morning at the weaving cooperative. Aiyana will go with me. We'll be home for lunch," said Starlight. "If you wake in time to go with us, you might enjoy it. If not, we'll see you at midday."

"Thank you for taking me in," said Cally.

"Anytime, sis," smiled Teddy. "Goodnight."

Exhausted as she was, Cally couldn't sleep. *What must Ryan think of me now? He won't want to continue our relationship after what I did. I can't blame him. And poor Felicity. I told her I wouldn't leave her again, and then I did. After the three of us had such a nice time in Rochester. Except for my nightmares, which no one else knew about. The whole Malcomson family gathered for Charlie's wedding knows by now what I did. How can I ever go back?*

Cally turned over. *It's like this every night. I can't get my thoughts to stop tormenting me.* She got up, went to the window, and looked out at the night. Stars sparkled in the sky.

So many people have been kind to me. But they don't know . . . Dear Charlie, oh, I'm so sad that I missed your wedding to your talented, beautiful Laoise. If my absence made the event even a tiny bit less joyful for you, I am so sorry. But you don't know what might have happened had I gone. You don't know I did this to protect you and everyone there.

Cally lay down again and made herself as comfortable as she could. *Wonderful Cathleen. Oh my. I am so ashamed, because how could you possibly understand? Precious, precious Felicity. I told you I wouldn't leave you again, and then I did. How can you ever trust me again? How can I trust myself?*

Cally couldn't bear the wheeling of her thoughts any longer. She rose from her pallet, pulled on her dress, and as quietly as she could, crept down the stairs. She opened the front door and slid into the star-spangled darkness, mercifully a shade cooler than daytime had been. She moved to sit on the front step, but jumped as someone cleared their throat. Shock poured through her body. She whirled around and saw Teddy sitting on the porch with his back to the wall of the house, watching her.

"Couldn't sleep?" he asked, patting the floor beside him.

Cally's breath came out in a whoosh. "No. Couldn't get my brain to turn off."

"Would you like to tell me what you were thinking about?" asked Teddy.

"If you'll tell me why you aren't sleeping," said Cally.

"I've been remembering the day in Albany, New York when you made us run away from the Malcomsons instead of letting them take us back to Uncle Dugan and Aisling. I never understood it, Cally."

"I'm sorry, Teddy. How could you? You were so small."

"Can you tell me now? It's a grief I have carried all my life."

Cally took a deep breath. *I don't want to talk about this. I don't want to remember how much I hurt him. But I owe it to him to at least try.*

"Do you remember when Mammy died, Teddy?"

"I remember," said Teddy. "I remember Da didn't speak to us or care for us. You were father and mother to me. You took care of all of us, Da, me, even Uncle Dugan. You weren't any bigger than me, even though you're a little older. Too small to carry so much responsibility."

"Uncle Dugan helped. And Aisling. After she started spending time with Uncle Dugan, Aisling taught me so many things. And when they were married, and Da came back to us, life seemed magical."

"Cousin Mickey and Louise helped too. They taught you to read, and you read to me after I hurt my leg."

"Yes."

"Those were good times. Even though my leg hurt. But I think you were going to tell me something else."

"Teddy, before Mammy died, she said to me, 'You'll be the death of me yet.' I still remember her face when she said it. And then I heard her tell Da that she didn't like me, and she wanted her new babby to be nothing like me. She wanted a lassie who would love to sew and be with her in the kitchen and be a wee princess, instead of a tomboy like me who preferred to be outside running around. I felt so hurt I said out loud when I was by myself milking Daisy, 'I hope the babby will die.'"

"So," said Teddy slowly. "When Mammy and our baby sister did die, you believed it was your fault?"

"I knew it was. And I knew it was my fault too when Da was so sad and didn't want to speak to us anymore. It seemed obvious he knew Mammy's death was my fault, so I understood his treatment of me. But I couldn't bear the fact that he turned away from you, too. So, I went to speak with Miss Hilda."

"Miss Hilda? I don't remember her," said Teddy.

"Do you remember a day I left you alone on the mountain with the sheep, and when I came back, I brought you sweeties that you hadn't had in a long time, since before Mammy died?"

"And then there was a storm, and we had to get the sheep into their fold."

"Yes. Before the storm, I left you alone so long because I went to Miss Hilda's house. I asked her to find out whether the faeries were angry with me and if they were, what I could give them to stop hurting our family. She did ask them, and when I went to see her again, she told me they wanted my mirror."

"The wee mirror I threw in the river? You smashed your head on a rock going after it."

"I didn't know you would remember all this, Teddy. That mirror was my treasure, the only pretty thing I owned. I thought the faeries were cruel to take it from me. So, I told Miss Hilda I would think about it and let her know. But I never did. I just kept the mirror. And then—this is hard to tell you, Teddy, and I don't know whether you can ever forgive me."

"Forgive you for what?"

Cally took a deep breath. "When we were at the beach visiting Cousin Mickey, Da started talking to me. I wasn't watching you well enough. And you broke your leg."

"You believe that was your fault too?" asked Teddy.

"I do. It was my fault. You were my responsibility. And I knew the faeries did that because I didn't give them my mirror."

"Da was there. Why wasn't it his responsibility to look after me? Anyway, it was an accident, Cally. I was jumping on the rocks, like any boy would do, and I fell. It would have happened even if you were right beside me."

"Maybe . . . but maybe not, Teddy. I was bad, as I heard Mammy tell Da—and my selfishness in not giving the faeries what they wanted—my treasure—confirmed that. So, they hurt the people I loved. And then Da decided to come to America and—"

Cally could not contain her tears. Teddy rubbed her back until she calmed.

"You believed Da's drowning was your fault, too? Oh, Cally. How awful. Have you ever told this to anyone?"

"No. I knew—it was crystal clear in my mind—if I went back to Ireland, something even more terrible than your leg would happen to you. Or to Uncle Dugan or Aisling. Or to all of you. Because the faeries were taking away one by one everyone I loved, to punish me."

"Oh, Cally. The pain you have borne is so huge and so deep."

"I wanted to go back to Dugan and Aisling too, just like you. I longed for that comfortable and easy way out. I knew they loved us. But don't you see—that's the very reason I couldn't take you back. Because I loved you. And I loved them. I had to protect all of you by staying in America, far away from the faeries."

Teddy put his arm around Cally. "Thank you, Cally. I know it's been hard for you to tell me, but it is such a relief to finally understand. As a child, the not knowing grew inside of me until I couldn't bear it anymore."

"And you ran away," said Cally.

"Yes. I wanted to go to Ireland and find Uncle Dugan and Aisling. But I couldn't remember the name of the village close to their farm. On my way to New York, I ran into River Runner. He took me in, and after a while, I started feeling at home with his family. It felt easier to stay with them than to try to go back to Ireland by myself."

"He was always kind to us," said Cally. "And you were so young. I grieved your leaving me. I grieved so much. But I understood I had not been able to give you what you needed."

"The main thing I needed was an answer to why you wouldn't let Captain Malcomson take us home," said Teddy. "And now finally, tonight, you've told me. Thank you."

"I'm sorry—so sorry you've been troubled by this for all this time."

"So, the reason you panicked over going to Ireland for Charlie's wedding was your fear that you would cause something terrible to happen to them."

Cally nodded, her head down. She whispered, "For weeks, in my nightmares, horrible things happened. At the wedding and to the people I loved who attended. I watched them happen over and over. In my dreams, my being there spoiled everything." Tears flowed again.

Teddy pulled her into his arms.

"Even—even Laoise's mum died because of me. In my dreams." Cally sobbed into Teddy's shirt, for so long that he grew alarmed.

"Cally, listen to me." He stood, grasped her shoulders and pulled her upright. "I know those were horrible dreams. But there's a difference between dreams and real life. And there's a difference between what we believe when we are children and what we believe as adults."

"I know, Teddy." Cally gulped, sniffed, and wiped her nose on the back of her hand. "I know this logically. But there's a part of me that's still certain—even in the daytime—that it was my fault, Mammy's and the baby's and Da's deaths. And your leg. It was my fault that you didn't have a home to grow up in, that you had to live in the streets of a big city and then on a barge with a drunken captain where you didn't have enough to eat and—"

"Cally, stop. Take a deep breath. Now another. And another. Better?"

"I—I guess so."

"There's another way to look at this story, one Starlight has helped me understand. Let's walk by the river, and I'll try to help you see it too."

"All—all right," gulped Cally, following him down the steps.

"I want you to try to open your mind to a different point of view. I want my words to be like seeds planted in the soil of your heart that can bloom into beautiful flowers, displacing the weeds of guilt and fear that have flourished there for too long. Will you try to really listen to me, Cally?"

"I'll try."

"Cally, when children face terrible things they can't control, in order to cope with their pain and fear, they often believe they have more power than they do. For example, Felicity might believe right now it was her fault that you ran off the ship. Was it her fault?"

"Of course not."

"But in her mind, if it was her fault, she can do something about it. By changing herself, she can control you and keep this from happening again. Felicity may be thinking if she is only 'good' enough in her thoughts and her actions, she can get you back and prevent your leaving her again."

"Oh, poor Felicity. I'm so sorry I did this to you. How can you ever trust me again? That's one of the thoughts that swirls through my head over and over and over when I try to sleep."

"Right." Teddy said. "Like Felicity, when you were small, you believed that if you had been good enough, terrible things wouldn't have happened. You believed you were bad, and selfish, but if you tried hard enough to be good, perhaps you could prevent other horrible things from happening. The truth, though, was that the people you needed weren't there for you. It must have been unbearable."

"But Teddy, I didn't consciously think or know any of that. I just knew what happened had to be my fault. I didn't see anyone else to blame but me. It terrified me."

"In the same way, perhaps Felicity just 'knows' it was her fault you left. That's child-logic. Starlight explained to me that child-logic takes over when the adults children most love and depend on prove undependable—even if it's through abandoning them by dying, like our Mammy and Da. In child-logic, it's easier to feel some control than to feel unprotected and helpless when the universe seems to hurt us unpredictably and arbitrarily."

Cally sighed. "I'm trying to understand what you're saying, Teddy. But I'm not quite grasping it yet in my heart. My soul."

"Children aren't capable of the responsibilities that fall to them in a situation like ours, Cally. It's easier if they believe themselves to have almost magical powers. Like the ability to cause a baby's death just by thinking it or saying it. If that's the case, they also have the ability, they believe, to not cause death. To protect life. Your faery story helped you maintain that belief. You had—in your mind—a logical way to explain the bad things that happened. You didn't do it directly, no. The faeries did it. Because you didn't give them your mirror."

"Wait—are you saying faeries don't exist? But Miss Hilda talked to them! How could she have known to tell me they wanted my mirror? I never told her about my mirror."

"Whether they exist or not almost doesn't matter, Cally. I'm talking about your belief in them as part of your own magical powers."

Cally stopped walking. "My head is spinning, Teddy. I don't think I can take in any more tonight. I must think about all this in the light of day. It's like you're shaking up everything I've built my life on. My entire understanding of who I am."

Teddy turned around and tucked Cally's hand into his arm. "I'm sorry I've said so much all at once, Cally. It's taken me years to unscramble my own head on some of these things. I can't expect you to absorb my work of years in just one conversation. I'm glad to talk again about all this, in small doses and when you're ready. Starlight is the one who has most helped me sort it out. Perhaps she can explain it better."

"I'm still afraid to go to sleep," said Cally in a small voice.

"Because you're afraid of your nightmares?"

"Yes. In the daytime, I know I didn't cause Mrs. Murphy to die. Charlie had told me it could happen any time, because of her defective heart. But at night it still seems like I would have hurt her family if I went to the wedding. How could I go on living if I did go and the things I dreamed about came true? The risk was too great." Cally began weeping again.

Teddy guided Cally up the steps. After a moment, as she wiped her eyes, Teddy said, "I don't suppose you told anyone about your nightmares."

"Of course not."

"They just went round and round in your own head, becoming every day more unbearable."

"True. How could anyone understand? They have a wrong idea of me, that I'm a good person. They've told me and shown me again and again how much they love me. But they don't really know me."

"Maybe that's what you feared most of all," said Teddy. "That they might discover things about you that you don't want them to know. About believing yourself a danger to people you love. But Cally, why don't you have the same fear here in America?"

"Because—because the faeries don't have power here. Only in Ireland. At least that's what I've always thought. Maybe I worry Cora and Thomas and the rest of the Malcomsons will think badly of me. And Ryan . . . "

Teddy took her by the shoulders again. "Cally, look at me. No, don't start crying again. Listen. You're not alone anymore. You've been brave enough to tell me about your nightmares and your fears, at least some of them. For tonight, let me hold them for you. And just—sleep."

"But it won't be fair if you can't sleep."

"I can sleep, don't worry about that. I can hold your bad dreams and your fears for you without believing them myself. And tomorrow you can decide if you want them back. I suspect you haven't slept deeply and peacefully for a very long time. Receive sleep tonight as a gift."

"I—I'll try. Thank you."

"You're welcome. Good night, Cally."

Cally reached out and hugged him. "Good night, little brother. I love you."

Grove, Oklahoma, Sunday evening June 18, 1905

A knock sounded on the door of Teddy's bungalow. "Telegram," shouted a young voice.

Teddy opened the door. "Thank you." The lad waved as he pedaled away on his bicycle.

"It's addressed to me, but it's actually for you, Cally." Teddy handed her the paper.

"It's from Ryan," breathed Cally, holding the paper to her heart. "He wants to talk to me. I can't believe it. Is—is that possible? And the Malcomsons will return a week late because of repairs needed on the ship."

"There's a telephone at the post office," said Starlight, who sat rocking Aiyana. "I'll go with you when it opens in the morning to ask them for a time you can receive a call. And then we can send a reply to Ryan."

"Wha—what will I tell him?"

"I recommend the truth," said Starlight. "I've found it the most effective way to communicate in the long run."

Cally sat down. "My mirror is in the bag I packed for Ireland, which they must have with them. Should I ask Ryan to ask Dugan to take it to Miss Hilda to give to the faeries?"

"Teddy told me about your mirror. You think maybe that will solve everything?" asked Starlight.

"It's something I can do," said Cally. "And Miss Hilda can ask them if they are satisfied and will stop hurting our family. And then I'll know whether that piece of things can be resolved."

"You truly believe in these faeries," said Teddy, taking Aiyana from Starlight before he sat down. The baby gurgled and patted his face.

"You don't?" asked Cally, surprised. "Maybe you were too young to remember . . ."

"Remember what?"

"The stories Da and Mammy told us, about all the people in Ireland who saw faeries and leprechauns and púcas and selkies. Mammy saw a faery herself. And Miss Hilda talked to them. She was called a wise woman. Everyone went to her for advice. I never told her about my mirror. She must have learned about it when she asked the faeries what they wanted from me."

"Interesting," said Starlight. "The Oneida see little people too. But for us, they are always good. Their job is to help humans, not ever to hurt them."

Teddy grabbed a carved wooden doll for Aiyana to play with, set her on the floor, and turned his attention to Cally. "Before our talk last night, I didn't know you believed in faeries. I do remember some of Mammy and

Da's stories. But I always thought they were just bedtime stories, like in those fairy tale books Miss Anthony loaned us. I never thought they were real, or true, or whatever the right word is."

"I suppose it wouldn't do any harm to give your mirror to Miss Hilda," said Starlight slowly. "At least then you might be able to separate in your mind the harm you believe the faeries caused and the harm you believe you yourself caused to people you love. Those two things seem to me to be separate, but for you they are tangled together."

"If I return to Ireland, the faeries will remember they are angry with me and then they will hurt the people I care about," said Cally.

"I know how much that little mirror has always mattered to you, Cally. Can you tell me more about that?" asked Teddy.

Tears brimmed in Cally's eyes. "Did you know that Cathleen gave me that mirror?"

"Cathleen Malcomson?"

"Yes. She and Charlie were on a trip, and needed a repair to their carriage right when they passed through Killeagh. I went into Killeagh with Uncle Dugan that day to take my eggs to the market. I must have been three or four years old. We were walking by the Old Thatch Inn when a carriage stopped, and a beautiful lady and a lad got out. The lady was looking into a mirror fixing her hair. She saw me watching her and asked Uncle Dugan if I could look in her mirror. It was the first time I ever saw my face. Then she gave it to me."

"How did you figure out that lady was Mrs. Malcomson?"

"I didn't. Cathleen did. When she and Charlie went to Killeagh to tell Uncle Dugan and Aunt Aisling that Da had drowned, they met at the Old Thatch, and Cathleen remembered being there before. Uncle Dugan looks so much like me, she figured it out."

"Amazing."

"Yes. To me, that wee mirror seemed to say I mattered in the world somehow. The lady was so beautiful and rich, and she *saw* me. Do you know what I mean? She looked into my eyes, and smiled, and I felt seen. Cherished.

Cared for. I don't know the right words." Cally sucked in air to keep from crying again.

"So, giving away your mirror felt like giving away your sense of worth?" asked Starlight.

Cally released her breath. "Yes. You understand. I'm so glad someone understands."

"Then how do you feel about it now? The idea of giving your mirror to the faeries?" asked Starlight.

Cally frowned and thought for a moment. "I—I'm not sure—but I think it might be all right. I know now there are people who love me, for whom I'm not invisible. I have a vocation. I know what I'm good at. I've survived hard things. I have Felicity, who needs me. Ryan—dear Ryan—sees a future for us together. Or at least he did, before—" Again, Cally sucked in air to keep herself from crying.

"Before you left the ship," said Teddy.

"Yes. And God—I hope you won't think I'm crazy, but God talks to me. He tells me things. He's been telling me not to be afraid. I heard him say that before I got on the ship. But my fear was so huge it drowned out his voice. Until after, when I was exhausted from running and didn't know where to go, he told me again not to be afraid. And to come to you."

Cally sat back in her chair and took a drink of water. "Whew. I've never said all this to anyone."

"But when the faeries first asked you for the mirror—" said Starlight.

"I thought without it I would become nothing. I thought I would dissolve into a puddle on the floor. I thought I wouldn't be able to take care of Teddy."

Cally picked up Aiyana and cuddled the baby close. "I used to look in the mirror to confirm I was still *there* and alive and *someone.* Especially after Paddy made me become a lad. So often I felt invisible and wasn't sure if I—if I even existed. It's hard to explain."

"I think I understand," said Starlight. "You were small, and alone, with hardly any adult affirmation and support. From infancy we know who we are because of how others communicate how they see us. *That* they see us."

"And I had to care for Teddy. But I couldn't do it well enough." Cally gave up trying not to cry. She sobbed as if her tears carried all the unbearable weight of those impossibly lonely years.

Aiyana looked at her mother, who nodded to her. The baby threw her arms around Cally and nuzzled her neck, holding her tight while the tears flowed.

Scooting close to her husband, who wept too, Starlight sat with her arms extended, palms up, her lips moving in silent supplication.

Finally, an unmeasurable time later, quietness stole into the room. Aiyana released her hold on Cally and reached out for her mother. Teddy went to get them all drinks of water, then knelt before Cally's chair and lay his head in her lap. She stroked his hair and to her surprise, found herself singing their old bedtime song, the one Aisling had taught her an eternity ago:

In peace I will lie down and sleep, for you alone will keep me safe.

Without speaking more, each of them went to their place of rest.

The man at the post office scheduled their call for 9:30 Tuesday morning, 3:30 in the afternoon Dublin time. He click-clacked the information to Ryan at his hotel in Dublin and charged Cally three dollars for the telegram.

"Starlight, would it be all right if I—if I take a walk by the river by myself?"

"Yes, of course. You know how to get back to the house?"

"I think so. Yes."

"Then Aiyana and I will go home and weed before the day gets hotter."

Cally thanked the post office man and stood a moment outside, orienting herself by the direction Starlight had taken. *Then this way is the river. I need to think about Starlight's idea that I simply tell Ryan the truth. And I need to decide whether to give the faeries my mirror.*

Grove Post Office, Tuesday, June 20, 1905

While waiting for Ryan's call, Cally posted a letter to Sister Irmena telling her the voyage back from Ireland had been delayed a week. "I won't be back at the hospital until July 10. I'll work hard to make up the time," she wrote. *I don't want to tell her I won't be on that voyage. At least not right now.*

The post office attendant handed Cally the telephone.

"Ryan, is it you? I'm having trouble hearing you—must be because you're so far away . . . yes, that's a bit clearer—no, I lost you again. Oh, this is so frustrating. I want to hear everything . . . You want to hear me too? I want to tell you . . . Ryan, this isn't working. I'll send a telegram after we hang up, and then write you a letter. I hope you're well. I love you."

Cally hung up the telephone and glared at it. *SO disappointing!! I thought it would be as clear as when I call Kansas City from Idaho. But Ryan didn't sound angry.*

"All finished? That will be ten dollars," said the post office man.

Cally gasped. "Ten dollars? But I couldn't even hear him!"

"Ireland is far away, ma'am."

"I have to send another telegram with the most important things I needed to communicate, because he couldn't hear me either."

"Yes, ma'am. You can write your message here."

For the second time, Cally filled out the form for a telegram. "Ryan, love, stay Ireland. I'm fine. Give Dugan mirror from my bag to Hilda for faeries. Writing letter. Cally."

"Three more dollars for the telegram. That will be thirteen altogether, ma'am."

"But—you're taking all the money I have. How can you ask so much?"

"Ireland is far away, ma'am."

Cally trudged out of the post office and turned toward Teddy and Starlight's home. *I feel angry. I could be with Ryan and Felicity in Ireland. I want to go home, not to Kansas City but to Idaho. But I still have the rest of the summer with Sister Irmena before I can move to Hansen. God, why is everything so messed up? Why did I mess everything up?*

Receive my peace. Let it shield your heart.

Cally stopped. She said aloud, "Is that you, God?"

Again, the thought came clearly, not garbled like the telephone. *Receive my peace. Let it shield your heart.*

"I'm listening, God."

Rest. Trust me.

Cally turned around and walked to the river. She lay down on the grass and fell fast asleep.

Baby hands on her face woke Cally. Aiyana laughed when she opened her eyes. Turning away from the bright sun overhead, Cally looked into Starlight's dark smiling eyes and felt joy run through her, from her head to her toes.

"We found you! And we brought a picnic! Are you hungry, Cally?"

Thank you, God, for giving me this precious sister. And this precious niece.

Let my peace surround you, Cally. Rest. Trust. Enjoy.

Dublin, Ireland, Tuesday evening, June 20, 1905

Ryan knocked on Thomas and Cora's hotel room door and handed Cally's telegram to Thomas. He heard Cora ask, "Who is it, Thomas?"

Thomas turned and said, "It's Ryan, Cora. He has a telegram from Cally. Can he come in?"

"Just a second," said Cora. She appeared a moment later in her dressing gown, her hair damp. "Come in, Ryan. Sorry, I just took my bath."

"We can wait until morning to talk about this," said Ryan.

"No, let's do it now," said Thomas. "We have an early outing tomorrow with the children, and then Dugan and Aisling will start back to Killeagh. If we find Cally's mirror, we should give it to them at breakfast."

"Cally's mirror?" asked Cora.

Thomas handed her the telegram.

"I haven't opened her bag," said Cora. "We can do it now."

Thomas pulled a suitcase from the closet and set it on the bed. He undid the clasps and then stood back while Cora pulled back the straps and opened the case. On top was a large, carefully wrapped package with a card labeled "For Charlie and Laoise."

"Oh my," said Cora. "It's a good thing we didn't carry this all the way back to Kansas City!" She lifted the package and set it on the dresser. "I'll leave this with Colin. Now, where would Cally have put her wee mirror? Maybe in one of the pockets." She unsnapped the inside pockets one by one, until her fingers touched the cold round metal of Cally's mirror.

"Do either of you feel uncomfortable about this?" asked Ryan. "I don't know anything about Irish faeries, but I do know Cally loves this little mirror. She always carries it with her. Why would she feel she must give it up?"

"Perhaps that's the only way she can come to Ireland feeling safe," said Cora. "Whether the faeries are real or not, they are real in her mind. It's a way of paying what she feels is a debt."

"What about this Miss Hilda—is she honest? What would keep her from just keeping the mirror for herself?" asked Ryan.

"Does it matter?" asked Thomas. "Either way, Cally will feel she did what she could. I believe it can give her a measure of relief from a burden she has carried since she was small, before she left Ireland."

"All right," said Ryan slowly. "But it makes me sad to see Cally give up something so precious to her."

"Perhaps she doesn't need it anymore," said Cora. "In any case, it's Cally's request of us. I have a small cloth bag I can tuck it in. There. We'll give it to Dugan and Aisling at breakfast."

"Ryan, after the huge disappointment of your telephone call yesterday, what are you thinking now about how long you'll stay in Ireland?" asked Thomas.

"I think I'll go back with you on Friday," said Ryan. "With Priscilla's help today, I found out a great deal about my relatives. With Cally, it would have been fun to try to visit them, but by myself—"

"You seemed quite engaged with the conversation yesterday with Colin," said Thomas.

"Yes, Irish nationalism fascinates me. Were you surprised at how involved Colin is? He's not Catholic—he's in the Church of Ireland, a part of society the

Catholics seem to view as oppositional to Irish freedom. Colin's son Desmond certainly seemed surprised."

"He was, yes. I was gratified to learn Colin hopes to achieve Irish independence without violence."

"That's what his hero, Arthur Griffith, who is starting the new political party Sinn Féin, seems to want. Like Desmond, I wonder whether it's realistic."

"Well, we won't solve this tonight. I'd love to talk with you more about it another time, though, Ryan. There certainly does seem to be a groundswell of enthusiasm for trying once more to achieve separation from England," said Thomas.

"You two can talk as long as you like. I'm going to bed," said Cora, yawning. "See you at breakfast, Ryan?"

"Maybe. If I can sleep, I may skip breakfast. I haven't slept well since we got here."

"That's understandable," said Thomas. "Sleep as long as you can. We'll look for you at luncheon, then. Good night."

"Good night," said Ryan. "And—thank you for taking care of Cally's request about the mirror. I'm not sure I would have reached the same decision, but I honor your confidence you're doing the right thing."

Ryan shut the door quietly behind him. *God? Are you there? Did we make the right choice?*

Don't be afraid, my son. All will be well.

Ryan, halfway down the hallway to his room, stopped, stunned. *Is that you, God? I've never heard you speak to me before.*

Don't be afraid.

☙❧

"Good morning, Dugan, Aisling, children," said Cora, smiling at each one. "Mmm, those look like grand choices for breakfast. Are you all ready for our outing to Dublin Castle?"

"Good morning, Cora," said Aisling. "We're ready and excited. I've never been there myself."

"Dugan, could I speak with you for a moment?"

Cora and Dugan stepped a few feet away from the table. Cora handed Dugan the small cloth bag containing Cally's mirror and asked him to take it to Miss Hilda to give to the faeries.

"But Cora," said Dugan. "Miss Hilda died of old age several months ago. We've lost our contact with the faeries."

CHAPTER 23

Billy

Fermoy, Monday, June 5, 1905

BILLY KNOCKED ON MR. MACDONAGH'S door. "Excuse me, sir. I've been studying for my Gaelic exam, and I don't understand the verb conjugations. I wondered if you could help me?"

Mr. MacDonagh pulled out his pocket watch. "I can give you fifteen minutes, William. I see you have your notebook. Show me what you don't understand. . . . Yes, I see. Your problem is not so much the verbs, but the word order. Come in. Sit down."

Ten minutes later, Billy gave a sigh of relief. "I get it now. You are such a good teacher."

Mr. MacDonagh smiled. "It's my theory that anyone can teach what they love. We have a few more minutes, William. Tell me about your conversation with Mr. Murphy."

Billy's brow wrinkled. "I have one question for you, sir. Do you support a violent revolution, or do you believe like Mr. Murphy that it may be possible to achieve independence peacefully?"

"I would like a peaceful process, of course, if it can yield results. But, William, that approach has been tried for centuries. It has never worked. Did Mr. Murphy explain how he hopes this time may be different?"

"He seems excited about a new political party. I think it's to be called Sinn Féin."

"Ah, he's been influenced by Arthur Griffith."

"He did mention that name, sir."

"I can see this must be a longer discussion than we have time for now. William, would you be willing to go with me to a Gathering in Kilkenny next weekend? I promise, I will protect you from whoever it was who tried to hurt you."

"Tried to kill me, sir. I don't see how you can make that promise."

"All right. I will do all in my power to protect you, William."

"I'll have to think about it. You weren't there. You don't know how terrifying it was."

"Yet you returned here without a scratch, William. Something about your story doesn't add up."

The old woman. What will Mr. MacDonagh think if I tell him about her? I think I better ask her first. She seems to want to stay out of sight.

"William?"

"Yes, sir. I'll think about it, sir. I do have exams. I planned to study."

"You're right. Perhaps this isn't the best place or timing. But when your exams are over, let's plan to go to another Gathering, so you can hear firsthand some of the great thinkers of our movement. I believe there is one scheduled for Galway at the beginning of July."

"That sounds interesting. Thank you, sir, for your help with the Gaelic."

"You're welcome. I expect you to do well in your exams, William. Not just Gaelic. All of them."

"I'll do my best, sir. Good night."

Thursday, June 22, 1905

Billy opened the door of his classroom after his maths exam and bumped into Mr. MacDonagh, causing Fred, behind him, to bump into Billy. Fred was just saying, "If I passed that exam it's because of all your help, William. Oh, hello, Mr. MacDonagh."

"Hello, Fred. William has been helping you with maths, eh? Good for you, William. I need a word with you, please." Mr. MacDonagh turned toward the stairs.

"Can Fred come? We're on our way to throw some balls around. Bleed off some stress from all these tests."

"He may if you wish him to. I've received a telegram. From your uncle."

Billy stopped. Fred bumped into him again.

"Wh—what did he say?"

"Let's go to my rooms and talk there."

Billy turned worried eyes to his friend. Fred squeezed his shoulder.

When the boys were seated on his sofa, Mr. MacDonagh handed the telegram to Billy. He read, "Send Billy home. His mother very ill. Must see him. Cecil Avery."

Billy turned as white as he was capable of turning. "My mother . . . " he whispered. "But how? What about my exams?"

"That's what we need to figure out," said Mr. MacDonagh. "I—"

A knock sounded on the door. "A telegram for you, sir."

Billy gripped Fred's leg. "Maybe she already—"

"No, William. She didn't already die," said Mr. MacDonagh after reading the telegram. "This is the answer to your 'how.' Your uncle asks you to travel this Friday on the *Lion III* from Waterford with his friend Thomas Malcomson. You're to meet him at the wharf at eight a.m. He has already bought your ticket."

"Uncle Cecil has a friend who is a Malcomson?"

"I don't know, William. Read for yourself."

Billy accepted the telegram, glanced at it, and began to tremble. "Wh—what about my last exams, sir?"

"You have done excellently in each one so far. We can make up the last two at the beginning of the next term. Assuming you return to us."

"I want to return, sir. The—the ship sails tomorrow."

"Yes. You'll have to catch the train tonight. I'll take you to the station right after supper and send a return telegram to your uncle telling him you're on your way."

"But—sir—what if my mother—" Billy's eyes flooded with tears.

"We will pray for her. And for your travel. Won't we, Fred?"

"Yes, sir," said Fred. "Every day."

"I—I don't have many clothes," Billy realized out loud. "I don't have money for the train."

"I can give you a set of my clothes," said Fred. "You know my mum—she'll be happy I helped you."

"And I'll pay for the train and give you some money for breakfast when you reach Waterford," said Mr. MacDonagh. "Now, William. You have two hours before supper. I suggest you do as you had planned with Fred—go throw some balls around. You have even more stress to bleed off now. I suggest a fast run around the practice field as well. Return in time to bathe and pack before supper. Then you'll be ready to go."

"Yes, sir." Billy breathed deep and squeezed his eyes shut.

Fred stood, grasped Billy's hand, and pulled him to his feet. "You can do this, William. I know you can. Come choose a set of clothes to pack."

"I'll see you after supper," said Mr. MacDonagh.

I wish I could talk to the old woman.

Billy finished the roll and tea he had bought for his breakfast at the Waterford port, then walked out of the shop and looked around the pier, hoping to identify someone who might be Thomas Malcomson. In the crowd of people, he finally spotted a family gathered around a sign saying, "Lion III Departure 10:00 for New York City."

"One, two, three, four children," Billy counted aloud. *One boy, three girls, and one extra adult. I wonder what it would be like to grow up in a family like that.*

Suddenly the boy broke away from his parents and ran full tilt in Billy's direction, yelling "Billy! Billy! I know it's you!"

Startled, Billy pulled back as the boy threw himself toward him, arms wide open for a hug. The boy stumbled, and Billy grabbed him before he fell.

By then, the rest of the family, also running, had reached Billy, all talking at once. The mother noticed his confusion, and with the help of the father, stopped the girls from piling into a group hug. Only the second man stood back.

"Children, give Billy some space," she said. "He doesn't know who we are. Billy, my name is Cora Malcomson. This is my husband, Thomas, and my children, Shane, Shauna, and Josie. And this is my niece, Felicity, and her soon-to-be father, Ryan."

Soon-to-be father? Grasping the name Thomas, Billy nodded to them. "Who—how—that is—I don't know—"

"Of course, you don't," nodded Thomas. "We—"

"But we know all about you!" interrupted Shane. "We've been looking for you for almost a year!"

An older woman joined the group. "This is my mother-in-law, Cathleen. She's not trav—" said Cora. She noticed Billy staring and stopped.

"I know you," said Billy.

"Yes. We met on the ship last year. I came to ask your forgiveness for how I treated you. I am so very sorry. A great deal of suffering could have been avoided if I had given credit to what you told me. Can you forgive me, Billy? I know now that you belong to us. You're part of our family. You are our cousin. Your father was my husband's uncle."

Billy's eyes streamed with tears. He rubbed his eyes, trying to compose himself. A blast sounded from the ship's horn.

"It's time to board," said Thomas. "Come, children."

Cathleen stood with Billy as Thomas and Cora steered the children toward the gangplank, Ryan holding Felicity's hand.

"I—I forgive you," managed Billy. "You're the first Malcomson who has believed me."

"You belong to a whole big family who believes in you and wants to welcome you, Billy. Thomas and Cora are only one part of our clan. They'll tell you the whole story. May I just say a prayer for you and for your mother Melody before you board?"

Billy nodded, wiping his eyes while Cathleen prayed a short prayer for healing and for blessing on the trip. She gave him a quick hug, waved to the family waiting by the gangplank, and walked away through the crowd.

Shane once again broke away from his parents and ran to accompany Billy to the ship, talking excitedly all the way. Billy didn't register anything he said.

Thomas walked beside him up the gangplank. "You've been traveling all night, is that right?"

"Yes, sir."

"You must be exhausted. And all this is quite a shock. Shane and Ryan will share a stateroom with you, but would you like a little time to yourself? I know our family can be rather overpowering when a person first meets us."

Billy nodded, relief flooding his body. He followed Thomas to a door, walked in, and collapsed on the lower bunk.

He only woke when Shane knocked on the door and then entered to say, "Billy, it's time for lunch. Are you hungry? Come on. After lunch I can show you around the ship. The captain is my friend."

He doesn't know I'm already familiar with this ship. But last time I boarded her, I slept with the sailors, not in a stateroom. And I worked harder than I ever had before in my life. I don't want to see the captain. He might remember that I deserted after Mrs. Malcomson didn't believe me. I could be in some kind of trouble.

"Billy, come with me."

Billy pushed himself out of the bunk and allowed Shane to lead him to the dining room.

"Billy, we're so sorry your mother is sick," said Cora, when everyone settled at the table with their food. "The last time we saw her she already wasn't well, but apparently, she's taken a turn for the worse. Since we heard, I've been praying for her. A lot."

"You—you know my mother?" asked Billy, eying his plate. *I've never in my life eaten food like this. How many more surprises will there be this day?*

"Yes!" exclaimed Shane. "We met her in Idaho last summer. And we visited her after she moved to Fish Haven with your grandmother and Ebony and—" Shane stopped, as Cora looked at him. "I'm sorry. Mummy says I must tell you everything more slowly."

"We'll have lots of time while we sail to tell each other our stories," said Cora quietly. "I know it's a lot to take in. We can take it as slowly as you like."

"Thank you, ma'am. Mrs. Malcomson."

"Hmm. Thomas, what should Billy call us? Mister and missus seems too formal."

"We're cousins, right? All of us are Billy's cousins," said Thomas.

"Like Felicity is my cousin?" asked Josie.

"Yes. Like that," said Thomas.

"If Billy is my cousin, is Ebony my cousin too?" asked Shauna.

"You know Ebony?" asked Billy.

"Yes! She came to help us when Aunt Cally was sick," said Shauna.

"Ebony is my second beautifullest person," said Josie. "Aunt Laoise is my first beautifullest and Ebony is my second. I wish I could look like her."

Billy laughed, then stopped when he realized Josie was serious.

"No one answered my question," said Shauna. "I want Ebony to be my cousin too."

"Hmm. Technically, I don't think she is. Right, Thomas? She has no Malcomson connection," responded her mother.

"Except by friendship, kindness, and generosity," said Thomas. "But we can love her just the same."

"Aww," said Shauna and Josie at the same time, both frowning.

"So, what do we call cousins from an older generation?" asked Cora. "What did you call Silas and Priscilla when you were a child, Thomas?"

"I called them Cousin Silas and Cousin Priscilla. That seems to work better in Ireland than in the United States, though. I don't remember when I started calling them just Silas and Priscilla."

"Then shall we be just Thomas and Cora for Billy?"

"I think that would be simplest. Is that all right with you, Billy?" asked Thomas.

"I guess so, sir. It might take some getting used to," said Billy.

"Good, then that's settled," said Thomas. "Now, I've been thinking we should tell Billy the story of the treasure hunt, and how I met his Uncle Cecil."

"You're the treasure, Billy!" yelled Shane.

"I'm—what?" said Billy.

"He'll understand everything better if we tell it in order, don't you think?" said Cora. "We could tell him about one clue each meal. How about that? But let's start the treasure hunt story at supper, all right? For this lunch, I would love to know anything you want to tell us, Billy, about your time in Ireland. Where are you living? Are you going to school? Do you like Ireland?"

Good. Something familiar I *can tell* them. *I think this voyage will be as challenging as learning Gaelic.*

ଔଷ

Billy and Shane ran down the gangplank to the New York City pier laughing and talking.

"Back in America! That was a long trip!" yelled Shane as his feet touched the dock.

"I've been gone even longer than you," said Billy.

"How long?" asked Shane.

"Almost two years. I left Idaho on my thirteenth birthday. Now I'm almost fifteen."

"Are you more American or more Irish?" asked Shane.

"I don't know. Some of both, I guess." Billy looked around the busy port. "I'm glad I can travel with your family as far as Kansas City."

"I wish you could stay longer with us. But I know your mother is sick," said Shane.

"I hope she's still alive," said Billy.

"Billy! Shane! Time to go to the train station!" called Cora. "Ready, girls? Thanks for your help with the baggage, Ryan."

As they walked behind a porter pushing a wagon loaded with their luggage, Thomas said, "I'll call Cecil from the train station, Billy, to find out how your mother is doing."

ଔଷ

Montpelier, Idaho, Wednesday, July 5, 1905

Billy paced the Montpelier train station, quiet now since the bustle of arrivals and departures had eased. *I wonder how long Uncle Cecil will take to get here. Whew, I'm tired. What a long journey. Almost a week on the ocean, overnight in New York City, then six days on the train to here. My mother was still alive when Thomas called Uncle Cecil in New York, but I don't know what's happened since then. It was hard leaving everyone in Kansas City.*

Billy sat on a bench, watched a dog sniff around the empty station, then stood and paced again the length of the platform. *It's hotter than blazes, and I already drank the water I got at the station in Salt Lake City. I'll ask the ticket seller. Oops, no I won't. His sign says, "Back at 2:00." Oh, I see a pump kind of thing. I wonder if it works.*

Billy lifted the handle and lowered it a few times, and to his delight a gush of water poured out. He managed to put his whole head under the stream while still pumping with one hand.

"Don't take the water for the whole city," said a voice, laughing.

"Uncle Cecil!" Billy threw his arms around the big man, wetting his shirt.

"Let me have a look at you, Billy." Uncle Cecil held his nephew away from him and looked him over. "You've grown up, boy. You were a small child last time I saw you. You'll need all your strength for these next days, but I'll be with you. And God will help us."

"My mother?"

"In her last days. Just waiting for you, I believe."

"I'll get my bag." Billy ran to the bench where he had left it, plump now with the suit Ryan had given him in Kansas City as a farewell gift, saying "You may have need of this."

"How long will it take to get to Fish Haven?"

"About two and a half hours, I figure, since you haven't done this before. Do you know how to ride a bicycle? I borrowed one from my friend Ezra Martin."

"I do, yes."

Billy followed Uncle Cecil around the station and saw two bicycles parked by the road. One had a large metal crate attached to the back.

“I started using a bicycle when my horse died. It’s faster and cheaper than a wagon. Can’t carry as much, but for the most part it works quite well,” explained Uncle Cecil.

“It will feel good to ride a bicycle, after all those days sitting on a train,” said Billy. Mr. Martin’s bike was blue, with wide wheels. “I haven’t seen a bicycle like this in Ireland.”

“The wide wheels are better for the sandy road,” said Uncle Cecil. “I don’t know whether we’ll be able to talk much on the way, so let me just say this: Melody has been desperate to see you. I think she wants to ask your forgiveness before she dies.”

“My forgiveness?”

“Yes. She told us she had not been a good mother to you, and she has mourned that since you left. You have a couple of hours now to think about that, and about whether you can extend grace and mercy to her.”

“Grace and mercy?”

“Mercy for what she did, and grace for what she didn’t do. She’s changed since you last saw her, Billy. She repented of the life she led and allowed God in to heal her deep wounds. She reconciled with your grandmother Minnie and has made amends as well as she could for the long years of estrangement. I hope you will be able to find some love in your heart for her. She’s walked a long, hard, road and is ready now to meet her Maker.”

I’ve walked a long, hard road too—mostly alone. She wasn’t much of a mother to me. I guess that’s what Uncle Cecil means by extending mercy and grace.

“I’ll think about it, Uncle Cecil.”

“I’m heartened by the fact that you dropped everything to come all this way to see her. I’m grateful, Billy. Now, put on this hat to protect you from the sun. If you need a rest, just yell at me and stop. I’ve put a bottle of water in the basket of your bicycle. I make this trip almost every day, so I’m used to it, but I know it may be challenging for you. Mary and Ebony will have a meal ready for us when we arrive. All right? Ready to go?”

“Yes, sir.”

This bike is a little different from my dragonfly bicycle—I should say the old woman's dragonfly bicycle. And the road is kind of powdery. But if Uncle Cecil can do it, I can do it.

ᘓᘐ

"Mama, they're here!"

Billy saw his cousin Ebony, a year younger than him, run from the front porch into the house, and then come out again with his Aunt Mary just as he and Uncle Cecil pulled up to the fence around their property. For the last half hour, the road had run near Bear Lake, and the sand had changed to small pebbles, not easy to navigate on a bicycle. Billy could hear small waves lapping the back yard of the house.

Aunt Mary and Ebony ran down the porch steps and out the gate to greet them. An elderly woman emerged from the house, waving and smiling.

This is my family. The thought stunned Billy. *I never thought I had a family. I only remember meeting my grandmother once, a very long time ago. When I was small, and my father was still with us. There was a big fight between my mother and my grandmother. We never saw her again.*

Billy gave his head a shake as Ebony grabbed his hand and pulled him up the steps to where his grandmother had sat down in a rocker.

"Here he is, Miz Minnie, our wandering boy," said Ebony.

"Come close, Billy. My eyesight ain't what it was. I haven't seen you since you was three years old."

Her voice is ancient. Creaky.

Billy came close and leaned in to hug her. She threw her arms around him and wept.

"My long-lost boy. Lord God, I praise you. I praise you! For you are good, and your mercies are everlasting. My precious child, how I have prayed for you. How I have longed to see you."

When his grandmother let him go, Billy knelt beside her, holding her soft, wrinkly hands in his. "Truly, you prayed for me, Grandmother?"

"We call her Miz Minnie," said Ebony. "Because she says us calling her Grandmother makes her feel old."

"But—"

Miz Minnie's laugh cackled. "Of course, I'se old, child. But you don't have to rub it in. Miz Minnie suits me just fine." She sobered. "Yes, Billy. I have prayed for you every day of your life. If I'm not mistaken, you had a birthday yesterday. Fifteen now, isn't that right?"

Yes. I turned fifteen all alone on the train. Felt quite sorry for myself too. "Yes, ma'am. Miz Minnie."

"Well, fifteen is worth celebrating, and I believe Mary and Ebony have prepared a birthday feast for you. But we'll all enjoy it more if you take a bath first, young man."

"My mother?"

"She's asleep right now. Ebony, show your cousin where to take a bath. And don't tarry, young man. There's fish chowder and I don't know what all waiting for us."

"Yes, ma'am." *A bath will feel amazing. And I'm so hungry my navel is touching my backbone, as Miss Trent at the brothel used to say.*

The meal was indeed a feast, topped off with a huge chocolate cake and fifteen candles and everyone cheering and laughing and telling jokes. *Why did I miss all this growing up?*

The noise must have woken his mother, because Aunt Mary disappeared down the hallway and returned beckoning to Billy. For a moment, he froze, staring down the hallway as if a wild beast awaited him.

Ebony took his hand. "It will be all right, Billy," she whispered. "Do you want me to go with you?"

Billy nodded and held her hand tight. The pressure on his chest seemed to chain him to the floor, but Ebony gave a little tug and walked with him to a half-open door at the end of the hallway. She pushed the door open and then stood aside, nodding to him. "You can do this," her eyes seemed to say.

Taking a deep breath, Billy walked in. The curtain was pulled open to a beautiful view of the lake. His mother lay propped on several pillows, her eyes fixed on his face.

"Billy, thank you for coming." Her voice, though quiet, was still vibrant.

Billy sat in the chair beside her bed, taking her outstretched hand. The mother he remembered had been strong and beautiful, looking much like Ebony did now. This woman was frail, her eyes the only live thing in her ravaged face.

"Mother," said Billy, and couldn't say anything else.

"My beloved son," said Melody. "I have longed to see you. I only realized how much I love you after you left me. Can you forgive me, my child? I have asked God to heal you from the harm I caused you."

She started coughing and pointed to a glass of water on a small table beside her bed. Billy helped her sit up enough to drink, feeling her ribs through her nightgown. She lay back, her eyes closed, exhausted, giving Billy a moment to think about her question, one he had wrestled with during the long bicycle ride from Montpelier.

"I forgive you," Billy said softly when his mother opened her eyes.

"Thank you, my son. I have an idea of what that has cost you. Now I can die in peace. But I want to give you my blessing." She stopped and gathered her energy. "Billy, my child, I bless you. May you grow strong and good. May you know God's wonderful joy. And may you be a blessing to others."

Her voice faded away and her eyes closed. Billy waited, unsure whether she wanted to say more. But her eyes remained closed, her hand lax in his. "Mother?" He touched her face. There was no response. "Uncle Cecil!" Billy yelled, and threw himself over her body, sobbing. "Mother, don't leave me now! We haven't had any time—it's too soon!"

Uncle Cecil touched Billy's shoulder, and knelt beside the bed, reaching for his sister's wrist. "She waited for you, Billy," he said gently. "She's been holding on for days, in the hope that you were coming. Look at her face, son. She died in peace."

Uncle Cecil gathered Billy into his arms, lifted him as if he were a small child, and sat in the chair with Billy in his lap as they wept together. Aunt Mary and Ebony helped Miz Minnie into the room and seated her in a chair on the other side of the bed.

Later, Billy gave a name to the sacred time that followed. He called it, "Homecoming."

ଔଷ

The funeral took place on Friday in a tiny church in Fish Haven, Melody's body buried in a cemetery beside the lake. Billy wore the suit Ryan had given him. The church choir sang, "Give Me Jesus" and "There's a Wideness in God's Mercy": *For the Love of God is broader than the measures of the mind, and the heart of the Eternal is most wonderfully kind.* Billy repeated the words in his mind, wondering if they were true. Uncle Cecil spoke about his sister's life—most of which Billy didn't know—with tenderness that surprised him. The fisherman-pastor spoke of mercy and of grace. Then the congregation sang with the choir, "I'll Fly Away."

Billy heard "I'm sorry for your loss" and said "Pleased to meet you" more times than he cared to count. Along with the church people, Uncle Cecil's friend Ezra Martin was there, and his daughter Connie, and her husband Michael, and a handful of friends from Fish Haven and Dingle, Miss Minnie's old home on the other side of Bear Lake.

Billy did not weep as he finally found a moment to himself, pressed against the wall of the church. *I don't feel anything at all. I hardly feel my own body.*

The fisherman-pastor seemed to understand. "Be kind to yourself, son," he said. "It's a shock to lose your mother, no matter how prepared for it you may have thought you were. Give yourself time and gentleness."

Billy heard the pastor's words but couldn't fathom how to do what he said. His body, though, seemed to know what he needed. He went home to Uncle Cecil's house and slept for seventeen hours straight. He awoke feeling like he might be able to take the next step. Whatever that was.

ଔଷ

On Saturday, Billy weeded the garden with Ebony and tried to teach her to play whist on the back porch with a deck Fred had given him. She had no experience with cards because Miz Minnie considered them sinful. They ended up laughing hysterically and building a tower from the cards.

The family went back to church Sunday morning. To his surprise, the service began with “Praise God from Whom all Blessings Flow.”

“People sing this in America, too?” Billy whispered to Ebony beside him.

“What did you say?” she whispered back.

“Never mind.”

Sunday afternoon, Billy pulled from the bookcase *The Marvelous Land of Oz* by L. Frank Baum. When he tired of reading, he worked on a drawing he had started on the train. This one was a bicycle with dragonfly wings.

“What gave you that idea?” asked Ebony.

“I’m trying to draw the bicycle I use in Ireland. When I ride it, I feel like I’m flying. I like the dragonfly because it molts. Do you know what that means?”

“Molting is a creature shedding its outer skin or shell to grow larger.”

“It’s my way of thinking about changing and growing,” said Billy. “Every so often something happens that changes me or—don’t laugh—makes me grow up a little more. To embrace what’s new, I must leave something behind, like the dragonfly leaves behind its old shell.”

“That’s interesting,” said Ebony. “Hmm. Like leaving behind our old house to move to this one, with space for Aunt Melody and Miz Minnie. I didn’t like the idea at first. But Miz Minnie lived in a shack. This house is so much better. It even has room for you! Tell me about something you’ve left behind.”

“I’ve had to leave behind lots of unhelpful ideas about myself,” said Billy.

“What do you mean?”

“Well, I thought I had to find my father to understand who I was. So, when I learned my father was dead, I was devastated. But kind people along the way helped fill that gap in my life. Coming back and seeing my mother again was another kind of molting, I think. Hearing her ask me to forgive her, and realizing I *did* forgive her, freed me from a burden I carried all my life. It left me freer to fly.”

“I like your drawing, Billy.”

“Thanks. I can’t seem to get the wings right, though, so they look like they’re flying the bike instead of the bike carrying the dragonfly. See what I mean?”

"Mmhmm. What if you—wait, I'll get another piece of paper, so I don't ruin your drawing . . . So, what if you change the angle. Like this."

"Ebony, I didn't know you could draw! That's fantastic. I'm not sure I could have figured it out."

"Things are a little slow around here sometimes, Billy. Drawing is one way I entertain myself."

"Can you show me your drawings?"

"If you promise not to laugh."

"You didn't laugh at mine. Why would I laugh at yours? I love sharing this hobby with you, Ebony. We can send each other drawings through the mail!"

Tuesday evening, after two days of fishing with Uncle Cecil, Billy sat on the back porch swing after supper staring at the lake. *Why do I miss my mother? I hardly saw her when I lived at the brothel, and haven't missed her at all the last two years . . .*

"Billy, may I join you?" Uncle Cecil sat in the rocker opposite the swing. "I've been wondering, son, what you're thinking about Ireland? Do you want to go back? You know you're welcome to stay here. We have years of life to make up for when we didn't know where you were. You're a comfort to us, after my sister's death."

Billy turned his gaze from the lake to his uncle, giving the swing a push with his foot. "I'm not sure, Uncle Cecil. I'm confused. When I left my school in Ireland, I planned to go back. It's a good school, and they're letting me study there without charging me. I guess you could say I'm their charity case. But they don't treat me any differently than the other students."

"Are you doing well in your studies?"

"I am. I've heard some say they think I'll come out of our exams at the top of my class. That's amazing, given how far behind I was when I started there. Mr. MacDonagh gave me special tutoring to help me catch up. I feel like I owe them something."

"Mr. MacDonagh is the one who sent me your letter. I can't describe for you, Billy, how excited, thankful, and relieved we all were to know you were alive, safe, and thriving. Those are words Mr. MacDonagh used in the note he sent us along with your letter. I agree. You owe them a great deal.'"

"I want to become a doctor, Uncle Cecil, a pediatrician. If I return to St. Colman's, I see my path clearly. It's a highly respected school, and if I do well, I should be accepted at a good medical school. I don't know whether that's possible if I stay here. How is Ebony studying?"

"Ebony is being tutored by Connie, Ezra Martin's daughter who came to Melody's funeral. I take Ebony with me to Montpelier once a week when I make my deliveries, and shop for the family that day to give her time with Connie. The studying she does on her own, fulfilling the assignments Connie gives her each week. Connie says she's doing well."

"Is there no school in Fish Haven?"

"Only elementary school. And they didn't want a student who looks like Ebony. Neither does the high school in Montpelier, even though Mr. Martin tried to persuade them. The closest school that will take her is in Pocatello. After Melody moved here, we lost our connections in Pocatello. And anyway, Ebony is very attached to her grandmother. She doesn't want to leave home while Miz Minnie is still with us."

"I see. So, my situation at St. Colman's is even more unusual than I thought."

"Yes, it is. You mustn't throw it away lightly, Billy. Tell me, what is giving you second thoughts about returning?"

"It's you, and Aunt Mary, and Ebony, and Miz Minnie. I have no experience of living with a family, a family I can call my own. I don't want to give that up either. It feels like—how can I explain this? Like something was missing inside of me and now I've found it." Billy's eyes filled with tears, and he roughly brushed them away.

"When you lived with your mother, that didn't feel like family?"

"At the brothel? I suppose . . . hmm . . . I guess the women created a sort of family for each other. They were very kind to me—spoiled me, actually. Gave me more attention than my mother did. She seemed happy they took care of me, so she wouldn't have to. But it wasn't—wasn't the same as this.

At all. That's why I ran away. I thought if I found my father, I would find what was missing inside of me."

Billy stopped and stared out at the lake. "I don't know how to explain it better than that."

Uncle Cecil's eyes never left Billy's face. "Do you know what I think, son? I think your grandmother's prayers protected you. She has prayed for you every single day of your life. She loves you with all her heart, even though these last days have been the longest she has ever been able to spend with you. And because Ebony is so close to her, she learned to pray for you too. Every night in her bedtime prayers."

Billy's eyes teared up again, and this time he let them flow. "I didn't know, Uncle Cecil. How can I give this up, this feeling that I matter, that my life is worth something to people just because I'm me, not because I do well in school or score in rugby or hurling."

"Come here, son," said Uncle Cecil.

Uncle Cecil stood and pulled Billy into a hug. Billy sobbed, pouring the pain and confusion and loneliness of years into tears, wetting Uncle Cecil's strong shoulder.

After a time, Billy realized that Aunt Mary, Ebony, and Miz Minnie had come out to the porch. He stretched out his arms, and all three joined Uncle Cecil's hug.

ঙ্গ

Billy carried his early breakfast dishes to the sink, ready to help Uncle Cecil prepare his gear for another day of fishing. Aunt Mary and Ebony were still asleep. But Miz Minnie, lingering over her coffee, asked him a question.

"So, boy, when're you going be back to school?" Her wrinkled hand trembled as she set her coffee cup back on the yellow checked tablecloth.

"I'm not sure yet whether I'm going back," said Billy.

"Nonsense. What's here for you? God ain't destined you to become a fisherman."

"What's here is my family."

"And we'll be here, delighted to welcome you back every summer holiday. During the school year you must go to school. That's your job."

"But it's so far away," said Billy, taking a step toward the door.

"Not so far a letter can't reach you. And I'll expect a letter from you every week from now on, young man." Miz Minnie looked so stern, Billy laughed and took a step back toward her.

"It's no laughing matter. You left us day after day, week after week, month after month not knowing whether you were alive or dead or even what country you were in. I like to used up all my tears weeping and praying over you, boy. I ain't got the energy to keep on doing it. So, I'll expect that weekly letter, and don't you let anything keep you from writing and sending it."

"Yes, ma'am." Billy looked at the floor and whispered, "I didn't know you cared, all that time."

"Speak up, boy. What did you say?"

"I said I'll try to write you every week."

"Trying ain't enough. You got to do it."

"Yes, ma'am." *I will try.*

"You never answered my question. When do you need to be back at your school?"

"The first day of the new term is August twenty-fifth. Mr. MacDonagh made me repeat that over and over so I wouldn't forget it."

"How many days do you need for the train and the ship?"

"Almost two weeks."

"And you must stop in Kansas City on the way, to spend a day or two at least with your other family. I calc'late we have about a month with you."

"My other family?"

"The Malcomsons, boy. Ain't that your last name? Didn't you travel with them all the way from Ireland? From now on, you can have Christmas with the Irish part of your family and your summers with us and visit your American Malcomsons going and coming. We'll count on it."

Billy sat down, his head reeling. "From having no family, now that I'm an orphan, I have three? You, one in Kansas City and one in Ireland?"

"You always had them. Don't tell me some of them weren't praying for you too. I know about the treasure hunt—I was part of it, you know! I was clue number one. Nice people, your other family. Cally and little Felicity, Charlie, Thomas and his family . . . I didn't get to meet the others, but I heard about Miz Cathleen. She prays, so I'm told."

Billy's eyes had grown wide. "Oh no. I—I can't believe it. I totally forgot!"

"Forgot what?"

"When I left the Malcomsons in Kansas City, Thomas gave me a package. I stuck it in my bag. I was thinking so much about getting here in time to see my mother, I forgot about it. Maybe it was food for the train. It must have fallen to the bottom of my bag when I pulled out Ryan's suit to wear for the funeral. If so, it's probably terribly stinky by now."

"Well, go get it, boy. What are you waiting for?"

Billy walked down the hallway to the room that used to be his mother's. *At first, I thought it would be scary to sleep in a room where someone had died. But instead, I've felt comforted, sleeping in the bed where she slept. Like a piece of her—a good piece—is still with me.* He went to the closet where he had thrown his bag and sniffed. *I don't smell anything stinky.*

Billy reached into the bottom of the bag and pulled out the package. *Since I told Miz Minnie about this, I might as well open it with her.*

As he re-entered the kitchen, Uncle Cecil came in through the back door. "Carlos is here and I'm ready to go. Are you coming with us, Billy?"

"He's just going to open this package first," said Miz Minnie, pointing to the packet that Billy had set on the table. "It's from his other family."

Uncle Cecil sat down next to his mother. "All right, then. Open it, Billy."

Billy unwrapped the package to reveal a slim envelope and a larger packet. Hesitantly, he opened the envelope. "It's a letter. From my father." Billy sat staring at the letter, as if it were a foreign object, willing himself not to cry. "I—I think I want to read it by myself."

"What else is there?" asked Miz Minnie.

Billy opened the packet. "It's money. A lot of money. Here, Uncle Cecil. I don't know what to do with this." Billy pushed the packet toward his uncle.

"I know what that's for, boy," said Miz Minnie. "It's to pay for your medical school."

"Tomorrow, when we go to Montpelier to make deliveries, we'll go to Ezra's bank and open an account for you," said Uncle Cecil. "Ezra will keep it safe for you until it's time for you to use it. Do you want some time to read your letter now?"

Billy shook his head. "He wrote it a long time ago. It can wait a few more hours."

Leaving the money with Uncle Cecil, Billy ran to his room and tucked the envelope under his pillow. He grabbed his hat and ran out the door to go fishing.

All day in the boat, Billy chatted and laughed with Uncle Cecil and his assistant Carlos, who helped Uncle Cecil manage the net. Billy caught more fish than the previous days combined. All the while, he felt the presence of the letter like a physical thing in his gut. *What will my father say to me? Why do I feel so afraid? I'm not sure after all that I want to read it by myself.*

Uncle Cecil yelled, "You have a catch, boy! A big one. Reel it in slowly. Let it play. Watch the net, Carlos. Billy will need help with this one."

Uncle Cecil crossed the boat to Billy's side. "Looks to be a bluenose—too big to be whitefish. Usually, I catch bluenose only in winter. That's it, tire it out. If you try to rush it, you'll lose it."

Billy flushed with the effort of holding on to the pole as the fish darted and dipped trying to get away. Uncle Cecil kept talking.

"The so-called French restaurant in Montpelier will be thrilled to have a large bluenose trout. This will bring a handsome price, son. Do you need me to take a turn?"

Billy shook his head, breathing hard. "I . . . I can do it."

"You know, Billy, the bluenose trout, like the two kinds of whitefish we usually catch, and the cisco and sculpin they feed on, live only in this lake. Nowhere else in the world. It's our claim to fame. That's it, the trout's getting tired. Reel him in slowly, slowly. I have the dip net ready."

Billy stopped trying to reel in the big fish. He put all his effort into holding on to the pole. The fish helped him by darting close to the boat.

"Look at the size of him! You've earned your keep with this one, Billy! Hang on . . . I got him! Congratulations, son. Well done! Put him in the tank, now. We want him as fresh as possible for the Frenchie restaurant. There now, take a breather, Billy. Go ahead and eat some of that lunch your Aunt Mary packed for us."

"I need help, sir!" yelled Carlos. "The net—it is too heavy!"

"We've run into a school of whitefish!" shouted Uncle Cecil. "That must be what attracted the bluenose. You pulled the line to close the bottom, yes, Carlos? Here we go . . . Billy, come help us!"

Grunting and using all their strength, the three together managed to haul the net over the side of the boat, filling its bottom with writhing, flapping fish. Uncle Cecil sat down and laughed. "Did you ever see such a thing, Carlos? Let's head on in. By the time we process all these, the workday will be almost over."

"Yes, sir." Carlos pulled anchor and headed the boat toward Fish Haven.

Uncle Cecil sat by Billy and reached for a sandwich. "I live for days like this. They happen only once or twice a year. And you got to be part of it!"

"Pretty exciting, Uncle Cecil!" *But Miz Minnie is right. I'm not meant to be a fisherman my whole life. It's a lot of waiting for one big catch. And so much work, caring for the fish for the nets, for the boat—*

"I'll take the helm now, Carlos. Come eat your lunch. Tell Billy your plan to become my partner, in time."

Carlos beamed. "I hope so, sir."

"Good for you, Carlos," said Billy, chewing. *I'm glad we're heading in early. I'm distracted by my father's letter. Who do I want to read it with me? Miz Minnie? No. She'll tell me what to think and how to feel about it and what to do with it. Aunt Mary? She's very kind, but I haven't had any personal conversations with her.*

"The sandwich, it is good," said Carlos.

"Yes, Aunt Mary's a great cook. Tell me about your family, Carlos."

"I am the only one here. *Todavía.* If I do well, maybe I help my family come here too. Your uncle—he is helping me."

Should I ask Uncle Cecil to read the letter with me? I can't explain why I don't want to—he's been more of a father to me than anyone else has. Maybe . . . maybe it feels like a competition somehow, between Uncle Cecil's care for me and my real father's, even though my father left me. Ebony? Maybe. She's close to my age. Maybe she'll understand what I feel more than the old people can.

Billy sighed, finished his lunch, and went to look at his trout, thrashing away in the tank. *I hope you make a lot of people happy at that restaurant.*

ଔଓ

After a supper of pan-fried whitefish, Billy asked Ebony to talk with him on the back porch.

"Is something wrong, Billy?" Ebony asked, her brow furrowing as she followed him to the swing.

"Not exactly. I received a letter, and I don't want to read it by myself."

"Who from?"

"My father."

"The one who took Aunt Melody from the Walled City?"

Billy looked puzzled. "I don't know about that."

"Never mind. How did your father send you a letter? Hasn't he been dead a long time?"

"He wrote it before he died and left it in the treasure hunt. The Malcomsons just gave it to me."

"Thomas and Cora?"

"Yes. I forgot. You know them."

"I spent a few weeks with them when Cally was sick. Helped with the children. They helped me, too."

"They did? How?"

"They gave me books. There aren't many books around here. Practically all the books you see in our house came from them. Or Miz Connie loaned to me. You can read them if you want."

"I already read *The Marvelous Land of Oz.*"

"Already? I haven't read it yet. When I do, can we talk about it?"

"Of course! But now, I want to read my father's letter."

Ebony shifted in the swing. "And you want to read it with me?"

"Yes. I thought, since you're close to my age . . . "

"Maybe I'll understand how it makes you feel, more than all the old people?"

Billy breathed a sigh of relief. "See—you already understand me. Do you have any friends, Ebony? What do you do for fun?"

"Yes, I have friends. All the other young people in Fish Haven. Would you like to meet them? Carlos is one of them."

"I would, yes. I'm not used to being around just old people."

"In a few minutes, I need to help Miz Minnie get ready for bed. So, if you want to read your letter—"

Billy pulled the envelope from his pocket. "Shall I read it out loud? Here goes . . . "

My precious son Billy,

Since you're reading this letter, you've met someone from your Malcomson family. I don't know who it will be—I fear, not one of my sons, your half-brothers. I doubt they can be bothered to cross the ocean for an old man's silly treasure hunt. And I doubt they'll appreciate the importance of this to me. The treasure hunt is the way I've thought of leaving some of my wealth to the people who have been important to me in America. Your mother, your grandmother—and most of all, you, my beloved youngest son, late-coming treasure of my heart.

Billy's voice choked. "I don't—I don't think I can go on."

"Do you want me to read it for you?" asked Ebony.

"Yes, please."

Billy, it's one of the greatest sorrows of my life that I must leave you. I hope your mother will remember to give you all the letters I am leaving with her for you, so you can be reminded as you grow that I love you and miss you and wish I could be with you.

"My mother never gave me any letters," blurted Billy. "I wonder what she did with them."

"Shall I go on?" asked Ebony.

"Yes, please."

It was your grandmother Minnie who persuaded me I must return to Ireland, to seek to make amends with my wife and my sons there before I die. You see, Billy, I left Ireland with my whole family upset with me. They blame me for the failure of Malcomson Brothers. They thought they would always have endless wealth to count on, and that is no longer the case. Whether this was my fault or not, history will judge. But I said things in anger I should not have said. Now I must ask their forgiveness and seek to end my life in peace with them.

My deep grief is that I must leave you. I had imagined watching you grow up, providing a home for you and your mother, a peaceful and happy life together. It seems, though, that my prior commitments, my earlier vows, must be honored. I go to my son William's home, which used to be mine, Coolroe, in Portlaw, County Waterford. I fear he may not welcome you, Billy. Please try to understand that for him, your life represents a betrayal on my part.

As I must ask his forgiveness, I also ask yours, my dear son. I can only pray that you will forgive me. My father's heart hopes you can be freed from any anger and bitterness you have experienced because of my leaving. I hope and pray you can live a good and faithful life, make allowances for other people's faults, use your gifts to bless others, and, if possible, honor my memory.

I will pray for you daily as long as I have breath, always for your happiness. May Father God, who loves you even more than I do, watch over you, provide for you and for your mother, and pour out on you the abundance of grace Miz Minnie has convinced me to believe in.

Your loving father,

William Malcomson

P.S. Please use this money for a grand purpose, not for whims or daily pleasures. Perhaps it may help you to study at a university, so that you can enter the profession you choose. I give it to you with great love. WM

"What profession do you want?" asked Ebony, folding the letter and returning it to Billy.

"I want to be a doctor. A pediatrician," said Billy, wiping his eyes.

"And now you have a way to do it," said Ebony wistfully. "I wish—"

"What do you want, Ebony?" asked Billy.

"Don't laugh. I want to be a lawyer."

"Why would I laugh?"

"Look at me. I live in a tiny place in a forgotten part of a brand-new state. My father is a fisherman. And I have the wrong color of skin."

"Don't say that. God made you, didn't he? And me. He doesn't make mistakes. My friend Fred's mother told me that. And anyway, Ebony, you are beautiful. Shall I tell you what Josie Malcomson said about you?"

"What did she say?"

"She said you are her second most beautifullest person and she hopes to look like you when she grows up."

Ebony laughed. "No chance of that! Who's her first most beautifullest person?"

"Laoise, Charlie's bride. Of course, Josie was enchanted by the whole wedding thing. But it's you she said she wishes to look like, not Laoise."

"I hope Josie doesn't lose her innocence—and her ignorance of how the world works—for a long, long time."

"Why do you want to be a lawyer?"

"Perhaps I could make things better for us—for all the dark-skinned people. Why do you want to be a pediatrician?"

"At the brothel in Pocatello, where I lived, there was one other child, a little girl. She died of an infection. I think her death could have been prevented. I want to care for other children so they can grow up healthy and happy."

"We both have big dreams. I'll support you in yours, cousin."

"And I'll support you in yours. Maybe we can split my father's money."

"You would do that for me?"

"Why not? I have more chance of other people helping me, I think. My other family, the Malcomsons, are rich. They've already been very generous to me. Maybe they will truly accept me as part of their family. Miz Minnie thinks so. In that case, my father's money can be yours."

"Ebony," Aunt Mary came to the back door. "Your grandmother wants to go to bed."

"Coming right now, Mother." Ebony stood, and bent to whisper to Billy, "Partners and pals?" She held out her little finger.

"Partners and pals," agreed Billy, linking his little finger with hers. "I look forward to meeting your friends."

CHAPTER 24

CHARLIE AND LAOISE

Millhouse, Dingle, County Kerry, Ireland, Tuesday, June 20, 1905

LAOISE OPENED HER EYES TO early morning sun sparkling on the gentle ripples of Dingle Harbor. She slipped out of bed, pulled on her dressing gown and sat in the easy chair by the open window of the hotel.

What a perfect place for a honeymoon! No ocean voyages involved. I hope I'm up to Charlie's plan for the next three days. Learning to ride a bicycle yesterday was comical, but the rental man assured me I'll conquer it within a few miles of Dingle. I'm glad Charlie decided to break up the loop—just thirteen miles to Dunquin today, with stops along the way. About the same tomorrow to Ballydavid. Then just eight or nine back to Dingle on Thursday, depending on where we decide to stay.

Laoise stood and moved closer to the window as a sailboat came into view. She watched it dock at the Dingle pier and the sailors climb the gentle grade toward Millhouse.

They must be coming here for breakfast! I'm delighted with this chance to know part of our own island I've never visited. Where people have never heard of Charles Malcomson or Laoise Murphy. A perfect getaway! And probably the longest time I've ever spent not practicing the violin, since I started playing at five. Charlie assures me I won't lose my touch in two weeks.

She sat down again, glancing toward the bed as Charlie sighed and turned over, then settled back into sleep.

I am worried about the other thing, though. Will the vinegar douche actually keep me from getting pregnant? It seems to have worked so far, but I feel uneasy, and that does keep me from fully enjoying our times together. I CAN'T get pregnant. It would spoil everything we've planned. When I think about this, all I see is blood and Mummy screaming and Da yelling. And my poor dead baby brother. I can't do it. I can't.

Laoise sighed, and Charlie sat up. "Good morning, love. Do you want to come back to bed?"

Laoise walked over to give Charlie a kiss. "I thought we were going to get an early start on the adventure of the day. And I'm hungry."

"You're always hungry when you wake up. All right, sweetheart. Do you want the first bath?"

As they walked down to breakfast, Charlie commented, "It's a funny thing. I visited Dingle in Idaho before I even thought of traveling to the Dingle in my own country."

"Wasn't that where you met—give me a moment—Billy's grandmother?"

"Your memory amazes me. Yes. Miz Minnie. And Billy's cousin Ebony."

☙❧

Charlie and Laoise's apartment, Dublin, Sunday, July 9, 1905

"Laoise, remember that meeting we went to at AE's house? Would you like to go again?"

"Your friend Liam keeps inviting us, doesn't he. I loved the people and the Conversation. Let's do it! Remind me what time it starts?"

"An hour from now."

"I can be ready to go in ten minutes."

"I'll go flag a carriage."

☙❧

"There's Liam," said Laoise, as they walked into AE's sitting room.

"You came!" exclaimed Liam. "I want you to meet a couple visiting tonight for the first time. Charlie and Laoise Malcomson, this is Mrs. Anna Haslam and her husband Thomas."

"I've heard of you," said Laoise, shaking their hands. "Aren't you working for women's suffrage? That makes so much sense!"

"Indeed," said Charlie, grinning at Laoise. "If my marriage is any kind of model, life works much better with a woman in charge."

"Haha," said Laoise, poking Charlie in the ribs. "Tell me, is there any hope we'll get the vote?"

"Indeed," twinkled the small, white-haired Mrs. Haslam. "Are you a member of the IWSLGA, Mrs. Malcomson? If you join, you can receive all the latest news about our progress."

"IWSLGA?" asked Charlie.

"The Irish Women's Suffrage and Local Government Association," replied Thomas Haslam. "In some places women are now allowed to vote in local elections and be elected to district councils. It's a big step forward."

"But that's not what the Haslams are here tonight to discuss," said Liam. "They're going to talk about Thomas's revolutionary method for choosing the size of one's family."

Laoise's mouth fell open. She gripped Charlie's arm.

"I have pamphlets that describe the method. Please take as many as you like and distribute them to your family and friends," said Mr. Haslam. "It's so important that women and their husbands decide together how many children they can adequately care for. I believe this method can transform our homes and families."

AE clapped his hands and called everyone from the refreshment table to the circle of chairs in his large sitting room. "Shall we begin our Conversation, friends? We have invited Thomas and Anna Haslam to be our guests tonight, and we hope they will become regular attenders. They likely need no introduction since their suffragist work is well known. What you may not be aware of is that Thomas has invented a revolutionary method of family planning. He will explain it to us. Thomas?"

After his introductory remarks, recommending his pamphlets, Mr. Haslam said, "The first thing to know, friends, is that women ovulate at the time of menses and remain fertile for a few days following. Now, since most men do not prefer intimate relations during the days of menses, they are often eager to resume relations in the days following, the very time a woman is most likely to conceive. The result is the high number of babies born into our families."

Mrs. Haslam passed out a brochure to each participant.

Mr. Haslam continued. "As you can see in the illustration, if a husband is willing to wait a week, he can be sure to avoid this fertile period. And when a couple desires another child, they can choose to take advantage of this time. So simple, yet so effective. I've asked Anna to describe how this has worked for us."

All heads turned toward the vivacious septuagenarian.

"At the time Thomas and I married, we shared a very low income, not enough to support a child. And we were both passionate about the causes we have worked so very hard to achieve."

Laoise's attention was riveted. *Like Charlie and me with our music.*

"As well, my darling Thomas has suffered ill health most of his life. We determined not to have children, and for many years we chose to remain celibate. This did not detract from our marriage. Rather, our friendship was enhanced, for we invested so much more in matters of the spirit and the soul."

Charlie looked at Laoise, frowning. She glanced at him and blushed.

Mr. Haslam reclaimed the narrative. "However, we know not every couple is called to such a radical stance. Therefore, based on the most reliable medical evidence, we designed the method I have described to you, and for years we tried it ourselves, with complete success. When we were confident of its effectiveness, we began recommending it to others."

Mr. Haslam leaned forward, looking earnestly into the faces of his male listeners. "Men, for too long we have been self-indulgent, at the expense of our wives and families. Not just in the matter of intimacy, but in all areas of life. We must learn discipline. It will make us better marriage partners, better fathers, better workers, and better citizens."

He stood straight, without losing his eye contact with his audience. "I encourage you, men, to take this seriously. No woman should have to bear and care for twelve, thirteen, fourteen children. Sharing the family resources with only one or a very few children is better for everyone. This makes logical sense, does it not?" He stepped back.

"We must admit, however, that some who tried our method have found themselves in a family way," said Mrs. Haslam. "Thomas and I are quite certain they must not have followed the method rigorously. We have no hesitation about commending it to you."

AE stood. "Thank you, Thomas and Anna. This is most interesting, as in the new Ireland we dream about, we will doubtless wish women—half of our population after all—to be as free as men to make choices for their lives and for their families as well as for their nation."

The Haslams bowed and took their seats.

"Who else would like to share a topic with us for discussion this evening?"

For the rest of the Conversation, Laoise smiled and nodded as appropriate, but her head was spinning. *I can't wait to discuss the Haslam method with Charlie. Surely it is the answer we've been looking for!*

꧁꧂

Charlie opened the day's mail. "Look at this, Laoise! We've been invited to play a benefit for our old school, the Dublin Academy of Music. August fifth."

"Both of us," said Laoise, quickly reading the letter Charlie handed her. "How lovely! I didn't think I would ever feel this way, but I miss performing."

"Shall we do it, then?" asked Charlie. "Perhaps some of our classmates will come."

"We could try out the new pieces we've been practicing for Desmond and Deirdre's wedding reception a week later. Before we take them to larger stages this fall," said Laoise.

"Good thought. I'll send an acceptance letter tomorrow."

Laoise smiled, delighted. "Charlie, I have an idea for our repertoire. I just got the sheet music for Paganini's "Cantabile for Violin and Piano." Do you want to try it?"

"Sure! If we like it, we can play it all season."

ଔଷ

The applause after "Cantabile," the final piece at the benefit, simply wouldn't stop. Laoise and Charlie bowed once more and left the stage.

"They want an encore," said Laoise. "What shall we do? We didn't plan for this."

"I suggest our old favorite, 'Méditation' . . . by Thaïs. I think we could play it in our sleep."

"All right. Ready?"

The audience quieted when Charlie took his place once more at the grand piano. As he accompanied Laoise's passionate performance, he watched her, lost in the music, her eyes closed, the sapphire and diamonds on her finger flashing. *How beautiful she is, inside and out. I don't deserve her. Thank you, God, for such a precious, precious gift.*

Laoise's Academy friend Betsy approached her at the reception following the concert. "That was stunning," said Betsy. "I always knew you'd go far."

"Tell me about you," said Laoise. "What's happening in the cello world?"

"I'm auditioning for the London Symphony Orchestra," said Betsy.

"Oh! We heard them play one of their first concerts, just a few weeks ago. We're in London often, so we can keep in touch with you."

"If they hire me," said Betsy. "I hope so. I should know within a month. We're both ambitious, aren't we, Laoise."

"All students at the Academy were trained to be ambitious," said Laoise. "Are you married, Betsy?"

"I was," Betsy replied. "I couldn't figure out how to reconcile marriage to a banker with my career." She looked around and lowered her voice. "My career won out after I got pregnant."

"Oh! You have a child? How old?" *I would love to know how she makes this work.*

Betsy looked around again and lowered her voice further. Laoise leaned in to hear her. "I decided not to have the child. If you ever get into that situation, Laoise, I can give you a recommendation. Motherhood and performance are incompatible."

Laoise tried to hide her shock and the sliver of fear that pierced her gut. "Yes, I—I feel the same way. It makes sense, after all we've invested personally and all that's been poured into us by our families and schools. Well, best wishes, Betsy. I'm sure it will hit the news if you're hired by the London Symphony. I look forward to seeing your name up in lights!"

"It's lovely to see you again, Laoise. Your performance was truly spectacular."

The applause at Desmond and Deirdre's wedding reception was no less enthusiastic than at the benefit concert. Charlie and Laoise bowed, then purposefully moved away from the piano toward the bride and groom, dressed to depart on their honeymoon. Charlie directed the applause to them by joining in the clapping and shouting, "Congratulations, Desmond and Deirdre! God go with you!"

The crowd echoed Charlie's sentiments. Desmond bowed and Deirdre waved. Their parents and Laoise gave them final hugs, and they were gone.

Laoise turned wearily to put away her violin. Cathleen approached. "Are you all right, my dear? You played gorgeously, as always, but you don't seem quite yourself."

"I'm fine, thank you, Cathleen."

"I won't press you. But I will pray," said Cathleen. "And if you want to talk, you have my—or I should say, Percy and Margaret's—telephone number."

"Thank you," said Laoise again, closing her violin case.

"A hug?" asked Cathleen.

Tears wet Cathleen's shoulder. But Laoise wiped her eyes, smiled, and said "Thank you" once more. *What's said can't be unsaid. I don't know yet. Not for sure. Now to pull myself together so Charlie doesn't suspect. He's not as intuitive as Cathleen, I don't think. I hope. My, I'm tired. I hope Charlie's ready to go home.*

CHAPTER 25

CALLY AND RYAN

Grove, Oklahoma, Tuesday, July 4, 1905

RYAN STEPPED OFF THE TRAIN and looked around the station. *How interesting—no patriotic decorations, no red, white, and blue . . .* He sought out the station master for directions to Teddy's house.

"That's it," said the station master after Ryan repeated the directions back to him. "But Blue Eyes and Starlight will likely be at the longhouse. I'll be going there myself as soon as my shift is over."

Maybe Cally stayed home—but perhaps they invited her to go with them. "Could you give me directions to the longhouse as well, then?" requested Ryan.

Finding no one at Teddy's house, Ryan turned toward what the station master called the Neosho River, passing (though he didn't know it) Cally's favorite picnic spot. *I'm glad the Oneida have such a lovely place to live. Aha, that long, bark-covered building must be it. How interesting. The Shoshone don't build longhouses.*

The front door stood open. Ryan stopped just inside to look around, careful to step to the side since the doorway seemed to be the main source of light. Despite the heat of the day, a fire burned in the center of the floor. The attention of all those gathered was focused on the speaker, an elderly man in full regalia.

Ryan looked around the dim room and quickly spotted Cally, holding a baby, sitting on the floor across from him. Her coloring stood out among her darker-skinned companions. A woman next to her whispered to Cally and pointed.

Cally looked up and for a moment, a shadow crossed her face. She frowned and looked down. Ryan held his breath. *Will she let shame defeat her and spoil our reunion?*

The woman next to Cally whispered something to her. Tears glistening on her face, Cally looked at Ryan again, and this time she smiled. His heart soared. The contrast between her face, at peace now, and the terror he had seen on the ship brought sudden tears to his own eyes.

Ryan pointed to himself, then to her, extending his hands palm up and raising his eyebrows to make it a question. She nodded, scooting closer to the woman next to her and patting the place on the floor beside her. Ryan eased around the circle, trying to be as inconspicuous as possible.

Just as he reached Cally and sat down, Teddy spoke in the same language the old man had used. "Oneida?" whispered Ryan.

She shook her head. "Seneca," she whispered back. "I'll explain later."

Ryan smiled at the woman beside Cally, and at the baby, who examined him curiously. "Aiyana," Cally whispered. The woman frowned at her. Cally put her finger to her lips when Ryan repeated the name.

The longhouse conversation seemed to go on and on. *Of course, it feels longer because I don't understand it. And because I'm so tired from traveling. Good thing I'm hungry—that's helping me stay awake. That and how hot I feel. I'm dripping sweat. Everyone else seems perfectly comfortable.*

Aiyana apparently completed her examination and found Ryan acceptable, because she reached her arms toward him. Ryan took her from Cally and entertained himself with the baby until she giggled, and the woman frowned at them both.

Teddy participated in the conversation several more times. Once, what he said made everyone laugh. Women spoke as well as men, and overall, the tone of the gathering was lighthearted. Ryan noticed when the station master entered and took his place in the circle.

Suddenly there was a stirring. People stood up and began chatting and moving around. When Cally stood, Ryan gratefully did so as well. Aiyana reached for the woman, and Cally said, "Welcome, Ryan. I want you to meet my dear sister-in-law, Starlight. You've already made friends with my niece Aiyana. And I'm sure you remember my brother Teddy from the trial in Kansas City."

Ryan smiled at each one in turn. "Would you two like to be excused?" asked Teddy. "This will go on for a while yet. Everyone will understand. I'll explain that you have just come on a long journey from across the ocean and are very tired. Would that be accurate?"

Ryan nodded. "It would. Thank you, Teddy."

Cally took Ryan's arm and nodded at the people she knew as she guided him around the circle and out the door. "I am so glad to see you!" she exclaimed when they could no longer be heard from the longhouse. "Thank you for coming to find me—not just at the longhouse, but here in Oklahoma. I know you're tired. Are you hungry as well?"

"I could eat," admitted Ryan.

"That means you're ravenous," laughed Cally. "We saved food for you from lunch. We weren't sure exactly when the train would get here. I suppose you've already been to the house?"

"Yes. The station master gave me instructions for both places. I assumed I would find you at one or the other."

"Right now, we're passing a place where I've spent a lot of my time here," said Cally. "Isn't it beautiful?"

They stood for a moment admiring the deep tones of the river and the lighter blue of the sky, flowers and trees growing in profusion along the river's edge and up a bluff on the far side. "Beautiful and peaceful," said Ryan. "There's obviously more rainfall here than in Idaho. At least where I live."

"Every place has its own loveliness," said Cally. "How long can you stay? I'm sure you're anxious to return to your farm and to Brian."

"I'll stay as long as it takes," said Ryan. "I need to reconnect with you. When you're ready to return to Kansas City, I want to travel back there with you. After that I'll travel on to Twin Falls."

"Thank you for caring, Ryan." said Cally. She turned and started walking again. Ryan stepped up beside her. "I told you I would explain about the people speaking Seneca instead of Oneida in the longhouse," said Cally, taking his arm.

"Yes—I thought Teddy had joined the Oneida."

"He did, and alone at home, he and Starlight speak Oneida. But this is actually a Seneca-Cayuga reservation."

"Then, why—"

"The Oneida man Teddy is most connected to, River Runner, married a Seneca woman, Maiana. When his wife's clan was pushed off their land in New York and decided to come here, River Runner persuaded his mother and her Oneida family, including Teddy, to come as well, so he could look after his mother."

"I see. I think."

"River Runner is highly respected by both the Seneca and the Oneida, and their customs are similar, so it has worked out. Teddy and Starlight have learned Seneca, and they speak some Cayuga as well, since there are many Cayuga living here. All three languages are Iroquoian and have many features in common."

"Amazing," said Ryan. "The only language I speak is English, and that not very well, I often think. Perhaps if I keep reading a lot, I'll become more eloquent. But in my simple way, I want to tell you, Cally, you're a sight for sore eyes. I've been so distressed for you. The look of terror on your face when you jumped ship has haunted my dreams ever since. I don't have words adequate to tell you how relieved I am to see you strong, well, and at peace."

"Dear Ryan," said Cally, taking his arm again and pulling close. "I'm so very sorry I put you through that. You and Felicity and everyone else. What happened surprised me too."

"We knew you didn't plan it, Cally. We felt totally helpless, though, as the ship chugged steadily away from shore. The captain told us he couldn't go back or let me take a boat. All we could do was send messages to the people we guessed you might go to."

Cally shook her head and said again, "I'm so sorry."

Ryan covered her hand on his arm with his other hand. "Our first sense of relief came when Cathleen explained that perhaps your fear had to do with the faeries. Then the night before the wedding, we received a telegram from Max saying you had been home in Kansas City and were coming here to Teddy. Even before we received the confirmation telegram from Max, I guessed that's where you would come."

"I hope Max's message allowed you to relax and enjoy the wedding. What made you think I would come here?"

"If your fear was related to the faeries, I thought you would want to be with someone from that world, someone who knew firsthand some of your story in Ireland before you came to America. That reasoning pointed to Teddy. It's clearly been good for you to be here."

They reached Teddy and Starlight's home and climbed the steps to the porch.

"It has, yes. I'll tell you more about it, but first let's get you something to eat." Cally opened the door and invited Ryan in.

The sense of peace and order in Teddy and Starlight's home seemed palpable to Ryan. He breathed deeply, raised his hands in thanks to God, and followed Cally to the kitchen. She warmed on the stove a food he didn't recognize but proved to be delicious—a spicy corn and squash dish, with peaches and grapes on the side. Cally watched him eat, smiling at his evident pleasure.

"More?" she asked.

"Yes, please," said Ryan. "Now that you've taken the edge off my physical hunger, I'm hungry to hear more about your time here."

"I'm anxious to hear about your time in Ireland as well. First, though, how is Felicity? She's been on my mind constantly."

"Reserving space in your mind for me, too, of course," grinned Ryan.

"Of course," smiled Cally.

"Felicity took your departure very hard. She kept saying you had promised not to leave her again. She attached herself to Cora and wouldn't detach except when sleeping—and even then, when she had nightmares, only Cora could comfort her."

Ryan took another bite. When he looked up from his plate, he saw tears in Cally's eyes. "At the family dinner before the wedding, Cathleen seated herself beside Felicity—with Cora on her other side, of course—and had a talk with her. I don't know what she told Felicity because I couldn't hear their conversation. But whatever it was, transformed her."

"That sounds like Cathleen," said Cally, not taking her eyes from Ryan's face, though tears ran down her cheeks.

"I was across the table from them and could literally watch a burden fall from Felicity's shoulders. She straightened up, began to smile, to eat, even to laugh. She began to interact with Dugan and Aisling, which meant the world to them. She even went to the wedding song practice after the dinner without Cora in tow."

"I'm so grateful," breathed Cally, wiping her face.

"Truly, it was amazing. She still misses you terribly, but since that dinner it's been a normal sadness, rather than a debilitating one. She wanted to come with me to see you, but I wasn't sure whether you would be ready for that, and I wanted to find out for myself whether you were still feeling as much fear as the last time I saw you. I wanted to protect Felicity if that was the case. And, selfishly, I wanted you to myself, at least for a little while."

Cally reached for Ryan's empty plate, and he took her hand between both of his. "I love you, Cally. It was very hard seeing you in so much pain. Whatever has brought you peace in Grove, Oklahoma, I am grateful for."

Cally looked down at their clasped hands, and when she looked up, tears shimmered again in her eyes. "I was afraid—" She swallowed and started again. "I was afraid you wouldn't want me anymore, after—"

"After you jumped ship? Oh, darling girl. Come here."

Ryan held her for a long time, soaking in the sweetness and solidness of her.

Finally, Cally drew back and sat at the table, her eyes damp. "Did my little mirror make it into the hands of Miss Hilda?" she asked.

"Sweetheart, I hope this won't be too much for you to hear right now. Miss Hilda died a few months ago. Aisling told us they have lost contact with the faeries. I have your mirror in my satchel."

Cally sat staring at Ryan, trying to absorb this information. "So, now there's no way to appease them."

"Aisling told me she believes the faeries have largely withdrawn from the places humans live and gather. There are still occasional sightings reported in remote parts of Ireland—mostly in the far northwest and southwest—but increasingly, people don't even believe in them. She thinks, and Dugan affirmed as well, you need not be afraid to return to Ireland on their account. Whatever debt you think you owe them has most likely been forgotten."

"So, maybe I could have gone to the wedding," Cally whispered. "I didn't know." She buried her face in her arms and wept. Ryan moved over to sit beside her and put his arm around her shoulders, waiting for the emotion to pass.

"Can you tell me what made you so afraid?"

Slowly, Cally recounted the same history she had told Teddy and Starlight. Ryan did not interrupt until she had finished.

"I think I understand, Cally. If I believed it was my fault my family died or got badly injured, and that those tragedies were linked to a debt I had incurred, and that those conditions only applied in a certain geographical place, I would be afraid to go back there too."

Cally reached out and squeezed Ryan's hand where it lay on the table. "Thank you, Ryan. Thank you for caring. Thank you for listening. Thank you for understanding. I didn't think anyone could. I can't tell you what it means to me to no longer be alone."

"Did Teddy and Starlight understand?"

"Starlight told me the Oneida see little people too, but theirs are beneficent to humans. Teddy was grateful to understand for the first time why I had refused to take him back to Dugan and Aisling after Da's death. That really mattered to him."

"Dugan and Aisling send their love."

"Do—do you think they can ever forgive me?"

"I don't think they feel there is anything to forgive, Cally. They too were relieved to feel they understood why you didn't go back. They do hope you will return someday. And they want to know whether, until that's the case, they could come here to visit you."

"They would do that?"

"Yes. They love you, Cally. You and Teddy. You're a part of them. They're your family."

"In some ways, more my family than the Malcomsons, even though I haven't seen them since I was seven," said Cally. "If the faeries have gone away, maybe I can someday return to Ireland without feeling terrified of what they might do."

The front door opened. Teddy stopped by the kitchen, a sleeping Aiyana in his arms, and gestured that he would take her upstairs. Starlight blew Ryan and Cally a kiss and followed Teddy.

"Cally, I have no idea what time it is, but I'm exhausted. Can we continue our conversation tomorrow? Do you know where I'm meant to sleep?"

"If you don't mind, on the couch," said Cally. "Starlight left a pillow and bedding for you."

"I don't mind at all," said Ryan. "Sleep well, precious Cally." He kissed her gently and turned toward the sofa. *I think right now I could sleep absolutely anywhere I can lie down and stretch out.*

Despite his fatigue, Ryan woke early. The house was quiet. He stood up from the couch and stretched, turning in a circle to appreciate the living room. *I was too tired last night to notice much of anything.* Plaques hung beside the front door, one in English and the other presumably in Oneida. As he walked over to read the English one, Teddy came down the stairs, treading softly.

"That's a tiny part of the Great Law of Peace of the Iroquois Confederacy, which so impressed Benjamin Franklin, he used it in framing the United States Constitution," he told Ryan in a low voice.

Ryan mouthed, "Wow!" and read, "With endless patience, the Haudenosaunee shall carry out their duty. Their firmness shall be tempered with a tenderness for their people. Neither anger nor fury shall find lodging in their minds, and all their words and actions shall be marked by calm deliberation." He crossed his hands over his heart.

"Breakfast in ten minutes," whispered Teddy. Ryan nodded.

"I think we can talk normally here in the kitchen without waking anyone," Teddy said as he served Ryan scrambled eggs and cornbread.

"Thank you. What is 'Haudenosaunee'? I've no idea how to pronounce that."

"It means 'people of the longhouse.' The five nations who originally formed the Iroquois confederacy used to live in longhouses, the oldest woman of a family and her descendants all living together. If a new family was formed, it was easy to add twenty more feet to the longhouse. I can tell you more when I get home from work if you're interested."

"I'm very interested," said Ryan. "I didn't know the customs of the Oneida would be so different from the Shoshone of Idaho. What kind of work do you do?"

"I'm an apprentice carpenter-finisher. Many people are moving into our town, so there is much building to be done." Teddy took his last bite of cornbread. "So, Ryan. I understand you have intentions toward my sister."

"I do," said Ryan. "Cally and I traveled all the way to Rochester, New York, to secure Miss Mary Anthony's permission for us to marry. Should I ask yours as well?"

"The fact that you're here speaks well for you. Cally's—what shall we call it, terror attack?—didn't scare you off."

"No. It only made me want to jump in the ocean and find out what was causing her such agony. The fact that I've never swum in water that deep interfered with that idea."

"You don't know how to swim? We'll have to do something about that. Today, when I get home from work. I'll give you a swimming lesson in the river."

"Oh, I misled you. I do know how to swim, in river water. Just not in an ocean. But I would love to go swimming with you if you have time." Ryan looked down at his long pants. "I don't know what I could wear, though."

"Hmm, I'll ask Starlight to figure that out for you. I'm off. Tell Cally I'm glad she was able to sleep in this morning. Sometimes she shares my early breakfast. See you this afternoon."

How interesting! We both like to work with wood. Ryan looked around and noticed several lovely things Teddy might have made, starting with the kitchen table and chairs. Picture frames, a lovely cutting board, a block on the counter holding sharp knives.

I think I'll follow Teddy out the door and go for a walk by the river. I need a little time to myself to try to absorb the fact that a childhood fear could have such a powerful hold on a person as smart and practical and self-giving as Cally. I'll leave a note for her. Maybe she can come find me once she's up and has her breakfast.

જ્ઞ

Cally looked so far ahead along the path by the river trying to spot Ryan, she almost stumbled over him. He was lying flat on his back on the grass at "her" quiet spot, staring at the sky. He sat up immediately and jumped to his feet to give Cally a hug.

"Sleep well?" asked Cally.

"Like a rock," said Ryan. "Amazing the difference sleep makes. You?"

"I had difficulty falling asleep. It's hard to accept how much worry I caused everyone. But when I finally did, I slept late."

"I'm glad for that. I think all this emotional conversation takes a toll on our energy. Necessary though it is." Ryan picked up a flat stone and skipped it into the river, then reached for Cally's hand.

"I would love to hear everything about your time in Ireland," said Cally as they turned to walk along the riverfront.

"I have some news I think you'd like to hear," said Ryan. "Laoise's father, Colin Murphy, had an encounter with Billy! They discussed Irish nationalism."

Cally stopped walking, her eyes huge. "Our Billy? The treasure hunt Billy? He's been found?"

"Yes! And he traveled with us on the *Lion III* and the train because his mother Melody was very ill. He left us in Kansas City for the last ride on to Idaho. I haven't heard news since then."

"What is he like? He must be—let me think—oh, his birthday was yesterday, July fourth! He just turned . . . maybe fifteen?

"Yes, I think that's right, though I didn't know it was his birthday. He would have been all alone on the train yesterday."

"Perhaps his family will celebrate when he gets there. Unless—do you think Melody is dying?"

"Yes, that's what I understand."

"Poor Billy. What is he like? We thought about him so much, but I don't really know."

"He was quite overwhelmed by meeting the Malcomsons. Cora helped everyone take it slowly and tell him about the treasure hunt. That was fascinating for me, too. I never heard the whole story beginning to end. For me, you are the treasure I gained from that hunt. But most everyone else felt Billy was the treasure. Especially Shane."

"The family had a lot of time on the ship and the train to get to know each other."

"Yes, and even before we sailed, Cathleen came to the port in Waterford to ask Billy's forgiveness." Ryan stopped and skipped another flat stone. "Aha, seven skips that time. These are interesting stones. In Idaho, we don't have flat, thin stones like this."

"I hope Cathleen feels relieved now about her part in Billy's story."

"I think so. But you asked what Billy is like. He's very intelligent. He wants to become a pediatrician. I think he'll succeed in that goal. He's strong and tall and apparently good at Irish sports. He's been attending a Catholic school, St. Colman's. Doing very well."

"Amazing! I wonder when I'll get to meet him."

"Perhaps he'll stop by Kansas City on his way back east when he returns to Ireland in August. Thomas invited him to do so."

"I hope he does. Tell me about the wedding! Was Charlie terribly disappointed I wasn't there?"

"Of course, he was disappointed. But he told us you would be the most distressed if we didn't enjoy the wedding." Ryan described the family dinner and the ceremony, including the children's song, then grew animated as he told her about the discussion of Irish nationalism at Mr. Murphy's club Monday morning after the wedding.

"The main question we discussed is whether violence is necessary to achieve independence from Britain. Mr. Murphy handled the conversation like a debate, asking volunteers to explain the main arguments for each point of view. He only revealed his own belief, that violence should not be necessary, at the end of the time, letting everyone else present their views and questions first."

"I didn't know Mr. Murphy is involved with nationalism."

"No one knew, apparently, not even his own son, Desmond. Mr. Murphy's more pacifist view is shared by Arthur Griffith, whom Mr. Murphy admires immensely. Mr. Griffith plans to launch a new political party this fall, based on the hope of achieving separation peacefully, through political negotiations. His party will be called Sinn Féin. It means 'of the people.'"

"What is the chief argument of those who think violence will be necessary?"

"The fact that multiple attempts at negotiation have been made over the years, none of them successful. Desmond seemed convinced that more talk will achieve nothing. Did you know that Cathleen's grandfather was Daniel O'Connell, the great Irish hero? But even all he achieved in the end came to little since the British clamped down with the power of their immense army. Dugan said of course he doesn't want violence, but since nothing else has worked, it may come to that. Thomas, while acknowledging he's quite removed from the struggle, living in America, said Mr. Murphy's and Mr.

Griffith's perspective appeals to him, and he would like to do what he can to support it. Charlie, of course, wasn't there. He was on his honeymoon."

"Did you reach any conclusions yourself?"

"I want to plant myself firmly in the no-violence camp. But I empathized with Dugan's sympathy with Desmond's argument: nothing so far has worked. What basis is there really to believe more talk will be effective?"

"Oh, Ryan."

"It's not like I'll be directly involved, Cally. I live in Idaho, not Ireland."

"I know. But there's been so much violence already in Ireland's history. I hate the thought of more."

"I do too."

Cally frowned, thinking back to what Ryan had first told her about finding Billy. "So—if Billy was in Dublin talking with Mr. Murphy about nationalism, he must be getting involved in some way."

"Yes. He's been a messenger boy for some of the leaders. It's become dangerous for him at times. He asked us to swear we wouldn't tell anyone in Ireland about this. So, I guess now you need to swear too."

"I swear not to tell anyone Billy is involved with the nationalists," said Cally dramatically. "Changing the subject, were you able to learn anything about your family?"

"Yes! Cathleen asked Cousin Priscilla to take me to the Quaker archives on Tuesday. Priscilla spent the day with me there, searching their records for Byrnes. Unfortunately, Michael Byrne, my father's name, is rather common. But she eventually found a note of my family departing for America in the company of a group of Quakers from Cork City. I was called 'wee Ryan.' I finally know the names of my brother and sister and mother!"

"Oh, how exciting, Ryan!"

"Yes. My mother's name was Annabelle. My sister, four years older than me, was Kezia, and my brother, two years older than me, was Isaac. I feel almost as if I can picture them, just by knowing their names."

"Dear Ryan, I'm so happy for you."

"Apparently, I do have aunts, uncles, and cousins still living in Cork City or nearby. Cally, I've been thinking . . ." Ryan looked at Cally, needing some encouragement to continue.

"You've been thinking?"

"What if we plan a honeymoon in Ireland next summer, after you finish your nurse's training? We could visit Dugan and Aisling, and your Malcomson relatives, of course, as well as my Cork City relatives. Wouldn't that be grand?"

Cally laughed. "You're talking like an Irishman already. Yes, I think it would be grand."

"So, on Wednesday after the wedding I wrote to all my relatives in Cork County I had addresses for, asking them to write me back at my farm in Idaho. Won't it be fun if they respond?"

"Grand fun," grinned Cally.

"And on Thursday, I joined a Malcomson family outing to the beach at Bray, and Friday we took the early train to Waterford in time to board the *Lion III.* And here we are!"

"So, today is Wednesday, July fifth," said Cally. "What if we spend another day here, and travel to Kansas City Friday? I told Sister Irmena I would be back at the hospital Monday, July tenth. You could spend Sunday there, possibly discussing next summer's plans with Thomas and Cora. And then go home to Idaho. You must be anxious to see Brian."

"I am, yes. I feel it more now that I'm less worried about you. So, you're ready to think about a date for our wedding?"

"Yes! How about toward the end of June, a couple weeks after I graduate from nursing school?"

"When we get back to Teddy's house, we can look at a calendar. Where do you want to get married, Cally?"

"Hmm. The options, I guess, are Kansas City or Idaho. I'll have to think about that."

"Of course, I think Idaho would be grand. But you probably favor Kansas City."

"Not necessarily. We don't have to decide now, do we?"

"Not at all. What we need to do now is stop by the post office to send Thomas a telegram about our plan to arrive in Kansas City on Saturday. They deserve to know you're feeling better. Do you know where to go?"

"Yes. Turn right here."

"Remind me to give you your mirror when we get back, Cally. I was so tired last night I completely forgot."

Kansas City train station, Saturday evening, July 8, 1905

"Where is Felicity?" asked Cally, after hugging Cora.

"She didn't want to come," said Cora. "Try to understand how upsetting this has been for her."

Tears filled Cally's eyes. "I'm so sorry," she whispered.

Ryan put his arm around her. "Let's take it a step at a time." He turned to Cora. "We owe you an enormous debt. You have cared for Felicity with such tenderness. We are deeply grateful, Cora."

"I'll ease your way with her as well as I can," Cora said to Cally. "It may take a while."

"I understand," said Cally.

"Max is waiting for us," said Cora.

Felicity was already asleep, in Cora and Thomas's room instead of her mother's. Cally stood watching her for a long time. *I need you so much, God. Never more than now.*

Don't be afraid. I am with you.

Thank you.

Sunday morning Ryan suggested to Cally that they stay home from church with Felicity. "We need some time to ourselves. Perhaps I can help mediate."

"We can invite her. But she may not want to be with me yet."

Indeed, Felicity chose to attend church with Thomas and Cora. Cally felt too upset to go, and Ryan stayed home with her.

"I feel like she's punishing me," said Cally.

"More likely, she doesn't know what to do with all her feelings," said Ryan. "Perhaps if she doesn't want to see you yet, she would be willing to go for a walk with me this afternoon."

Cally sighed. "I never imagined this would be so difficult."

"She feels betrayed and abandoned," said Ryan. "It makes sense that rebuilding trust will take time. We need to be patient, and gentle, and available whenever she chooses to come our direction."

"Thank God for Cora," said Cally.

Felicity did go for a walk with Ryan but refused to talk about Cally. They giggled over a squirrel's antics, made friends with a puppy, and picked wildflowers in an empty field.

"I need to go home to Idaho tomorrow, Felicity," Ryan told her as they approached the house. "I've been gone from Brian a long time and I miss him terribly."

"Take Mummy with you," said Felicity. "I don't think she wants me anymore."

Ryan stopped and sat down on the sidewalk. "Come here, honey."

Felicity looked at him and slowly walked toward him. He gathered her in, and she burst into tears. She cried for a long time.

"Better?" Ryan asked her when the torrent slowed. She gave a nod. "Can I talk to you a little bit?"

Felicity sat up and wiped her eyes.

"Your mummy found out she didn't have to be afraid anymore of what frightened her in Ireland," Ryan said. "She's sad now that she didn't go with us. She's especially sad because she has missed you so much. Like I miss Brian."

"Is that true?" asked Felicity. "Or are you just trying to make me feel better?"

"It's true," said Ryan. "Do you think you can give her a chance to tell you so herself?"

"Will you be there?"

"If you want me to be."

Felicity nodded, took Ryan's hand, and walked with him into the house.

"Shall we see if she's in her bedroom?" asked Ryan.

"All right," said Felicity. She stopped. "But I'm a little bit scared."

"I understand," said Ryan, squeezing her hand. "I'll be right here with you."

Felicity walked with him toward Cally's bedroom and knocked on her door.

"Come in," said Cally in a muffled voice.

Ryan opened the door. Felicity looked at her mother's tearstained face and ran to her. They hugged each other and wept together for a long time.

Ryan watched for a while, then eased out of the room and gently closed the door.

Kansas City Train Station, Monday, July 10, 1905

"Goodbye, Ryan! I'll see you in a few weeks! Give Brian and Flora hugs for me!" Cally yelled, running alongside the already-moving train, Ryan's head stuck out the window.

"I'll count the days. Goodbye, precious Cally!" And the train rumbled away.

Cally stood for a moment, then made her way through the station and back to the carriage where Max waited for her. Impulsively, she climbed onto the bench beside him. "I don't feel like being shut up inside," she said. "Thanks for taking me to the hospital, Max. Can I drive?"

Max looked at her, his eyes raised. "I'm not sure—"

"Dr. Flora and I drive ourselves everywhere in Idaho," said Cally, smoothing her uniform. "But there, it's a wagon, not a carriage."

"Would you mind terribly if I consult Mr. Thomas about this first, Miss Cally? I mean no disrespect. Miz Cora has never asked me such a thing." Max guided the horses away from the curb.

"Please don't worry. I love to drive, and soon I'll be back in Idaho where it's a necessity, not a luxury. It's good to be back here for a few weeks, though I miss Ryan already."

"Of course, you do. He's a fine young man."

"Then you approve?"

"One hundred percent. If I may say so, you've come a long way since I first met you, a fevered heap dressed as a boy passed out beside the road to Olathe."

"Thank you for helping rescue me. And for all you've done for me since."

"It's been a pure pleasure, Miss Cally. I pray for you every day while I'm driving around. You and every person in this family."

"You do? Max, you should come to our wedding! It will be toward the end of June, at Ryan's farm in Idaho."

"Well, that's an invitation I never expected. I'll have to consult—"

"Thomas. I understand. He and Cora will be coming, and the children."

"So, they may need me to care for the house and the horses while they're gone. But I do appreciate the invitation, Miss Cally. Here you are. Let me come around and help you down."

Cally grinned. *It's not necessary, but—* "Thank you, Max."

"You're welcome, Miss Cally. Here's your nurse bag. God bless your day."

"And yours. Max, it means a lot to me to know that you pray for me. Like I'm safe or protected or something."

"Because God loves you. Don't ever forget that."

ଔଷ

"So, Sister Irmena has completely mapped out my next weeks," said Cally at dinner. "I have a lot to make up for. And she wants this alternate training program to be a success. She's been talking to Flora about sending more students to Idaho next year."

"It's good to see you back to normal," said Thomas.

"Being busy will be good in a way," said Cally. "I won't have time to miss Ryan."

"When you go back to Idaho, I want to go with you," said Cora.

"Me, too!" yelled each of her three children. Josie added, "I want to see Ebony."

"I miss her too, Josie. We could visit Cecil and his family on the way back. Or on the way, if there's time."

"Billy will already have left," said Thomas. "To get back to St. Colman's on time, he'll have to leave early in August."

"I know," said Cora. "But I want to personally extend my condolences for Melody's death. And I've been collecting books for Ebony."

"I'm sad I didn't get to meet Billy," said Cally. "Do you think he'll stop through Kansas City on his way back to Ireland?"

"We're expecting him," said Thomas. "Sometime in the first week of August, I think."

"I can't wait! Ryan thinks he is wonderful!" said Cally. "The whole treasure hunt feels more worthwhile."

"I agree with Ryan. I know you'll be delighted," said Cora.

"I'm going to stay in Idaho, because Mummy's getting married!" exclaimed Felicity, climbing into Cally's lap. "I'm going to have a daddy and a baby brother!"

Cally grinned and hugged Felicity. The other three children changed "Mummy" to "Aunt Cally's getting married," and chanted it until Cora stopped them with, "Anyone want dessert?"

CHAPTER 26

BILLY

Montpelier, Idaho, Wednesday, August 9, 1905

"GOODBYE, EBONY. I CAN'T WAIT to see you next summer! Happy tutoring," said Billy as Uncle Cecil stopped the wagon in front of Miz Connie's house on the way to the Montpelier train station. Connie waved to them from her doorway.

Billy jumped down from the bench to give his cousin a hug. "Send me your drawings and I'll send you mine."

Ebony nodded and wiped a tear, then turned toward Miz Connie.

"We have an hour before the train. Anything you want to do, Billy?" asked Uncle Cecil.

"There's something I want to talk about before I go back to school," said Billy.

"All right. Why don't we drive to the station, so we'll already be there when the train arrives."

Uncle Cecil guided the horses to a shady place near the tracks. "Now then. What's on your mind, son?"

Billy took a deep breath and plunged in, telling his uncle about his role as messenger boy for the nationalist movement in Ireland. "I'm confused about whether I should continue doing this, Uncle Cecil. I learned the hard way how dangerous it can be. On the other hand, it's something I can do for the country, and especially for the school, that has taken me in, fed, housed, and educated me. I found out shortly before I left that nationalism is St.

Colman's philosophy, not just Mr. MacDonagh's. That's why they host the Gaelic League, and why all their students are learning Gaelic."

"Is the danger your main concern, son?"

"That, and the fact that Mr. MacDonagh believes the struggle for independence may result in violence. And he believes a true Irishman should be willing to pay what he calls the 'ultimate price'—he means death. He is willing to do so himself."

"Violence seemed necessary to free the United States from Britain," observed Uncle Cecil.

"I know. And to free the slaves. I honor what you did, Uncle Cecil. I do," said Billy.

Uncle Cecil bowed his head. Billy put his hand on his uncle's arm.

"I'm not an Irishman, Uncle Cecil. I was born here in Idaho. I don't want to die. I have plans for my life. So, should I continue supporting something I don't truly believe in? If Mr. MacDonagh thought like Mr. Murphy—"

"Mr. Murphy is—"

"He's the man who talked with me about what nationalism means. He is also, I learned on the ship, the father of Laoise Murphy, who married Charles Malcomson. That's the wedding the American Malcomsons, Thomas and Cora and their children, went to Ireland to attend."

"I know about Charlie. And Cally and Felicity. I know the Kansas City Malcomsons, remember? So, what does Mr. Murphy believe?"

"He and a man named Arthur Griffith believe independence from Britain can be achieved without violence, through politics. Mr. MacDonagh says that's been tried for centuries and has never worked, so why would anyone think it will work now? But I heard Thomas and Ryan talking on the ship. They said the Quakers—that's the Malcomson family background and Ryan's too—they don't believe violence is ever justified."

"So, you prefer the thought of working for someone who doesn't espouse violence," said Uncle Cecil.

"Yes. But it's Mr. MacDonagh who has done so much for me. Without his tutoring, I wouldn't be where I am academically at St. Colman's. In fact,

I wouldn't be there at all, because he's the one who convinced the board to take me on as a charity case."

"About that, I'm so proud of you, Billy. You're doing so well. You're a credit to yourself and to all who love you."

Billy blushed. "Thank you, Uncle Cecil. I'm doing my best."

"It makes me happy to think you have a path ahead of you for becoming a doctor."

"It makes me happy too, Uncle Cecil. If you have any thoughts or advice for me about what I've told you, please send me a letter. All right?"

"I'll think and pray on it, son, and send you any thoughts the Lord gives me. One thought I have right now is to tell you what I say when I feel afraid. I say, out loud, if possible, 'I am safe. I'm secure. I am strong, cuz I belong.' Sometimes I have to say it over and over to turn my mind away from my fear. Maybe it will help you, too."

"What does the 'secure' part mean?"

"I think of it as an anchor holding a boat in waves and wind. I'm anchored to God, and I'm anchored to my family. And I hope you are now, too."

"That's what you mean by 'I belong.'"

"Yes. I'm not strong by myself. I'm not strong all alone. But I'm strong in God, who is always with me. And I'm strong in the interwoven strength of my family. Like a fishing net. A single strand of rope can't hold anything. But woven together with other strands, even a small net is strong."

"'I am safe. I'm secure. I am strong, cuz I belong.' Thank you for giving me this gift to take with me."

"You're welcome, son."

"I'm glad I could spend the summer with you, even though my reason for coming was sad, and I still feel confused about my mother. I loved fishing. I already told Aunt Mary, but please tell her again how much I appreciate her kindness. And tell Miz Minnie I look forward to seeing her next summer."

"Billy, it's possible that—"

"I know. But I also think Miz Minnie will live for as long as she sets her mind to do so. Oh, I hear the train. Goodbye, Uncle Cecil."

"Goodbye, son. Give my love to Thomas and Cora and their family. Please send us a telegram once you've arrived safely back at St. Colman's. And keep in touch, Billy. I'll be in no end of trouble with my mother if you don't."

Billy laughed. "I know. I'll do my best. Goodbye!"

Uncle Cecil said nothing more. When Billy turned for a final wave before boarding, he was wiping his eyes.

A skinny man and his plump wife boarded the train ahead of Billy. As Billy followed them into the car, the man turned and gave Billy such a look of hatred, it felt like a physical blow. *Wow. I think I'll go to another car.*

Billy found a seat in the next car back, exchanged nods with the man beside him, and settled in for the long ride with *The Red Badge of Courage*, a book Ebony had loaned him, to be returned next summer. *Ebony thinks this will help me better understand Uncle Cecil's experience as a Civil War soldier.* He turned to the first chapter. *I thought of telling him about the old woman. And the dragonfly bicycle. But probably Irish nationalism is enough for him to think about right now. I'm glad Ebony knows, though.*

ঔ৯

Billy glanced up from his book as the train slowed coming into the station at Cheyenne, Wyoming. *Oh my. It's evening already. I've almost finished this book—not sure I like it, though. It's well written, but the Youth doesn't even know why he's risking his life. The supposed glamor of fighting doesn't make any sense to me. It seems stupid. It seems like some high-up people are using these poor men to achieve something they want, not caring very much whether the soldiers live or die. I know this is about the Civil War, and that Uncle Cecil fought hoping to gain freedom from slavery for Black people. But the whites—what were they fighting for? There's no clue to that in the book.*

Billy shifted his gaze from the window just as an old woman sitting in front of him turned and looked straight into his face. He gasped. "Are—are you—no, it's not possible. I'm sorry, ma'am." He ducked his head in embarrassment.

Billy found his heart racing. When he glanced up again, the old woman was bent over, as if gathering her things. She rose as the train stopped, sidestepped past the passenger beside her, and walked down the aisle to the exit.

"Cheyenne. Half hour stop," announced the conductor.

Half an hour—that's long enough to get out and stretch. And buy something to eat, maybe. I already finished most of what Aunt Mary packed for me. I wonder whether there's a bookstore in the station or nearby. I still have a day and a half of travel to Kansas City.

Billy stood and pulled his bag from the overhead compartment. *Maybe it's safe to leave it on the train—I didn't see that old woman carry anything with her—but I would be sad to lose any of these things. They're all the possessions I own.*

He stood in line to use the restroom, then stood in line at the station café, looking around the depot. *I don't see a bookstore.* Someone bumped him from behind. Billy turned and just caught a glimpse of the face of the skinny man who had boarded with him in Montpelier before a fist crashed into his face.

Billy fell to the ground, his nose spurting blood. The man pulled a knife, raised it, and yelled, his face contorted with rage, "We don't want yer kind in Idaho, ye hear? Nor Wyoming neither." His wife yelled, "Harry, no!" and grabbed his arm.

Billy tried to roll but bumped into a large waste basket as someone shouted, "Help, police!" Hands grabbed Billy under his armpits and yanked him away just as Harry's knife, jerked from its intended destination, plunged into his wife's thigh. She screamed, footsteps came running, and Billy passed out.

A woman's voice said, "It's all right, sir. He's my son. He's not badly hurt. I'll take care of him. Don't want to lose our place on the train—people expecting us at the other end, don't you know."

"If you're sure . . . " The policeman's voice sounded doubtful.

"If you could just help me get him on the train, sir, I'll care for him there. It would help to have a whole bench."

Billy felt himself lifted and carried. He opened his eyes, but they were covered by something. *We're going up steps, I think. Must be into the train. . . . Yes, this is definitely a train seat.*

A man must have moved, because the policeman said, "Thank you, sir, for changing seats."

"I saw it happen," a man said. "One never knows these days. Everything seems peaceful and then suddenly—"

"Well, the perpetrator will be on the next train back to Montpelier where he came from." *That's the policeman.* "He'll go to jail there. His wife has been taken to the hospital here. I think this young man should have been too. Let me see, ma'am, whether the bleeding has stopped."

Pressure lifted from Billy's nose. He blinked. A man in uniform bent over him.

"Broken," said the policeman. "But the bleeding has slowed. Hold it a little longer, ma'am."

"Yes, sir." Pressure on Billy's nose again, the cloth covering his eyes. "We'll take him to see a doctor in Kansas City." *Who is "we," I wonder. Who is this woman who's claiming I'm her son? Couldn't possibly be the old woman from Ireland. Could it? How? If that cloth weren't covering my eyes, I could see her.*

"I wouldn't want to be in her place, married to that brute." *The man who said he saw it happen.*

"Sadly, this is not a rare occurrence," said the policeman. "Some people think they're better than others."

"Departing for Big Springs," announced the conductor. The train started to move.

"Thank you for your help, sir," said the woman.

"It's my duty, ma'am. I hope this ends well." Running feet. The train door shutting.

Billy moaned. "Can you not push on my nose quite so hard?" he managed.

"Now that man is gone, yes," said the woman. The cloth released and Billy found himself staring into the face of, *yes!* the old woman from Ireland.

The one with the bicycle. *That* old woman. But now she had dark skin like his. She sat in the seat opposite him. Looking forward, whereas his bench faced backward.

"How do you always show up when I'm hurt?" Billy asked, trying to sit up.

"No, no, ye must stay down for a while yet. We don't want the bleeding to start again."

"Who are you? I demand to know." Billy started to slide off his bench as the train gathered speed. The woman, incongruously, lifted both feet to anchor him. Her shoes pressed against his arm and his abdomen.

"Tsk, tsk. Ye're in no position to make demands, Billy. Now, I have a pack of ice here somewhere." The woman pulled a bag from under the seat. "Lie still and don't try to talk. I'm going to hold this on your face for fifteen minutes. It'll help with the swelling."

How on earth can the old woman have ice? There wasn't time to get any at the station, I'm quite sure of that. And anyway, why would she? It's almost as if she knew I was going to get hurt.

"Too cold," Billy protested.

"All right. I'll wrap it in my handkerchief."

Not much better. I wonder what it means that my nose is broken. Will I look strange forever, my nose all crooked?

Billy squirmed against the cold. "Now, Billy, settle down. Ye must do yer part. It's cold but it won't kill ye. All in all, I'd say ye came out of that little incident quite well. Better than the man's poor wife."

Little incident?! That man wanted to kill me! But when Billy tried to protest, his voice came out all garbled and muffled by the ice pack.

"Settle down, I said. Ten minutes to go. I'll be glad too, when I don't have to hold ye in place."

"May I help you?" A female voice. Young? No, but not old either. Hands replaced the old woman's feet holding Billy on his bench. Strong hands. "I'm a doctor. When your ten minutes are up, will you let me look at his face?"

"Certainly, and I thank ye," said the old woman.

"My name is Flora," said the doctor. "I'm on my way to Kansas City."

Flora. Flora. Didn't I hear that name on the ship? When the Malcomsons were telling me about the treasure hunt?

"We're headed to Kansas City, too. This is my son, Billy. He encountered a man's fist at the Cheyenne depot."

Her son, ha. How long will the old woman keep up this deception? But I'm happy to have a doctor look at me. Maybe she'll predict the future of my face . . .

"Now, then," said Dr. Flora an eternity later. "Let's see what you look like, Billy. Keep your eyes closed. I'll be gentle but this may hurt a little. Uh huh. Not too bad, but I need to ease your bones and cartilage back into place. I think I have some laudanum in my bag . . . Let me lift your head so you can swallow this."

I remember this taste. From when I got hurt in Knocklong.

"We'll wait a few minutes for it to take effect. Ma'am, it will swell less if your son raises his head. Could you sit beside him and hold his head on your lap? You can help hold him still. Despite the laudanum, it will hurt. You'll have to be brave, Billy."

This is like getting my lip stitched. I'll count to one hundred and see if she's done by then.

"We'll also need a bandage . . . Sir, since you seem so interested in this procedure, could you find the conductor and ask him whether he has a first aid kit? I don't know whether Johnson & Johnson has distributed them to the railroad."

Billy blinked his eyes and saw a man leaning over his seat from the bench in front of them.

"I'll find out. Glad to help," said the man.

Billy couldn't help squirming under the doctor's fingers. The old woman put her hands firmly on his cheeks and somehow, the pain eased.

"There. I would call that a successful manipulation. Thank you for helping me, Billy. Here comes our bandage."

The conductor swayed down the aisle holding a red box, the helpful passenger following him.

"Thank you, sirs. Can you please open the kit for me? . . . Hmm, not exactly what I would choose for a dressing, but we'll make do."

"This passenger described for me what happened in Cheyenne. Shame, that," said the conductor.

"His mother described it as an encounter with a man's fist on our last stop," said Dr. Flora. "I stayed on the train at Cheyenne, so I missed seeing it happen."

"A passenger didn't like the color of my son's skin," said the old woman. "His intent was to kill Billy, judging from the way he brandished a knife. But his wife grabbed his arm and suffered the injury herself."

"Killed?" asked Dr. Flora, her eyes wide.

"No, just a deep wound in her thigh. They took her to the hospital in Cheyenne and the man is in custody. He'll be returned to Montpelier to face justice."

"That may or may not amount to anything, depending on the judge and jury," said Dr. Flora. "Well, I'm glad you sustained only a broken nose, young man. It will take a few weeks to heal. No sports or activity more strenuous than walking for at least two months."

Billy struggled to sit up. "Two months? But I can't—it's hurling season. My team needs me."

Flora gently pressed him back down. "I'm almost finished, Billy. Hurling, is it? I've never heard of hurling in Kansas City. In fact, I don't know what hurling is."

"It's a complicated sport played in Ireland," the old woman responded for Billy. "It's been played there for at least two thousand years. My son studies at a school in County Cork."

"Ah, now I understand your accent, ma'am. You're Irish too."

"Ye could say that," said the old woman noncommittally.

"We need to figure out a way you can sleep sitting up, Billy, to reduce the swelling."

"We have an empty sleeping car," said the conductor. "Would that help?"

"It would, if you have enough pillows," said Dr. Flora. "Rest is the best thing for him the next day or two. That and more ice."

"I'll check for ice in the dining car. Can the young man walk?"

"I believe so," said Dr. Flora, sticking on a last piece of tape. "Ready to try it, Billy? I'll come with you and help you get situated. Another dose of laudanum will help too. And a drink of water for him, please, conductor. I don't know how much blood he lost. With enough fluids, his body will make more blood for him while he sleeps."

"Amazing how bodies work," said the old woman.

How bodies work? She has a body—I'm lying on it. Why didn't she say, "Amazing how our *bodies work." No point asking her.*

The helpful passenger carried Billy's bag and opened the doors between train cars. They walked through three cars before reaching the sleeper car.

"The second door on the right," said the conductor. "I'll fetch ice, if there is any. And water. And see whether we have more pillows."

"You've been so helpful, both of you," said Dr. Flora, taking Billy's bag from the passenger. "Thank you."

"Shortly we'll arrive at Big Springs," said the conductor. "Only a five-minute stop there, though. Unless you have a particular need, doctor?"

"No, we'll be fine with ice and water and pillows. Thank you, sir."

The old woman had eased Billy onto the bottom bunk of the sleeper, where he sat hunched over to not hit his head on the top bunk, waiting for more pillows.

"Thank you, Dr. Flora," Billy said, his voice sounding wheezy.

"You're welcome. Don't try to talk. I'll leave you in your mother's care. Please use ice fifteen minutes of every hour. And make him as comfortable as he can be sitting upright. Here's another dose of laudanum, Billy. Your job now is to rest."

Billy opened his mouth and the doctor squirted in a few drops of liquid.

"I'll check on you in the morning, but if you need me during the night, I'll be three cars up." Dr. Flora left and closed the door gently after herself.

"You're falling asleep where you sit," said the old woman. "Here, lean back into these two pillows, and once the conductor brings them, I'll tuck more behind you."

"I'm your son, eh?"

"For all the trouble you give me, you might as well be," said the woman, removing Billy's shoes and tucking a blanket around him.

Billy remembered nothing more.

Kansas City, Friday, August 11, 1905

Carrying his bag, Billy carefully deboarded, the old woman behind him, and looked around the Kansas City train station. *Nice I don't have to wait for luggage. I guess I'll walk down to the end of this track. No one told me exactly what to do when I got here.*

He looked around to suggest to the old woman they walk toward the lobby of the station. She was not there. *Hmm, maybe she forgot something on the train.* He waited while a stream of people descended the steps, then stuck his head into the car. *Nope. Empty. Maybe the sleeper car.*

He walked three cars back to the sleeper they had used the last two nights. *No one here, either. Maybe I missed her somehow.*

Exiting, he was swarmed by passengers boarding the train to continue east. *How will I ever find her?*

He walked to the end of the track and into the lobby just as Cora came in through the door opposite him. While he worked his way toward her through the crowd, a woman threw her arms around Cora. *Aha. Dr. Flora IS connected to the Malcomsons. I thought I remembered her name.*

Cora and Flora talked a few minutes, then Cora's eyes flitted around the station. *Now she's looking for me. What shall I do about the old woman. Maybe—maybe she doesn't want to be found. She seems to appear and disappear on her own timetable.*

Billy smiled when Cora caught her first glimpse of his face. "Billy, what on earth did you do to yourself?"

He walked the last few steps and gave Cora a sideways hug. "You can ask Dr. Flora, Cora. She probably knows more about this than I do."

"So, you two met on the train."

"In unusual circumstances, yes," laughed Dr. Flora. She lightly punched Billy's arm. "I suspected you might be THE Billy, the treasure hunt Billy. But getting you stabilized seemed to be the priority."

Cora looked from one to the other. "I want the whole story, every detail. But first let's see to your luggage. You can tell me on our way home."

"This is all I have," said Billy, lifting his bag.

"I only brought this small valise," said Flora. "Oh, it's so lovely to see you, Cora. Such fond memories of last summer. Especially once I was on my feet again after that long illness."

At the curb, they found Max chatting with his horses. Cora introduced Flora and Billy, and they climbed into the carriage. Max showed no surprise at the condition of Billy's face.

"So, Flora, before you tell me Billy's story, I'm curious about this visit. Delighted and curious," said Cora.

"I've been wanting to see Cally ever since Thomas told me about her desertion from the ship," said Flora. "I couldn't leave Hansen, though, until I found a doctor to take my place for a couple of weeks. I need a rest, so this is good timing. I also look forward to talking with Sister Irmena in person about her plans to expand what she calls the 'Frontier Nursing Extension.' Since I'm being contracted by the St. Joseph Nursing School, I need to make sure we're in agreement about my plans and responsibilities. Cally is the trial case. Next year, Sister Irmena hopes to send me at least five nurses in training who feel called to work on the western frontier."

"I see. Cally, a rest, and Sister Irmena," said Cora. "Now you can tell me what Billy ran into."

"A man's fist," said Flora, grinning at Billy.

"You didn't! What does the man look like?" asked Cora.

"If there's any justice in Idaho, he's behind bars," said Flora. "His intention, apparently, was not just to wound Billy but to kill him."

Cora gasped. "What?"

"Because of the color of my skin," said Billy. "I was in line for something to eat at the Cheyenne train station when someone bumped me from behind. I turned around and the man's fist smashed into my face. Then he pulled a knife. His wife yelled and grabbed his arm, but I guess it was already in motion because instead of hitting me, he plunged it into her leg."

"Merciful heavens!" said Cora. "That settles it. Shane is NOT going to travel to Idaho by himself, much as he thinks himself old enough to do so."

"Fortunately for me, Dr. Flora was on the same train and took care of me," said Billy.

"Along with—where is your mother, Billy?" asked Flora, looking around the carriage as if she could conjure the old woman.

"She's not actually my mother. She's a friend who has an odd way of showing up when I'm in trouble."

Flora frowned. "I don't understand what you're saying, Billy."

Billy laughed. "There's no way to understand that old woman. I asked her why she said she was my mother and she said I give her so much trouble I might as well be her son. I don't even know her name."

Flora shook her head. "I must be more exhausted than I thought."

"She comes and goes as she pleases. That's all I can tell you," said Billy. "Believe me, I've tried many times to get her to explain herself to me." *I won't mention that she can make herself and her cottage invisible. They may think the blow to my head has addled my brain!*

"How very interesting," said Cora. "It sounds almost like she's your guardian angel, Billy."

"What's a guardian angel?"

"I guess it's a heavenly being assigned to a person to take care of him. Or her. I don't know exactly," said Cora.

"Well, I don't know anything about angels, but that makes as much sense as any explanation I've heard so far," said Billy.

"We're almost home," said Cora. "The children should be arriving from school about the time we get there. Then Max will pick up Thomas from work and Cally from the hospital. We'll have supper about an hour from now. Would you like to go to The Eldridge for a rest, Flora? Billy is going to bunk in with Shane."

"A rest would make me a better companion for the evening," said Flora. "Thank you. How is the pain, Billy? Do you need another dose of laudanum?"

"No, thank you. I'd rather have my head clear."

"I know you'll want to bathe, but don't get your face wet, Billy. We mustn't disturb those bandages. Your nose needs time to heal."

"Yes, ma'am."

Cora tapped on the window of the carriage and Max pulled over to the side of the street. Cora opened her window and stuck her head out. "Please take Dr. Flora to the Eldridge first, Max. Then we'll go home."

"Yes, ma'am, Miz Cora." Max eased the horses back into the stream of traffic and turned left at the next corner.

଒ଓ

Shane seemed as delighted to see Billy as when they had first met on the wharf in Waterford. *As if I'm some kind of hero in his eyes. I'm worried that I'll disappoint him.*

The first night, Shane understood Billy was wounded and needed to rest. The second night, though, he wanted to talk. Billy put his pillow over his head, but it hurt his face.

"I'm sorry. What did you say, Shane?"

"Did Uncle William give you a lot of money in that packet Daddy gave you?"

"Yes."

"What are you going to do with it?"

"I put it in the bank to save for college."

"Do you think people in Ireland talk funny?"

"I did at first, but I got used to it. I even started saying some things like they do."

"How long can you stay with us?"

"Just tonight. I have to take the train to New York City tomorrow, and you know what a long trip that is. Then sail to Waterford, take a train to Cork City and a coach to Fermoy. All in time to start school August 25th."

"Ugh. It's too long of a trip. Why don't you just stay here? You could go to school with me! And anyway, don't you think you should let your nose heal first so you can get rid of that bandage? Won't your friends laugh at you?"

"They might. Even worse, they'll ask what happened, and I don't want to tell that story again and again. Hey, Shane, maybe you could help me make up a funny story to tell. What could I say I bumped into that will make people laugh?"

"Won't that be kind of like lying?" asked Shane.

"Well, I suppose if they ask me if it's true, I could say no, but it will be more fun than to tell what really happened. Then I can ask about their summer, and they'll only remember that it was a fun conversation."

"What if you say you were fishing, and the fish was so big that when you tried to reel it in the fishing pole hit you on your face? I think that's a funny story. Especially if you make the fish really huge."

"Good idea! Any others?"

"You could say you were trying to ride your bicycle with no hands and hit a rock and flew up into the air and then crashed right on top of your handlebars."

"Ouch, that really sounds painful."

"Worse than what actually happened to you?"

"Only if it wrecked my bicycle at the same time. Any other tall tales you can think of?"

"You were walking while reading a book, and you walked smash right into a light pole."

"This is great. I can tell a different story to each person who asks me. Pretty soon my friends will realize they're all made up and I don't want to talk about what really happened. After a day or two something else will come up that's more interesting."

"Like what?"

"Like hurling or rugby or Gaelic or what one of the teachers said or a practical joke or plans for the next weekend. There's always something going on."

"I guess you love your school. That's why you're making the long journey back."

"I guess I do. But I'm glad I got to meet you and your family. And finally got to meet your Aunt Cally. I didn't know I had so many cousins. I only knew about my cousin Ebony."

"The second most beautifullest person in the world," said Shane, mimicking his sisters. Then he said soberly, "Billy, I'm sorry your mother died."

"Thank you, Shane. I'm sorry too. Are you ready to sleep now?"

"No. But I'll be quiet so you can."

"Thanks. Dr. Flora says sleep is the best thing for healing my face. And I have to get up before you do to catch my train in the morning."

"I know. Good night." Shane was quiet for a moment. Then he whispered, "I'll miss you. I wish you didn't have to go."

"Good night, Shane."

Billy made his way out to the carriage in darkness. Impulsively, he asked Max, "Can I ride on the bench with you? I'll be stuck inside a train for days. The fresh air feels so good."

"Of course, Billy. Throw your bag into the carriage and climb on up."

"How long have you worked for the Malcomsons?" Billy asked as they pulled away.

"They hired me when they first came to Kansas City. That will be—hmm, let me think. The twins were born soon after Thomas and Cora bought this house, and they will be twelve in December. So, almost twelve years! Time goes fast. It's been good."

"They seem to depend on you a lot."

Max chuckled. "You're observant, son. I'm glad you asked to sit up here with me. I've been thinking about something I might mention to you."

"Please tell me."

"Billy, what just happened to you—suffering violence for the color of your skin—it's an opportunity."

"An opportunity, Max? What do you mean? I've tried not to show it, but I feel angry."

"I'm sure you do, understandably so. I've been where you are many times, Billy, in my long life. I've learned that my anger offers me a choice."

"Please explain, Max. I don't understand."

"Anger can be a power for good, giving us energy for change. Or it can be a huge time waster. If we allow anger to become bitterness inside, all it does is chew us up and spit us out. That kind of anger only convinces us the whole world is against us."

Billy nodded. "I do feel that way sometimes."

Max pulled on the reins to avoid running into a milkman's cart. "That's understandable, son. But if we believe we're just victims, we push people away. Or they take on our outrage at the injustice we've suffered and become angry themselves. In the end, anger we hold on to and feed just burns up a chunk of the precious time we have on this earth."

"It sounds like you made that choice at some time in your life," said Billy.

Max chuckled. "Didn't I say you're perceptive? Yes. I wasted a lot of years feeding my bitterness. The problem was, it didn't stay contained in one little part of my heart. It grew and spread. It ended up costing my marriage and my relationships with my children. And it accomplished nothing. That's why I say it's a time waster."

"I didn't know you were married, Max." Billy waved and yelled at a ragged child stepping into the street. "Be careful! You almost got hit!"

"I was married, to the loveliest gal you would ever hope to meet," said Max, after the child ran down the side of the street away from them. "But I let bitterness over racial injustice poison my soul and destroy our happiness."

Max guided the carriage around a corner through the growing traffic of early commuters, then continued. "I wish someone had spoken to me this way when I was your age, Billy. It could have saved myself and people I love immense heartbreak. Perhaps I would still have my family."

"But my anger is growing stronger inside me, Max. I don't know how to stop it. What that man did to me seems unforgiveable. If I let it go, I'll be disrespecting not just myself but all people who look like us."

"Forgiveness doesn't mean saying 'Oh, what that person did doesn't really matter.'" Waiting for a carriage to pass in front of them, Max turned to look at Billy. "Forgiveness is only necessary when wrongdoing has been done."

Billy frowned. "I don't understand."

Max tried again. "Forgiveness says what was done was wrong, sometimes terribly wrong. At the same time, it says, 'I refuse to give that person the power to ruin my life. I release him to God so I can preserve my own integrity and my ability to make choices for myself.'"

"You mean, if I don't forgive him, that man can go on hurting me every time I think about him?"

"Exactly. I'm not saying it's easy. Forgiveness requires a deliberate act of courage."

Billy took a deep breath. "But what do I do with my anger?"

"Don't deny it. Use its energy. Choose not to see others the way that man saw you. Think about what a closed, dark space his mind must occupy and ask God to give you compassion for him."

"Compassion for the man who wanted to kill me?" Billy's voice rose until he was almost shouting.

"Yes," responded Max calmly. "When I asked God for compassion, I didn't feel it all at once. But gradually I started praying for the people who wronged me. They will come under God's judgment; he promises that. I wouldn't want to be in that man's place when God judges him. Would you?"

"No." Billy settled back on the bench. He took a deep breath, his mind whirling. "Not at all."

"I see myself there, under God's judgment, son," said Max quietly. "If I had not forgiven the people who hurt me, I'd have become violent myself. I could have struck out at a stranger because of the rage inside of me. Who they were wouldn't matter."

Billy nodded. "I can imagine that happening to me, too."

"What that man did reveals the condition of his heart, not who you are. I will pray for you, Billy, as you think about what I've said and the example of my life."

Max pulled up at the station. He turned and looked into Billy's eyes. "I hope you won't make the same mistakes I did. But even if you do, there is always, always the possibility of turning it around. I'm grateful for that grace every day. Don't give up, Billy. Don't despair. Use the energy of your anger for good. You will be the one who reaps the greatest benefits."

Max reached out and gave Billy a sideways hug. "One more thing. When I'm afraid or angry, I say out loud, 'I am safe. I'm secure. I am strong, cuz I belong.'"

Billy's whole body jerked. "How is this possible? I can't believe it. My uncle told me the exact same words. Do you know my Uncle Cecil?"

Max chuckled. "No, I don't. Isn't that the way the Spirit works, though? A marvel."

"I am safe. I'm secure. I am strong, cuz I belong," repeated Billy. "Who do you belong to, Max?"

"First, to God. Then to this family. I pray for each of them every day. Thomas and Cora, Cally, Shane, Shauna, Josie, and Felicity. They are part of me and I'm part of them. Ryan's easing his way in there too. And you."

Billy hugged Max back. "Thank you. I'll think hard about everything you've told me. Goodbye."

"Next time you're here, you can tell me how things are going. Goodbye, son. Travel safely. God goes with you, and he loves you. Never forget that."

CHAPTER 27

CHARLIE AND LAOISE

Dublin, Sunday, September 3, 1905

"IN TEN DAYS, WE CAN celebrate our three-month anniversary in Paris! Then we can eat the real thing," Laoise said brightly as she handed Charlie the omelet she had labored to create for him and sat down to her own.

"Depends when you count from," grinned Charlie. "We've been legally married since January third. That means today is our nine-month anniversary. Nine months—the time it takes to create and birth a baby."

Laoise blanched and set down her fork.

Charlie's eyes opened wide, and he put his hand to his mouth. "I'm sorry, Laoise. It's just what came to mind when I said nine months. It didn't mean anything. Instead of a baby, we've birthed an amazing itinerary. I look forward to performing with you this fall more than I have any season in my career so far."

Laoise swallowed and smiled, fighting to respond normally.

Charlie kept talking. "May I tell you, sweetheart, what profound joy I have experienced being married to you? I live in awe every single day of your beauty, inside and out. I have no doubt I'm the most blessed husband in the whole world. Thank you for your kindness, your vision, your inspiration musically, and your fundamental belief in goodness. I love you, Laoise, with all my heart."

"Excuse me," managed Laoise before running to the bathroom.

Charlie called through the door. "Are you all right, darling? Are you feeling sick?"

No. I throw up for pleasure. Of course, I'm feeling sick! Laoise wiped her mouth, forced a smile and opened the door.

"Just a little off kilter today. Must be the lamb I ate at the restaurant yesterday. I'm sure I'm fine. We need to discuss our plans for the week, who will do what to prepare to travel to London Thursday." Laoise returned with Charlie to the breakfast table.

Charlie brightened. "London, with you—always a delight. And Paris as well. And Marseilles, Milan, Rome . . . This will be such fun, Laoise!"

"It will! So much more delightful doing it together. I never liked going to a hotel room by myself after a concert. Of course, when I traveled with your mother, I enjoyed her companionship. That was one of your best ideas, Charlie."

"I'm glad, sweetheart. And your omelet is as good as anything I've eaten in France. Congratulations!"

"I tried to follow the recipe to the letter. I may master this cooking thing yet!"

Charlie chuckled. "Neither of us learned some of the basic skills of life, did we. We always had people to do things for us. I'm glad we decided to live on our own these first months, Laoise. It's been an adventure, and I'm proud of us both for conquering as much as we have."

"Yes—you even learned to sweep the floor," Laoise smiled. "Although you made me learn how to use a broom first, so I could teach you."

"Much the most efficient way, my dear. You're a wonderful teacher."

"Well then. This morning is the day for you to learn to wash dishes. I'll let you figure it out for yourself while I take a little rest before church, all right? Tomorrow we must consider what we need to pack, and whether there's anything we still need to shop for."

"Speaking of that, I have a surprise for you. Would you like to see it now?"

"A surprise? I love surprises!"

Laoise followed Charlie into their bedroom. He reached under the bed and pulled out a large, flat white box.

"Oh, Charlie," breathed Laoise as she lifted a stunning sapphire evening gown. "It's absolutely gorgeous."

"It matches your eyes," said Charlie, beaming. "Try it on."

"If you'll help me with the buttons," said Laoise. She shrugged off her dressing gown and lifted her arms as Charlie eased the dress over her head. "Oh my.""

"I want the world to see how lovely you are, a reflection of your inner beauty," said Charlie.

"I'm stunned," said Laoise. "Thank you."

"You're welcome. Let me help you out of it now so you can rest."

"I think what we need is a matching shirt for you, Charlie, to wear with your tuxedo."

"Like this?" Charlie pulled a smaller white, flat box from under the bed.

"You already thought of it! Perfect! I can't wait to see photographs of us together."

Charlie grinned. *That went well. Her pleasure thrills me.* "All right. Dishes for me, rest for you. Then we'll get ready for church."

Laoise climbed back into bed, but she couldn't relax. *I'm scared. What if—what if missing my second period and feeling sick in the mornings means what I think it does? But how is that possible? We've followed Thomas Haslam's plan to the letter. I even checked with my doctor, and he approved it. What if something else is wrong with me? We leave on our tour in four days! What am I going to do? I can't tell Charlie what I suspect. This could ruin everything.*

☙❧

"What are your plans today, Charlie?" Laoise asked at breakfast two days later.

"I'll practice for a couple of hours, then I'm meeting with my solicitor at ten thirty," said Charlie. "I want his advice about how to organize our finances. Would you like to go with me?"

"No, thanks. We agree on our priorities. I trust you to make good financial decisions for us." *Perfect! I can see Dr. Dennison and Charlie won't have to know.*

"This afternoon let's run through our whole repertoire. I'm still not satisfied with the 'Cantabile,' despite the audience response we've received." Charlie took his last bite of toast and stood.

"Especially the ending," said Laoise. "While you practice, I'll pop over to see Deirdre, all right?"

"Lovely. I'm delighted she's become such a good friend. Until this afternoon, then." Charlie kissed her and walked to the grand piano in their living room.

Laoise tidied the kitchen, threw up in the bathroom, the sound covered by Charlie's playing, then called for a carriage.

I'm grateful Deirdre agreed to go to the doctor with me. This is too hard to do alone. I miss my mother!

ঙ্গ

Dr. Dennison beamed. "Congratulations, Mrs. Malcomson! You are with child! About two months along, I would say. You'll have a spring baby, late March or early April."

Laoise clutched Deirdre's hand as the doctor began talking about vitamins and rest and caution with exercising and maintaining emotional calmness.

"Dr. Dennison," interrupted Deirdre. "Are you aware that Laoise is a world class violinist and leaves on a European tour Thursday? What do you have to say to her about that?"

"Oh, surely the stress of such a tour would be too much, my dear. I advise you to cancel and stay home. Pregnancy is a state of delicacy. No amount of pampering is too much, especially for ladies of means and position in society. From now on, your first vocation is motherhood, Mrs. Malcomson. Surely others can fill in for you on the stage. Now, as I was saying, for the nausea, keep crackers beside your bed and eat a few of them before you try to get up. Many women tell me this helps them."

"Thank you, Dr. Dennison," said Laoise, rising. "I will carefully consider all of your advice." She walked toward the door and Deirdre followed.

When they were seated in a carriage, Laoise said, "I can't do this. I can't. Swear to me, Deirdre, you'll say nothing to anyone, not even Desmond, and especially not Charlie. I need some time to figure it out."

Deirdre stared at Laoise, opened her mouth, closed it, and opened it again. "Laoise, you wouldn't . . . " Deirdre took a deep breath. "You can't—"

"I need time to think about what I can and can't do," said Laoise. "Thank you for coming with me today, Deirdre. Please don't worry. Oh, I do so wish my mother was alive . . . "

"Cathleen strikes me as a good person to talk to, Laoise."

"I'll think about it. Now swear to me, Deirdre."

"I swear," said Deirdre, frowning. "I won't tell anyone, not even Desmond, and especially not Charlie. But I hope you'll soon choose to do so yourself."

ଓଃଛ

"The person I know is here in Dublin," said Betsy on the telephone. "I'll ask her whether she knows a doctor in London and send you by courier what I find out, let's say by the end of the day tomorrow. You'll need some recovery time, you know."

"That's why I'm thinking Paris. But London might be possible too. Maybe better. In both cities we'll have a few days between concerts."

"So, London or Paris, next week or the one after. Right?"

"Yes. Thank you, Betsy."

"What are friends for?" Betsy ended the call.

Laoise wandered around the apartment. *I can't believe I'm considering this. Mum would be appalled. But I've gone over and over it in my mind, and I don't see any other way out. Betsy says people of our class receive excellent care, so in that way I'm fortunate, I guess.*

She stopped by the piano and played the opening theme of "Cantabile." *I'll make it look like a miscarriage. I don't think Charlie will know the difference. . . . I'm doing this for him as much as for me. He's so looking forward to doing this tour together.*

ଓଃଛ

"A message for you," said Charlie, handing Laoise a sealed envelope delivered to their door.

"Thank you." Laoise opened the letter and scanned it quickly. "It's from Betsy, wishing us well on our tour. That was a lovely reconnection."

"How nice of her," said Charlie. "As I was saying before the doorbell rang, I've arranged for a carriage to pick us up at 6:00 a.m. That will give us plenty of time to get settled on the ship before we sail."

"Isn't this exciting?" said Laoise, putting as much energy as she could muster into her voice.

"A dream come true," said Charlie. "Your father has invited Desmond and me to his club after their work today for a farewell drink, but I'll be home early. Too bad he didn't choose a place where you can go too."

"I saw Da yesterday," said Laoise. "Enjoy yourself!" *It's the opportunity I've been looking for to call the doctor in London. And if he can't do it next week, I'll call the one in Paris. But—what will we do afterwards? How can I keep from getting pregnant again?*

London, Sunday, September 10, 1905

"Look at this, Laoise," said Charlie the morning after their two-concert series with the London Symphony.

Laoise leaned over his shoulder to read the review in the London *Daily News*. "Stunning . . . gorgeous music matched by the beauty and charm of the performers . . . Who will ever forget the loveliness of Laoise Murphy swathed in sapphire blue, or forget the passion and purity of her performance, supported and supplemented by the inimitable Charles Malcomson?"

"I guess they liked us," said Laoise. "Well, this was only the beginning, eh, inimitable Charles?"

"I guess so, beautiful and charming Laoise!" Charlie turned to kiss her. "We have the whole day, Mrs. Malcomson. Anything you'd like to do?"

"Let's order room service, so we can go back to sleep after breakfast," said Laoise, yawning. "I'm tired."

"Me too. They didn't let us go last night until almost midnight, when the concert hall people finally chased the last ones out."

"Charlie, once we wake up again and have lunch, let's go to the Royal Botanic Gardens. We must enjoy this beautiful weather before it starts to get cold!"

"Grand idea, sweetheart. Tell me what you want for breakfast."

"Hmm. Something cold and light. Fruit and yogurt."

Charlie looked at Laoise. "Truly? I've never seen you eat a breakfast like that. You've always said a hearty breakfast is the foundation for good health."

Laoise yawned again. "That's all I want today. Quick and easy so I can go back to sleep. Bring it to me in bed?"

"All right. Well, I'm hungry. I'm ordering the full spread."

"I'm glad we have three more days in London," said Laoise Monday morning. "I know we need to practice, but can I go for a walk while you write your letters?"

"Of course, dear," said Charlie. He blew her a kiss, then dipped his pen, muttering as he wrote. "Dear Cally and Ryan, I hope you are both well. Laoise and I have begun our joint European tour! I wish you could have heard Laoise play for our London audience. I could hardly keep my mind on my own part of the performance. Next, we go to Paris, then Marseilles . . . "

Laoise dressed to go out and waved to Charlie as she left. "See you in an hour or so, darling."

That was easy. Now to find the address . . . I'm to make the powder into a tea, and when I begin to bleed, tomorrow or the next day, go to the Royal London Hospital emergency room and tell them Dr. Stuart is my physician. He'll admit me, do what needs to be done, and that will be that. He'll give Charlie his condolences on my miscarriage. Can anything go wrong? I don't know. But today is too beautiful to worry about it.

The bleeding began slowly, but soon it seemed to pour from Laoise's body. She shook with terror. *It's like seeing Mum all over again.* "Charlie! Charlie! Help!"

Charlie ran into the bathroom, shaking both sleep and his hair from his eyes. Laoise saw them grow wide.

"What's happening?" Charlie croaked.

"I'm bleeding," cried Laoise. "I need help!"

"I'll call the desk and ask them to send an ambulance," said Charlie, galvanized from his initial paralysis.

"Then grab supplies from my bag, and clothes. My navy jumper and white blouse. And get dressed yourself, Charlie."

Dr. Stuart approached Charlie, pacing back and forth in the Emergency waiting room. Charlie grabbed his arm. "How is she? Will she be all right? How could this happen?"

"I'm sorry to have to tell you your wife has had a miscarriage. I must admit her at least overnight. She's lost a great deal of blood."

"A miscarriage? You mean she is—was—expecting a child?"

"She didn't tell you? Well, at this early stage, many women don't realize they are pregnant. This is not unusual, Mr. Malcomson. She must rest, though, while we monitor her flow. We may need to give her a blood transfusion if her bleeding doesn't ease."

"But—but she can't be—we took every precaution! We're just starting our tour!"

"Ah. I thought I recognized her. Of course. Laoise Murphy, the violinist who played this weekend. I was there Friday evening. She was spectacular. As were you, Mr. Malcomson. It was one of the loveliest concerts I have ever attended."

"Thank you, sir, but can you tell me how far along she was?"

"My guess is about ten weeks."

That must be why she was sick in the mornings. She tried to hide it from me. I saw, but I didn't understand. I never suspected . . .

"Mr. Malcomson, would you like to see her before we take her upstairs? She will have a private room, of course."

"Yes." Charlie realized his whole body was trembling. He put his hands behind his back.

"I understand your anxiety, Mr. Malcomson. Fear not. We will have your wife's condition under control within a day or two. Take a deep breath. Blow it out slowly. That's it. Once more. In . . . out. Better? You must be strong for her, Mr. Malcomson. We don't know how she will respond to this loss."

Charlie took another deep breath in, then slowly blew it out. "Yes, sir. I'm fine now, sir."

"Through those doors, third room on the right. I will see you again upstairs."

"Thank you, sir."

Charlie found Laoise in tears. He bent down and wept with her.

"Dr. Stuart, we need your counsel before Laoise is released from the hospital," said Charlie Thursday morning. "We are scheduled to travel to Paris today, for concerts tomorrow night and Saturday. My agent just informed me the concert hall is sold out. What shall we do?"

"That is a difficult question, Mr. Malcomson. As a physician, I would much prefer that Laoise simply rest through the weekend, and even next week. As a music lover, I want Parisian concertgoers to have the same experience I did last Friday. Tell me, what will next week be like for the two of you, after the weekend concerts?"

"Similar to this week, in that we'll stay in Paris until Thursday to rest and to practice. Then we'll travel to Marseilles and perform Friday and Saturday evenings."

"Then I would say it depends on your energy level, Mrs. Malcomson. If you feel you are up to performing tomorrow night and can rest all day Saturday and then for a few days following that evening's concert, I think you will be fine. But if you feel exhausted, and especially if you start bleeding heavily again, then it's too soon, and you, Mr. Malcomson, will have to perform without your wife."

"But—"

"I understand, sir. It will be a blow to you personally and to your audiences. But if she doesn't rest adequately, she won't heal, and you'll be chasing this for weeks. If she stops long enough to heal now, she can likely do well for the rest of your itinerary."

Charlie looked at Laoise, wiping tears from her face. *It's not like her to have nothing to say through this whole conversation.*

"Sir, isn't it true, or at least likely, that my wife will need to heal emotionally as well as physically after this shocking event?"

"That's very true, Mr. Malcomson. This has been a loss and must be grieved. I suspect her music is the best way for her to heal. But healing must happen naturally. It cannot be forced. She herself, combined with your knowledge of her, must be your guide. In her discharge papers, I will leave for you the name and address of my colleague Dr. Jean Pierre Armand in Paris. You may go to him with any crisis or questions. I believe you will be wise enough to choose the best path to take at each moment of decision. Good day, sir, ma'am."

The doctor bowed and left. Laoise burst into tears. Charlie sat on the bed beside her, offered his handkerchief, and rubbed her back.

Laoise wept for a long time. *This is all my fault. I did it so I wouldn't interfere with our itinerary. So I could continue wearing his beautiful dress, and make marvelous music together. And now it looks like I'm doing exactly what I didn't want to do. I don't feel at all ready to perform with Charlie in Paris.*

Laoise looked at Charlie and tried to stop crying but seemed to have no control over her emotions.

I can't get out of my head the blood pouring out of my body. Like my mother birthing the baby who died. I thought taking this action would free me from the fear of childbirth I've felt all my life. I wonder if there is a way to make it impossible for me to ever get pregnant again.

Laoise blew her nose and hiccupped. Aloud she said, "I want my mother."

"Oh, sweetheart. I can only imagine how hard this is for you."

You have no idea.

A nurse entered and said, "I have your discharge papers, Mrs. Malcomson. Your orders are to rest, eat and drink, and if there is increase rather than decrease in your blood flow, you are to return to the hospital at once. Do you have any questions, ma'am?"

Yes. Many questions. But none I can ask you. "No. I understand. Thank you, nurse."

"Then you may leave as soon as you are ready. Goodbye, Mrs. Malcomson. Mr. Malcomson."

"Thank you. Goodbye."

"Charlie, what are we going to do?" asked Laoise in the carriage on the way back to their hotel. *I don't mean what are we going to do today or this weekend. I mean, how can we have a marriage in which I don't get pregnant. But I can't ask him that. Not today, at least.*

"We must take this one step at a time. If we get you a sleeper car on the train, do you think you could handle traveling to Paris?"

"I—I think so."

"Then that will be my first task when we get back to the hotel: change our ticket to an overnight sleeper tonight. You can rest all day and tell me this evening whether you feel able to make the journey."

"All right."

"But we need to decide now about the concert tomorrow evening, Laoise. I believe the Paris Orchestre's first violinist could fill in for you. It's terribly last minute, and it won't be the same, but I believe we must in fairness give him as much time as possible to prepare. I would rather do that than pressure you to perform too soon."

"That sounds wise. Charlie—I—I'm sorry."

"My precious darling, it's not your fault. We just need to give you time to get over this."

It is my fault. All of it. But how can I ever tell him?

CHAPTER 28

CALLY

Kansas City, Friday, August 11, 1905

CALLY SHADED HER EYES AGAINST the setting sun as she watched for Max to arrive with the carriage. *Whew, I'm tired. Thank you, God, for this weekend off, my first one since I came back a month ago. It's perfect timing so I can spend time with Flora. I wonder, though, why she decided to come.*

Max waved from a distance away. *I see. He can't get through the traffic. I'll go to him.* Cally picked up her bag and ran, dodging people on the way. She pointed to the bench by Max, and he shook his head. *He must have picked up Thomas first.*

Opening the door to the carriage, Cally slid in opposite Thomas. "Cally, how was your day?" he asked.

"All right. But the hospital is flooded with influenza patients. Usually this doesn't happen until the weather changes, around November. Oh, I guess I can take off my mask now. How was your day?"

"I heard unsettling news about an incident in Cheyenne, Wyoming on Wednesday. A man pulled a knife on a boy, but accidentally stabbed his wife instead. From what I can tell, the railroad people handled the incident appropriately, but it's making me wonder whether we should screen passengers for weapons before they board. This kind of racist incident seems to be increasing."

"Racist?"

"Yes. The intended victim apparently had dark skin."

"How awful."

"Yes. And although this happened in Wyoming, it's under my jurisdiction. I've written headquarters asking their advice on screening for weapons. We would lock them up and return them when the passenger leaves the train."

"That would give your people a lot more work."

"True. But if it saves even one life, I think it would be worth it. Well, the decision will be handed down to me—I don't have to make it. I do need to educate our people to be on the lookout for odd behavior that might signal trouble."

"You've done so much, Thomas. Like ensuring people of all races receive equal treatment on your trains."

"Unfortunately, that's not true yet further south. Oklahoma Territory is mine, but Texas and other states in the far south are not." Thomas sighed. "Help me make the transition to father and husband and host, now, Cally. What shall we do to ensure Billy's brief time with us is good for him? And do you know what Flora most wants to gain from her visit?"

"How about a picnic at West Terrace Park?"

"Grand idea, Cally. I think everyone will enjoy that. I'll talk to Cora about it as soon as we get home. Oh, Max is turning. I know. Flora must have gone to the Eldredge to rest, and he's picking her up now for dinner."

"What would we do without Max?" said Cally.

"And Nora. She settled in nicely. How do people make it who can't afford assistance?"

"Well, they probably don't create beautiful art like Cora or manage a railroad like you."

"Or devote their lives to caring for sick people like you. Here we are. Welcome, Flora."

"Thank you for having me, Thomas. I am delighted to be here."

"Flora! How wonderful that you came to Kansas City!" Cally gave her friend and mentor a warm hug. "How long can you stay?"

"I found a doctor to fill in for me for two weeks. This is my vacation, Cally! I find myself quite weary. I can't wait until you join me, and we can work together in Hansen."

"Does Sister Irmena know you're here?"

"Yes. I'll meet with her on Monday to make sure we're in agreement about the remainder of your training. She wrote me saying she hopes to send me five students next year. I need you to help me figure out how that can work. I can't spend all my time teaching and supervising them."

"Perhaps I'll be able to help," said Cally. "With the students as well as patients."

"I'm counting on that," said Flora. "And I'm hoping the doctor who is filling in for me will find himself drawn to the frontier. If so, and if he does well while I'm gone, I intend to offer him a job. I can't seem to cover my responsibilities anymore without running myself ragged. The only reason I'm the least bit coherent right now is the nap I just took."

"Look—the children are all outside to greet you, Flora!" said Thomas. "Shane keeps asking me when we can return to Idaho. We're trying to figure it out."

"Come with Cally and Felicity at the end of the month," said Flora.

"We're considering that. We want to visit Cecil and his family too."

"You are always welcome," said Flora. "Thank you, Max." She accepted his help to climb down from the carriage and was immediately surrounded by four children, who escorted her into the house all chattering at once.

"Felicity will have a big adjustment to make," said Cally, watching them.

"She seems excited about it," said Thomas. "But we'll miss you both, Cally. Oh my. There's Billy. Look at him. It looks like his nose may be broken." Thomas stopped, his head down, breathing hard. Cally put her hand on his arm.

After a moment, Thomas looked up. "This brings the whole problem too close to home. It's exactly what I feared, because of the timing of his travel, Cally. He must have been the intended victim on the train. But it could happen to anyone. We must find a way to protect our darker-skinned patrons, even if it does give more work to our employees. You haven't met Billy yet, have you? Let me introduce you."

"You must be the famous Cally!" said Billy before Thomas had the chance to speak. "I've heard so much about you, from the Malcomsons and from my Idaho family."

"I can't tell you what it means to me that we've found you, Billy," said Cally. "Now finally, the treasure hunt is complete."

Hansen, Idaho, Saturday, September 2, 1905

Cally, her hand in Ryan's, stopped for a moment to survey the group that had organized a luncheon to welcome her, Felicity, Cora, and her children. *Too bad Thomas had to stay in Kansas City. What good friends these dear people have become. All because Uncle William devised that amazing treasure hunt. We would never have thought of coming to Idaho otherwise. And so many good things are coming from it, including the plan to train nurses for the frontier. Thank you, God. And thank you that Billy is safely back at his school in Ireland. Thank you that he got to see his mother before she died, and for the flourishing of the Avery family in Fish Haven. That too is fruit of the treasure hunt.*

"Cally?" Ryan asked.

Cally took a deep breath and smiled. "Just remembering old times with these precious people," she said. "My heart is overflowing with thankfulness."

Ryan squeezed her hand. "There is a great deal to be thankful for. Including our new physician, Dr. Brandt. Ready to meet him?"

"Yes, and ready to give lots of hugs to dear friends."

Hansen, Idaho, Monday, September 25, 1905

Cally, Aaron Brandt, and Flora sat at the kitchen table in Flora's home. Cally dipped her pen in ink and waited to take notes.

"Our focus this week will be prenatal care. Next week we'll proceed to labor and delivery, and the week after to postnatal care. These are all critical topics on the frontier. Skilled midwives have traditionally been the main providers of care for pregnant women, and we have much to learn from them. That's why I've invited Sunrise, Falling Water's protégée and daughter-in-law, to join us today. She should be here soon."

"I'm curious to discover what she can add to our understanding of these topics," said Aaron. "In medical school—"

"Come in, Sunrise," said Flora. "Thank you for being willing to spend time helping us this morning. Would you like anything to drink?"

"A glass of water would be lovely," said Sunrise, sitting next to Cally.

"You've met Dr. Brandt, haven't you?" asked Flora.

"Not formally, no. I'm happy to meet you, Dr. Brandt."

"Please call me Aaron," said the doctor. "If we're going to work together, I prefer first names."

"All right. My name is Sunrise, Aaron. I am so pleased that you have joined us here in Hansen. I was getting concerned for Flora. We have too many people settling in this area for one doctor to care for."

"Thank you. I am very interested in what you will share with us today, Sunrise."

"I want to begin with the topic of family planning," said Flora. "An interesting case study has come to us from Ireland. We may run into the concepts advocated by this brochure among our Irish patients. Unfortunately, I have only one copy, so you'll have to pass it around. Tell me, what is the basic assumption behind Mr. Haslam's plan to avoid conception?"

"That ovulation occurs in conjunction with a woman's menses," said Aaron promptly. "That's common knowledge. This looks like a good plan to me."

"Thank you for setting up the problem," smiled Flora. "Can you tell me the scientific basis for the assumption that ovulation occurs along with menses?"

Aaron frowned. "I don't remember any explanation. It was simply presented to us as fact."

"Then you would agree that it's a belief we can challenge?" asked Flora.

Aaron's eyes widened. "I presume you have reason to doubt its veracity."

"We do, yes. The Shoshone healers believe differently, and I would like Sunrise to explain their perspective to us."

"We look at the woman's cycle as a whole," began Sunrise. "The Creator designed it for procreation, so we place ovulation at the center, like this." She began to draw on a piece of paper. "What the fertilized egg needs in order to thrive is a uterine lining rich with new blood. The act of menses drains away the old uterine lining when conception has not occurred. So, menses and the days following are the worst time for a fertilized egg to find safe haven and nourishment. We believe the Creator is wise and would not devise a system like that."

"Interesting," said Aaron. "Though not scientific."

Sunrise looked at Flora, who smiled and nodded. "Please continue, Sunrise."

"Following menses, the uterus begins to rebuild the uterine lining in preparation for the possibility of conception. We believe this takes about a week. It coincides nicely with a mid-cycle ovulation, so that by the time the egg travels through the Fallopian tube to the uterus, it has optimal opportunity to be protected and nourished. Thus, we believe a woman's most fertile period begins about ten days after the onset of menses and continues for about a week. A woman can still conceive the last few days before menses, but it is less likely, as the uterine wall begins to degrade." Sunrise took a deep breath. "That is our belief."

"If you are correct, Mr. Haslam's recommendation for avoiding conception is exactly wrong," said Aaron. "As well as the whole medical profession."

"True," said Flora.

"Hmm. My pregnancy occurred about two weeks after my period," said Cally. "You don't know, Aaron, so I might as well tell you as a fellow medical professional. Felicity's conception resulted from rape, a unique and memorable event. I remember that my period prior to that assault began in the middle of a lecture on suffrage by Miss Susan Anthony in Buffalo, New York. I had traveled there with her and was annoyed that I had to miss part of her lecture. On the way home she talked about how fast time was going by and how could it be February already. That's why I remember the date. The rape occurred eleven days later—not within the window of fertility Mr. Haslam identifies. For whatever that is worth."

"That's interesting. It lends credence to the Shoshone understanding, don't you agree, Aaron? Thank you for letting us consider your case, Cally. It's helpful because it was a unique event."

"Most women trying to plan their families do not have that frame of reference," said Aaron slowly. "They will not usually be able to identify the specific day of conception, so it's difficult scientifically to pin down the time of ovulation from their experience. I'm intrigued. It seems the Shoshone starting place, their belief that the Creator would provide optimal conditions for conception to be successful, might prove instructive."

Cally drummed her fingers lightly on the table. *If Laoise was following Thomas Haslam's recommendations rigidly, it's no wonder she got pregnant. And suffered that terrifying miscarriage. I wonder how she's doing now, and what she's thinking about the future. Perhaps Sunrise's perspective may help her . . .*

"Cally, I can tell you're thinking. Would you like to tell us what's on your mind?" asked Flora.

"I know a woman, the one who sent us this brochure from Ireland, who followed the plan to the letter, yet got pregnant. She ended up having a traumatic miscarriage. I was just thinking perhaps Sunrise's knowledge might help her avoid another pregnancy until the time she desires and is ready to conceive."

"So, with Cally's observation we have a direct application of the value of what Sunrise has shared with us. You will have women ask you how they can avoid pregnancy, Aaron and Cally. You must decide which of these models you believe to be more accurate, and what you will advise your patients as a result. The examples Cally has brought to us this morning—her own, and her friend's—reinforce my leaning toward the Shoshone perspective."

"But how can we know for sure?" asked Aaron. "This flies in the face of accepted medical understanding. And ought we be giving this kind of advice? In the faith tradition I'm from, women are expected and encouraged to have children. Indeed, they are commended for it above all other endeavors. Won't their husbands object and say we're interfering with what should be their own decision?"

"Educating people does not imply making their decisions for them," said Flora. "We are simply increasing their understanding, giving them a broader basis upon which to make their decisions. I believe these choices should be made jointly between a wife and her husband. We will greatly reduce the number of abortions if more pregnancies are undertaken intentionally. And don't tell me abortions do not occur. We cannot serve our patients well if we turn a blind eye to this reality."

"But abortion is morally wrong," said Aaron.

"Whether it is morally wrong or not, desperate women always have and always will seek to end unwanted pregnancies, despite the vagaries of the laws," said Flora. She leaned forward. "The question is, will our patients trust us enough to come to us for medical help if they attempt abortion and it goes badly? Or will they add to the numbers of women each year who die because they do not receive adequate care, often leaving young children behind them?"

"The Shoshone do not view abortion as you do," said Sunrise. "We know which herbs to use to restore a woman's flow, when that is better for any number of reasons. But we only do this prior to quickening. That is the time we believe a baby's life begins. After quickening, we treat the unborn child with all the love and care we give to all our children. Our babies are deeply valued and cherished. We don't experience the tension over this that I have observed in European families."

"This has been a most enlightening conversation," said Aaron. "You've given me a great deal to think about."

Flora stretched. "Returning to the topic of a woman's fertility, I intend to note from now on all information I can gather from the women I care for about the timing of their pregnancies, especially how long after menses they believe they may have conceived. They may not be able to pinpoint it exactly, Aaron, as you've said. But I've noticed that many women, especially multiparas, do have a keen sense of when they become pregnant. Their bodies tell them."

"Multipara means a woman who has been pregnant more than once?" asked Sunrise.

"A woman who has given birth more than once," said Flora. "A woman who has been pregnant more than once is called multigravida."

"Thank you, Flora. Shoshone women, also, often know when they conceive," said Sunrise. "I will ask our women to contribute to this gathering of information."

"Will you two embark on this discovery project with me as well, Aaron and Cally?" asked Flora. "The more information we can glean, the more quickly we can reach consensus on this important topic and the more helpful advice we can offer our patients."

Aaron and Cally both nodded.

"Thank you," said Flora. "Now, let's turn to prenatal care. To begin, please share with us the basic training you received, Aaron, and we'll compare that with our practices here on the frontier."

Cally had difficulty concentrating on what Aaron told them. *I'm going to write to Laoise about what Sunrise explained to us today. She may like to know there are other ways of thinking about the timing of conception than what they learned from Mr. Haslam and likely from their doctors. I'm glad we'll have more to go by because of Flora's "discovery project" before Ryan and I need to think about this for ourselves.*

Ryan's farm, Twin Falls, Idaho, Saturday, December 2, 1905

Cally watched Felicity playing with Brian, and laughed out loud when her daughter successfully mounted the toddler on the back of a surprised goat. The goat began to run around in circles to free itself of its unaccustomed burden. Felicity managed to keep pace, holding Brian in place, until finally they fell in a laughing tangle on a heap of hay.

"You two look like little porcupines," chuckled Cally, pulling bits of hay from the matching moss-green sweaters she had knit for the two children.

"Can I go for a ride, Mummy?" asked Felicity.

"On the goat? No. But you can ask Ryan for a pony ride when he finishes his chores."

"I'll go ask him now!" Felicity ran to the barn.

Brian toddled toward the goat, now in the far corner of the pen. Cally ran to scoop him up.

"Enough goat rides for today, baby," she said. "Let's go stir your daddy's soup."

Cally hummed as she set the table and sliced a loaf of Ryan's homemade bread. "I love our life here," she said out loud, to engage Brian. "It will be even better when Ryan and I can live together. Only about six more months. Then you can learn to call me mama."

"Mama," said Brian. "You mama."

"Oh, you already know, do you? Well, that makes me very happy, Brian."

"Dada," said Brian, pointing to the door just before it opened.

"I'm going to take Felicity for a short ride, Cally, all right? We'll take Chestnut around the perimeter of the farm to check my fence. About thirty minutes, a few more if I need to examine the fence more closely at any point."

"Enjoy," said Cally. "Brian just called me mama!"

"Good boy," said Ryan. "Back soon."

I'm so glad we love each other's children. And they love each other. Makes joining our two families so much easier.

After supper, Cally said, "Ryan, I've received an invitation from Cora to celebrate Christmas with them. The four of us. What do you think?"

"That sounds lovely. If the weather is amenable—not too much snow for the trains to run."

"Good. I'll let them know," said Cally. Felicity, it's time for us to go home to bed."

"Aww, can't we stay here? I could sleep on the sofa."

"In about six months the answer to that question will be yes," said Cally. "Oh—Ryan, did I tell you Starlight is expecting their second child?"

"You didn't, but that's lovely. Teddy must be delighted. Good night, Felicity. I love you," said Ryan. "Brian, you and I will walk our girls out to Flora's wagon. He lifted his son. As they walked, he said, "I love you, Cally. I hope these six months go by fast."

"Shall we start telling people our dates?" asked Cally. "I can include them in my response to Cora. And in the Christmas cards I'm sending to other friends and family. I think it would be all right now that we've had a positive response from Uncle Dugan and Aunt Aisling."

"June twenty-third wedding here. July fourteenth reception in Killeagh. Fine with me," said Ryan. "Unless we decide to elope sooner." He gave her a long kiss.

"You know that won't work," laughed Cally, pushing him away. "All my energy must go into helping Flora for one more semester. And learning from her all I can."

"I know, I know," fake-grumped Ryan. "Give your mama a kiss, Brian."

The baby planted a wet kiss on Cally's cheek, then put his head down on his father's shoulder. Cally helped Felicity up, climbed onto the bench beside her and picked up the reins.

"Time for bed for all of us," said Ryan. "Good night, Cally. Good night, Felicity."

CHAPTER 29

BILLY

St. Colman's, Fermoy, Friday, September 1, 1905

ON HIS WAY FROM CLASS to hurling practice, Billy nodded to Mr. MacDonagh as he passed in the hallway.

"How was your first week of school, William?"

"Good, sir."

"My condolences on your mother's death."

"How did you know my mother died?"

"Your uncle sent me a telegram informing me of her death and telling me you would stay with his family for the summer."

"Oh."

"We must schedule the two exams you missed at the end of the last term. Please stop by my rooms after practice so we can choose a time."

"Oh. Yes, sir." *Last term seems an eternity ago. I don't even know which exams I missed.*

Billy hurried to the field to join Coach O'Brien. *I wish I could play. It's kind of Coach to let me help him train the lads, but it's not the same. The school doctor says six more weeks. That's the whole season, really. The team will figure itself out without me.*

Billy knocked on Mr. MacDonagh's door and entered when he said, "Come in."

"First, William, tell me what happened to your face. An accident? I presume Dr. Foster has examined you?"

"Yes, sir. He changed the bandage. I was assaulted. Because of the color of my skin. The man wanted to kill me. His wife intervened and received the knife in her leg instead of in my chest."

Mr. MacDonagh's eyes opened wide. "I'm so sorry this happened to you, lad. Was it here in Ireland or in America?"

"It was in the state of Wyoming in America, but the man was from Idaho, near where my uncle lives."

"Outrageous. I imagine you feel safer here."

"At the school, yes. In Kilkenny, no."

"Speaking of that, William, have you given more thought to the role you want to play in our movement? We need your message deliveries more than ever."

Billy sat down on Mr. MacDonagh's sofa. "I've thought a lot about that, Mr. MacDonagh. I talked with my Malcomson relatives and decided I'm a pacifist, like my father, who was a Quaker. I don't believe in war or violence as the best ways to solve problems. I think innocent people will always suffer in those conditions, and I don't want to be part of anything like that."

"I see," said Mr. MacDonagh. "In your conversation with Mr. Murphy in Dublin, did you discuss alternate ways to be involved with the nationalist movement?"

"Yes. Mr. Murphy and Arthur Griffith and Bulmer Hobson want to achieve Irish independence from Britain, but they believe they can use political means. I do see why separation from England is worth pursuing, but I think I disagree with you about how to do it."

"Even though your country, America, used arms to achieve its own independence from Britain?"

"Yes, sir. That was a long time ago and I don't know yet what I think about that. I just know what I myself don't want to do."

"I see," said Mr. MacDonagh once more. "If I were to send you as a messenger in matters that do not involve violence, you might still be willing?"

"I might," said Billy. *I do miss the fun of going to new places. Of flying down the open road on the dragonfly bicycle. Of having a secret from the other lads.*

"But?" said Mr. MacDonagh.

"But if I get into another situation like the one in Kilkenny, and I survive it, that's it. I won't do it anymore."

"I see," said Mr. MacDonagh again. "I'll take all that you've said under advisement. Now, about your exams. Next week on Tuesday and Thursday after classes. Please inform Coach O'Brien you will miss practice those days."

"Yes, sir. Can you remind me what subjects the exams will cover? I don't remember."

"I'm not surprised, William, with all that happened to you this summer. The two exams are algebra and biology."

"Thank you, sir."

"You may go, William."

I did it. I said it out loud. I'm a pacifist, like the Quakers. Like my father. I want to heal people, not hurt them. As he walked toward his room, Billy touched the bandage over his nose. Anger rose inside him, and he remembered his conversation with Max. *Anger is an opportunity. I choose to use my anger for good. I am safe. I'm secure. I am strong, cuz I belong.*

Beside the door, Billy saw a stack of mail. One, a fat one, was addressed to him. *It's from Ebony! She must have sent me some of her drawings!*

Billy greeted his new roommate, George, who had taken Harry's place, then sat on his bed and opened the envelope. He found a letter from Miz Minnie, a note from Uncle Cecil, and a drawing by Ebony: a dragonfly painted with shiny green paint, hovering over a blooming lily pad on the edge of a lake. Ebony had used watercolors for the background and oil for the dragonfly. *It looks like the dragonfly can dart away at any moment.*

The painting was labeled "Flying Free." Ebony had drawn a tiny heart beside her signature.

Billy smoothed the creases as well as he could and tucked the drawing into the back of his notebook. *So I can look at it every time I need to be reminded that hate and anger limit my freedom and I must let them go. Once my exams are over, I'll write a letter back to all of them.*

The road to Clonmel, County Tipperary, Saturday, September 23, 1905

Billy whooped as he stretched out his arms and pedaled as fast as he could down a smooth, straight piece of the road from Fermoy to Clonmel. The wind rushed past him, and a curious starling, which briefly settled on his handlebars, flitted away on its own flight.

"I'm flying free, Ebony!" Billy shouted. "The dragonfly has molted again!"

At a curve where the road began to rise, Billy lost momentum. *I still cannot believe what happened yesterday. If Fred had not been with me, I might imagine I dreamed it.*

Billy leaned into the climb and remembered every detail he could. *I was notified to go to the director's office after class because I had a visitor, who called himself my brother. This must be a prank, I thought. I have no brothers. Or sisters either, though Ebony is like a sister to me. I asked Fred to go with me to share the fun, whatever it would be. In the director's office, an oldish man stood to greet me. I had no idea who he was. None.*

"Billy," he said. "I've come to apologize to you for the way I treated you a year or so ago."

"Sir?" I replied, mystified. I looked around to see which of my classmates was behind this charade. Where had they found this man?

"Ah, perhaps you don't remember me. It was a very brief meeting, after all. I am William Malcomson, your half-brother. At the time you came to my home, I could not imagine you were telling me the truth, that my father was your father. I must say you don't look quite as I remember you either. Your face—"

I was so stunned I could only stand there gaping at him. Fred stepped forward and held out his hand. "I'm William's friend, Fred," he said pleasantly. "We call him William here. I'm pleased to meet you, even though Billy, as you call him, seems to be nonplussed. Billy suffered an accident, a broken nose, which unfortunately for St. Colman's has kept him off the hurling team for the season."

I almost laughed, which must have been Fred's intention, to relax me a bit. "Nonplussed" was a new vocabulary word for us in English class that week. I managed to close my mouth and extend my own hand for the gentleman to shake.

"Is there a place we could go to talk?" asked William-my-half-brother.

"It's a beautiful day. We could go to the garden." Fred came to my rescue once again.

We found a bench and sat.

"How—how did you figure it out?" I stuttered.

"I had a visit from a cousin, or to be precise, a cousin's wife," said WMHB, as I've started calling him for short.

I frowned, sorting through the Malcomsons I had met, trying to make sense of who this woman could be. Cathleen! I concluded, just as WMHB began explaining his cousin Peter had died, but his wife Cathleen had traveled from Waterford to speak to him.

"Cathleen explained the whole situation to me. She told me about making the same error herself when she met you on the ship. That helped me forgive myself, but I knew I had to ask your forgiveness as well, Billy. William."

"Please call me Billy. All the Malcomsons do. It keeps me distinct from all the other Williams," I said. "And yes, I forgive you. How could you have known? I was so upset to learn my—our—father had died that I imagine I was quite incoherent."

Fred grinned at me. "Incoherent" was also one of our vocabulary words last week.

"I confess it took me some time after Cathleen's visit to wrap my mind around what my father had done in America," continued WMHB. "I knew when he disappeared from Ireland he was quite upset, and with good reason, after the way my brother and I and our mother had treated him. I can only suppose he thought his life in Ireland and his relationships with us had ended, and that he would live the rest of his life in America. Even so, it's such a departure from the behavior I would have expected from the father I knew. It's been hard to reconcile in my mind. Yet here you are."

"Here I am. Very grateful, sir, for your visit."

*"I'm not sure, Billy, that you need call me 'sir.' Even though I could be your grandfather. I must say I am quite gratified—" (Fred and I grinned at each other upon hearing him use the word "gratified.") "*Quite *gratified to find you studying here at St. Colman's, a school with such a sterling reputation. And the director assures me you are one of the top students. When Cathleen told me who you were, please forgive me, but I imagined you as I had perceived you to be that day, a hungry vagabond. Yet here you are."*

"Here I am," I said again, as Fred elbowed me and grinned.

"Please tell me more about your life," said WMHB. "Where do you go, for instance, on holidays?"

"I spent last summer with my aunt, uncle, cousin, and grandmother in Idaho. My mother's family," I said. "I arrived in time to speak to my mother before she died, and then I stayed until it was time to travel back to school. On the way I stopped in Kansas City to visit Thomas and Cora Malcomson and their children. Thomas is Cathleen's second son, who has settled in Kansas City and works for the railroad there. I've been invited to Cathleen's daughter Margaret's home for Christmas. Cathleen lives with Margaret's family in Waterford."

"I see," said WMHB. "Is there a time you could come to visit my family?"

I almost fell off the bench. Fred anchored me and spoke up. "We have a whole week off school for the October Holiday. I invited William home with me, but if he prefers to go to your home, I'll find another time for him to visit my family again. My mother is proud of me for having such an erudite friend" (I poked him for fitting in yet another of our vocabulary words) "who is keeping me from drowning academically. The dates are October 30-November 3. Plus the weekends on either side."

"Perhaps we could split that holiday, Fred," suggested WMHB. "I must travel to the Continent the first week of November. What do you think, Billy? You could come to us the first weekend, and travel to Fred's house for the November days."

"I-I guess so," I said, too stunned to express myself more eloquently.

"It will be a privilege for us to get to know you better," said WMHB.

"And I you, sir. I mean—"

WMHB laughed. Until then I didn't know he was capable of laughter.

Fred spoke up again. "You may be interested in knowing that Billy will be competing in an interschool scholastic competition on Friday before that holiday, October twenty-seventh. He is one of three students who have been chosen to compete from our school. The event will be held in Cork City. Perhaps you and other family members would like to attend and cheer him on. My own family plans to do so. You could even invite Mrs. Catherine—"

By then I had turned scarlet. As scarlet as my skin tone allows. "Cathleen," I said.

"Forgive me. Cathleen. And any other Malcomsons out there," finished Fred.

"Thank you, Fred. I believe that will be educational for my younger children. Perhaps we can take Billy home with us directly afterwards. Billy, please send us the specifics of time and place. Perhaps Cathleen will want to attend with Margaret and her family."

Fred looked like a cat that had swallowed a canary. THAT expression I learned at the brothel in Idaho.

"It seems to me, Billy, you have a grand friend in Fred. Be good to him." WMHB stood and extended his hand to Fred and then to me. Clearly, we hadn't yet reached the hugging stage.

Coming abruptly out of his reverie, Billy swerved to avoid a cart clattering quickly downhill toward him. As he came over the top of a hill, he glimpsed the cotton mill in the valley, on the edge of the town of Clonmel.

I wonder whether Lucy will meet me there again. And whether she will remember me. THIS holiday weekend—called in Ireland the Autumnal Equinox and Samhain, not Halloween—I'm happy to be a messenger boy.

ᏈᏭ

Lucy was there. She looked Billy up and down and pointed to his face.

"An accident," Billy said. "Hello, Lucy."

"Hello, Billy. It's been a long time since you came. The weather's more pleasant, I must say. You were more than half frozen, as I recall. I suspect whatever happened under that bandage is less troublesome than that was."

Billy laughed. "By far. It's lovely to see you again." *One thing hasn't changed. She's as easy to talk to as I remembered.*

"I bet you're hungry. Lads your age are always hungry. Let's go see what Mum has prepared for supper."

"Are you still working at the cotton mill, Lucy?"

"Probably for the rest of my life," she sighed.

"If you could do anything in the world, what would you like to do?" asked Billy.

Lucy brightened. "I would go to a music school."

"You would? What instrument do you play?"

Lucy pointed to her throat. "I carry my instrument with me. But I know I don't know how to use it properly."

"Isn't there anyone in Clonmel who can teach you?"

"There might be, I don't know. But my father considers singing frivolous. Not a worthy investment. What about you, Billy? What do you want to do with your life?"

"I intend to become a doctor. A pediatrician," said Billy. "Don't give up on your dream, Lucy. Miracles can happen. They have for me." *Like what happened just yesterday with WMHB.*

 css

St. Colman's infirmary, Tuesday, October 10, 1905

"All right, lad. Let's have a look." Dr. Foster carefully loosened the bandage he had applied a week earlier. This time, he touched Billy's nose, first gingerly, then more boldly. "Any pain?"

"No, sir."

"The nice thing about this kind of break is that it doesn't require physical therapy after it heals." Dr. Foster chuckled at his own joke. "Now, lad, without the bandage to remind you, you may forget your nose still needs time for the new bone and cartilage to solidify. I'll tell Coach O'Brien you may not play for two more weeks. But you can practice again in a limited way. No tackles or punching, no catching the sliotar with your nose." Dr. Foster chuckled again. "Give this paper to Coach O'Brien. Congratulations. Your face looks quite respectable."

"Thank you, sir." *I need to find a mirror. And remember when I'm a physician not to make lame jokes. Although, for children and their families, a sense of humor might ease the intensity of what they're going through. I must learn all I can from Fred.*

Billy walked into class and all the lads cheered. He bowed, gratified, and took his seat. *The man who punched me and wanted to kill me had no idea who I am. No idea at all.*

ଓ୪ഋ

St. Colman's, Thursday, October 26, 1905

"I understand you won't be available to me these next days," said Mr. MacDonagh, passing Billy in the hallway. "That's all right. I've found someone else to go in your place. Good luck at the competition tomorrow. We'll all be cheering for you. Even the school board officials plan to attend. Make us proud, William."

"I'll do my best, sir." *He's making me nervous. The school board? WMHB and his family? Cathleen, Margaret, and her family? I'll just look at Fred. He'll keep me calm and focused. I hope. I'm more nervous about going to WMHB's home afterward. How to behave in a mansion like my half-brother's? I have no idea.*

ଓ୪ഋ

Queen's College Cork City, October 27, 1905

"Billy, I'm so proud of you!" exclaimed Cathleen, giving him a warm hug. "William, isn't it amazing to have someone so gifted in our family? Children, congratulate your cousin."

"Congratulations, Billy!" and "Congratulations, William!" sounded from all sides. Billy couldn't stop grinning. *I guess I did what Mr. MacDonagh asked of me, to make St. Colman's proud. I hope I can do as well with WMHB's family as on the Queen's College stage.*

Billy looked around for his teammates. They too were receiving enthusiastic acclaim. He waved to them, and they waved back. Fred and Ben rushed over and pounded his back.

"Whenever you're ready, Billy," said WMHB. "Our carriage is waiting outside."

Billy barely had time to appreciate again the loveliness of the university's sandstone towers before he was tucked into a large carriage with WMHB, his wife, and the two children he had long ago glimpsed running out of their house and past him without a glance. The butler had called them Llewellyn and Susan.

"Find out what you have in common—try sports first, then hobbies and games," Fred had advised. "You could teach them whist if they don't know it. You've become quite good, you know. Cards can be terrific icebreakers. Let them teach you something they like. You'll be fine."

I hope so, he said to himself in the carriage.

WMHB helped. "Billy plays on the St. Colman's hurling team, son."

Llewellyn brightened. "You do? I play too. What position?"

This might turn out all right after all.

CHAPTER 30

CHARLIE AND LAOISE

Livorno, Italy, Monday, October 2, 1905

"THE SUNSHINE IS DECEPTIVE," SAID Charlie, stepping back into the hotel room from their balcony. "The breeze is chilly. We'll need jackets."

Laoise smiled and pulled a warm wrap from her case. "It's not the Livorno beach time we imagined. Still, it's lovely to be here. I love the sea. So open and free and ever-changing."

"Ready?"

"Ready."

Charlie tucked Laoise's hand into his arm as they walked to the beach. "How do you feel about our tour so far, Laoise?"

"I think it's gone well. Once we got past London. And Paris."

"I do too, though in Marseille the Mendelssohn Concerto took a lot out of you."

"Yes. Milan was better. Oh, Charlie, look at the dolphins!"

Charlie shaded his eyes. In the distance he saw sleek silver figures leaping from the water. "They're so playful. I miss that."

"You miss dolphins?"

"No. I miss the playful side of you. I haven't seen it since—let me think. Since Desmond and Deirdre's wedding."

Laoise's face fell. "I've tried to be cheerful."

"You have been, sweetheart, but only on the surface. As always, our audiences love you. But your interactions feel forced. In Milan, I watched your face after the last person left. As soon as he turned away, your face changed. You looked so sad, my heart broke. You're not yourself, darling. I feel like you've pulled away from me."

Laoise said nothing. She picked up a pebble and tossed it into the waves stirred up by the breeze.

"Do you want to talk to me about it?" asked Charlie. "Have I hurt your feelings in some way? Are you grieving the loss of the baby?"

Laoise responded quickly. "Oh, no, Charlie. Everything's fine."

Charlie smiled at her, then sobered. "Do you know what I hear in what you said?"

"That everything is fine?"

"No. I hear that you don't want to tell me. And that makes me sad. I used to feel we could talk about anything. Now there's a barrier between us. Invisible but definitely there."

Laoise climbed a boulder, sat, and looked out to sea, her chin in her hand. Charlie climbed up beside her and sat quietly. It seemed the dolphins had moved on.

For a long time, Laoise stared without speaking. *How can I distract him from what I don't want to tell him? I feel so empty inside I can't think of anything. I'm exhausted. Mummy's death and then all the fuss in London . . . I wish I could sit here in peace without having to give an account of myself. Though I know he only asks because he cares.*

Finally, she said, "Charlie, how are we going to avoid going through the same experience again? Getting pregnant and then miscarrying, with all the drama of being hospitalized, missing concerts . . . I just don't know how to make this work."

"Most pregnancies don't end in miscarriage, Laoise."

"True. But didn't we agree not to have children? A pregnancy that doesn't end in miscarriage is a child."

"Would that be so terrible, Laoise? To have a child?"

Laoise jumped to her feet. "Charlie, what are you saying? That my career isn't important? That it would be all right with you to leave me at home tied to a baby while you travel around being famous? Would *you* want to stay home and give up your music?"

Charlie opened his mouth and gripped his abdomen, as if he had been punched. "Laoise, I've never heard you use that tone of voice. Not once."

"Well, you asked me."

Charlie stood up, balancing on the rock. *She's in pain. That's obvious. I need to calm down and listen. This is a complex situation, and I haven't given it enough thought. It was easy, before we were married, to say yes to not having children. I would have said yes to anything Laoise had asked of me, I think.*

He glanced at Laoise, sitting again, her head buried in her arms. *I assumed she would feel differently after we were married. That a maternal instinct or whatever it's called would set in and she would change her mind. Then I would be a loving husband and support her in having the child* she *wanted.*

Laoise rubbed silent tears from her eyes and stared again out to sea.

Clearly, that's not the case. I need to think seriously about how I feel regarding having children. Am I truly willing to never have a son or a daughter? A daughter with Laoise's sparkling sapphire eyes looking up at me? A son calling me Da, thinking I'm his hero?

Charlie sat beside Laoise and offered his hand. After a long moment, Laoise took it.

"Can you tell me more about your feelings regarding having children, Laoise? I know that what you witnessed with your mother made you terribly afraid of childbirth itself. And you're afraid a baby would ruin your career. Is there anything else you want to tell me?"

Laoise bowed her head, then shifted on the boulder to look at him. "I feel called to be a violinist, Charlie. I don't feel called to be a mother." Her voice grew more strident with each word she spoke. "I feel betrayed by Thomas Haslam's system. We followed it exactly. We didn't waver, even once. Yet I got pregnant. So, I know it can happen again."

Charlie stared at Laoise. *I did ask her. But I didn't expect this—this avalanche of anger.* He focused again on what she was telling him.

"Yes, I'm afraid of the birthing. But I'm more afraid of losing my place in the world of music performance. Right now, you and I are in demand everywhere. All that would change if I have a child. How could I ever recover professionally? A son or daughter is forever. We would be parents, with responsibilities to him or her for the rest of our lives."

Charlie pulled back as if Laoise had struck him. *She said "the rest of our lives" as if she would be doomed to a terrible fate. What is going on in her beautiful, gentle soul?*

"Are you sure there isn't something more troubling you, Laoise? Because you've said those things before. I understand they're huge issues, and though you didn't mention her, I know you miss your mum terribly. But I have the sense there's something else beneath the surface. Something you haven't told me and for some reason, don't want to tell me."

Laoise stared at Charlie with tears puddling her sapphire eyes, but she said nothing.

"Laoise, I want to know. I want us to face whatever this is together. You don't need to carry this alone."

Laoise shook her head and again buried her face in her arms.

"All right, sweetheart. But if you change your mind, I'm here. I want to understand. I want to be a support to you, in whatever is causing you so much pain."

Laoise said nothing. She stood, brushed off her skirt, and climbed down from the boulder, ignoring Charlie's outstretched hand. As he clambered down beside her, she said, "I'm tired, Charlie. I want to take a nap."

"All right, darling." *I'll use that time to journal about my feelings regarding children. She deserves a clear and honest statement from me. And maybe if I'm more forthright, she'll be willing to be the same.*

≈

After wild acclimation of their concerts in Rome, Laoise made a show of being energetic and enthusiastic about Charlie's proposals for how to spend their time there. She was affectionate and even laughed out loud sometimes. But she engaged in no more discussions about the subject of children.

And every time there was an opportunity for intimacy, she was too tired. Or had a headache. Or cramps when her next menses occurred.

Charlie gazed at her still sleeping after he woke one morning. *What if she never wants to be intimate again? It's been a month since her miscarriage. Surely, she has healed by now. I wish we had a reliable way to avoid pregnancy. I wish she could trust me enough to tell me what is troubling her beneath the surface. I wish we were as free and easy together as we were before—before she lost our child.*

Laoise woke, and in her first unguarded moment, she smiled at Charlie. His heart leapt. But a shadow quickly crossed her beautiful features, and she turned over, closing her eyes again.

"I'll be in the lounge downstairs reading the paper," said Charlie. "When you're ready for breakfast, please join me."

A slight nod was all the response she gave him.

We have three more concerts—Venice, Munich, and Amsterdam—then we head home. I wonder whether Mum can help us. I know Laoise misses her own mum terribly. They were always so close.

☙❧

Dublin, Thursday, November 2, 1905

"Home again! That was an exhausting two months!"

Laoise said nothing. She walked into their bedroom and began unpacking.

Charlie pulled a few personal letters from a huge accumulation of mail on a table in the vestibule of their apartment. *Perhaps Laoise and I can tackle at least some of the fan mail after our supper with her family, identifying those that require a response.* He sighed as he regarded the large stack of envelopes from strangers. *Nice words are lovely, of course, but this is a bit much. Perhaps we should hire a secretary. I know Terry doesn't have time to deal with all this.*

Charlie carried their personal letters, a stack in each hand, into their bedroom. "Laoise, these letters are for you."

"Oh, good. I'd like a break." She sat beside Charlie on their settee as each opened the letters addressed to them from Thomas and Cora, Cathleen, Margaret, Daniel, and Liam.

"Here's one from Cally!" said Laoise. "An apology for missing our wedding, I imagine. I wonder what she'll say for herself."

Quickly perusing the letter, Laoise sat up straight. "Charlie, listen to this! Cally thinks Thomas Haslam is all wrong!" She read aloud Cally's description of Sunrise's beliefs about female fertility.

"How interesting!" Charlie said in a neutral tone. *This is the most exciting news I can imagine receiving! But I must stay noncommittal. This is about Laoise, not about me.* He pulled out his pen, made notations on the back of an envelope, and showed them to Laoise. "If Sunrise is correct, this month for you looks like this."

Laoise stared at his dates, her mind whirling. *This seems so much more sensible. The optimal fertile period should be after the lining of the womb is restored. Is it possible? I wish I could be sure . . .*

She looked up at Charlie's face. "I wonder if there's any way to corroborate this."

"I suppose we could ask the mothers of my family whether they can identify when in their cycles they got pregnant. My mother would be the most likely to know, I suppose, since my father was gone so much. Shall we ask her about it when we travel to Waterford next week?"

"We have nothing to lose, right?" Laoise thought for a minute. "I've wondered how Meghan managed to have just two children. We could ask what their secret is, too."

"Shall I write to Daniel?" asked Charlie.

"Yes, please," said Laoise.

The next evening, Charlie knocked on Desmond and Deirdre's door.

"Welcome home!" exclaimed Deirdre, hugging Charlie and Laoise.

Desmond beamed behind his wife. "Da should be here soon," he said, guiding his sister into the sitting room. "So, tell us all about your time on the Continent!"

"I'm making a scrapbook for you," said Deirdre. "Let me show you." She extended a book to Charlie, who shared it with Laoise. It was half-filled with newspaper reviews of their tour, including Laoise's hospitalization and missing the concerts in Paris. A reporter had interviewed concertgoers and communicated the sympathy for Laoise they had expressed.

Tears came to Laoise's eyes. *They don't know I did it to myself. I don't deserve these kind words. But how could I have coped with a pregnancy and then with a child?*

Laoise kept her eyes on the newspaper clippings, many of them including photographs of her, until the wave of emotion passed, and she could smile at Deirdre. "Thank you so much! What a gift, Deirdre! It's kind of you to do this for us."

"It's fun," smiled Deirdre. "I feel famous myself, knowing I'm related to celebrities. Oh, there's the door. It must be your father."

Colin hugged them both, then held his daughter by the shoulders and looked into her eyes. "Are you well again, Laoise? I am so very sorry for what you have suffered."

Laoise smiled, blinking back tears. "Thank you, Da. I'm fine. We were just looking at the lovely scrapbook Deirdre has made of our tour."

As Laoise intended, her father turned his attention to the articles Deirdre had collected, carefully reading each one. "Your mother would be so proud," he said.

When supper was announced, Deirdre hung back with Laoise while the men entered the dining room. "I'm sorry you lost the baby," she whispered. "I just learned I'm with child myself. I'm so happy I thought of announcing it tonight, but I don't want to hurt your feelings."

"Congratulations!" said Laoise, hugging her sister-in-law. "That's wonderful news! Please, share it with everyone." She breathed deep. *Thank God. This will divert attention from me. I don't want to talk about the "miscarriage."*

❧

"Do you have enough energy to look at some of our fan mail?" asked Charlie as they prepared for bed.

"I'm tired. Can we do it tomorrow? We could read a few of them at breakfast. Do you have other plans?"

"Just the meeting with Terry at 11:00. That still works for you? If not, I could call him and try to reschedule—"

"It works. Terry's been a wonderful agent, taking me on as well as you. After that I'll meet Alice Jacob for a late luncheon," said Laoise, yawning.

"The Quaker artist we met at AE's? How delightful! Shall we join AE's Conversation again this Sunday?"

"I'd like to. But what if the Haslams are there?"

"What if they are? Someone needs to let them know their system isn't perfect."

"Well, I'm not going to discuss it. You can if you want to."

Charlie climbed into bed. "I'll think about it. They are doing amazing work for women's suffrage—I read an article about it this morning. You could talk to Mrs. Haslam about that, Laoise. Perhaps before long, you'll be able to vote!"

༄༅

Laoise sighed as she sipped her breakfast coffee and opened her seventh fan letter. "They all say pretty much the same thing, don't they? Do we have to read all of them?"

Charlie didn't answer. Laoise glanced at him and froze. The expression on his face was one she had never seen before.

"Wha-what's wrong, Charlie?" she asked.

Charlie looked at her, clearly fighting for control. "This isn't a fan letter. It's from your friend Betsy. I don't think I was meant to read it."

He handed the paper to Laoise. She looked at it and blanched.

"I'm sorry I opened it," said Charlie. "I didn't associate the name Elizabeth Mallory with your friend Betsy. I only thought the famous cellist would be congratulating us on our performance with the London Symphony, where she's just been hired."

"Charlie, I—"

"Before we talk about this, I need to go for a walk to calm down. I'll come back in half an hour." Charlie pulled on his jacket and closed the door gently behind him.

Laoise looked again at Betsy's brief note. *It's dated before the news of my "miscarriage" would have hit the news.* "You haven't told me what happened. Did you contact the doctor I recommended? Were you able to rid yourself of the fetus? Tell me all! Bets."

Laoise crumpled the note, threw it on the table and began to pace, gripping her abdomen. *An hour and a half until Terry gets here. Charlie will be back any minute. I feel like running away. But delaying this conversation will only make things worse.*

She walked to their bedroom and knelt beside the bed. "God, please forgive me for my sin of not being honest with Charlie. I'm frightened by what I saw in his face. Please help us to hear each other and find a path forward. Please."

The door to their apartment opened. Charlie walked in and stopped. "Laoise?" he called.

"I'm here." Laoise rose, smoothed her dress and hair, and stood for a moment, trembling. She took a deep breath and walked into the front room.

Charlie reached out a hand and Laoise, trembling even more, extended hers. He guided her to the sofa and sat for a moment, his head bowed.

Finally, he looked at her, tears glistening in his eyes. "Laoise, what hurts me the most is that you didn't trust me. What have I done that made you hesitant to talk to me about this? Afraid to share your struggle, to the point of deliberately deceiving me?"

"I—" Laoise stopped and cleared her throat. "I'm sorry, Charlie. I thought it would be something so simple it needn't disturb our happiness. I imagined it would be like menses. I didn't imagine hemorrhage, and hospitalization, and cancelled concerts. Apparently—" She stopped and cleared her throat again. "Apparently, the doctor here in Dublin prescribed too large a dose. He never asked me how much I weigh."

"But even after all those awful things happened, you didn't tell me. Nor in Livorno when I begged you to tell me what had created a barrier between us. I thought—" Charlie bent, his face in his hands. After a long moment, he spoke again. "I thought our marriage was more solid than that. I thought we faced challenges together." He looked at Laoise. "You don't conceive a child alone. It takes both of us."

"I was wrong to deceive you," said Laoise, tears brimming. "I'm sorry."

"Then please help me understand your secrecy."

"I was afraid," said Laoise. "I was afraid you would insist I keep the child. I was afraid of what you might think of me for wanting to end the pregnancy."

Charlie stood and walked from one end of the room to the other. Then he knelt in front of Laoise. "Have I given you reason to be afraid of me, sweetheart?"

"Yes. No. Oh, I don't know, Charlie. You're a man."

"What does that mean to you, my being a man?"

"It means you think yourself superior to me, your goals and dreams more important than mine."

Charlie frowned and Laoise blushed. "No, Charlie, you've never expressed anything like that. I guess when it came to something so important to me, I thought—"

She stopped for a moment. "I guess I thought you would respond like any man would."

"A two-level view of humanity, eh? Males on top and females beneath them?"

"Isn't that how our whole society is organized?" said Laoise. "Men lay down the law to favor themselves. Women can't even vote."

Charlie took a deep breath and sat beside her on the couch. "That's not how I want our life together to be, Laoise. I don't regard you or your goals or dreams as inferior to mine in any way. I admire you with all my heart and all my soul. I want us to figure things out together. I want—"

He pressed his hands against his eyes, then looked into Laoise's. "I want you to be able to trust me. I want to prove myself worthy of your trust."

"Oh, Charlie. I'm sorry, so sorry. It was wrong of me to let myself be controlled by fear." Laoise swallowed. "This whole situation is showing me how accustomed I am to living life as *I* choose. Even if my goals and dreams are admirable—and I hope they are—I've been extremely self-centered in my pursuit of them. I've wronged you, Charlie. Can you forgive me?"

Charlie breathed deep. "I can forgive you, darling. But I still feel—I feel betrayed. Disillusioned. Deeply disappointed. And I feel profound grief." He stopped. "I can't talk about this anymore right now, Laoise. I need time to gather myself before Terry arrives."

"I understand," said Laoise. "Can you handle the meeting with Terry without me? Later you can tell me his proposal." She stood, walked into her bedroom, and closed the door. A few minutes later, she heard Terry's knock and his voice.

The joy has gone out of the idea of us touring together. I can't deal with it right now.

An hour later, the murmur of voices stopped, and the door closed. Prepared for her luncheon with Alice, Laoise walked out to an empty sitting room. Charlie hadn't even left her a note.

He's even more upset than I thought.

After chatting with Alice about a variety of interesting topics, Laoise said, "Alice, I've run into an interesting situation. I would love your perspective."

"Tell me," said Alice, setting down her fork.

"I recently learned that a musician friend of mine—a cellist—chose to end a pregnancy because she didn't think she could be both a professional musician and a mother. It shocked me, and I've been thinking about it a lot. What do the Quakers believe about this?"

"Quakers tend to take the Jewish position, Laoise, though there's not universal thinking among us on this issue. Some of us believe it is always wrong. Others believe there can be mitigating circumstances that make such a decision understandable."

Laoise leaned forward. "What is the Jewish position?"

"The Talmud calls an embryo 'mere water' until forty days of gestation. After that, it is viewed as part of a woman's body, until the fetus is separated from her by birth. They believe it becomes a 'person' when the soul enters its body through the baby's first breath, as in the Genesis account of creation."

"Does the Jewish tradition point to any other Scriptural basis for this position?"

"Yes. There's a passage in Exodus—forgive me that I don't remember chapter and verse—stating the penalty for an assault on a woman resulting in the death of a fetus. The aggressor must pay a fine. But in the same chapter, the penalty for murder is a life for a life. The rabbinic interpretation therefore does not equate the loss of a fetus with murder. The primary concern in such a case would be any injury done to the woman."

"Interesting," said Laoise, sitting back in her chair. "Since Christianity is based on Judaism."

"Yes. Nothing in the New Testament references abortion. Of course, we Quakers are pacifists, opposed to violence of any kind and committed to protect the wellbeing of every living thing. The loss of a potential child is a serious matter, especially when it is caused by violence, and must never be undertaken frivolously. At the same time, for us as for the Jews, care for the woman is primary. Her life outweighs her fetus's potential life. The fetus should not be allowed to kill the mother."

"Thank you. You've helped me a great deal, Alice," said Laoise. "I don't yet know how I feel about all this, but I'm glad to know the Quaker and Jewish perspectives."

Laoise heard Charlie come in late that night, after she had already gone to bed. She waited for him to join her. When he did not, she tiptoed into the dark front room. A bit of moonlight profiled Charlie's body on the sofa, an arm flung over his face.

Laoise crept back to bed, leaving the door open. A long time later, she fell asleep. When she woke, Charlie was gone. This time he left a note: "Dearest Laoise, I walked for hours yesterday afternoon, and believe I understand myself better. I'm taking some time this morning to journal and pray. I'll bring lunch home for us. Love, Charlie."

Charlie appeared at noon with a meat pie and a multi-colored rose bouquet. Laoise set aside her violin to greet him. As they ate, they discussed Terry's proposal for their spring concert tour, a trip across the ocean to

America—familiar territory for Charlie, but except for the New York Philharmonic, new for Laoise.

After lunch, they moved to the front room. Charlie sat quietly, took a deep breath, then asked Laoise whether he could read for her some of his journaling.

"If that's what you wish," said Laoise.

Charlie read, "I'm trying to sort out why I feel so devastated by the news I learned from Betsy's note. First, of course, I wish Laoise could have shared her distress with me herself, so that we could work it through together. She didn't allow me a voice in whether to allow our child to grow, to become a person. A child unique in the world. Ours. Hers and mine. A brand-new person blending the two of us."

Charlie looked up at Laoise.

"Please continue, Charlie."

He nodded. "This grief feels separate from the decision to have or not have a child in the future. It's specific to that child, the one we've lost, the one who will never be. Who I lost before I even knew he or she existed."

He blew out a breath, then read, "I thought God had taken our child from us, through miscarriage. Knowing Laoise *chose* to end his or her life—maybe it's the part of me formed by my mother's Catholic beliefs. It feels—" He looked up at Laoise again.

"Go on," she said. "How does it feel to you?"

"It feels wrong," he said.

"I didn't think of it that way at all," said Laoise. "I felt no attachment to it. I simply saw my pregnancy as an insurmountable threat to my career. I wanted to be free of it, to leave it behind me. To end my dread of sabotaging all that I've worked so hard to achieve."

Charlie stared at her. "Laoise. If your mother had done what you did, *you* wouldn't exist. We will never know what gifts and talents, personality traits and quirks our child might have had. Does that mean nothing to you at all? I'm trying to understand. Truly."

"I didn't think of it like that at all."

"But Laoise, you are a deeply loving person. I *know* this about you. I think—I think I didn't care well enough for you, and that's why you didn't trust me to face this together, to consider whether it might have been possible for you to have both—a flourishing career *and* our child." Charlie's voice caught. He bent his head and sobbed. A series of emotions crossed Laoise's face as she watched him.

Finally, Charlie took a deep breath and stood. "Let's both take more time to think and pray about this, shall we, Laoise? We need to talk more, but I feel quite wrung out."

"All right," said Laoise. "I do love you, Charlie, though I'm discovering love means more than I thought it did. I didn't mean to hurt you. Truly."

Charlie pulled her up and wrapped his arms around her. They stood together for a long time. Then he went to the piano, and she to her favorite chair, in their bedroom by the window overlooking the park.

Laoise gazed out the window at two children and a dog chasing each other. *I think you were with us just now, God. Thank you. Surprised as I am by it, I feel Charlie's pain. You're growing me up, showing me how spoiled I have been. Now that the secret is out, I feel . . . I once again feel hope for us. For us together. Though it may take as much time for Charlie to heal as for me.*

Laoise stood, to see the children more clearly. *God, how can Charlie and I feel so differently about this? Please show me how* you *feel about what I did. I will wait here for you to answer my prayer.*

Someone must have summoned the children because they called the dog and walked toward the street in front of Laoise and Charlie's apartment building. *Hmm, perhaps they're our neighbors.* Just before they disappeared from her view, the wee lassie looked up at Laoise, smiled, and waved. Laoise's heart jerked, and unexpected thoughts tumbled into her mind.

It was a wee lassie you sent to Me before her time. She is precious. I am healing her from the trauma of her death and will care for her until your time to join her.

Laoise couldn't breathe. She doubled over, clutched her stomach, and stumbled back to her chair.

A gentle knock sounded at her door. Charlie peered in.

Laoise waved at him and turned back toward the window.

"Our neighbor Marian is here to welcome us back. Shall I tell her you'll greet her later?"

Laoise nodded without turning around, tears suddenly streaming down her face.

*

"I understand now. God showed me. At least a little bit," Laoise said in response to Charlie's anxious face after Marian said goodbye.

Charlie said nothing. He opened his arms, and she went into them, and they grieved together. For the child they both had lost.

Finally, Charlie said, "Laoise, I have something I must say to you."

She lifted her head and wiped his tears with her hand.

"Laoise, I've realized in the last two days that I do want to have a child. That doesn't mean we ever should. Certainly, we shouldn't for as long as you do not wish it. Meanwhile, since intimacy is meant to be safe and free, can we agree that until we can be joyful and free together, we choose together not to be intimate? Until we figure this out—until you feel safe."

Laoise lifted her head. "Truly? You will not feel resentful?"

"My feelings may come and go," said Charlie. "But I am asking for this because I love you. I want you to feel safe with me. I want us to share and bear each other's burdens. I want us to find solutions together—real solutions. I want *you* back."

*

"That's a question I've never considered," Cathleen told Charlie on the telephone early Sunday. "Thank you for giving me time to think about it before you come. I did keep journals faithfully through all these years, so I may be able to figure it out. I think I understand how important this is to you and Laoise. Please give her my love."

"Thank you, Mum. We plan to arrive by supper time Tuesday."

"I can't wait to see you both," said Cathleen.

Charlie relayed this to Laoise then listened again.

Laoise squirmed. *I wonder whether she would say that if she knew what I've done. She is Catholic. She might not ever be able to understand . . . or forgive me . . . Nor do I deserve her forgiveness. Though Charlie, somehow, has loved me through all of this.*

Charlie turned to Laoise. "Mum says Wednesday morning will be a good time to talk, because Margaret will be helping supervise a school outing to the glassworks factory."

"Wonderful. Please tell her thank you, Charlie." *Is this a good idea? I do hope so. Though I'm a little bit anxious about how Cathleen will react to our questions.*

☙❧

Sunday evening, Charlie and Laoise climbed the steps to AE's front porch. "I look forward to this Conversation," said Laoise. "The other times we've come, I've been a bit nervous, wondering if we would fit in and have something to offer."

"I know what you mean," said Charlie, ringing the doorbell. "Oh, there's Liam."

"I'm so glad you came tonight!" exclaimed Liam, bounding up the steps to join them just as the door opened. "These Conversations become more interesting to me by the week."

Laoise glanced around and didn't see the Haslams. She did spot her new Quaker friend, walking toward her. "Hello, Alice! I thought you couldn't come tonight."

"When I found out you were coming, I rearranged a few things to make it possible," smiled Alice. "I so enjoyed our luncheon."

"Then we must do it again," said Laoise. "We're basically home now until March, with a few excursions here and there in Ireland and Eng— . . . Charlie? Are you all right?"

Charlie, still chatting with Liam, had stopped mid-sentence and was staring across the room. Laoise followed his gaze to two men walking in from an adjoining room. Her eyes widened.

"Da! What's he doing here?"

Liam laughed. "You refer to Mr. Murphy, I presume, not Vicar Greer. Colin is a regular, and invited Vicar Greer as his guest tonight. Colin's been the speaker for us several times."

"Speaking about what?" asked Laoise.

"Various things, mostly to do with how to organize society once we're free of England," responded Liam.

Laoise frowned. "My father is a nationalist? I had no idea. None."

Across the room, Colin turned and saw Charlie and Laoise. His mouth opened.

"He looks as surprised as we are," said Charlie. "Let's greet him."

Colin had already walked half the way toward them, trailed by the vicar. "Laoise and Charlie? How did you learn about AE's Sunday Conversations? Are you here for the first time?"

"No, sir. We've come several times. My friend Liam invited us." Charlie motioned toward Liam. "Good evening, Reverend Greer. Thank you again for officiating our wedding."

"It was my pleasure," responded the Vicar with a bow.

"The connections in this group never cease to amaze me," said Colin. "I suppose it's been happenstance that we've attended on different dates. Well, now you know how I spend part of my free time."

"Da, Liam says you're a nationalist!" exclaimed Laoise. "I never would have imagined that."

"It's been growing on me, since your mother died," said Colin. "I've always been interested in the movement, but I didn't want to cause anxiety to Muriel. Or to you, Laoise. Then I had the opportunity through Vicar Greer to meet Andrew Griffith, and, well, things have developed from there. I've had an ongoing discussion with Desmond about this since your wedding."

Laoise breathed a sigh of relief. *If Da is aligned with Mr. Griffith, he must not be in favor of violence. I couldn't bear it if—*

"Desmond knows?" asked Charlie.

"Yes. I got to talking about nationalism with the young man from America. Ryan, I think? That led to a breakfast conversation after the wedding with several of the men—Daniel, Thomas, Desmond, Dugan the farmer, Ryan . . . I don't recall anyone else."

"We had already left for our honeymoon," Charlie noted.

"Yes. So, AE seems to regard my understanding of Irish law as an asset to these Conversations. I love imagining life without the constraints England imposes on us."

AE clapped his hands. "Shall we gather, friends? Our speaker tonight is well known to most of us. I've asked him to set up for us a provocative topic: In the new Ireland we all hope is coming, how shall we deal with Catholic-Protestant relations? You may not know Colin is a member of the Church of Ireland. He invited his vicar, the Reverend Greer, to join us."

"Who could have guessed?" whispered Charlie.

"Not me," Laoise whispered back.

Waterford, Wednesday morning, November 7, 1905

Cathleen fluffed the cushions on the settee for Charlie and Laoise in a small room Margaret used for prayer. She took the rocking chair for herself, placing pages of notes and several tattered notebooks on a small table beside her.

"This has been a most interesting question to pursue," Cathleen began. "It had never crossed my mind to wonder exactly when my children were conceived—even our surprise child, Charlie." She smiled at him and continued. "I believe you know, Laoise, that Peter sailed regularly to New York and back."

Laoise nodded.

"In my journals I noted each interval Peter spent away from home. I also, coincidentally, noted the dates of many of my menses, simply because I suffered with them. I was on a quest to practice graciousness despite my discomfort, so I often tried to evaluate in my journals whether I had been successful or not. I believe you will understand that it mattered to me also whether I was in the middle of menses during Peter's brief interludes at home."

Charlie and Laoise nodded.

"So, counting back from each of my children's birthdates, I found it easy to identify, within a few days' time, the possible dates of conception for each one. I was surprised to discover I had registered enough information to know where I was in my cycle on the dates Peter was home."

"Amazing, Mum!" exclaimed Charlie. Laoise didn't speak. She was holding her breath.

"I've written it out for you," said Cathleen, rising and handing them a sheet of paper. "You'll see that each of my children was conceived mid-cycle. This discovery so intrigued me that I charted where I was in my cycle each time Peter was home six months prior to and following these dates. I've written that information on a separate page for each of my children."

Cathleen extended four sheets of paper. Charlie jumped up to take them from her.

"Oh my," said Laoise, after she and Charlie studied the pages. "You were rarely mid-cycle when he was home. You were more often experiencing menses or coming out of menses."

"If the accepted medical wisdom is true, that fertility is linked to menses, it would have been expected that you would conceive at almost any other time Father was home than when you did," observed Charlie.

"Exactly," said Cathleen. "Isn't that interesting? There's a pamphlet going around in Waterford by a Mr. Thomas Hastings—no, that's not quite right—"

"Thomas Haslam?" asked Laoise. "We heard Mr. Haslam and his wife speak on this topic. They convinced us to try their method. We did so scrupulously, but I got pregnant anyway."

"And then you had that horrific miscarriage. I'm sorry you suffered so, sweet Laoise. I believe my data indicates something amiss with the prevailing medical wisdom and with Mr. Haslam's plan."

I doubt she would extend such compassion if she knew what I did . . .

Laoise looked questioningly at Charlie, who nodded. She pulled Cally's letter from her pocket. "Cally sent me a fascinating letter. Please tell me what you think of it, Cathleen."

Cathleen leaned forward, her eyes fixed on Laoise's face as she listened. "The Shoshone understanding of things makes so much sense. Especially considering what I've discovered was true of my own experience."

"This really matters to us, Mum," said Charlie. "We're seeking a way to protect Laoise from conceiving while she's so enjoying her career. This may be the answer we're looking for."

"I am delighted you are considering options together," said Cathleen. "That's so much more rewarding than leaving all the responsibility to Laoise, Charlie, as so many husbands do. I'm also happy that you value and want to protect Laoise's very special giftedness on the violin."

Charlie and Laoise looked at each other. "I haven't done this as well as I should, Mum," said Charlie. "But I'm learning."

"*We* are learning," said Laoise.

"Do you know, when I heard about your miscarriage, Laoise, along with my grief over your suffering, the thought crossed my mind that should you have a baby at some point, I could be the child's nanny when you travel. I could go with you to care for him or her. I quite liked the idea. So, if that day comes, please feel free to invite me!"

Laoise stared at Cathleen with her mouth open. "I never imagined . . . so, both might be possible? . . . I didn't know . . . "

"Laoise has felt that having a child would be incompatible with her career," explained Charlie. "It didn't seem realistic to imagine being a musical performance artist and a mother."

"Well, I know it would be more complicated than just the demands of touring," said Cathleen. "But if you decide you want to be a mother, and if I can help, please let me know."

If I decide? I thought she would say, "If God gives you another child" or something like that. Maybe someday I can tell her what I did. Maybe?

Charlie whispered to Laoise. "Could we tell Mum about your fear of childbirth? I think she would understand."

Laoise thought for a moment, then nodded. "I'll tell her," she whispered back. She flushed and sat up straight when she noticed Cathleen watching them.

"That was rude. I apologize, Cathleen."

"You have no need to apologize for speaking with your husband, dear."

"Could—could I tell you another dimension of our situation?" Laoise asked.

"Of course."

Laoise took a deep breath, then told Cathleen about her experience of seeing her mother giving birth to her dead baby brother, blood pouring from her mother's body.

"Oh, Laoise, what a difficult experience for a young child!" said Cathleen.

"Ever since, I've been terrified of giving birth," said Laoise, swallowing hard. "And then, in London—"

Laoise gave up fighting the tears. She buried her face in Charlie's shoulder and wept.

Cathleen waited, her hands open in her lap, her lips moving soundlessly.

When Laoise's sobs eased, Charlie repeated, "In London—"

"In—in London, I saw blood pouring out of my own body. I—I don't ever want to go through that again."

"What a frightening experience for you," said Cathleen. "I understand your distress, precious Laoise. I understand better now your fear of becoming pregnant again."

Laoise nodded and accepted a handkerchief from Charlie.

Charlie said, "It doesn't really help to know that most birthing isn't like that, because severe bleeding has featured in both of Laoise's only experiences related to childbearing."

"I—I have nightmares," said Laoise. She pressed her palms against her eyes, her whole body tense. "Sometimes I'm afraid to go to sleep."

"When I remember to pray for her before we sleep, it seems to help," said Charlie. "I don't always remember . . . "

"May I pray for you now, Laoise?" asked Cathleen.

"Yes, please."

"Can you extend your hands, palms up like mine, as evidence of opening yourself to the Lord, Laoise?"

Laoise did so. Cathleen added, "Why don't you do this also, Charlie" and then began her prayer. "Lord, you see and understand Laoise's suffering and fears. Charlie and I join her in offering them up to you. Will you please take each one?"

She paused and then said, "Now, Lord, will you grace Laoise's heart and soul and mind with your peace?"

After another pause, Cathleen continued. "We don't know the future, Lord, but we do know you love and care for Laoise. You sympathize with her from your own experience, Lord, when blood flowed from your body, from the crown of thorns on your head, the stripes on your back, the nails in your hands. You *know* how this feels, Lord. Release, then, your beloved daughter from her suffering. Come to her in your gentle compassion, to take her fears upon yourself."

"I see him," whispered Laoise. "He's touching my forehead. Oh my." Her body relaxed, the tension in her face softening into a smile. "Thank you, thank you," she whispered.

Cathleen sat quietly until Laoise opened her eyes, brimming now with tears of relief and gratitude. She said softly, "Laoise, our Lord's love is always available to us. When these fears raise their heads again, with Charlie or by yourself, give them back to the Lord once more, and ask for his peace in their place. He wants us to live freely, joyfully, confidently."

It was Charlie's turn to weep.

"There's still your sense that you're not called to be a mother," said Charlie as they chatted in bed that night. "As Mum said, it would be challenging even with her help."

"The biggest challenge for me is your desire to have a child someday," said Laoise. "I still haven't absorbed that idea."

"Well, I'm in no hurry," said Charlie, stifling a yawn. "We don't have to decide tonight."

"Your mum's research gives me hope, though. It lines up with Sunrise's beliefs. It seems we can have some control and make decisions for ourselves instead of leaving it all to fate."

"To fate? Or to God?" Charlie turned over, then looked back at Laoise. "I feel hope because we're figuring this out together. No more secrets. Unless you're hiding something else from me."

"Only what I'm planning to get you for Christmas," said Laoise.

Charlie tickled her.

"Sleep well, dear husband."

Charlie chuckled. "You too, dear wife."

Walking into their apartment after their visit to Waterford, Charlie and Laoise found another large stack of cards and letters forwarded by their agent Terry.

"This is crazy," muttered Charlie. After tipping the bellboy who brought in their luggage, he began flipping through the mail. "Oh. Laoise," he called into the next room. "We have a response from Daniel!"

"Read it to me while I start unpacking," she called back.

Charlie pulled the pages from the envelope while he followed Laoise into their bedroom.

> "Hey, little brother. I'm glad you felt you could write to me. These are big questions, not easily answered, and I hope our experience can be of help.
>
> "Once Meghan and I decided two children was the number we could best care for, I started using condoms because we didn't like the other two most obvious options, abstinence and interruption of the act. Due to Catholic sentiment about contraception, I doubt you'll find condoms in Dublin, unless you discover back channels. I have an easier time buying them here, so I'll send you a package, and you can pay me back with one from London next time you're there.
>
> "It's important to check often to be sure there are no leaks. The rubber tears quite easily. But we've used them for many years now and the quality seems to be improving.

"One thing I like about this is taking responsibility myself for our family planning. Too often the burden rests on the woman, which is not fair. At least, we don't think so.

"With fond memories of your Belfast concerts and Laoise's, I followed your tour through the press. I was sorry to hear about Laoise's difficult miscarriage. I hope she is truly feeling better now, both physically and emotionally. Wishing you all the best, Daniel"

"Now we have two options!" said Laoise.

"What if we combine the two?" said Charlie. "Double insurance."

"Sounds good to me," said Laoise.

"Whew," said Charlie. "A relief of huge stress on our marriage. I hope."

"I hope so too, Charlie. With all my heart."

CHAPTER 31

CALLY AND RYAN

The Lion III, July 2, 1906

CALLY BOOSTED FELICITY AND RYAN held Brian to see over the *Lion III*'s railing as the ship pulled away from the New York City dock.

"This time we're all together," said Felicity, squirming around to hug her mother. "That's because now Ryan is my real daddy and Brian is my real little brother."

Ryan shifted Brian to one arm and with the other, hugged Cally and Felicity. "That's right, sweetheart. And we're going to Ireland to celebrate at Uncle Dugan and Aunt Aisling's farm in Killeagh, where your mummy was born and grew up!"

Felicity frowned. "Have I been there before? I only remember Dublin."

"No, you haven't been there before. Neither have I, nor Brian. This will be so special!" Ryan set Brian down on the deck. He immediately toddled away. Felicity chased after him and grabbed his hand.

"How are you doing, Cally?" asked Ryan.

Cally leaned into him. "A flood of memories. But I'm ordering my mind to pay attention to *this* memory. The four of us. Together. Happy."

"We're facing the faeries," said Ryan. "Together."

Waterford, Saturday, July 7, 1906

Cathleen, Margaret, and all three of her children cheered as Ryan, Cally, Felicity, and Brian appeared at the top of the gangway in Waterford. "You made it! Hurrah!!"

Tucked into a carriage with her family and her mother by adoption while Margaret and her three rode in Percy's brand-new Rolls Royce Silver Ghost, Cally said, "Thank you for coming, Cathleen. What a happy homecoming."

"I am filled with joy," said Cathleen. "I want to ask you about your wedding, but we should wait until Margaret is with us, so you won't have to say it all twice. I will observe, though, that you are more beautiful than ever, Cally, my dear."

Cally blushed as Ryan grinned at her. "What a sweet thing to say! Thank you."

"Brian is asleep," said Ryan. "Can I stretch him out onto your lap, Cally?"

"Of course!"

Cathleen smiled at Brian, kissed her finger, and gently touched his forehead. "Tell me about your plans. I know, of course, the reception will be a week from now, July fourteenth at Dugan and Aisling's farm. I can't tell you how excited they are."

"We're excited too," said Ryan. "From Waterford, we'll make a stop overnight with Cousin Mickey and Louise at Youghal on the way to Killeagh. Cally has never made that trip by train before. After the reception, we plan a few days in Cork City, meeting some of my relatives."

"And we return to America from Waterford July twenty-third, to begin the long trek back to Idaho," completed Cally.

"No plans to visit Dublin?" asked Cathleen.

"Not this time," said Ryan. "Cally begins work with Flora as a full-fledged nurse August first. I'm glad the Dublin folks can attend the reception."

"I haven't said congratulations on your pinning!" said Cathleen. "I'm so proud of you, Cally. If I were sick, there's no one I would prefer to care for me."

"Thank you, Cathleen! This trip is our honeymoon. Ryan and I had one day and one night together before we started traveling east to New York. You know what that journey is like."

"I do," said Cathleen. "I remind myself how fast it is now, compared to the olden days when it took weeks to cross the ocean and months to reach Idaho by wagon."

"That's a good perspective, Cathleen. Thank you," said Ryan. "A generation ago, we wouldn't be having this double celebration, the wedding in Idaho and the reception in Ireland."

"True. I find it special that both events are taking place on farms, and that I'm familiar with them both. The one where you were born and spent your first years, Cally, and the one where you'll live as an adult. Both such lovely and beloved places."

"We have photographs of the wedding in our luggage!" said Cally. "Flora gifted us with a portrait of us in our wedding finery. Of course, the artist needs a few weeks to finish it."

"I'm in the picture too!" said Felicity. "And Brian!"

"Yes," said Cally, smiling at her daughter. "The portrait will preserve the lovely shade of green of your flower girl dress and Brian's ring bearer shirt."

"I brought it to wear at the reception, too," Felicity confided to her grandmother. "But Mummy didn't bring her wedding dress. She says it was for one day only. But when I get married, I want to wear it. It's so bee-yoo-ti-ful."

"So, at your reception you expect Daniel and his family from Belfast, Charlie and Laoise and Colin from Dublin, Margaret and her family and me from Waterford, Mickey and Louise from Youghal, and of course Dugan and Aisling and their family. And Cousin William and his family from Portlaw, who have become quite friendly to the rest of us since taking in Billy. Billy himself, as you know, is in Idaho with his family for the summer. Anyone else?"

"We also expect a few close friends of Dugan and Aisling's. Eamon, Conner, and Toby are the names I remember," said Ryan. "And a cousin I've never met, who lives in Limerick. He and his wife will go with us to Cork City for the first ever Byrne family reunion."

"Well done, Ryan. It sounds like your interest in knowing your family is motivating them to have more connection with each other."

"I hope so," said Ryan. "Isn't it interesting that Colin Murphy met Billy before the rest of us did? Apart from you, of course, Cathleen."

A shadow flitted across Cathleen's face before she smiled. "Truly amazing," she said.

"I'm glad Thomas and Cora and their children, and Billy and his Idaho family were able to attend our wedding," said Cally. "Billy is doing so well. Just one more year at St. Colman's and then he'll begin medical school."

"Yes, he's really flying!" said Cathleen. "The last time I talked with him he hadn't settled on whether to study at Cornell in New York or at Trinity College in Dublin. A professor at St. Colman's—a Mr. MacDonagh, I believe—told me he expects Billy to graduate first in his class."

"I think he's leaning toward Trinity," said Cally, shifting Brian's weight on her lap. "He says New York is so far from his Idaho family that he might as well be in Ireland. It's too bad there aren't medical schools closer to Idaho who will accept students like him. At Trinity, he'll be near his Ireland family. I'm glad he'll have this summer with Miz Minnie. She sends you her love, Cathleen. She has aged a great deal this last year."

"The world will lose a treasure when Minnie passes," said Cathleen. "I feel quite overwhelmed right now thinking about the experiences we shared on that treasure hunt. And the fact that it led you two together. With your precious children." She wiped her eyes and smiled at Ryan and Cally. "Who could ever have guessed that the wee girl I met in Killeagh all those years ago would become my beloved daughter? We have so very much to celebrate."

"All joy," agreed Cally, reaching her hand out to Cathleen. Turning toward Ryan, Cally saw herself reflected in his eyes. *I no longer need my wee mirror to know who I am.*

"And here we are at Margaret's," said Cathleen. "I'm glad for the traffic that allowed us time for this special conversation. I will treasure every word."

EPILOGUE

Trinity College, Dublin, Ireland, June 10, 1916

"I'M GLAD WE CAME EARLY enough to sit close to the stage. But how can we hold all the emotions at one time?" Cally asked Ryan. She smoothed their five-year-old daughter Chloe Flora's dark curls as they waited for the Trinity College conferring ceremony to begin.

"Our pride in Shane's graduation today. And in Billy's achievement of specialization in pediatric surgery," said Ryan. "And his being chosen as commencement speaker. And his and Lucy's wedding next week, while we're all here and can celebrate with them!"

"The joy of Laoise's birthing of healthy twins," said Cally. "Even though people feared she was too old to bear children."

"It was so special that she and Charlie could play the 'Irish Fantasy' for several years first," said Charlie. "What an honor that Hamilton Harty wrote it for them."

"I'm glad Cathleen could be with Laoise for the birthing. Like she was with me for Chloe's and Michael's. Such a comfort, since our mums are gone," said Cally.

"She plays the mum role well for me, too," said Ryan. "She's adopted us all as her own children. Including Dugan and Aisling and their family."

"The bitter grief of Desmond's death in the Easter Rising," Cally added to their litany of strong emotions.

"And the execution of Billy's old professor, Mr. MacDonagh. I wonder how Billy will hold himself together enough to be able to speak," said Ryan.

"He must share our anxiety regarding what the future holds for Ireland," said Cally.

"And our anger at the executions," said Ryan. "It feels like the whole country is boiling with rage and grief."

"Mama, lots of people are coming into the seats we saved," said Brian.

Cally turned. "I see Daniel and Margaret and Thomas and their families. And Cousin William and his family. And Lucy and her family. And Cecil, Mary, and Ebony. We might not have saved enough seats." She smiled and waved as their row and the one behind them filled with familiar, beloved faces.

"An usher is with them. She'll help figure it out," said Ryan. "Is it acceptable for you to nurse Michael in this setting?" He handed Cally their six-month-old, who had begun to cry.

"That's why I have my shawl," said Cally. "As well as to show off your lovely wool."

Ryan grinned and put his arms around Felicity's and Brian's shoulders, seated on either side of him. "Thank you both for wanting to be here with us."

"Look—people are walking onto the stage. There's Billy! He's dressed up in his black academic robe. The green of his hood is so shiny!" exclaimed Felicity, pointing with one hand and hugging her grandmother with the other as Cathleen sat down beside her. Chloe scrambled over to climb onto Cathleen's lap.

After greeting each family member, Cathleen asked the child on her lap, "Did you know Chloe means hope?"

"You tell me that every time!" said Chloe. "And Cathleen means pure. And Michael means gift from God. And Felicity means happy. And Brian means strong. And Ryan means kingly. I didn't forget, Grandma."

"I bless you all," said Cathleen, smiling at each one.

"And Callandra means lovely one," whispered Ryan to Cally. "I'm so glad you're mine."

"The usher is walking onto the stage," said Brian. "I wonder what she's doing?"

"She handed something to Billy," said Felicity.

"And he winked at her," said Brian. "Why would he do that? I'm going to ask him at the reception."

ঙ্গ

"She's an old friend," explained Billy when Brian managed to pose his question amid the hugs and congratulations both Shane and Billy received from the gathered family and friends after the ceremony.

"It seemed like she gave you something," said Felicity.

Billy smiled and pulled a small metal piece from his pocket.

"It's a green dragonfly," said Shane.

"It looks old," said Brian.

"It's from a special bicycle I used to ride," said Billy. "I'll tell you about it sometime."

"Why not now?" asked Brian.

"Because it's a long story," said Billy. "A good story, but it would take a while. Don't worry, I'm sure we'll find the right moment."

"Is the dragonfly the reason you talked about flying in your speech?" asked Shauna, pushing between her twin and her cousins to examine the metal circle.

"And dreaming and growing even though we're sad?" wondered Josie, pressing in beside Billy.

"What happened to the bicycle?" asked Shane, not waiting for Billy's reply.

"The last time I rode it, I smashed it into a wall trying to escape from someone chasing me," said Billy.

"Did he catch you?" asked Felicity.

"Yes. But I escaped."

"How did the usher get the dragonfly from the bicycle?" asked Brian.

"That's part of the long story." Billy smiled and turned to look for Lucy.

Discussion Questions

Prologue and Chapters 1-7

1. The Prologue is based on records about William Malcomson I and his son Willliam Malcomson II preserved at the Quaker library in Dublin. In what way did it give you insight into Uncle William (William I) as you met him in the first two books, *Horse Thief 1898* and *Treasure Hunt 1904*?
2. If you've read the first two Cally and Charlie novels, recap for each other what you know about the main characters, including Cathleen.
3. Though Billy became important to the Idaho treasure hunt, we didn't meet him until now. What do you think of him so far?
4. A theme in *Facing the Faeries 1906* is the healing power of kindness. What examples can you cite in these first chapters?
5. What foreshadowing can you identify in regard to each of the main characters?

Chapters 8-16

1. What is your favorite scene from these chapters?
2. A theme that continues from the first two books is family. List the main characters and their family situation by the end of Chapter 16. What significant losses has each one suffered?
3. In what ways does each find personal support within their families? Discuss Billy's situation.
4. How did you feel through Cally and Ryan's conversation about who he should ask for permission to court her?
5. In Chapter 16, we see again Cally's fear of the faeries, first mentioned in Chapter 2. What "faeries" do you see troubling the other characters?

Chapters 17-22

1. What does his growing friendship with Fred mean to Billy (Chapters 17 and 20)?

2. "Then we are his family," says Father Jancey about Billy in Chapter 20. In what ways might this be true and in what ways not?
3. What did you like best in Chapters 18 and 19?
4. What are your thoughts at this point about the old woman?
5. Were you surprised by what Cally did? Do you think there's more Ryan could have done in response?
6. Have you ever reacted to something like Felicity did to her mother leaving her? Why did her conversation with Cathleen help her so much?
7. Why did Cally's conversations with Starlight and Teddy help her so much?
8. What else do you want to discuss from these chapters and the book so far?

Chapters 23-31 and Epilogue

1. "Partners and pals," Ebony says to Billy. Discuss the ways Billy learns he's not alone.
2. What do you think of Laoise's friend Betsy and her influence on Laoise?
3. Do you think Cally was adequately "punished" for how her actions hurt Felicity?
4. Chapter 30 is long and complex. What most caught your attention?
5. The author believes God is always with us, even when we can't see him. How do you notice this borne out in the characters' lives?
6. The bittersweet emotions identified in the Epilogue reflect the grief of the 1916 Easter Rising in Ireland. What current situations, over a hundred years later, indicate there is still work to be done to heal our world?
7. In what ways did Billy and the other main characters learn to "fly free"? Are you flying free?

Historical Notes

Note: These simple introductory comments belie dozens of books and hundreds of hours of research for Facing the Faeries 1906. Additional information is easily obtainable.

AE, the name preferred by the poet, writer, editor, literary critic, painter, and Irish nationalist **George Russell**, who held Sunday Conversations in his home attended by well-known people in the early twentieth century, including the historical figures cited in this story.

Anna and Thomas Haslam, like their Quaker counterpart in America, Susan B. Anthony, are best remembered for their commitment to women's suffrage. A memorial seat to them in St. Stephen's Green, Dublin, honors their "long years of public service chiefly devoted to the enfranchisement of women." Their efforts in favor of family planning are less well known, perhaps because of the faulty medical beliefs undergirding their plan.

The **faeries** of Ireland are sometimes distinguished from the good fairies by their spelling. It is said that when Lucifer rebelled against God, a third of the angels refused to take sides. God banished them to Ireland, where they demonstrate whether they deserve redemption (by behaving well) or condemnation (by behaving badly). This determination is to be made at the Last Judgment. A fascinating and complex mythology developed over centuries in Ireland, where regular sightings of faeries/fairies and other mystical creatures reinforced belief in their existence and their roles in Irish history. In this novel, the old woman is either a fairy or a guardian angel, one of those "ministering spirits" whose interaction with humans is frequently noted in both the Old and New Testaments of the Bible.

The Iroquois Confederacy or **Haudenosaunee** was originally a joining of five northeastern tribes: the Seneca, Cayuga, Oneida, Mohawk, and Onondaga. They so impressed Benjamin Franklin with their manner of living and decision-making that he borrowed from them ideas for the United States Constitution, declaring an eternal debt and goodwill toward the Confederacy. This declaration was shortly betrayed by "manifest destiny" and the State of New York, which coveted Confederacy lands, eventually forcing the tribes out of New York. The Oneida went mostly to Wisconsin or to Ontario, Canada. Some, however, as in this story, joined the Seneca-Cayuga in northeast Oklahoma.

The six-day 1916 Easter Rising, an armed rebellion against English rule undertaken by some 2500 Irish nationalists, counted on a limited reaction because Great Britain was heavily invested in World War 1. However, the Rising was brutally suppressed by 20,000 British troops using incendiary bombs and heavy artillery to rout the rebels. Some two thousand people were wounded and 458 killed, mostly civilians. Fifteen leaders of the Rising were swiftly and publicly executed, shocking the Irish into passionate support of independence from Great Britain. The dead leaders were regarded as martyrs, their blood seeding the Irish Civil War, 1919-21. The Anglo-Irish Treaty was signed on December 6, 1921. A year later, Ireland's lower thirty-two counties became the Irish Free State. Dozens of books, both historical and fictional, have been written about this period of Irish history.

Thomas MacDonagh, one of the 1916 Easter Rising's leaders and martyrs, was a gifted teacher, not quite so gifted poet, and passionate nationalist. He established and nurtured chapters of the Gaelic League in several places and taught at St. Colman's in Fermoy from 1903 to 1908. He is an Irish hero. His wife and children, however, suffered greatly from his single-minded devotion to Irish independence. He expected not to survive the Rising, yet left his family impoverished, having devoted his resources to the Irish cause. His wife eventually committed suicide, leaving their children orphans. Much has been written about MacDonagh's life and his death.

Charlie and Laoise's Repertoire and other songs mentioned in this book

Link for playlist (find it also at the top right of horsethief1898.blog)
https://www.youtube.com/playlist?list=PLPKlZ6WXGYq8ucSEeMrwTbofoYg4xU08J

Chapter 3: "Gloria" by Antonio Vivaldi, Monteverdi Choir with John Eliot Gardiner
https://www.youtube.com/watch?v=wXx_1pZV8tE

Chapter 15: "Jesus, Lover of My Soul," by Charles Wesley, music by Joseph Parry, sung by Fernando Ortega
https://www.youtube.com/watch?v=NsXcCdWjsmg

Chapter 15: "All Through the Night" traditional Welsh lullaby sung by Aled Jones and the Notre Dame Folk Choir
https://www.youtube.com/watch?v=yReZCAKv4xU

Chapter 16: "A Little Bit of Heaven" by Kate Smith, sung by Connie Francis
https://www.youtube.com/watch?v=hThpC6Sm8ZM

Chapter 21: "All Creatures of our God and King" by St. Francis of Assisi, tr. by William Draper, first published in 1906 with the 1623 German hymn tune Lasst uns erfreuen. Westminster Abbey sings an arrangement by Ralph Vaughn Williams
https://www.youtube.com/watch?v=VF12LkUS25c

Chapter 24: "Cantabile" by Niccolo Paganini, played by Esther Abrami and Iyad Sughayer
https://www.youtube.com/watch?app=desktop&v=2lIF6u_H7Cs

Chapter 24: "Méditation" from the opera Thaïs by Jules Massenet, played by Rusanda Panfili and Donka Angatscheva https://www.youtube.com/watch?v=7QtGOWemQhY

Chapter 30: "Concerto for Violin, Piano, and Strings in D Minor" (also called the "Double Concerto") by Felix Mendelssohn, played by the Orquesta de Camara de la Sierra de Guadarrama with Fumika Yamamura and Daniel del Pino https://www.youtube.com/watch?v=Qz7O54orjLc

Epilogue: I didn't find Harty's "Irish Fantasy for Violin and Piano" on YouTube (nor his "Trio" from Ch. 15), so I'm substituting his "Irish Symphony," which Charlie and Laoise heard when it came out in 1905 (Chapter 15). This recording is by the Ulster Orchestra. The idea that Sir Harty wrote the "Irish Fantasy for Violin and Piano" for Charlie and Laoise is, of course, pure fiction. https://www.youtube.com/watch?v=k6iag2N5ytw

With Thanks

FOR THIS THIRD BOOK IN the Cally and Charlie Series, I especially thank my husband David for his support, including traveling with me to Ireland and helping me with research there. I think warmly of the lovely people in Ireland who spent time with us on behalf of this book, including Roy Pearson and others at the Friends Historical Library in Dublin. Mary Phillips and other staff members helped me with research at the Carnegie Library of Pittsburgh.

Each person who read the manuscript gave me invaluable suggestions: Elaine Elliott, Meredith Dobson, Megan Sateia, Timmy Podnar, Rhonda Herman, David and Bonnie Liefer, Janice Griswell, Rachel and Brian Becker, and David Kornfield. My writing critique group, Page 29 of Word Weavers International, gave me consistently good input and instruction.

I'm delighted with Marissa Bowles' creative, precise, and beautiful cover image. As always, I'm thankful for "my" team at EA Books, Marsha, Rebecca, Ardythe, and Robin. They make publishing a joy and my books beautiful.

I do hope the living Malcomson descendants can enjoy this book despite the fictional liberties I took with their ancestors! It is true that William Malcomson I, son of David and Mary Ffennel Malcomson, took leadership of exorbitantly profitable Malcomson Brothers Shipping and Trading upon the early demise of his talented brother Joseph (fictional Peter's father). It is true that the Society of Friends, rather than excommunicating him, exonerated William I when the company went bankrupt under his leadership. It is true that William I's wife and sons, along with the extended Malcomson family of the time, were so unhappy with him that he disappeared for three years before reappearing and making amends with his family before his death. I was unable to discover any record of where William I went and what he did during those absent years. So, the story I tell about him and about his son William II, in all three books of the Cally and Charlie series, is entirely the fruit of my imagination.

About the Author

DEBRA KORNFIELD PUBLISHED FOUR NONFICTION books in twenty years of mission work in Brazil while pioneering abuse recovery and raising four children. She framed her memoir *Karis: All I See Is Grace,* now in Portuguese and Spanish too, around her daughter Karis's luminous journals and poetry. *Horse Thief 1898,* her first novel, was followed by *Treasure Hunt 1904. Facing the Faeries 1906* concludes the Cally and Charlie series. Debra has contributed chapters to various books. Her current project brings to life several children's books she wrote over the years, some of them crafted with Karis. Debra enjoys adventuring with her grandchildren, hiking, and keeping up with her husband David, her seven sibs, and many South American friends. Follow her on HorseThief1898.blog and personally on ButGod.blog. She lives with Dave in Pittsburgh.

Made in the USA
Middletown, DE
23 February 2024

50213437R00220